# the Emerald Heart of COURTENAY

## OTHER BOOKS AND AUDIOBOOKS
## BY ANITA STANSFIELD

*First Love and Forever*
*First Love, Second Chances*
*Now and Forever*
*By Love and Grace*
*A Promise of Forever*
*When Forever Comes*
*For Love Alone*
*The Three Gifts of Christmas*
*Towers of Brierley*
*Where the Heart Leads*
*When Hearts Meet*
*Someone to Hold*
*Reflections: A Collection of Personal Essays*
*Gables of Legacy, Six Volumes*
*A Timeless Waltz*
*A Time to Dance*
*Dancing in the Light*
*A Dance to Remember*
*The Barrington Family Saga, Four Volumes*
*Emma: Woman of Faith*
*The Jayson Wolfe Story, Five Volumes*
*The Dickens Inn Series, Five Volumes*
*Shadows of Brierley Series, Four Volumes*
*Passage on the Titanic*
*The Wishing Garden*
*The Garden Path*
*Legally and Lawfully Yours*
*Now and Always Yours*
*Heir of Brownlee Manor*
*The Color of Love*
*Lily of the Manor*
*Love and Loss at Whitmore Manor*
*The Stars above Northumberland*
*The Heart of Thornewell*
*The Lady of Astoria Abbey*
*The Empty Manger*
*The House of Stone and Ivy*

# ANITA STANSFIELD

# the Emerald Heart of Courtenay

a novel

Covenant Communications, Inc.

Cover image: Woman Among Trees © Mark Owen / Trevillion Images

Cover design copyright © 2019 by Covenant Communications, Inc.

Published by Covenant Communications, Inc.
American Fork, Utah

Printed in the United States of America
First Printing: July 2019

25 24 23 22 21 20 19     10 9 8 7 6 5 4 3 2 1

ISBN 978-1-52440-969-2

# Chapter One
## THE MYSTERIOUS KEY

*Surrey, England—1806*

SARAH COURTENAY HAD NO CHOICE but to put more effort into breathing evenly and more deeply, hoping to ease the sharp pain in her side as she quickened her pace in order to return home before the diffusing gray of dusk transformed into the dark blanket of night. She'd started out more than an hour earlier with the intention of simply taking a brisk walk to ease her nervous energy and get some much-needed fresh air. Following the disturbing conversation she'd had with her father sharing tea together in his room, her head had been spinning with confusion, astonishment, and perhaps even fear. Without a doubt, Oswald Courtenay was a reasonable and rational man; he'd always been known for his kindness and was well-liked by everyone who knew him. Sarah and her father had always been close, and they'd become even closer as they'd shared the common grief of losing her mother to an unexpected illness two years earlier. They'd enjoyed many outings together and had even done some traveling, which had aided their healing process. Sarah had just begun to feel hopeful that she could get beyond the grief of losing her mother when Oswald had taken ill. The symptoms of dizziness and weakness had come on slowly but had continued to worsen. Consulting three different doctors had given them no answers to his mysterious ailment. Sarah and her father were apparently meant to simply accept that there were many illnesses that even the best doctors didn't know about or understand; therefore, nothing could be done except to try odd tinctures that might soothe Oswald's symptoms. Some things they'd tried had proved worthless; others had helped, but their effectiveness had worn off. Subsequently, Oswald's illness had grown steadily worse over the last few months; nothing had eased his growing weakness, and he'd been confined to bed for many weeks now.

Sarah spent a great deal of time in her father's room—at least when he was aware enough to enjoy her company. They shared tea together every day and occasionally shared other meals, and they talked about a great many things—as if he knew he was likely dying and wanted to give her every piece of advice he could think of. Sarah indulged him in such conversations, even though she was convinced he would get past this and make a full recovery. But today Oswald had spoken things to Sarah that almost made her wonder if his illness was causing him to hallucinate or become somehow hysterical. She had not previously seen signs of any such anomalies, but how else might she explain his sudden need to tell her about family secrets and a supposed curse on the Courtenay name, as well as a great treasure that was coveted enough to kill for? He'd rambled about the reason she was an only child, since her mother had miscarried three babies, losing them before the halfway point of her pregnancy—as if that somehow indicated that a curse existed in the family rather than simply being a medical problem, as it had always been referred to before now. Her father also jabbered almost incoherently about the tragic death of his grandfather, as if he'd always believed it had been caused by the very fact that he had borne the Courtenay name, which had therefore cursed him, rather than simply being a tragic accident. In addition, he referred to two other incidents in the family, difficult things that had happened to both himself and his father, as if they too were indications of a curse, when Sarah had always believed these were easily categorized as the typical challenges human beings encountered during the course of their lives. Had her father suddenly come to see them as evidence of a curse? Or had he carried this belief all his life and simply hadn't spoken of it? Sarah had never heard her father refer to these things in this way before and she was more than taken off guard. She had listened and asked some questions, which he'd answered in ways that hadn't helped clarify her understanding at all. Once he'd fallen asleep, Sarah had sat in a chair near his bed stewing over everything he'd just said, wondering what on earth she was supposed to do about it. She'd finally concluded that they would simply have to talk again after supper and had impulsively decided some fresh air would help clear her head.

The days were getting shorter as autumn marched steadily toward winter, but it had been a particularly pleasant day and Sarah felt plenty warm as she stepped outside, wrapped in a lightweight cloak as black as her unmanageable black curls that hung far past her shoulders in complete disarray. Her hair had been partially put up and pinned into place at the back of her head to keep it from hanging in her eyes, but it had been decided a long time ago that attempting to put all her hair up in a more proper style was generally a waste of time since it never stayed in place for long, no matter how many pins were used. And with the weight of her hair, having it pinned up often caused headaches, which Sarah simply wouldn't tolerate. So she defied society and left her hair hanging in its unruly state and didn't care if anyone considered her doing so was improper.

Sarah's intention had been to take a quick walk around the grounds, but she'd become lost in her heavy thoughts and had wandered much farther from home than she'd realized until she found herself far into the woods with the sudden awareness that the sun had gone down, and its remaining light was quickly diminishing. She'd hurried out of the woods and across the vast expanse of moors and meadows toward her home. Not keen on being outside and alone in the dark pushed her forward with haste, despite her growing breathlessness and the ongoing sharpness in her side, which seemed to be taunting her over the fact that she wasn't accustomed to walking so far and so fast, and she'd do well to acquire better habits in that regard.

Sarah was relieved to come over the crest of a hill and see Castle Courtenay come into view, with glowing lanterns illuminating her goal of the front door, and lights flickering in many of the uniquely shaped windows. She was glad to share her surname with that of her home, since it was a fine and beautiful structure, and she'd known much happiness within its walls and in the surrounding gardens and open fields that spread out around the castle in every direction like a cozy quilt displaying a brilliant variety of color in spring and summer when the flowers were in bloom—but those colors had faded now with the cold winds of autumn. Still, Sarah believed that her ancestor—a few centuries back—who had built and named the house, must have been an arrogant man. By no means could this structure—as spacious and beautiful as it was—be defined as a *castle*. It had lovely turrets at each corner that rose into peaked roofs, and the gray stone had been forged and structured in a way that lent an air of what she imagined to be the legendary palaces of centuries gone by. But Castle Courtenay was smaller, if anything, than other elegant manor houses in the county; therefore, referring to it as a castle often felt a little embarrassing. And she blamed her ancestor centuries back for putting the family in the position of having to apologize for their home bearing a far more grandiose name than it needed or deserved. Now,

Sarah wondered over the things her father had said about family secrets and curses, and she wondered if her father was losing his mind, or if this house with which she shared a name actually had menacing qualities she'd never thought possible.

Sarah didn't really care about the name of her home; she was simply glad to be able to call it home and to feel safe and loved there—a fact she focused on as she pushed away the nonsense her father had been sharing with her earlier. She far preferred to consider it nonsense, which was easier to digest than any other possible explanation. By the time she reached the door it was completely dark, and she breathed deep relief to step into the well-lighted foyer. She sat down in a conveniently placed comfortable chair where an unannounced guest might be left to wait. She was glad to be able to sit there alone and unnoticed for several minutes while she drew in deep breaths and blew them out slowly until her breathing returned to normal and the pain in her side slipped away.

Sarah became so completely relaxed that she hadn't realized she was close to dozing until the sound of hurried footsteps coming closer startled her back to full consciousness. She lifted her head and turned to see Poppy—her personal maid and cherished friend—coming briskly toward her. Poppy's expression of panic jolted Sarah to her feet.

"Oh, there you are!" Poppy said, as out of breath as Sarah had been when she'd come through the door and plopped into the chair.

"What is it?" Sarah demanded. "What's wrong?"

"It's your father, dearie," Poppy said between her attempts to take in even breaths. Having been born and raised in the Scottish Highlands, Poppy couldn't speak without her origin being readily evident. "He's taken a sudden turn for the worse; we don't know why. The doctor's been sent for, but . . ." Her attempt to explain faded into silence, perhaps because she didn't know what to say, or perhaps because Sarah was running toward the stairs and likely wouldn't have heard the rest of what Poppy had to say anyway.

Sarah lifted her skirts high and bounded up the grand staircase in a very unladylike manner, barely aware of Poppy coming behind her, both of them quickly becoming out of breath again. Sarah deliberately threw off any effort to be ladylike as she conquered the stairs and ran down one long hall, and then another, oblivious to whether Poppy was keeping up. Sarah paused for only a moment outside the door to her father's bedroom, which had been left open. She took one deep breath, then another, before she entered, still breathless but not caring. She stood for only a second just inside the door to take in the scene, which was typical—but never had it been so somber. A chill rushed down her back and made her shudder, as if the angel of death was declaring its presence in the room. She scolded herself for such a ludicrous thought, although she couldn't deny that her father looked paler and sallower than she'd ever seen him. He was propped up in his bed with a great many pillows, and she might have believed him to be dead already if not for the obvious rise and fall of his chest—but the evidence of his breathing caused her even more concern, since it was clearly strained.

It was not unusual to find Mr. Halford sitting beside the bed, reading and willing to do anything to help Oswald, but his countenance showed his frustration over knowing there was nothing he could do, and his fear that the end was finally drawing near for this man he'd served loyally for decades. Halford had worked as a valet for Oswald Courtenay since long before Sarah was born. He was to Oswald what Poppy was to Sarah. They were inseparable, with a friendship that was deeply integrated into their working relationship. Halford's brown hair was thick for his age, and he wore it combed back off his face in a way that made him look younger than his years. But then, his leanness and agility also contributed to his youthful appearance, as did his soft facial features—completely devoid of the slightest wrinkle. Overall, he conveyed an image of a much younger man. He was old enough to be Sarah's father, but he could perhaps pass for her older brother—except that they looked nothing alike.

Attempting to not sound as if she'd been running, Sarah took in another deep breath before she stepped carefully to her father's bedside and put a hand on Halford's shoulder, which startled him from such deep thought that it was evident he'd not heard her enter the room.

"Tell me," she whispered, disconcerted with the way her father didn't respond to her voice. It was typical of him to turn his head toward any sound that indicated a newcomer to his bedside, and Halford often joked about how his lengthy illness had not affected his hearing. Sarah couldn't believe it had only been a couple of hours since he'd been speaking to her—weak and a little breathless, but certainly conscious and alert.

With his concerned eyes focused on Sarah's father, Halford said quietly, "After you left, we were talking and it's as if he just . . . fell asleep right in the middle of a sentence—and I couldn't wake him." Halford's voice cracked. "I couldn't wake him. I don't know what to do."

Sarah felt certain she should console him in some way, but she honestly couldn't think of a single word that might make any difference. She gently squeezed his shoulder where her hand was still resting before she sat on the edge of the bed and took hold of her father's hand, startled by how cold it felt. She attempted to wake him, even though Halford had already assured her it was impossible. Still, he observed her efforts expectantly, as if he hoped she might be able to accomplish what he'd been unable to do. But Oswald remained completely unresponsive and looking very much dead except for the evidence of his strained breathing—which was becoming noisier and more labored.

"What's happened?" Penelope Courtenay screeched as she burst into the room like some kind of large bird, her bright-pink taffeta gown rustling with her every movement. Sarah loved her father's sister dearly. She'd never married and had always lived here at the castle and had therefore been an integral part of Sarah's life. Penelope looked very much like Oswald; they both had the same long face and large eyes, and they'd both gone prematurely gray, which had made Oswald look more dignified since he wore it well. However, it had only made Penelope look older than her years, but perhaps that was due more to the way she wore it pinned up in an elaborate style that was common among the elderly. In spite of Penelope's tendency to be overly dramatic, and her many obvious eccentricities—such as being dressed in such an audacious gown when she had no intention of leaving the house or receiving guests—Sarah loved her beyond words. Penelope had a talent for being compassionate and supportive during difficult times—even if her methods came with a generous helping of drama.

"What's happened?" Penelope repeated, squeezing her slightly plump body between the bed where her brother lay and the chair where Halford was sitting. Halford eased out of the chair in order to avoid any awkwardness and began to slowly pace the room while he gave Penelope the same brief explanation he'd given Sarah.

Penelope's response to this information was to speak so loudly to her brother that she was practically shouting in his face, as if that alone might accomplish what Halford and Sarah had been unable to do. But Oswald didn't show the tiniest response to his sister's shouting, except perhaps that his breathing took on more of a rattling sound.

The doctor arrived while Penelope continued to shout at her brother to the point where Sarah felt hard-pressed not to shout at *her* and tell her to be quiet. As much as she loved her aunt, there were times when the woman's flamboyant personality grated on her nerves. But then, there were things about her father that elicited the same feelings. However, that didn't make her care for either of them any less. Still, she was relieved by the doctor's intrusion, which forced Penelope away from the bed—and to subside into silence—while the doctor examined Oswald closely, asking a few questions as he did so. Sarah explained her father's strange behavior when she'd last spoken to him, then the room became eerily still, especially in contrast to Aunt Penelope's attempts to shout her brother into consciousness. The doctor's examination seemed to go on and on, even though Sarah knew he was being quick and efficient. Dr. Turnlow was wise and sharp, and he'd cared for this family for so long that he'd delivered Sarah when she was born. He'd always been as kind as he was knowledgeable and thorough. If anything at all could be done for her father, Dr. Turnlow would know. Sarah observed impatiently while she prayed in her mind that *something* could be done; this couldn't be the end. It just couldn't. She felt as if she were barely recovering from the loss of her mother. How could she lose her father now? Like this? With so much mystery surrounding the very reasons for his illness?

When the doctor had apparently finished, he stood up straight and his eyes went first to Sarah. It took her only a moment to realize why. Her heart hammered painfully in her chest even before she heard Dr. Turnlow say, "There's nothing more to be done, my dear. He's very near to death as we speak." Sarah let out a mournful gasp which she forced back by clapping a hand over her mouth. "I don't know why, Sarah; I have no answers. But I know death when I see it. And I know you . . ." he took a quick glance around the room but set his eyes again on Sarah, "all of you . . . expect me to be honest and not skirt around the point." He sighed, and his expression held nothing but genuine compassion. "I would be surprised if he lasts more than an hour." Sarah whimpered behind the hand still covering her mouth. "But I don't believe he's in any pain. I'm so sorry, so very, very sorry."

The moment the doctor stopped speaking, Penelope burst into boisterous wailing. Sarah got hold of herself enough to swallow her own shock, walk across the room, and take hold of her aunt's shoulders. "Aunt Penelope," she said firmly, "you know I love you dearly, but if you cannot be still, I will insist on your leaving the room. I wish for my father to die peacefully. We will all do our crying later . . . in the privacy of our own rooms. Do you understand?"

Penelope gulped, then coughed, then nodded. "Forgive me, my dear," she said and sniffled.

They hugged tightly while Sarah said, "I know it's difficult, but we must be strong."

Sarah couldn't believe she was even capable of speaking such words. She didn't feel strong at all, and she couldn't begin to comprehend this was actually happening. She felt certain the only reason she was able to say such things to her aunt was the knowledge that if Penelope didn't keep still while they shared her father's bedside vigil—waiting for him to die—she would end up shouting at her, and she didn't want to mar her father's death by creating more drama.

The doctor took a chair in a far corner of the room, saying quietly, "I'll be right here if you need me." Sarah was distracted by the memory of him doing and saying exactly the same when her mother was dying. The idea passed briefly through her mind that perhaps this meant her parents would be together. The thought gave her the tiniest bit of comfort, although it was too tiny to compete with the volcanic rumbling of grief and horror that she was barely managing to keep suppressed—but she would not allow herself to become a hypocrite by losing control of her emotions when she had so firmly put Penelope in her place.

Sarah, Penelope, and Halford were the only people in the room— besides the doctor—while they waited for what Dr. Turnlow had declared was inevitable. The silence became increasingly eerie as Oswald's breathing became increasingly difficult. Each breath rattled more than the last, and the length between them grew longer. Sarah found herself holding her breath, waiting for her father to breathe again, until she found her lungs burning and she had to let the air out. When Oswald drew his last breath, Sarah glanced at the clock and realized it had been a little over half an hour since the doctor had declared Oswald likely wouldn't last more than an hour.

Sarah couldn't believe it. He was gone! He was really gone! Halford sat quietly and wiped at silent tears streaming down his face. Penelope pressed her face to her brother's shoulder and sobbed quietly—at least far more quietly than her normal sobbing, likely still mindful of Sarah's edict. Sarah bravely touched her father's face and hand, startled by their coldness and the immediate awareness overcoming her that this was no longer her father, but a lifeless shell. She kissed his cold brow, whispered that she loved him, and hurried from the room, knowing that the rumbling inside of her would refuse to remain in submission much longer, and she had no desire to burst into helpless sobbing in front of everyone else.

Sarah ran through long hallways, up one flight of stairs, and down another, and then through more hallways before she finally arrived at her own room where her breathlessness lurched into painful, heaving sobs.

She barely managed to get to her bed before she collapsed from the weight of the realization that her father was really dead. They'd had tea together not so many hours ago; they'd talked and laughed earlier today. How could this have happened so quickly? So horribly?

Poppy came to check on Sarah, tearfully telling her that she'd just heard the news. "Is there anything I can get for you?" Poppy asked with her usual tender kindness. "Anything I can do?"

"No," Sarah said, "but thank you. I just . . . need some time alone."

"Of course, dearie," Poppy said. "I'll check back a little later."

Sarah nodded, and Poppy left the room, clearly overcome with emotion herself. She was only a few years older than Sarah, and had grown up in this household, the niece of the head butler—a man who had passed away the year prior to the passing of Sarah's mother. Poppy had been taught the fine points of being a lady's maid—mostly because she was such a good friend to Sarah that Sarah had begged her father to make it possible for Poppy to be able to work directly with her so they could maintain their friendship more easily by spending time together every day. Poppy took very good care of Sarah, in ways that Sarah could have never imagined. She was like a mother, a sister, a friend, and a maid all mixed together into one amazing young woman. The two were a stark contrast in appearance, but in every other way they were perfectly matched. Poppy's hair was straight and blonde and stayed obediently wherever it was pinned, and she had a well-rounded figure that Sarah considered far more feminine than her own narrow hips and lack of waistline—something the dressmakers commented on each time she was fitted for anything new. But none of that mattered, because Poppy was an angel. Sarah knew she would likely return later with a supper tray, which Sarah would likely declare she couldn't eat, but Poppy would insist, and they would eat together—and cry together—and Sarah would be able to keep going because Poppy would make certain that she did.

Sarah cried until she felt all dried up, then her mind wandered through the strange conversation she'd had with her father earlier this afternoon. Recalling it now, she gasped. It was almost as if he'd known he was close to death, as if he'd passed on great secrets that would have likely been meant to be given to Oswald's son and heir—except that Sarah was an only child; therefore, she was the only one to whom he could pass *anything* on. Sarah convinced herself that what he'd told her was nonsense—which wasn't difficult considering that some of it made no sense at all—but she concluded there *was* one thing he'd told her that she could verify easily enough.

Sarah jumped off her bed and crossed the room to the beautifully carved wooden jewelry box that had been her mother's. Since her mother's death it had been right in this very spot, given to her by her father—along with all its contents. For Sarah, the sentimentality of the jewels meant more than their actual monetary value, and she'd rarely worn anything from the box. But her father had told her today that it had some kind of secret drawer or something where a key was hidden. She picked the box up, even though it was large and slightly heavy, turning it over to examine every angle, pushing and prodding at every line where wood met wood in the fine craftsmanship. When that proved fruitless, she opened and closed every drawer more than once. She took them all the way out and put them back—more than once. Then she noticed something unusual. She emptied the contents from the small, flat-bottom drawer and stuck her fingernail into a tiny notch at the edge where the bottom met the side. She was surprised by how easily the bottom of the drawer lifted up, and there before her was a key. Sarah gasped and stared at it, then gasped again. If her father had not been delusional about this key, what did that mean regarding everything else he'd told her? She hardly wanted to rethink the things he'd said, let alone repeat them to anyone. And given the secretive—even frightened—way he'd told her, she believed it wise to *not* tell anyone. Not even Poppy. Not yet, at least.

Glancing at the clock, Sarah knew the usual suppertime was nearly over, and Poppy would likely give her a little more time to get hungry enough to be convinced to eat. If she wanted to keep all this a secret from Poppy, Sarah had very little time to see if this key was actually what her father had told her it was. She tucked the key inside her bodice since she didn't have any pockets, and carefully put back the false bottom of the drawer and replaced its contents before setting the jewelry box back so carefully that even the bare hint of dust that would be cleaned away tomorrow didn't look disturbed.

Sarah was about to sneak out of the room when she heard Poppy's familiar knock at the door. Sarah took two huge steps and literally leaped onto her bed to give the appearance that she'd never left it. And she actually managed to do so before Poppy peeked inside, and when she saw that Sarah appeared to just be waking up, she offered a wan smile and opened the door more widely in order to come inside with a supper tray laden with enough food for both of them.

Sarah *didn't* feel any appetite, even though the growling of her stomach kept trying to convince her that she needed to eat, as if it were in solidarity with Poppy in her insistence that Sarah needed to keep up her strength because of the difficult forthcoming days. Sarah didn't even want to think about what would happen next. As she forced herself to dig into a steak and kidney pie that looked too beautifully crafted to eat, her mind was more preoccupied with whether or not the key she'd found would actually open what her father had told her it would. Oh, how she wanted to be able to go back to his room and talk to him about it! But he was gone. Her mind knew the truth, even though something in her spirit seemed hesitant to accept it. But he was gone, and whatever secretive messages he'd passed on to her were now her responsibility.

While Sarah ate far more of her piece of treacle tart than she'd intended, she convinced herself once again that her father's talk of secrets and family curses was nonsense. Still, she only had to go where he'd told her to go and see if the key worked. But she didn't know when doing so without being noticed might even be possible.

Later that evening, after Poppy had helped make certain Sarah had everything she needed for the night, Sarah felt a sudden urgency to return to her father's room and see his body again before it was taken from the place where he'd died. She'd become so caught up in her own grief, and the desire to not be observed in her frequent bursts of tears, that she'd overlooked her need to be assured that Oswald Courtenay had really passed from this world. She had her memories of touching his cold, lifeless hands and face, and she didn't doubt the truth of his death. Still, she felt drawn back to her father's room and put on a dressing gown and slippers to trek her way across the enormous structure to what had become her favorite part of the house during the months her father had been bedridden with his illness. They had talked and laughed, had shared meals and teas. But now it was all different. Even before she arrived at the door to his bedroom, she could feel the difference, and she entered the open doorway to see nothing but darkness except for the circle of light created by the lamp she'd brought along to guide her. Approaching the bed, she found her father's body gone and the bed made up as if nothing unusual had taken place here not so many hours ago.

Disappointed that the undertaker had already come for her father's body, Sarah reminded herself that she would be able to see his body in its casket before he was buried, but the very idea felt so strange and surreal that she shuddered and had to focus on breathing evenly, not wanting to break out in tears when she was so far away from the safety of her own rooms— even if no one else in the house was likely even awake. Then an idea occurred to Sarah, and with fresh energy she hurried back to her room and retrieved the mysterious key.

With the key tucked safely in the pocket of her dressing gown, Sarah took up the lamp again and moved quietly and carefully through the house and slowly down to a room she had never known existed. Even as she worked her way toward it, a part of her doubted its existence. She had lived in this house her entire life and had never been in any such room, but then according to her father's directions, it was well hidden and not meant to be found without being told about it—which was something passed on as an oral tradition from father to son, or in her case, *daughter*.

Sarah crept into a pantry-like room, feeling as if she were some kind of burglar intent on stealing its contents. She'd known there were many pantries in the house, but this one was some distance from the kitchen, and the door was set back from the hallway, as if it were trying to avoid ever being noticed. She stood in the center of the room and held the lamp high, surveying the back wall, which appeared perfectly normal with a few barrels and sacks stacked in front of it—as she would expect to find in a pantry where food for a large household was stored. But the room was thick with dust and cobwebs, and she knew no one had been in here for many years, which made her wonder what exactly might be stored here. She sighed at the realization that she would have to move those barrels and sacks herself in order to get to the wall, which her father had declared could be opened, revealing a secret compartment behind it. A part of Sarah doubted the validity of such a claim because it had sounded so ludicrous, but he'd been right about the key in her mother's jewelry box. And perhaps if nothing else, this little escapade was keeping her from thinking about her father's death. She knew it would be impossible to sleep right now, so she might as well be moving sacks and barrels.

Sarah took a deep breath and resigned herself to doing work that a strong manservant was likely meant to do. She knew there were men who worked in this house who were sent into town with a large wagon in order to acquire supplies, which would then be put into one of the pantries for storage. But this room hadn't been used for a very long time and she wondered if anyone in the household beyond her father—and now her—had even noticed its existence. Sarah steeled herself to just get this done, even if it meant aching muscles tomorrow. The two barrels that were sitting on top of other barrels were surprisingly light and she wondered if they were only here to make the room appear like a pantry, when in truth it had a different purpose. Moving every sack and barrel away from the wall took some time, but nothing was heavy enough to make her think there was anything significant inside of them. When she had moved everything, she stood before the wall, which looked completely ordinary, and sighed. Had all that work been for nothing? Had her father been losing his mind as he'd crept closer to death?

Sarah moved the lamp closer and set it down so that it illuminated the wall more clearly. She pressed her hands over every part of the smooth wood slats that comprised the wall—at least as far as she could reach—and felt nothing unusual. Sarah even stood on one of the barrels and moved it a couple of times to examine what she wouldn't have been able to reach otherwise, but that also proved unsuccessful. She moved her fingers carefully along the edges of the wall where they met with the adjoining walls and still felt nothing . . . except . . . She'd barely noticed the little notch against the edge of the wall and had to move her fingers over it several times to be convinced that it was anything more than a slight flaw in the wood. But she recalled how the false bottom of the drawer in her mother's jewelry box had been accessed by a tiny opening. Wondering if the same concept might be true here, she attempted to get her finger into the notch enough to see if doing so would make it possible for her to open some portion of the wall. But even her tiniest finger wouldn't quite fit. She looked around the room and saw a crowbar lying on top of a barrel on the other side of the room. It was surely here to open the barrels when needed. Unless . . . the barrels weren't meant to be opened. Sarah picked it up and put the end of the tool into the tiny notch, amazed at how perfectly it fit, and pushed on the handle, wondering if she might end up just damaging an otherwise fine wall. But she gasped when one of the long slats of wood that comprised the wall popped open as easily as the bottom of the drawer in the jewelry box. The wall had been carefully constructed for this purpose; she could see it now. When closed, the slats all looked perfectly even and unsuspicious. But now that one of them was partially open, it looked as if all the craftsmanship surrounding it had been purposely designed to hide this particular feature.

Sarah recalled again what her father had said, and how fantastical it had seemed. Would she really find here what he'd told her she would find? The thought seemed too incredible to be true. But if it *was* true, then she had to do as he had asked—which was to remove the contents from this place before someone he didn't trust got their hands on what was hidden here. Sarah had no idea who else might know about this, but her father had seemed convinced that what had meant to be a secret passed from one heir of Courtenay to the next had been discovered by someone else, and he didn't want what was rightfully hers to fall into the wrong hands. He'd told her to take it, keep it, guard it carefully—for he had declared that he truly believed the person who was in possession of what lay behind this wall would be protected and preserved from the evil curse that had been placed upon the Courtenay family many generations back. It all sounded like a fairy tale to Sarah, but she took a deep breath and reached out to open the wooden slat more fully, surprised by the way it swung on a cleverly hidden hinge. However long unused the hinge was, it still swung open with little effort, but Sarah couldn't see anything of what was inside the secret compartment. She lifted the lamp directly in front of it and saw a long box that fit so perfectly into the hidden space—with only less than an inch of space above it and at each end—that Sarah knew the compartment had been specifically designed to hide *this* box and nothing else. Sarah set down the lamp and carefully eased the box out, noting how much dust came with it, which fell on the floor and clung to her hands. The box had obviously been in there a long time.

Holding the box in her hands, Sarah felt an inner trembling—both her heart and her stomach were suddenly wobbling like a perfectly baked custard. She wanted to open the box here and now but felt hesitant to do so. Instead she leaned the long, narrow box against the barrels of a different wall before she carefully closed the secret compartment and assured herself that the wall looked as normal as she had found it. She moved the dust on the floor around with her foot so that it was scattered enough to not even be visible. Just as carefully, she put back the barrels and sacks exactly as she'd found them, more than once comparing their appearance to her memory and making small adjustments. She noticed a broom in one corner and used it to swirl the dust on the floor around enough to disguise any evidence that someone had been in here. Once she was satisfied that everything in the room looked exactly as it had when she'd entered, Sarah figured out a way to carry the long box beneath her dressing gown with her arm wrapped securely around it. She doubted she would come across anyone in the house on her way back to her room, and even if she did it would be impossible for anyone to not notice that she was carrying some strange object beneath her dressing gown—as large as it was—but she still figured that was better than carrying the box unconcealed and having someone see it—and see that she had it. According to her father there was someone in this house who could not be trusted; she had no idea who that might be, but she didn't want to take any chances.

After carefully closing the pantry door, Sarah hurried back through the maze of Castle Courtenay to her own room, carrying the lamp in one hand, and barely managing to keep hold of the box with her other arm while attempting to keep it concealed. Creeping silently through long hallways and up various staircases, it occurred to Sarah that she hadn't needed the key in her pocket to retrieve the box, and she wondered why. When she finally got back to her own room, she set the box on the floor on the other side of her bed with the thought that if anyone came into the room, they wouldn't be able to see it, or see her opening it. She knew the very idea of anyone coming to her room at this time of night was ridiculous, but the discovery of this box had brought on a sudden and severe paranoia. That same paranoia prompted her to lock both doors to her room—one that went into the hallway, and the other into her sitting room. She then checked behind the draperies, under the bed, and even inside her wardrobe to make certain she was completely alone. Even while she was carrying out this thorough search, a voice in her mind—which she knew was her own—told her she'd gone mad in the hours since her father's demise. Her precautions bordered on the ridiculous—or perhaps she had fully crossed that border and her behavior was just utterly absurd. Only a moment's thought convinced her of the latter.

Still, she felt unquestionable relief to know she was completely alone and safe while she knelt beside the box and examined it with the aid of the lamp she'd set nearby on the floor. The box was about as long as the front of a large overstuffed chair, as wide as a dinner plate, and a little deeper than the length of her hand from her wrist to her fingertips. Sarah quickly realized she was looking at three hinges along the edge of the box and immediately turned it around so that she was seeing the front where there was a latch directly in the center—and a keyhole in the center of the latch. Sarah gasped softly and reached into the pocket of her dressing gown for the key she'd found hidden in her mother's jewelry box. She looked at the key, and the keyhole, and the key again, surmising that they appeared to be a good match. But for some reason she felt hesitant to even open the box. Her determination to find the box suddenly felt a little foolhardy as her father's mostly nonsensical last words came back to her. Maybe she didn't want to know what was in the box, or maybe she just didn't want to be responsible for it—whatever it might be. But her father was dead now, and she was his only heir. If the contents of this box were an important piece of her heritage—of what it meant to be *the keeper of Castle Courtenay*, as her father had put it—then she needed to just exercise some courage, not let her imagination make more of this than it was, and find out what exactly her ancestors had chosen to keep hidden in such a way.

Sarah took a deep breath and put the key into the keyhole. She took another deep breath and turned it. The lock clicked open with no resistance and the latch popped up as if magically beckoning her to just open the box. Sarah lifted the lid, feeling a mild resistance from the hinges. What she saw inside was a length of green velvet fabric, which covered the contents and prevented her from seeing anything. Sarah held her breath and gently lifted the fabric as if it were so fragile it might disintegrate in her hands. Now that she was finally able to see the treasure she had in her possession, Sarah sucked air into her lungs and had difficulty letting it out again while she wondered what on earth she—a young woman not yet twenty—was meant to do with such a thing.

# Chapter Two
## SUSPICION

Sarah reached out to touch the magnificent sword gleaming in the lamplight as if it had been carefully polished just today. The accumulation of dust on the box when Sarah had found it was evidence that it hadn't been touched in a very long time, but clearly no dust had gotten inside. She *almost* touched the sword and drew her hand back quickly as if she feared it might burn her.

"It's only a sword," Sarah murmured quietly to no one in particular as she banished to stillness her father's jumbled talk of family curses and birthrights, labeling them as nonsense. And yet, when she took hold of the beautifully gilded golden hilt and lifted the sword to the level of her eyes in order to examine it more closely, she felt strangely empowered. It was crafted of metals both gold and silver in color, although she couldn't determine exactly what they were by their color alone; she knew nothing of such things. At first Sarah believed it was nothing but an ornamental piece, partly because of its breathtaking beauty, and partly because it wasn't very heavy. She had no trouble lifting it high above her head, and for some unknown reason she brandished it as if to fight an imaginary foe, even while she was kneeling on the floor of her bedroom. The movement of the weapon reflected the lamplight, almost sparkling in some places, and showing Sarah clearly that the blade was actually very sharp; she didn't have to touch it to know; she could see how fine the edges were.

But the most magnificent feature of the sword in her hand was the glistening emerald stone laid securely into the metal right at the center of where the hilt and the blade met, forming a cross with the intricately carved handle. The stone was the size of a ripe plum—at least—and crafted into the shape of a heart. Something her father had said burst suddenly into her mind, refusing to remain banished into silence. *You must protect the heart of Courtenay at all costs. Its value is more than you could ever understand, and I don't have time to tell you.*

Tell her what? Sarah wondered. This remarkable sword with its emerald heart was obviously very valuable. The stone alone had to be worth a great fortune. But Sarah knew there was more wealth in the family than she could spend in three lifetimes, even if she were ridiculously extravagant—which she was not. So, why would it be so important to protect *this*? Why had it been hidden away in such a secretive and mysterious way? And why—being the only child of the heir of Courtenay—had she never heard *anything* about this unusual treasure?

Sarah continued to study the sword in her hand, strangely fascinated—almost mesmerized—by it. Turning it over she noted that on the opposite side of the emerald heart was a beautifully crafted collection of smaller emeralds in different shapes and sizes that had been inlaid in a mosaic style to create the shape of a heart. Sarah concluded that each one of *these* stones—even as small as they were—had to be valuable. But she looked again at the enormous emerald heart on the other side and could hardly believe her eyes.

Sarah's arm became tired, even though her fascination had not diminished. Overcome by a growing nervousness regarding the box and its treasure, Sarah found herself breathless for no logical reason, and perhaps frightened—even if she couldn't define the reasons for her fear. Perhaps it was all just so very strange; perhaps it was the eerie shadows of the room created by the single lamp by which she had been examining the remarkable treasure she had found. Perhaps it was the memory of the strange things her father had said to her only hours before he'd died. Or perhaps it was the very fact that he *had* died, and the reality of his death hadn't fully sunk in. All things combined, Sarah hurriedly returned the sword to the box exactly as she'd found it. She locked the box with the key and looked around her room, wondering where she could possibly hide such a thing and know that it wouldn't be discovered—by anyone.

Sarah put the box at the back of the bottom of her wardrobe. The many long gowns and dresses hanging there completely concealed the box and removing one or two at a time—which was always the case—would still never reveal even a glimpse of the strange treasure. Sarah then put the key back into her mother's jewelry box where she'd found it, hidden beneath the false bottom of a drawer. She unlocked the doors of her room and forced herself to go to bed, knowing that sleep was vital. Her father had died; there was a funeral to be planned, and she wondered what all this meant in regard to the estate. She had no brothers or male cousins to whom the property would be bequeathed. Her father had told her more than once that she was his heir, and she needed to be prepared to care for Castle Courtenay and all things associated with it. But Oswald had not been anticipating death. Even with the illness he'd been experiencing, Sarah knew he hadn't expected to die, and therefore he'd told her nothing that would prepare her for what might be required of her. His mostly nonsensical conversation with her this afternoon had led her to the box now in the bottom of her wardrobe—a box filled with a monetary treasure she couldn't even fathom. But what good was that to her in regard to the management of a large household and estate, where a great many people resided and made their living? Sarah's worries about her responsibilities melted into the fresh realization that her father was really dead. Silent tears leaked from the corners of her eyes and gradually turned to a painful sobbing. She wrapped herself around her pillow and pressed her face into it, as if it could absorb her pain.

Sarah awoke to find the room filled with a gloomy daylight caused by cloudy skies. Her pillow was beside her instead of beneath her head, so she knew she'd cried herself to sleep. She sat up and noticed a covered food tray on the table near the window, which let her know that Poppy had checked in on her but had let her sleep. Sarah didn't feel like eating, but her stomach growled, and she actually felt a bit nauseated, which let her know that she definitely needed to eat some breakfast in order to be able to function through what could be a very difficult day.

* * * * *

During the days leading up to her father's funeral, Sarah was unspeakably grateful for the love and support of the people around her that helped make such a shocking and difficult situation almost bearable. Every person in the household was kind and extra helpful, but it was Halford, Poppy, and Aunt Penelope who were on hand to help make all the necessary decisions regarding her father's service and burial. And Sarah was especially grateful to have Halford and her aunt by her side while she visited with the overseers of the estate, the housekeeper, and the head butler, and to be reassured that everything was in order, and to at least take the first steps toward filling her father's role. She was glad to know that he had trusted these people he had worked with for many years, and she deeply appreciated how sensitive they were to her need to mourn her father's death and to simply make it through the funeral. They all agreed to meet again when Sarah felt up to it and assured her they would continue to care for everything as if she and her father might have been traveling. Sarah actually appreciated the analogy, since she knew that the household and estate always ran smoothly whenever she and her father had been away—even if she'd never given a thought to how that might be happening. Now she had no choice but to think about it a great deal, but at least she had some time to adjust and be more prepared to step into her father's shoes.

Sarah knew it was a rare occurrence for a young woman to inherit the whole of an estate, and she knew that if there was even one male relative, she would have had to give up her entire home and fortune to him. But there wasn't. And she was glad of it. This was *her* home, and this was the way her father would have wanted it. Even though she knew her situation was unusual, she was shocked by how many times well-intentioned friends and acquaintances mentioned the matter during the time before and after the funeral when custom mandated that she be available to receive condolences. People were kind, and their comments were sincere, but Sarah felt as if she might scream if one more person told her how sorry they were for her loss, or that her father's passing was such a shock. But even worse were the seemingly never-ending comments about how strange it was that she would be inheriting the estate. Did the entire county know the situation of her inheritance? Did they have nothing better to talk about? Did they not have enough decency to keep matters of inheritance and money out of their comments on the very day of a man's burial? Sarah actually began to envy the way Penelope was almost constantly crying into her handkerchief, which prevented most people from approaching her with their comments and condolences. She wished she could do the same. But her self-respect wouldn't allow for such behavior. Sarah felt compassion for Penelope, but she often found it difficult to know how to assuage this woman who frequently behaved like a child. Poppy and Halford on the other hand were always nearby, ready to fetch anything she might want or need, or to just make certain she was all right. Halford whispered more than once to her that he was ready to whisk her away at any given moment, but she felt committed to show respect for her father by representing him with dignity on this most terrible of days.

A moment finally came when Sarah couldn't take it any longer, and she only had to send Halford a firm gaze before he began making apologies to the people around her, declaring that she needed to rest. With Halford and Poppy accompanying her away from what seemed more like a party to

Sarah than an event to show respect to her father, she was relieved to soon have distance from the noise and heaviness that had been surrounding her.

A short while later, Sarah was securely tucked beneath the covers of her bed, already wearing a nightgown even though supper wouldn't be served for a couple of hours. But she had liked Poppy's suggestion to just get ready for bed and take supper in her room, since she surely had to be exhausted. Sarah *was* exhausted. Ever since the conversation she'd shared with her father not long before his death, her mind had been spinning and tumbling through so many things that didn't make sense, and she still couldn't grasp that her father was truly dead. All the tears she'd shed throughout these past days, combined with her disturbing discovery of the sword and its puzzling implications, contributed to her exhaustion, making it difficult for her to get the sleep she'd needed. Even now, as thoroughly drained as she felt, she found it nearly impossible to relax. Her mind went continually to the box in the bottom of her wardrobe—filled with a treasure more precious than she could imagine, a sword that was not only clearly *very* valuable, but had some kind of symbolism or meaning in regard to the Courtenay family. Sarah simply couldn't comprehend that she had inherited an entire estate; that in itself was sufficiently overwhelming—but then there was this secret box, hidden carefully away, which was purported to be associated with some kind of curse—or at least that was what her father had seemed to be saying. Oh, how she wished she could go back! Oh, how she wished she'd known it would be their final conversation! Oh, how she wished she'd paid more attention, asked more questions! The combination of regret and mystery and grief was just too much. She felt too numb to cry anymore, and too overwhelmed to sleep in spite of how badly she needed to do just that. Trying very hard to concentrate on going to sleep—certain that a nap before supper would do wonders— Sarah was nothing but frustrated to still be wide awake when Poppy arrived with the supper tray. She was glad that Poppy had brought enough food for two—as she usually did—since Poppy's company was both a distraction and a comfort. She could completely be herself with Poppy and had no problem complaining about the people who had made insensitive comments to her earlier in the day; nor did she hesitate to fully express her ongoing shock over the fact that her father was dead, a topic of discussion that was always accompanied by tears that seemed to come from an endless source.

Poppy was kind and understanding as always, and sometimes she even cried with Sarah. Poppy had been treated well by Oswald, and she too missed him very much. On top of that, she had a gift of perfect compassion for the suffering of others, and right now it was completely focused on the heartache she knew Sarah was feeling. Sarah felt inexplicably grateful for such a true and precious friend, but even as she thought it, a blanket of guilt threatened to smother her. She'd never kept a secret from Poppy before. Never! But there was a great big, shiny, valuable secret in the bottom of Sarah's wardrobe. A part of her wanted desperately to tell Poppy, if only so she wouldn't have to carry the burden of it alone. She also just hated having to be on guard with Poppy in any way. But telling her didn't feel right, at least not yet. She wanted more information about what she'd found and the family legends surrounding it. But she'd been too preoccupied with grieving and getting through the funeral to have time to go digging around in the family library for the records of the Family Courtenay.

As they were nearing the end of their meal, Sarah reached for a teapot that had remained beneath a cozy to keep it warm while they'd been eating, talking, and crying. Traditionally she enjoyed chamomile at bedtime because it helped her relax—at least it had before her father's death. And since Poppy preferred something different, there were always *two* teapots on the supper tray. But it had been the same with Sarah and her father. They had distinctly different preference in their tea; therefore, different teapots, signified by the different colors of yarn in the knitted cozies covering them, were always on the trays for meals and their teatime snacks.

While Sarah was pouring the still-very-warm tea into a dainty cup painted with a pink and green floral pattern, Poppy said, "I need to ask your permission for something. I was going to just do it *without* asking your permission, then I realized that I couldn't do such a thing in good conscience, and I would have a great deal of explaining to do in the morning."

"What*ever* are you talking about?" Sarah demanded.

"Dr. Turnlow was here today because one of the kitchen maids got a nasty cut on her hand that needed stitches. I pulled him aside and told him you'd hardly gotten a wink of sleep since your father's death, and he gave me something that might help. I was going to sneak some into your tea because I knew you'd argue with me about it, then I realized that if it were the other way around, I certainly wouldn't want you doing any such thing. So . . ." Poppy drawled as if she expected an argument with Sarah, "I'm hoping you'll be agreeable to taking something that will help you get some sleep." She nodded toward a little tincture bottle sitting clearly in the center of the supper tray. "I fear if you don't, you'll become ill, and we don't want that."

Almost defiantly Sarah picked up the bottle, opened it, and moved to pour some into her cup.

"Careful there!" Poppy said. "Not too much at once!"

"How much?" Sarah asked, and Poppy told her the number of drops the doctor had prescribed.

Sarah added the drops, closed the medicine bottle, stirred her tea, and leaned back to drink it while Poppy watched her with astonishment. "I thought you'd argue with me."

"I'm too tired to argue, Poppy," Sarah admitted. "I've never gone this long without any decent sleep before, and I appreciate your insight." She took a long sip. "Although I *am* glad you asked me." She heard Poppy sigh just before Sarah sighed even louder and longer and took another sip, imagining the glorious sleep she would enjoy tonight, thanks to Poppy's intervention.

\* \* \* \* \*

Sarah came awake slowly, feeling deeply rested but so much so that she also felt disoriented. The angle of muted sunlight peering through the draperies let her know that it was likely late morning, which meant she'd slept much longer into the day than she normally did. But she'd surely needed the rest and felt confident that once she came fully awake and adjusted to the day, she would feel better physically than she had since her father's death.

Sarah wasn't surprised to find a cloth-covered tray on the table. She pulled on a dressing gown and sat down to eat the boiled eggs, scones, butter and jam that had been left there. The tea was still warm since the pot had been snuggled inside a cozy, and Sarah knew it hadn't been terribly long since Poppy had left the tray. It was as if she had a strange sense about anticipating Sarah's needs. And thanks to Poppy, Sarah had gotten the sleep she'd needed so badly, and she was thoroughly enjoying every bite of the food on the tray. It seemed that getting some sleep—or perhaps getting the funeral behind her—had increased Sarah's appetite. She suddenly felt a hunger that implied its intention to make up for how little she'd eaten in recent days.

After clearing away every crumb and drinking every last drop of tea, Sarah got cleaned up and dressed. Poppy showed up at the very moment when Sarah needed help buttoning the back of her dress. Sarah then sat down in front of the large mirror in her room, fidgeting with the hairpins on the dressing table while Poppy gathered a handful of Sarah's unmanageable black curls from each side of her face and pulled them back, winding and pinning them securely into place and adding a large, ornamental hair clasp, which helped make her hair look as if this was a preferred and intended style, rather than a necessity, given the fact that Sarah's unruly hair would never tolerate being all gathered up and pinned into place in the fashionable way that most ladies wore their hair.

After sharing a few minutes of casual conversation, Poppy said, "I'm so very glad you got some good sleep, dearie. I'm afraid you might very well need it."

"What do you mean?" Sarah asked sharply, meeting Poppy's eyes in the mirror while she was careful not to move, knowing that Poppy hadn't quite finished making Sarah's hair look as good as possible.

"You father's solicitor arrived just before I came upstairs," Poppy said ominously. "He wishes to speak with you right away—not only you but your aunt and Mr. Halford too."

"What on earth . . ." Sarah began to ask but couldn't finish the sentence. "Why didn't you tell me as soon as you—"

"I told him you had slept late due to the stress of your father's death and you would be down as soon as you were ready," Poppy explained, not rattled by Sarah's impatience. "And I saw no point in telling *you* until you were nearly ready to go down, because that meant less time you had to be agitated over it. May I state the obvious and say that no one has any idea why he's here, but you'll know soon enough. So there's no need to get yourself into a state over it until you hear what he has to say."

"Then I'd do well to go hear what he has to say," Sarah said, rising to her feet the moment she knew Poppy had finished with her hair. Despite feeling an unsettling fear over the solicitor's unexpected visit, she took a moment to assess the present situation and paused on her way to the door, turning back to say to Poppy, "Forgive me for my foul mood, Poppy. You take such good care of me; I don't know what I'd do without you. My frustration is not with you. Forgive me if I've been unkind."

"You haven't been unkind," Poppy said, but her smile and the slight glimmer of moisture in her eyes let Sarah know that these days had been difficult for the maid. "I'm more . . . concerned about you, and . . . well, I'm here for you, my friend."

"I know," Sarah said, "and I'm grateful." They shared a long, tight hug before Sarah gave her friend the first smile she'd been able to muster since her father's death, then she hurried from the room and downstairs, wondering what on earth would warrant this unexpected gathering. Mr. Curtis, her father's trusted solicitor, had come to visit the day after Oswald's death, both to offer his condolences and to let her and Penelope know that Oswald's will was exactly what they had known and expected, and that all matters of the estate that fell under his responsibility were in order. He'd answered some questions and had promised to be there for Sarah should she ever need to consult with him over any matter that might arise. She'd known Mr. Curtis for many years—even if she hadn't had a great deal of personal interaction with him. But she knew her father considered him to be a trusted friend. Mr. Halford had attended that meeting, mostly because he had *always* been present for *every* meeting between the solicitor and Oswald—at Oswald's request. Halford was a lifetime friend and a trusted confidant, and Oswald had considered it prudent to make certain someone he trusted was privy to every aspect of his dealings in the event that he needed someone to speak on his behalf. Halford knew Mr. Curtis well and had not been at all surprised by the contents of the simple will, and he had gladly accepted Sarah's request to continue working for the household and to act as a liaison on her father's behalf to help her learn everything she needed to know. She was grateful for these two men and trusted them completely. Right now, she needed all the help she could get.

Everything had appeared to be completely in order and not at all confusing when Sarah had met with Mr. Curtis, Halford, and Penelope not so many days ago. She couldn't begin to imagine what might have come up in the meantime that would require all of them to meet together again so soon.

Sarah stopped at the bottom of the stairs to catch her breath and to muster the necessary dignity and propriety now that she was in charge of all she'd inherited from her father. Assuming an air of confidence she truly didn't feel, Sarah walked with trepidation toward the study where meetings with Mr. Curtis always took place. She found herself desperately wishing for an older brother right now. It wasn't the first time she'd indulged in such a wish, but she couldn't recall ever wanting it more than at this moment.

Sarah took a deep breath and opened the door to the study, stepping inside to see that she was the last to arrive. Halford and Mr. Curtis came respectfully to their feet, offering kind greetings. Penelope nodded and smiled toward her, but it was a nervous smile and Sarah knew her aunt shared her same questions and concerns. Penelope was dressed in a gown of bright lavender, which was typical. Sarah had noted that whenever her aunt left the house, she respectfully wore black to appropriately mourn her brother, but when at home she had continued to wear her normal, elaborate, and brightly colored gowns. Sarah had done the same, wearing her own normal attire, mostly because she didn't have enough black dresses to wear the color continually, and she also knew that her father wouldn't care a whit what his daughter and sister wore in regard to his recent death. Sarah smoothed her hands over the fabric of her own dark-blue dress that was dotted with little pink flowers in an attempt to soothe her nerves. Once she was seated, the men sat back down, and she was glad when Mr. Curtis said, "I'm certain you're all likely baffled over my visit today, so I will not waste any time with chitchat; I'll just come straight to the point."

"I think we would all appreciate that very much," Sarah said, feeling the need to assert herself as being in charge.

Mr. Curtis let out a long and heavy sigh, and his countenance was far graver than when he'd visited to offer his condolences for Oswald's death—a man who had been not only a client but a friend for many years. What on earth could make Mr. Curtis feel more upset *now* than he had been *then*? The question swirled in Sarah's mind while her quickened heartbeat made it difficult to sit still and remain dignified. It was taking great self-restraint not to shout at the man and insist that for all his promise to come straight to the point, he was taking a terribly long time finding the words to say whatever it was he needed to say.

"Mr. Curtis?" Sarah finally said, proud of herself for sounding so calm. "You seem to be having trouble getting to the point. We are all here at your request and obviously something is wrong, but—"

"Forgive me, m'lady," Mr. Curtis said. "I admit to feeling somewhat upset, but I shall do my best to remain professional and tell you what I learned late last night. You see . . . Dr. Turnlow came to my home at a very late hour, and he was quite upset. I can't possibly repeat all the details he told me—medical terminology that makes no sense to me—but we all know he is very good at what he does, and he has been a trusted confidant of this family for decades. He rehearsed all your father's symptoms, how they'd come on, how long they had been occurring, and how your father was in such a frenzy when he spoke to you that afternoon—with his death coming on soon afterward." He said nothing more.

"Yes," Sarah agreed when he hesitated too long. If she didn't hear immediately what Dr. Turnlow had said, she feared she might erupt into a very immature tantrum. "And what exactly did he tell you that was so upsetting?"

"You know that he attended your father throughout his illness," Mr. Curtis said.

"Yes," Sarah said again, finding it increasingly more difficult to sound patient.

Mr. Curtis took a deep breath and his words burst forth on the wave of a forced exhale. "He believes your father was poisoned—murdered—that someone in this house slowly and deliberately killed him."

"What?" Sarah barely managed to mutter, finding it difficult to breathe. It was absolutely the last thing she would have ever expected to hear. She was still finding it a challenge to even accept that her father was dead, but *murdered*? It wasn't possible!

Not surprisingly, Penelope burst into sobbing and pressed a handkerchief over her mouth, muttering over and over that it wasn't possible, it was too horrible to consider, who would do such a thing? As if from a great distance, Sarah heard Mr. Curtis explaining some of what the doctor had told him, but she found it difficult to hear him with the sound of her own breathing and heartbeat pounding in her ears. And Penelope's wailing didn't help any. Sarah tried very hard to focus on Mr. Curtis, hearing bits and pieces of the reasons for the doctor's conclusion; something about the way the illness had come on, the way symptoms would come and go, get worse and then better, and most especially the way he had died so suddenly when he had been doing rather well the day before. He said something about how easy it was to acquire substances that could be added to food or beverages in small doses that could cause such symptoms, and then ensure death with a larger dose. Sarah could feel the facts accumulating in her mind, even though she was hearing them through some kind of dense fogginess. She felt frozen, as if her body had turned to stone even while her mind was speeding repeatedly through endless pathways of information and questions. Her heart and lungs were working so hard it felt as if they might kill her simply by their efforts to absorb the shock of the information while allowing her to appear straight-faced and in control. As much as she loved her aunt, she would not reduce herself to behaving in such an undisciplined and dramatic way.

When Mr. Curtis apparently had nothing more to say, Sarah was surprised to see him take a handkerchief out of his pocket and dab at his eyes, something that Halford had been doing ever since the shocking news had been delivered. Sarah wanted to cry, but not here, not like this, not with these people present. Still, the silence prompted her to the fact that she *was* in charge; these people were looking to her for answers when she didn't even know what questions to ask. She forced herself past the horror of the words *poison* and *murder* being associated with her father's death, and asked Mr. Curtis with a trembling voice, "And what now? I can't even begin to comprehend such a thing being possible, and I certainly have no idea what's to be done about it. Do we report the doctor's suspicions to the police? Do we—"

"I already have, m'lady," Mr. Curtis said. "Dr. Turnlow and I went together early this morning to speak with the constable. They will be speaking with everyone in the house, with a special interest in those who had access to your father's food." He leaned forward, looking firmly at Sarah as if he wished to convey by his gaze more than he dared speak with his words. "You trust everyone in this room," he stated, even though she felt like he had intended it to be a question.

"I do," Sarah said with no hesitation; she didn't even have to think about it. "And you obviously do, or you wouldn't have requested the three of us particularly."

"I do," Mr. Curtis said. "So, I must ask . . . because I know that the police will be asking the same questions before the end of the day: Do you have any reason to *not* trust anyone who works in this house? Is there anyone you personally trust enough that you would absolutely know they had nothing to do with this?"

Sarah thought about that for a long moment. "I absolutely trust my maid Poppy. She loved my father, and she is good to the core. Beyond that . . . truthfully, Mr. Curtis, I know most of the servants' names, and our interaction is amicable, but I don't know any of them well enough personally to say one way or the other. I can't even imagine *anyone* in this house being capable of such a thing. I'm . . . in shock, Mr. Curtis. If I were not, I fear I would be in no condition to be speaking to you."

"I fear that when it sinks in, m'lady . . ." Mr. Curtis said, and Sarah was briefly distracted by the realization that since her father's death he'd stopped calling her by her name. All things combined, she felt as if her head might start spinning so fast it could easily just fall off. The solicitor didn't finish his sentence due to his own emotion, but Sarah understood his implication and she felt certain he was right. When the shock wore off and she could fully grasp that someone had *murdered* her father, robbed them of years together, stolen his life, she would likely either fly into a rage or become so crippled with emotion that she wouldn't be able to get out of bed. She anticipated likely needing more of whatever it was the doctor had given Poppy to help her sleep. She realized now that he'd surely suspected this when he'd been here the previous day to give medical assistance to a maid. But he'd obviously needed to speak with the solicitor and the police before he informed anyone else of his suspicions.

"M'lady," Mr. Curtis said, startling her from distant thoughts that felt like some kind of evil monster waiting at the edge of her consciousness, waiting to devour her. "Do you have any idea at all how this might have happened? Anything that might help us know where to begin an investigation?"

Sarah hurried to gather her thoughts. "I sincerely do not," Sarah declared, hearing once again a quiver in her voice that seemed to be letting her know that her ability to maintain her dignity wasn't going to last much longer.

Mr. Curtis's sigh was heavy with disappointment, as if he might have hoped to come away from this exchange with some kind of valid information that could have possibly helped solve the case this very day.

"Wait," Sarah said as her mind raced through dozens of facts all at once, "we always had different teapots because we had different preferences. The tea cozies over each pot were distinctly different, and we always knew which one was intended for each of us. We ate meals together from the same tray . . . ate the same food; but we never drank the same tea." As the idea fully sank in, she felt literally sick to her stomach. Could that possibly be how it had happened?

"And who had access to your father's tea?" Mr. Curtis asked.

"I have no idea," Sarah insisted, wishing she *did* know. "In a household such as this I assume it could have passed through many hands before it was served to him. How could we possibly know?"

Following yet another sigh, Mr. Curtis said, "I will give that information to the police and we'll let them do what they do best; I believe they will be here within the hour. They will be questioning every person who lives and works here, and I doubt their interviews will be brief; therefore, they are likely not going to be able to finish today. You understand, of course, that I have no control over this situation now that our suspicions have been put into the hands of the police; and of course, we had no choice but to inform the authorities, when Dr. Turnlow's information had so much validity."

"Of course," Sarah repeated blankly, wanting to both scream and silently disappear. Since she could do neither, she popped to her feet and declared,

"Thank you for keeping us abreast of what's happening, Mr. Curtis. I know you cared very much for my father, and he trusted you completely. This can't be easy for you."

"Nor for you," Mr. Curtis said, also standing.

"I confess it's . . . well . . ." the quavering in her voice became impossible to disguise, "I think I need to be alone. This is so . . . so . . ." She couldn't find the words.

"I completely understand," Mr. Curtis said with compassion, "but I must ask you to hear something else that I have to say. You need not feel any shame about expressing your emotion here, m'lady. However, I can't let you leave until I tell you something that I simply cannot allow to remain unspoken."

"What is it?" Sarah said, sitting back down with a huff that was more an attempt to swallow her need to cry, but it came out sounding impatient, or perhaps even indignant.

Sarah was glad that Mr. Curtis didn't seem affected when he sat back down and looked at her firmly. "M'lady, because we don't yet know the reasons someone would want to harm your father . . . kill your father . . . we can't be certain that you are not in danger as well."

"What?" Sarah blurted, her desire to cry suddenly and assuredly gone. Penelope and Halford repeated the word in quick succession, as if in a perfectly timed echo. Penelope was so astonished she actually stopped sobbing and stared at Mr. Curtis as if he'd said the world would end tomorrow. Halford looked upset, perhaps angry as his eyes darted back and forth between Sarah with concern, and Mr. Curtis with astonishment.

"Why on *earth*," she finally blurted, "would *I* be in danger? It's ludicrous!" Even as she said it, she consciously accepted that she'd not fully absorbed the possibility her father had actually been murdered. But to think of her own safety being an issue simply felt too ridiculous to even consider.

Sarah's heart quickened when she saw some kind of enlightenment appear on Halford's face. He looked at her as he spoke. "Your father told me on numerous occasions of a great family treasure that was hidden secretly away, and that in generations past, lives had been lost in dispute over that treasure. He believed the treasure was cursed. Perhaps all of *this* has something to do with *that*."

Sarah weighed her answer for a long moment before she said with confidence. "Since I have no idea what you're talking about, I don't see how something so . . . obscure and strange could have anything to do with me."

"But you are his heir," Penelope muttered sepulchrally from behind her handkerchief, looking horrified, as if she truly believed this family curse might come through the ceiling at any moment in the form of a bolt of lightning and strike Sarah dead.

"Yes, I am his heir," Sarah said, now feeling angry without understanding why. "The heir to his estate. This . . . mysterious treasure will likely remain a mystery given that his knowledge of it has gone to the grave with him. I know nothing of any such treasure." Sarah felt a tingle pass over her shoulders and down her back, as if her willful lies about the hidden treasure were having a physical effect on her. But she couldn't deny her firm belief that the secret her father had passed along to her must remain a secret. She couldn't fathom the idea that her life might be in danger because of it, but she was so overcome by the accumulation of strangeness surrounding her father's death that she felt as if her head might explode. Sarah stood up again, saying firmly, "Thank you for your concern, Mr. Curtis, but I'm certain I am not in any danger—especially here in my own home."

"In your own home where your father was poisoned?" Mr. Curtis countered respectfully.

Sarah couldn't find a retort for that. Penelope managed to suppress her sobs long enough to say, "We must take special care regarding everything she eats and drinks. I will gladly help see that—"

"Thank you, Aunt," Sarah said, "but that's completely unnecessary."

"Begging your pardon, m'lady," Halford piped in, "but I agree with Mr. Curtis; I believe it *is* necessary to take every possible precaution to protect you—at least until we figure out exactly how your father died, and why."

"And you may *never* figure it out," Sarah countered. "Am I to live in fear for the remainder of my life? Coddled and watched over like some piece of fragile porcelain? If that's what it takes to remain safe, I boldly protest. I assure you I am perfectly safe."

Sarah hurried from the room before she had to endure any more arguing. She ran toward the security of her own bedroom, grateful she didn't cross paths with anyone who might notice her complete disregard for any kind of propriety in the way she lifted her skirts to keep them from impeding her. She felt a storm rumbling inside her and wanted to be safely alone before she allowed it to erupt. But its force was growing stronger very quickly and it felt as if she were literally racing with the inevitable eruption, and the first painful sob leapt out of her before she reached the door to her bedroom. She hurried inside, closed the door behind her and leaned against it as another sob erupted, and another. The breathlessness she felt from her lengthy run contributed to a sudden weakness and she hurried to her bed, collapsing there on her side where she sobbed and gasped for breath in some kind of strange rhythm that coincided with horrifying thoughts pounding in her mind. Her father murdered? Her own life in danger? And if Mr. Curtis was right—in both cases—could it really have something to do with the treasure she'd discovered according to her father's instructions? If such was the case, she was certainly far better off to continue pretending that she knew nothing about it. She didn't even understand *what* the gleaming sword with its emerald heart had to do with *anything* related to the estate, and especially herself. The box was best kept hidden at the bottom of her wardrobe, and her knowledge of the box and its contents was absolutely best kept secret from *everyone*. It wasn't a matter of being able to trust certain people; it was more a feeling of not wanting to put this burden upon anyone else's shoulders. She didn't know why her possession of the sword felt like a burden, but it did. And if it was indeed a burden—and it was associated with her inheriting the estate—then it was her burden to bear.

Sarah had barely managed to calm down enough to breathe evenly, reducing her sobs to an occasional sniffle, when Poppy entered the room after knocking but not waiting for a response. It was the standard signal between them to let Sarah know she was coming in, but there was never any reason for her *not* to enter. If Sarah really needed privacy she would lock the doors—which she did very rarely, because no one but Poppy would ever enter the room uninvited, and Sarah relied on Poppy in every respect, and trusted her completely—except for telling her about the box in the bottom of the wardrobe, she thought with some degree of shame as Poppy closed the door behind her and moved to sit on the edge of the bed, taking hold of Sarah's hand.

"Halford just told me the things Mr. Curtis said; he felt certain you would want me to know."

"Of course," Sarah said, wanting to add that there were no secrets between them, but that was no longer true.

"I believe he also wanted me to know because . . . he wants me to help look out for you so that you'll remain safe."

"There is absolutely no need for that!" Sarah protested.

"I heartily disagree," Poppy said with the firmness of an overprotective mother. "I will be overseeing your meals and bringing them to you personally— whether you eat here or in the dining room." Sarah sighed, not knowing what she could say to convince Poppy that it wasn't necessary.

"You should also know," Poppy said, "that a few police officers are already here. They are questioning the servants as we speak, and we were all warned not to leave the house until they've completed their interviews."

"And then what?" Sarah asked, determined to remain in her room if only to avoid coming in contact with these officers in any way—although she felt certain they would want to speak with her, as well. She just couldn't grasp the concept that their presence here confirmed Dr. Turnlow's suspicions that her father had been murdered. Simply thinking about it made her head throb.

"Then there will be an inquest," Poppy stated. "That's what Mr. Curtis told Halford."

"And what if the outcome of this inquest is that it's true?" Sarah asked. "What if they truly believe he was murdered? Then what?"

"I have no idea, dearie," Poppy said with compassion. "But we'll get through it—no matter what."

Sarah tried to smile and tried to believe her, but at the moment she felt as if the world she lived in, where she had always felt safe and loved and secure, was now crumbling around her, and she didn't know how to fix it.

# Chapter Three
## THE INQUEST

FOR FOUR DAYS POLICE OFFICERS spent every hour of daylight at Castle Courtenay, observing, interviewing, and inspecting what seemed like every nook and cranny. Given the size of the house and the number of people who lived and worked here, Sarah found it remarkable it didn't take them a month. But having them in her home made her decidedly uncomfortable. Beyond her own thorough interview with two officers, she'd barely encountered them. It was a sizable house and there were plenty of places she could go to avoid them. But just knowing they were present left her feeling on edge.

When it occurred to Sarah that these men might thoroughly search her wardrobe, she panicked. Considering the size and intricacies of the house, which she knew far better than any stranger, she carefully moved the box to an unused guest room in another wing and slid it beneath the bed, pressing it against the wall beneath the headboard as far as it would go. She then cordially invited the officers to search her rooms before she guided them to continue their investigation in the remainder of the rooms in her wing, which were all left unused—the furniture covered to protect it from dust—except for her sitting room and Poppy's room which was across the hall. When they finished searching that wing, Sarah suggested that Poppy take the men down to the kitchen to have some lunch—since it was conveniently that time of day—which gave her just enough time to get the box and sneak it back into the bottom of her wardrobe without being seen. She was relaxing in her sitting room with a book when Poppy returned with a lunch tray for both of them to share, and they talked about what they'd mostly been talking about for days—the horror and absurdity that Oswald may have been murdered, the discomfort of having their home overtaken by the police, and the many unanswered questions that lay ahead regarding the matter. They didn't say anything that hadn't been said many times already, but it was all so much to take in that they both seemed to need to keep talking about it. Perhaps when the matter was resolved they could talk about something else. For now, there was no point pretending they could think about anything else; therefore, talking about it felt like the healthiest thing to do—rather than trying to pretend the situation was different than it actually was.

When the police finally announced that they were leaving Castle Courtenay, Sarah knew her relief was shared by everyone else in the house. Although, with the secret hidden in the bottom of her wardrobe, she doubted anyone could be more relieved than she was. She was informed that after they did some more investigating and put together all their information, a formal inquest would be held to determine whether Oswald Courtenay's death had been the result of a criminal act. Sarah felt freshly horrified to hear it put that way, and she wanted to ask what would happen after that—but she couldn't bring herself to pose the question. To her it seemed impossible to ever find out who had committed the crime. Someone clever enough to poison a person was not going to be stupid enough to leave clues for the police to find—especially so long after the fact. The very idea that a murderer could be living and working under this roof, calculating ways of disguising their hideous actions, left Sarah continually uneasy. But what was to be done about it? She'd considered a great deal—and discussed with Poppy—the advice Mr. Curtis had given her in regard to the possibility that her own life might be in danger. Even if it *were* true—which she couldn't even imagine—she didn't know what could be done about that either. She wondered if she would ever feel at peace again. She'd always felt safe and secure here in her home, but that feeling had vanished and now she always felt uneasy, which made it difficult to relax. And she certainly wasn't sleeping well at night. The entire matter was just so thoroughly absurd—and the absurdity increased dramatically each time she thought of what was hidden in the bottom of her wardrobe, and how she'd come to find it.

Eight days after Mr. Curtis had first revealed to Sarah and her trusted aunt and Mr. Halford his suspicions regarding the true reasons for Oswald's death, Halford informed Sarah after supper that the official inquest would be held the next day, and he told her that she had the option to attend; she didn't *need* to be there because her testimony of the events according to her perspective had been carefully taken into consideration in the investigation, but she was certainly welcome to be present if she wanted to personally see for herself how the inquest proceeded—and be there for the outcome.

Sarah only had to think about it for a moment. "I don't want to be there," she said firmly, "but I . . ."

"What, m'lady?" he urged in a tender voice he'd used with her throughout the whole of her life.

"Halford," she said with kind firmness, "first of all, let me make it clear that I do not wish to have you call me that. You've always called me by my name, and I find this formality highly uncomfortable."

"It's proper," he replied, unruffled.

"I don't care," Sarah stated with vehemence. "I'm asking you to simply continue calling me by my name."

Halford sighed, as if he were torn between his strict training on proper protocol versus his respect for her. "Very well," he said, "if that's what you wish. I'll agree to a compromise. There are times when certain people are around when it would be inappropriate for me to speak to you so informally. Only during such occasions will I revert to formality."

"That sounds reasonable," Sarah said. "Thank you. As for the inquest, I was wondering if you'll be attending."

"I will," he said.

"Then I know I can count on you to give me an accurate report of all that was said and also the . . . outcome."

"Yes, you can count on me," he said. "I will even take notes to help me remember important details."

"Good," Sarah said on an exhale of relief. "Do you need me to help convince my aunt to remain at home? I'm certain her being there could be very disruptive." She laughed softly but felt no degree of humor. "You know more than anyone besides Poppy how very much I love her, but her inability to restrain her emotions can be . . . challenging in certain situations."

Halford smiled knowingly. "I understand completely . . . . Miss Sarah." His smile twitched upward just a little more as if to declare he was following her orders to use her given name. "I have already spoken to her and assured her that it would be too difficult for her, and she was quick to agree. I do fear she will want to spend the day with you, and she might require a great supply of handkerchiefs while she considers the possibilities of what might be happening."

Sarah smiled at him, a little more naturally this time. "Don't worry. I've been close to Penelope my entire life; I can keep her calm—and well supplied with handkerchiefs. I still find that preferable over sitting in a stuffy room listening to men talk about the details of my father's death."

"I understand," Halford said and wished her a good evening before he walked away.

Sarah stood where she was—near the foot of the stairs—for a long moment before she decided to go to the library and try to find something she'd not already read that might hold her interest. Reading would be a good distraction from all that was happening, and nothing she had in her room at the moment had been able to hold her attention. But surely hidden amongst the many hundreds of books in this room lined with majestic bookshelves she could find *something* to help distract her from the unfathomable possibility that her father had been murdered. And perhaps if she was immersed in a book tomorrow while she waited with her aunt, she might be able to more easily convince Penelope to remain calm and quiet so that she could read; she could even offer to read aloud to Penelope which might help keep them *both* calmer.

By the time Sarah got to the library, the need for a good book had settled into her as something mandatory. She stood in the center of the room and turned in a circle, trying to feel drawn to some particular section, since she didn't even know where to begin to find a novel she hadn't read that might sufficiently intrigue her. As much as she'd read books from these shelves her entire life, she still had trouble understanding how they were organized—or perhaps they weren't. Her eye was drawn to some particularly large books that were stacked on their sides because they were too tall to fit upright on the shelves. She'd noticed them before but had never felt any curiosity over what they might be. However, at the moment she *did* feel curious and took the top book off the stack, blowing dust off of it, appalled by the evidence of the maids' neglect in keeping the books dusted. But then, there were so many books, and surely there were more important priorities for them elsewhere in the house.

Sarah felt her heart quickening when she read on the front of the very old book in her hands, *History of the Family Courtenay—Eighteenth Century*. On the day of her father's death—with all the strangeness that had occurred— she had wondered if such a thing existed here in the library, but then she'd forgotten all about the idea. And now a shiver rushed over her shoulders as she considered the way she had just been led to find this. She stared at the title while she considered that they were not so many years into the nineteenth century, so perhaps that volume was yet to be written. But who exactly was meant to write and compile such a record? Was this yet another of her responsibilities of which she'd not been informed? Hadn't anyone ever thought to keep a list in an obvious place in the office of the house that might make her duties and responsibilities clearer?

Sarah sat on the floor since the book was heavy, and she set it down on the carpet in front of her, carefully turning the pages and scanning some of them to quickly realize this was an incredibly boring book. Her forebears had lived bland and ordinary lives—at least in the eighteenth century. Then a thought occurred to her that made her gasp. Perhaps the eighteenth century had been boring for the Courtenay family, but what about before then? She now felt impatient and eager as she took down the other books in the stack, the oldest being the family history from the fourteenth century. Starting there, she carefully turned the very old pages and scanned them, realizing this was the story of her ancestor—William Charles Courtenay—a man who had personally associated with the royal family. He had been a brave warrior who had apparently saved the lives of more than one of the children of the king and queen during some terrible rebellion that had been kept from the knowledge of the public so as not to cause alarm. But because of William's bravery and sacrifice—having been severely wounded in the scuffle—he had been given a title and a great deal of property and wealth. Ironically, everything that had been given to William Courtenay was property that had been impounded from a titled and wealthy man who had committed treason in numerous ways, and therefore he'd been tried, found guilty, executed, and all of his property had been confiscated—and given to William. With such an enormous amount of wealth, he had decided to have the old home on the property torn down completely and have a new home built. Apparently, the queen herself had suggested putting turrets into the design of the house, and it was also the queen who had bestowed the name of *Castle Courtenay* on the house. Sarah felt taken aback by such a revelation, and a little sheepish about her inaccurate ideas regarding how the name of the house had been founded in some kind of grandiose arrogance. According to the book in her hands, the royal family had come here more than once while the house was being built. But before the house was completed a death had occurred and the crown had been handed down to the next generation. And the familiar connection William had shared with the royal family dissipated. But his wealth and title remained.

Sarah scanned through the pages, bored by details of building the great house in which she had always lived, and little anecdotes about happenings among the family and servants. Sarah concluded that perhaps one day she would take more of an interest in such stories, but right now she was still too preoccupied with her father's death. Still, she found herself methodically turning the pages to see if anything else from the fourteenth century caught her attention. She yawned and decided to return the books to their resting place, knowing they would be here whenever she found herself in the mood to learn more about the history of her family. She methodically turned one more page and froze as if a blast of bitter cold air had just rushed into the room, instantly turning her into something like unto a statue, unable to move and barely able to breathe. There it was. Right in front of her. Again, it felt as if she'd been mysteriously guided to this book and this page on this night.

Breaking free from her numbed state, Sarah looked in both directions as if she feared she might find the ghost of William Courtenay standing behind her, guiding her from the great beyond to this moment. Of course, she saw nothing, but a distinct shiver rushed over her entire body as she turned back to stare at the perfect drawing of the sword that was in a box at the bottom of her own wardrobe. She leaned closer to the page, examining the drawing carefully, amazed at the exact proportions, the details of the carvings in the hilt, and the perfection of the details of the emerald heart. At the top of the page were the words: *The Emerald Heart of Courtenay.* And below the drawing was a paragraph stating that a man who had worked closely with the royal family for many years—and whose life had also been saved by the bravery of William Courtenay—had presented William with the gift of this remarkable sword, which had been crafted by this man's brother, as an offering of immeasurable gratitude. All of this made sense to Sarah, and she was glad to know the history of what was now in her possession, but what she'd read so far didn't explain the reasons for how mysteriously the box with its precious contents had been hidden, nor the way her father had been babbling about it so strangely before he died. Sarah read on, gasping again as she took in the words before her: *This mighty sword has been blessed to hold great power to whomever shall possess it. To possess it is to possess great blessings upon the head of the possessor and all of the House of Courtenay, therefore if the rightful possessor of this great sword allows it to fall into the hands of evil, a great curse shall come down upon the House of Courtenay. So it has been blessed, recorded, and declared forevermore.*

"Good heavens!" Sarah muttered, pausing in her repeated reading of those last few sentences to ask herself if she believed in such things. Her father had rambled something about a curse upon the house . . . the family . . . he'd said both. The incidents in the family that her father had suggested might be somehow attached to a curse just seemed like natural events to Sarah.

But then her father had been so frenzied during that conversation that it was difficult for her to put together the pieces of his actual intentions. She'd tried so hard to remember exactly what he'd said that it only seemed to become more muddled in her mind. But she knew now—looking at the words directly in front of her—that he had said the phrase *rightful possessor*, and he'd said that person was *her*. Given that she knew he'd given her clues on how to find the sword, she had little doubt he was referring to *this* strange prophecy or tradition or whatever it might be related to the sword, and somehow, he'd known he was dying. But murdered? She became eerily haunted by all things combined and resisted the urge to again look around as if she might see the ghost of William Charles Courtenay. Or perhaps that of her own father.

Realizing how ridiculous her thinking had become, Sarah gave herself a chiding moan and looked once more at the page in front of her, the drawing of the sword, the strange words written about it, perhaps attempting to memorize them. When she realized she couldn't, she stood up and went to the writing desk in the corner to retrieve pen, ink, and paper, which she took back to the floor where the heavy book lay open. Sarah carefully copied down the exact wording of those last few sentences. She could recall the story behind the sword well enough, but she wanted to study these particular words more carefully when she wasn't so tired. She returned the pen and ink to the desk and folded the paper once she'd blown on the ink to dry it, tucking it into her bodice since her dress had no pockets.

Taking one last, long gaze at the image of the sword, Sarah truly had to wonder what on earth her father would have wanted her to do now—or to know. Oh, how she wished she could speak with him. She let out a gasp bordering on a scream when she heard Poppy say, "Oh, here you are!" She then giggled and added, "Sorry, I thought you would have heard me come in. And you know I can't go to bed until I make certain you're all taken care of."

"It's all right," Sarah said, now wanting to get these books put away as quickly as possible in order to avoid questions for which she had no answers.

But before Sarah could close the book, Poppy asked, looking over the top of her head, "What is that?" She'd moved closer than Sarah had realized, but she asked the question with complete innocence; of course, she would have no reason to think that a drawing of a sword in a very old book would mean anything at all.

Sarah slammed the book closed and carried it to the shelf, recalling that this volume had been on the bottom of the stack. "I came here looking for a novel that might distract me tomorrow." She put the other volumes of her family's history back in place, in their proper order. "And I found these old books about the history of the house and the family. I was just glancing through one of them."

"Oh, how fascinating!" Poppy said.

"Most of it was rather boring," Sarah said, leading the way out of the library.

"Did you find out why the house was called a castle?" Poppy asked, sounding amused. They'd joked about it a great deal, which made her question valid—and a mutual source of humor.

"Actually, yes," Sarah said as they headed together up the stairs.

Sarah told Poppy the gist of what she'd read about the story of William Charles Courtenay, and how the house had been built by him. Sarah found as she repeated the story—perhaps inspired by Poppy's enthusiasm—she felt rather fond of William who had been richly rewarded for his bravery. But Sarah said nothing about the sword.

Once Poppy had helped Sarah out of her corset and made certain Sarah had everything she needed, they said good night and Poppy went across the hall to her own room. But Sarah couldn't sleep. Her mind was smoldering with thoughts of tomorrow's inquest—with all its implications—combined with all she'd learned about the treasure she'd been guided to through her father's final jumbled conversation with her.

Sarah finally got up and lit a lamp. She retrieved the folded paper she'd hidden at the bottom of a bureau drawer earlier when Poppy had been distracted. As if reading it again and again might help her understand it, she did so until she concluded that it actually made no sense at all, so she hid the paper again and forced herself to go back to bed, even though it took her a long while to go to sleep.

Sarah awoke to the sound of rain falling, and the room heavy with the same dark gray of the clouds outside. A glance at the clock let her know she had slept late into the morning—which was not surprising. And as expected there was a cloth-covered tray on the table near the window; Poppy was nothing if not consistent in anticipating Sarah's every need, and she was sensitive enough in her care of Sarah that she would never want her to go hungry even for a short time.

Sarah lay in bed for a few minutes, looking toward the rain drizzling down the windows, thinking about the inquest taking place today regarding her father's death, and feeling deeply grateful that she had been able to remain at home. Not only had she been spared from having to wake up early and get ready after getting so little sleep, but she also didn't have to listen to the details of Oswald's illness and passing—details she'd already reviewed in her head way too much. The last thing she wanted was to hear them discussed freely by men who hadn't even known her father. She could only pray that the outcome would be favorable. But what might that mean exactly? She wanted desperately for an official conclusion that it was *not* murder, and that the doctor was simply mistaken. However, her deepest instincts were telling her that there was something foul regarding her father's death, and if it was officially declared murder, then what? Was her life truly in danger? And why? *Why?*

Unable to even think about it, Sarah forced herself out of bed and freshened up before she put on her most comfortable dressing gown and sat down to enjoy the tray of food Poppy had left for her, deciding that she preferred remaining in her rooms today for as long as possible.

Sarah had barely finished her breakfast when Poppy came with a few novels she had found in the library, thinking Sarah might enjoy them. Being the close friends they were, Poppy knew Sarah hadn't read these particular books. Sarah felt deeply grateful and told her so, because she very much needed a distraction but didn't feel like getting dressed and going down to the library herself. Poppy also reported that Penelope had left earlier in one of their carriages to attend a ladies' luncheon that was a regular occurrence. Sarah couldn't deny feeling some relief that she wouldn't have to feel obligated to check on Penelope—or sit with her while they waited for Mr. Halford's return.

When lunchtime came, it hadn't been that long since Sarah had eaten breakfast, but she still enjoyed sharing a meal with Poppy in the sitting room and was surprised by how hungry she was. They talked about anything *but* the inquest taking place—and all things remotely related to it. After lunch Poppy went to take care of some of her responsibilities elsewhere in the house and Sarah made herself comfortable on a sofa in the sitting room, diving into one of the novels Poppy had brought her. She was just beginning to lose herself in the story when Poppy returned, sounding a bit frantic as she informed Sarah that Halford and Mr. Curtis had returned from the inquest and wanted to speak with her and Penelope right away. Penelope had returned only a short while earlier and had gone to her room to freshen up; a maid had been sent to retrieve her.

Sarah hated the sick knot that immediately tightened in her stomach, and her quickening heartbeat that only tightened the knot further. With Poppy's help she hurried to get dressed and look presentable. Poppy hugged her before she headed down the stairs, assuring her that everything would be all right, but Sarah felt a deep dread that something was very, very wrong—and this was just the beginning. Three times on the way to the drawing room she told herself to stop being so paranoid, and three times she recounted a great deal of evidence that told her she had good reason to feel the way she did.

Sarah entered the room to see Penelope seated very ladylike in a bright yellow gown that was puffy to the point of overwhelming her. She looked as if she were trying to be brave, but the emotion just beneath the surface was evident. Sarah knew her aunt feared the worst, and the very idea of losing her brother this way was tearing her apart inside. Sarah doubted it would be long before Penelope was sobbing into her handkerchief—again. Halford and Mr. Curtis both came to their feet as she closed the door, and she felt as if she had intruded upon a silent tension reeking of awkwardness, and they were all glad for her arrival. But a quick perusal of their expressions told Sarah everything she needed to know.

"Gentlemen," she said with a nod. Then to Penelope, "Aunt." And another nod. She was pleased with her ability thus far to keep her voice steady, and glad to be able to move to a chair and sit down with at least as much poise as her aunt without revealing any evidence of the nervousness buzzing inside her.

"I'll get straight to the point," Mr. Curtis said as the men both sat back down. "The inquest concluded beyond any question that Oswald Courtenay was murdered."

Unsurprisingly, Penelope began to sob into her handkerchief, but Sarah could tell she was attempting to remain as quiet as possible. Sarah didn't know what to say, how to react. She was just barely becoming accustomed to having others look to her for answers and directions, now that she was officially considered in charge of all things Courtenay. Forcing her thoughts to stop swirling, as if she'd silently ordered them to be still, she found a reasonable question and did her best to ask it with dignity and composure. "Was there any information revealed that I'm not already aware of?"

"No," both men said, and she was glad to not have to endure learning about any more unexpected horrible details regarding her father's death. "I should clarify, however," Mr. Curtis added, "that it was the doctor's examination of your father's body following his death that bore the greatest evidence. I don't understand such things enough to be able to repeat what he reported, but the police seemed to know what he was talking about." A long silence followed as if he expected Sarah to comment, but she couldn't think of a thing to say. He finally cleared his throat and added, "I wish I had more to tell you, m'lady. I wish the news were different. Without the doctor's keen perception, we might not have *ever* known."

"Perhaps that would have been easier," Halford said and Sarah agreed with him—at least the part of her that preferred to just move on with her life as simply as possible agreed with him. But another part of her felt frightened of what might have happened had they *not* known the truth, of being caught unawares at some point in the future, considering that the murderer was still at large—and likely in this very house—and no one had any idea who it was or what their motives might have been.

Sarah tried to think of a way to say all she was thinking without babbling a myriad of comments and feelings that would likely make no sense. She settled on simply saying, "What now?"

"A very good question," Halford said. "We've been discussing that very thing. The police will continue their investigation, but it's evident they have very little to go on, and neither of us," he nodded toward Mr. Curtis, "believe they have enough information to find out who is responsible."

"And yet it seems evident it must be someone in this house," Sarah stated the obvious.

"Yes," Mr. Curtis said grimly. "Which is why we . . ." he hesitated and nodded toward Halford *and* Aunt Penelope, who had calmed down but wore a severe expression, "have taken the liberty of arranging protection for you."

"What *kind* of protection?" Sarah demanded, not liking the sound of this at all. As much as she hated the feeling that someone in this house might wish for her to follow in her father's footsteps, she couldn't imagine what might be done about it. And she didn't like the idea of these people— even as much as she trusted them and knew they cared for her—making plans on her behalf without consulting her.

"You need to remain safe," Penelope said with a forcefulness that rarely showed itself. But that didn't answer Sarah's question. "You are the heir to everything your father left behind, dear girl. Without you, everything would fall into . . . chaos." She nodded toward the two men in the room, then looked again at Sarah. "We all agree that until this mystery is solved, we must do whatever it takes to see that you are protected."

"And what if this mystery is *never* solved?" Sarah snapped, wishing her agitation wasn't so evident. "Am I to live my life in fear, always wondering if someone might want to do away with me? And how can I really be safe when we don't even understand the reasons why my father was killed? Perhaps it has nothing to do with me at all."

"Perhaps it doesn't," Mr. Curtis said, "but for the time being, I feel better assuming that it does and therefore taking the necessary precautions."

"And I agree with him," Halford said.

"So, I am outnumbered three to one," Sarah said, her voice still snappy.

"*Four* to one," Halford said. "We have spoken to Poppy and she has already been helping keep you safe. She is entirely in agreement with us."

Fury overcame Sarah as if someone had poured a bucket of ice-cold water over her head. She stood up both to try and stifle her temptation to shout, and to be able to turn her back toward the three people in the room who had been plotting on her behalf without her knowledge. She took a few deep breaths, reminding herself that it was her safety and well-being they were concerned about. She reminded herself that they genuinely cared about her, and their intentions were to do what was best. Feeling calmer but not calm enough to turn and look at them, Sarah asked, "What exactly—may I ask—does my being *protected* entail? Am I to remain locked up in my rooms every minute of my life? Will you provide weapons for all the stable hands and have them surround me even while I walk through the gardens?" Sarah couldn't help her sarcasm; she was only grateful to know that these people all knew her well enough to know that her anger was based more in frustration than in anything personal. And they all had to know that grief and shock over her father's death were still very close to the surface for her, for all of them. She couldn't begin to grasp why *anyone* would have wanted to kill her father, and she missed him so dreadfully that sometimes his absence created a very real pain in the center of her chest that could only be alleviated by a bout of sobbing that she would permit herself only when she was all alone.

"Please sit down, Sarah," she heard Halford say with a gentle firmness that reminded her of her father. She did so but remained at the edge of her seat. "We understand that this is very upsetting for you—for a number of reasons. You are accustomed to being very independent, and we all know that. However, the three of us discussed our concerns the very day we found out about the doctor's suspicions. I have written to a very good friend of mine, a fine man whom I have known most of my life. I wrote to *him* because he has a connection to a man with some very specific training and experience in protecting people who are in danger. While serving in the military he was chosen for his keen perception and excellent skills to help protect members of the royal family. When he grew weary of certain aspects of working in that situation, he became somewhat of an independent . . ."

Halford hesitated as if he were searching for the right word, or perhaps more accurately, a word to describe what this man did that would not make Sarah even angrier. She quickly came up with the most likely word he might have said and blurted, "Bodyguard? You've hired a *bodyguard* to what? Follow me around like some kind of bloodhound?" She resisted the urge to stand up again, mostly because her limbs felt a little shaky.

"In essence, yes," Halford said, remaining calm. "But he's discreet and he will be respectful of your privacy. He's a decent man or I would not be trusting your safety to his care. But you must do as he tells you, Sarah," Halford pleaded. "Even if his instructions might not make sense to you, you must trust him."

"You must!" Penelope pleaded. "You're a headstrong girl," her aunt added, somehow making it sound like a compliment and a reproach at the same time. "Your personality will serve you well as heiress to this estate, but you know nothing of being able to keep yourself safe when we're not even certain what or who exactly might be a threat to you. Mr. Halford knows what he's talking about. You must trust us. And you must trust this man and do what he tells you."

"I think I would rather remain locked in my rooms," Sarah declared.

"I can understand why you'd feel that way," Halford said, "but given the fact that your father's murder took place right here in this house, I'm not certain that's a safe option. Not to mention that we all know you well enough to know you would go crazy being stuck indoors for more than a day or two."

"Then what exactly are my options?" Sarah demanded.

Halford sighed loudly. Mr. Curtis and Penelope did the same, like an echo trying to release some of the pressure building in this conversation.

"For now, you need to meet Mr. Noble and hear what he has to say," Halford told her. "You may be the heiress, but you are still very young, and you need guidance from the people you can trust to help keep you safe. We are those people, and we are unanimous in this."

"So, the decision has been made," Sarah declared, now making no effort to conceal her disdain. "I have no say in this. You're just turning me over to this Mr. Noble, to do whatever this man tells me to do, whether I like it or not."

"That's exactly what we're doing," Halford said, "and quite frankly, I feel confident that if your father were still here and he had a say in this decision, this is exactly what he would have done. I'm more concerned for your safety than whether or not you are angry with me."

"And I can say the same," Penelope stated, unusually composed and firm.

"I'm just the solicitor," Mr. Curtis said, "but I have been made to feel a part of this family for a great many years, and I too am in complete agreement."

Sarah shook her head and closed her eyes, as if that might help her think more clearly, but it only let her know that she had no valid argument for everything she'd been told. It seemed all she could do for now was resign herself to being under the protection of this bodyguard that had been hired without anyone consulting her.

"Very well," she said and let out a long, weighted sigh, "when might I have the pleasure of meeting this Mr. Noble?" She couldn't help her sarcasm, especially when emphasizing the word *pleasure*.

"As a matter of fact," Halford said, now showing a smile that irritated Sarah, "he's here now; he's been waiting in the hall."

"What?" Sarah said more harshly than loudly, not wanting to be over-heard. Halford just stood up and walked toward the door, pulling it open with a triumphant glance toward Sarah, who felt nothing but dread.

# Chapter Four
## THE PROTECTOR

SARAH STOOD ABRUPTLY, IF ONLY to feel more dignified, or perhaps just taller. Mr. Curtis stood as well, but without showing any of the concern that Sarah felt. Penelope remained seated but looked entirely composed. But then, she had been conspiring about this for days; what reason did *she* have to feel uneasy?

Sarah watched Halford motion with his arm toward the hallway and felt decidedly unnerved to think that this man who had been hired to protect her had been out there all this time. She wondered if he'd been able to overhear their conversation, and she also wondered how much he knew about what was going on.

A man stepped into the room; his hair was as black and curly as her own, and clearly as unmanageable. He was a few inches taller than Halford, whom Sarah knew to be average height. He had hair on his face that could in no way be described as a beard; it was more like he'd been too lazy to shave for a day or two. After appraising his ridiculously perfect features and dark eyes for barely a second, Sarah hurried to take in the way he was dressed. His black boots and dark breeches looked well-worn and boldly declared that they had been chosen for comfort; his white shirt with blousy sleeves and a high collar looked dingy—not as if it were dirty, but more because it was old. However, his waistcoat, the front of which was predominantly black, woven into an exquisite pattern with small amounts of red and gold, looked as fine and new as if he intended to wear it to a grand social occasion. The contrast of his attire confused Sarah and took her slightly off guard, but as she met his gaze falling directly upon her, she had the distinct impression that the way he dressed was clearly intended to confuse people and take them off guard. She estimated him to be about a decade older than herself, and she couldn't deny that he was handsome. But she wouldn't have cared if he was as ugly as a pig. Either way, she didn't want her life to be controlled by him or any other man.

Before there was time for any introductions, he bowed slightly toward her and said with perfect respect, "Darius Noble, m'lady, at your service."

"And *are* you?" Sarah asked him, knowing the subtle sharpness in her voice was directed at the situation—not at him—but she hardly knew how to explain that in the moment.

"Am I what?" he asked, standing straight again. "At your s—"

"Noble," she said.

"I try to be," he replied humbly, which took her off guard again.

Sarah cleared her throat softly while she struggled to know what to say next; the silence of everyone else in the room made it evident they intended for her to handle the situation from this point forward. "I've been told," she began, "that you've been hired to protect me."

"How very convenient," he said with a slight twitch of his lips. "I've been told exactly the same thing."

Sarah didn't appreciate his attempt at humor, given her foul mood. "In light of all the unanswered questions regarding the present situation . . . I assume you've been informed of the present situation."

"I have," he said, completely respectful again.

"How do I know that I can trust *you*?" Sarah asked him.

"Sarah," Halford said, mildly reproachful.

"No, it's all right," Mr. Noble said, holding up a hand toward Halford. "It's a fair question." He motioned around the room with his hand. "Do you trust the people who hired me?"

"Yes," she said without having to think about it.

"I've known Mr. Halford for as long as I can remember," Mr. Noble continued. "I know how dear you are to him. I doubt he would put your safety into the hands of anyone *he* didn't trust."

"You make a fair point," Sarah said.

"Shall we sit down?" Halford suggested.

"I'd rather stand," Sarah said firmly. She was more than a head shorter than Mr. Noble, but standing to face him still boosted her confidence. "And when exactly will your protection begin?" she asked.

"My lady," he said with two little crinkles showing between his dark eyebrows, "I have been protecting you for days now."

Sarah gasped, then wished she hadn't. "How is that possible?"

"I have been here for days. I'm well aware of when you are settled in for the night, and when you leave the house."

"And yet I haven't seen you," she protested.

"That's what makes me so good at what I do," he said with a smile, but his words were more a statement of fact than any hint of bragging. "If I don't want to be seen, I won't be seen."

"And what of this . . . concern that my food or tea might be poisoned as my father's was?" Sarah asked, hating to consider how much that question above all others had been haunting her.

"I've conversed with Poppy more than once," he said. "She didn't tell you because she didn't want you to be alarmed, and we had decided to delay this meeting until after the inquest—with the hope that it wouldn't even be necessary. Although when I heard what the doctor had told Mr. Halford, I didn't need any official inquest to tell you he'd been murdered. And until we know who and why, you and I are going to be very good friends."

"Unless you don't want me to see you," Sarah said; she couldn't resist. "You won't be seen unless you want me to see you? Is that how it works?"

Mr. Noble smiled, however subtly, before continuing his explanation. "Poppy has been making certain that everything you eat or drink is coming directly from the pots and serving dishes in the kitchen—those from which all the household would eat—before bringing it directly to you."

"I see," Sarah said, feeling a little miffed at being kept out of this plan everyone else had been in on, but at the same time relieved to know that there *was* a plan; she couldn't deny that she'd been afraid, and for all that she wasn't keen on the idea of her and Mr. Noble becoming *very good friends*, she couldn't deny being grateful to know that someone with his skills would be watching out for her. More focused on her gratitude now, she said with less petulance, "I appreciate your efforts, Mr. Noble. I must admit this has all been rather . . . unnerving."

"Then I hope your knowing I'm nearby will offer you some peace of mind," Mr. Noble said as if it were his sincerest wish. "However, before we make this official, I have one absolute stipulation regarding those I am hired to protect."

"And what is that?" Sarah asked, sounding mildly defensive.

"Are you certain you don't want to sit down?" Mr. Noble asked, and she noticed Halford and Mr. Curtis were also still standing. Of course, it would have been impolite for them to sit while a lady was in the room and on her feet. But Sarah just wanted to hurry and get this over with.

"I'm fine," she insisted.

"You must do everything I ask of you—*everything*," Mr. Noble said as if it were a matter of life and death. Perhaps it was. "It doesn't matter whether you understand my reasons at the time; if you don't follow my instructions—precisely—I cannot keep you safe."

Sarah pulled her shoulders back, not liking this but unable to deny the logic. "And if I *do* follow your instructions, how can I be certain you'll keep me safe?"

He looked as if her question was difficult to answer, which made her slightly nervous. But he said with firm confidence, "There will always be things I cannot control, but I promise you I will do everything in my power to keep you safe; it will be my most prominent responsibility for as long as it's necessary."

Sarah sighed and knew she couldn't protest. But she hated it! She hated all of it! But she felt more scared than proud. "Very well," she said.

"Good," he said in a brief, triumphant syllable, as if that was all he'd needed to hear to seal their agreement. "Then we must be on the move as quickly as possible."

"What?" Sarah countered.

"For now, you cannot stay in this house and remain safe, m'lady," he said resolutely. "You, myself, Poppy, and Mr. Evans—a man who works driving your carriages and has come highly recommended by Halford as being trustworthy—will be leaving as soon as your things are packed. Poppy has informed the housekeeper that you need a holiday to recover from your father's death; however, it's not as if everyone here doesn't know by now that your father was murdered and there are other reasons for your leaving."

"But . . ." Sarah began until she immediately recalled that she had just agreed to do everything he told her to do.

"I know you don't want to leave your home, m'lady, but I can assure you that you are much safer elsewhere—in fact I would venture to guess that this is the *worst* place you could be right now. I daresay the entire county is likely unsafe for you and those traveling with you, which means the sooner I get you far away from here, the better for all of us."

Sarah pondered this for several seconds, attempting to come up with any reasonable argument. She *didn't* want to leave home, but neither could she dispute anything she'd just been told. The situation was deplorable, but that didn't mean any of the people in this room could change it—as much as they might want to.

"Very well," she said. "With Poppy's help we should be packed and ready within an hour."

"Excellent," Mr. Noble said, and Sarah hurried out of the room before anyone could say anything else to her. She had the sudden urge to cry and didn't want to engage in any further conversation that might tempt her tears to the surface.

By the time she'd reached her room she had wiped away a few stray tears and managed to choke back the remainder of her emotion. Right now, she had to focus on remaining safe, and leaving with Evans and Mr. Noble seemed the only feasible way to make that happen. She was glad to know Evans would be going with them. She'd been acquainted with him for years and he'd always been very kind to her.

Just before arriving in the hallway where her rooms were situated, it occurred to Sarah that she could not leave here without taking the box in the bottom of her wardrobe. It was conspicuous and would be awkward to carry. She knew because she'd carried it a good long way from the secret pantry to her bedroom. Thankfully an idea occurred to her before she reached the door of her bedroom.

Sarah wasn't surprised to find Poppy in her room, waiting to see what the verdict might be, both in regard to the inquest and what she'd known that Sarah hadn't—that she'd already been under the protection of Mr. Darius Noble.

"We're leaving within the hour," was the first thing Sarah said to her. "Please have someone bring my largest traveling trunk here and we'll both pack our things in it; it will be less complicated that way. We can talk while we're packing."

"Very good," Poppy said and hurried away.

Sarah tried to quell her nerves while she started gathering her most practical belongings and laying them out on the bed. She realized they needed to pack light, with only the minimum necessities, and surely they could acquire new things if they needed them. For that very reason she dug out some money she kept hidden and stuffed it into a deep, discreet pouch of her pocketbook. She assumed that Halford had arranged for Mr. Noble to be paid his fees—and traveling expenses—but she didn't want to be without money on the outside chance that they became separated for some reason.

A manservant brought in the large trunk she'd used when traveling with her father and left it on the floor. Sarah thanked him, and Poppy arrived only a moment after he left. Needing some minutes alone with the trunk, Sarah said to Poppy, "I hate to be a bother, but I admit this is all very stressful. Would you very much mind getting me some fresh tea from the kitchen, and perhaps some biscuits or scones to settle my stomach a bit?"

"I'd be happy to," Poppy said, cheerful as always—even though she too knew they were hurriedly leaving their home. "I'll get some for myself while I'm at it."

"I assumed you would," Sarah said lightly, and they exchanged a smile that let Sarah know Poppy would be by her side, helpful and supportive as always, no matter what happened.

As soon as Sarah knew that Poppy was no longer in view of the room, she carefully closed the door and locked it, along with the sitting room door. It took her only a minute to get the box containing the sword from the bottom of her wardrobe and put it into the bottom of the trunk, thankfully with inches to spare on every side. A few minutes later she had carefully placed one of her pairs of shoes at each end of the box which kept it from sliding from one end of the trunk to the other, and she put carefully folded clothing along the sides and over the top of it, concealing it perfectly, leaving plenty of space to add a few more things and all that Poppy would need. She knew that eventually she would have to tell Poppy about the sword—if Poppy didn't find it first. But they didn't have time for that conversation now. And for some reason Sarah felt as if the people she cared about were safer *not* knowing about it. For now, she was simply grateful to know that she'd found a way to take it with her, and no one would be the wiser.

Poppy returned with a tea tray after Sarah had unlocked the doors and made herself appear to be relaxing after having done most of her packing.

"Oh, you're practically finished," Poppy exclaimed, glancing at the trunk.

"I'll help you with your things," Sarah said, not only for the sake of getting packed more quickly, but also to make certain that Poppy didn't start rearranging things and inadvertently come across the strange box in the bottom of the trunk.

They sat down together and shared tea, taking enough time to enjoy it, but not dawdling since they needed to hurry. While Sarah checked her drawers and wardrobe to make certain she had everything she might need, Poppy went to her room to gather her own things. Within twenty minutes they had the trunk packed with room to spare, and Poppy closed the lid and latched it. Deciding they didn't need to wait for anyone to carry the trunk downstairs, they donned the cloaks they would need to wear outside on this brisk autumn day before they each took hold of one of the handles on either end of the trunk and carried it down the stairs, which wasn't difficult considering that it wasn't heavy.

When they set the trunk down in the front foyer of the house, they found Darius Noble pacing impatiently. Sarah was immediately struck by the coat he wore over the clothes he'd been wearing earlier. She couldn't recall ever feeling such an interest in a man's coat; but the way it seemed to wear *him*, as opposed to the other way around, forced her to stop and take notice. It was as black as his hair, which was evident from the way he had the collar turned up as if to stave off a cold wind from getting to his neck. The fabric appeared to be prepared to take on any kind of weather, and it looked well-worn but still rather fine. The top was well-fitted as if it had been tailored especially for him, and from the waist down it was full and hung nearly to his knees, with a slit in the back going to the waist, which she knew made it possible for him to wear it while riding a horse.

Sarah was surprised to feel Poppy nudge her with an elbow.

"What?" Sarah asked, startled from her thoughts.

"What are you staring at?"

"His . . . *coat*," Sarah answered honestly, not adding that she was inexplicably fascinated with the way he wore it so well, and how it moved around his legs as he paced and turned.

"His coat?" Poppy echoed and laughed softly.

Sarah was relieved to be saved from any further explanation when Mr. Noble noticed the women and said, "I would have gladly carried the trunk down the stairs for you."

"No need for that," Sarah declared, glad for an opportunity—if only a small one—to prove to him that she wasn't accustomed to being doted upon and coddled; and while she might need a protector, she certainly didn't need any kind of manservant following her around. Poppy was very good at seeing to Sarah's every need, but Sarah also helped Poppy each day with certain things; they could take care of each other and she wanted Mr. Noble to know that.

"Only *one* trunk?" he asked, glancing at both of them.

"We're sharing," Sarah told him with no further explanation.

"I'll just . . . secure it onto the top of the carriage," he said, and Sarah couldn't argue with the fact that she had no capability of doing *that*. She nodded and watched Mr. Noble pick up the trunk and hoist it onto one of his more-than-adequate shoulders. "I expected it to be heavier," he commented, heading to the door, which had been left open, and through which the wait-ing carriage could be seen, harnessed to four fine bays.

"Did you think," Sarah asked him, only slightly sarcastic, "we might pack some elaborate gowns on the chance that this adventure of running and hiding might include a fancy ball?"

"Maybe," he said, smirking at her in a way that surprisingly put her at ease instead of putting her on the defensive.

Sarah watched him walk out the door, and through the opening she could see Evans helping him secure the trunk to the top of the carriage, along with a couple of much smaller trunks, which she assumed belonged to the men. Sarah then turned her attention to the foyer in which she stood. She instinctively reached for Poppy's hand and they shared a tight squeezing of each other's fingers. No words were needed for Sarah to know that Poppy shared her feelings as she seemed to be silently bidding farewell to her home and all that she loved here. She wondered if anyone would come to see them off, but Mr. Noble came back in to tell them they needed to leave, and beyond the sound of his voice, the house felt eerily quiet. Sarah and Poppy followed him outside and just as they were about to get into the carriage Halford and Penelope burst out of the door in a run that had her aunt gasping for breath.

"Oh, good," Halford said. "We're not too late."

Sarah ignored all propriety and hugged Halford tightly, feeling some-how as he returned her embrace that something of her father might be present. He looked into her face and took her shoulders. "Noble will take good care of you, and he will communicate with me your whereabouts and such through a safe method. Try not to worry."

Sarah nodded but couldn't speak. Penelope took a turn at hugging Sarah as her breathlessness turned to sobbing. Sarah just hugged her aunt tightly and forced a smile as she pulled back, saying with a positive lilt that felt hypocritical, "Everything will be all right."

Penelope nodded and pressed her handkerchief over her mouth as Sarah turned to find that Poppy was already in the carriage, Evans was comfortably situated on the box seat, reins in hand, and Mr. Noble was standing at the door of the carriage, holding out his hand in a silent offer to help her inside so they could be off. Sarah gave her aunt and Halford one final wave and turned to look at her protector. When their eyes met, he seemed to read her mind as he said quietly, "We will hope and pray that all of this gets solved as quickly as possible, and in the meantime, I will do everything in my power to keep you and Poppy safe. I swear it." Sarah nodded and put her hand into his, grateful for his help. Stepping into a carriage while managing skirts and petticoats was always a challenge. Any determination to show him she could be independent didn't seem to matter as she felt the strength of his hand practically lifting her up the step and into the carriage. The moment he let go of her he folded the step out of view, closed the carriage door, and stepped onto the wheel to launch himself onto the box seat next to Evans. Sarah could only see his boot as he did so, but she felt the carriage rock with his movements, and the second he was seated they were in motion, as if Mr. Noble believed they couldn't get away from here fast enough. Sarah couldn't deny feeling that way herself. Her sadness over leaving home was definitely overpowered by her fear of staying. And perhaps it wasn't until she'd been confronted with the results of the inquest, and the realization that someone had been hired to protect her that she had allowed herself to honestly face the depths of her fear. Tucked inside the carriage as it moved away from Castle Courtenay, she was surprised to note that she felt more relaxed already. She only wished she had any idea of what exactly Mr. Noble's plans might include from here. She had no idea where they were going or what they might do when they got there, but for now she simply breathed in the fresh air of safety and tried to relax.

\* \* \* \* \*

Sarah and Poppy were both delighted to realize that a hamper of food had been left on the seat of the carriage. Since they stopped only once before nightfall—and that was barely long enough to use the personal facilities at a pub, and to feed and water the horses—they were glad to have generous helpings of fruit, raw vegetables, and sliced, buttered bread. There was also an abundant variety of biscuits. During their brief stop Sarah asked Mr. Noble if he and Evans would like some of the food; they certainly had plenty to share and she didn't want the men going hungry.

"You're very kind," he replied, "but we were supplied with our own hamper filled to the brim and we've been enjoying it very much."

"Are the two of you doing all right up there?" Sarah asked, glancing toward Evans who was carefully attending to the horses.

"Very well, indeed," Evans declared.

"And you?" Sarah asked Mr. Noble who was also standing nearby.

"I am supposed to be looking out for you, m'lady," he said with a smile, "not the other way around."

"You're supposed to protect me," she clarified. "But I don't want either of you going hungry while we're . . . going wherever it is that we're going."

"Again . . . you're very kind," he said, "but I can assure you we're fine. The weather is perfect for traveling and we're making good time."

"Excellent," she said, not daring to ask where they were going—and perhaps not wanting to know.

"So, m'lady, we shall—"

"Will you do me an enormous favor?" she asked.

"If I can," he replied, and she noted how he didn't agree without knowing what she might ask.

"I would prefer you not call me . . . m'lady. I don't like it at all, and if—as you put it—we're going to become very good friends, I would prefer less formality."

"Very well," he said, sounding surprised. "What would you prefer that I call you?"

"You call Poppy by her given name; I would prefer the same. Sarah."

He looked even more surprised and she wondered if such a request was so unusual. Thinking about the people she knew who were in the upper social classes, she could well imagine that it *was* unusual. But she didn't care.

"Very well," he said again, "Sarah. And I would add that such preferences should be regarded equally; therefore, I insist that you call me Darius. Truthfully, *Mr. Noble* makes me feel as if I should be a banker or a barrister or something, and as you can see, I am not."

"Darius it is, then," she said. Poppy had been close enough to hear their conversation, even though she hadn't commented, and Sarah saw her toss a little smile in their direction, although Darius didn't see it.

At that very moment, Evans approached to announce that they were ready to move on. Darius took Poppy's hand to help her into the carriage, while at the same time Evans said quietly to Sarah, "Are you well, m'lady? Halford threatened me about making certain you were well cared for." He said it with a little smile, and Sarah knew that Evans and Halford were trusted friends and had been for many years.

"I am quite well," she declared, not willing to admit that she felt nervous and filled with uncertainty; given everything these men were doing for her—and Poppy too—she would not reduce herself to complaining.

"I'm glad to hear it," Evans said and took her hand to help her step into the carriage, even though Darius had been hovering nearby to do that very thing.

Sarah's foot was barely on the step when she heard a deafening sound crack the air and before even a second had passed, she found herself on the ground, feeling the weight of a man over her shoulder and arm. She realized that a gun had been fired nearby, and she wondered if it had been aimed at her. She didn't know if it was Evans or Darius who had pushed her to the ground, going down with her to keep her safe. For a long moment she wondered if she'd been hit by a bullet but hadn't yet been able to feel the pain. Then she found Darius kneeling beside her, demanding in a voice that was fiercely frantic, "Are you all right? Were you hit?"

"I . . . think I'm fine," Sarah murmured and tried to get up, then a horrible realization settled in and she wanted to scream. Instead she began to breathe so sharply she feared she might lose consciousness, but she was even more afraid that screaming might put them in further danger.

While she was trying to find the ability to tell Darius that she now believed Evans had been hit and she'd gone to the ground beneath the weight of him falling, she realized that Darius had figured it out and rolled Evans onto his back, away from her.

"Is he . . ." she sputtered. "Is he . . . all right?"

"No, Sarah, he's not all right. He's dead."

"No, no, no," Sarah muttered, finding it even more difficult to believe. She was barely aware of Poppy stepping out of the carriage to investigate when Darius shoved her back in just before he physically picked Sarah up off the ground and shoved her into the carriage as well.

"Stay on the floor!" he ordered in a whispered panic. "And hold on tight."

"But . . ." Sarah heaved. "Evans! He . . . he . . ."

Darius put his face close to hers and she realized that he too was finding it difficult to breathe. "He's dead, Sarah. There's nothing we can do for him. He'll be found and taken home. But if we don't get out of here *now*, you will be next." Still hesitant to leave Evans's body lying on the ground she attempted to speak again but Darius said more hotly, "You promised to do what I tell you! Now stay on the floor while I get us out of here."

"But . . ." she whimpered, hearing Poppy just behind her, gasping for breath.

"Sarah!" he growled, taking hold of her shoulders and shaking her gently, "do you think they were aiming at *him*?"

Sarah sucked in her breath and couldn't let it out. The shot *had* been aimed at her! *Had Evans died in her stead?* The very idea was inconceivably horrible!

Darius didn't bother with any further conversation. He slammed the door closed and she felt the carriage rocking as he stepped up onto the box seat and then they were moving—very fast. The speed at which they were traveling made the ride far bumpier, which was also worsened by the fact that Sarah and Poppy were on the floor of the carriage, both of them barely able to breathe, clinging to each other as their breathlessness turned to sobbing.

Sarah's mind exploded with thoughts she could barely keep track of as they darted around and bounced back and forth inside her head. Her father's death had been devastating; the strange discovery of the key and the treasure it unlocked had been eerie and confusing; the discovery that her father had been murdered had been too horrible to comprehend; having to leave her home to remain safe had felt challenging but important enough to take seriously. But this? *This?* Evans dead? Shot while he'd been standing right next to her? Recalling how it had felt to fall to the ground—now realizing it had been due to the weight of Evans's body pushing her down—she once again found it so difficult to breathe she feared she would lose consciousness.

"Breathe with me," Poppy said firmly, taking hold of her shoulders. "Breathe! Breathe!"

"I . . . I . . ." Sarah tried to say. "He . . . He . . ."

"I know, dearie," Poppy said with compassion and comfort, even though it was evident she too was very nearly as upset as Sarah. "I know," she repeated and sobbed. "But . . . everything will be all right. It just has to be."

Sarah gave up trying to speak. She wanted to believe what Poppy was saying, but doing so felt impossible in that moment. Evans was dead, his body left outside a pub on the edge of the road. She knew he had no family, but he had a great many friends at Castle Courtenay—and in the nearby village. Many people would be heartsick over his loss. And for what? Could his death have been any more meaningless? Who was *she* to have the value of her life put above that of a good man like Evans? He didn't deserve this! And now what? Did Darius Noble actually have a plan to keep them safe, considering that their driver had been shot to death not many hours after leaving Castle Courtenay? She couldn't believe it! She just couldn't believe it!

Sarah lost track of how long she and Poppy lay on the floor of the moving carriage, clutching each other's hands. Their mutual difficulty in breathing gradually settled to a point where Sarah almost felt as if she were barely breathing, barely alive, barely able to think or feel. Soon after Sarah was able to stop crying, Poppy too fell into a silence that felt as if it might shatter if either

of them dared to speak of the horror that had occurred, and the tightening fear of what this now meant for both of them.

Sarah and Poppy let out a soft gasp at the same time when they felt the carriage coming to a halt. As Sarah tried to sit up, her body ached in protest, reminding her they'd been huddled on the hard carriage floor for hours. Only moments after the carriage halted, the door came open and Sarah heard Darius say, "We're in a place a short distance from an inn I know well, away from the shine of any street lamps. I want you to come with me and crouch down as much as you can when you walk. I'm taking you to a safe place to wait while I talk to the innkeeper and arrange for a place where we can safely rest."

Sarah said nothing. She felt as if her voice had left her since the realization that Evans had been shot and left dead on the side of the road had fully sunk in. She sat up and reached a hand toward Darius's shadow in the darkness. He took it firmly and pulled her toward him, as if he instinctively knew she would have a difficult time moving—for both emotional and physical reasons. The strength of his grip—combined with his confidence in the plan he'd laid out—helped Sarah feel slightly better, at least in regard to knowing they *had* a plan. Even if the plan was only for the next several hours, it was better than nothing. And oh! How she longed for a safe place to rest!

Darius pulled her out of the carriage and held to her arm long enough to make certain she was steady on her feet before he helped Poppy out and did the same. They followed his instructions and crouched down as they walked, their bodies hugging the wall of one building and then another, before emerging into a narrow alley, which smelled rather foul. He helped them find what seemed to be one of the cleanest spots in the alley—at least according to the smell, for they could see very little—and Sarah and Poppy sat on the ground with their backs against the wall. Sarah felt like a defense-less little mouse hiding from the likelihood of a bunch of cats that might pounce at any moment.

"Wait here and be still," Darius whispered, squatting down in front of them. "This inn is open to travelers any hour of the day or night. I will be back as soon as I speak with the innkeeper, and I'll make certain your belongings are safe."

Until that moment Sarah had forgotten about the treasure hidden in her trunk, but she was grateful she didn't have to ask Darius to keep the trunk safe—certain it would have sounded ridiculous for her to be concerned about a few clothes and personal belongings at a time like this.

"Thank you," she croaked, making it evident how long and hard she had been crying. At least she knew her voice could still function.

"I won't be long," he said and moved away in the opposite direction from which they'd come.

Sarah wanted to say something comforting to Poppy, but she couldn't find the words. She wanted to talk to her dearest friend about what had happened and how upsetting it was for both of them. But she couldn't think of what to say or how to say it, so she just took hold of Poppy's hand and squeezed it, feeling her squeeze in return. Right now, it seemed that knowing they were there for each other was all that really mattered.

Sarah prepared herself to wait a long while for Darius to return, even though he'd said he wouldn't be long. True to his word, he came back much sooner than she'd expected.

"Come along," he said, holding out both his hands, offering one to each of the two women. Sarah and Poppy took his hands and he lifted them to their feet, his strength compensating for how aching and tired they were. She wondered how he could have so much strength and energy when he'd been driving the carriage for hours. Her gratitude for his resilience deepened when he put an arm around each of them to guide them out the back of the alley and along the edge of one building, then another, and another. Now that they were at the back of the buildings, he apparently wasn't concerned about them standing up straight as they walked.

"We're here," he said, stopping beside a door that had no window in it. But Sarah noticed a window nearby where a dim light was shining. Darius opened the door and motioned the women inside. He closed the door behind him and locked it before he led them up a long hallway, motioning with his arm for them to follow, and putting a finger to his lips to remind them to be as quiet as possible. A lamp that was barely emitting enough light to allow them to see where they were going had been left on a table in the hall, and Darius picked it up as he passed it. He turned a corner and headed up a narrow flight of stairs. Sarah impulsively slipped off her shoes and Poppy followed her example; she felt certain their stockinged feet would be much quieter on the stairs and the wooden floors. At the top of the stairs they went right down a long hallway to a door that had the number *four* painted on it. He opened the unlocked door and guided Sarah and Poppy into the room, closing the door quietly behind him.

Whispering, Darius said, "There should be everything here you need to freshen up and get some rest." He motioned toward a washstand and a

curtained area in the corner of the room behind which she assumed was a chamber pot for which she was very grateful after such a long and harrowing ride. He also motioned to the large trunk belonging to her and Poppy, and she saw the other two trunks that had been on the carriage, which she assumed belonged to Darius and Evans. *Evans.* She couldn't think about it. She was too exhausted to fall apart now. "The two of you can share the bed," he said, motioning toward a large four-poster with curtains that could be closed around it. "And I will take the floor." He motioned to a rug in front of the fireplace. "And just to be clear, I'm quite accustomed to sleeping wherever I can, and if you might be concerned about having a man sleeping in your room, let me remind you that it's my job to keep you safe—in every respect. I'm here to protect you. That's it." He took hold of the doorknob and added, "I'm going to see to the horses and I'll be back. I want you to lock the door when I leave and unlock it for me when I come back." He demonstrated a unique knocking sequence quietly on the wall next to the door. "Once I'm back we'll all get some sleep and when we're more rested we'll consider what to do next." He turned to leave, then turned back. "I know you both must be terrified and upset—understandably so—but everything will be all right."

Sarah felt a single tear slide down her cheek before she could even think about holding it back. She didn't know if it was a spontaneous response to his description of exactly how Sarah was feeling, or the very fact that he was offering compassion as well as protection. Either way, Sarah quickly wiped away the tear and simply said, "Thank you . . . for everything."

"Of course," he said and hurried out of the room, quietly closing the door behind him, which Sarah hurried to lock.

For a long moment Sarah just stood there, frozen, not knowing how to actually function now that she was someplace safe. She heard a strange sound and turned to see that Poppy was crying but she'd pressed a hand over her mouth in an attempt to hold back the full torrent of her emotion. Sarah wrapped Poppy in a sisterly embrace and Poppy returned it with fervor. They held to each other and wept as the fear and horror they'd experienced in just the short time since leaving home washed over them like a cold, heavy downpour of rain. Within a few minutes they both were able to calm down, but still neither of them said a word.

Not certain how long Darius would be gone, Sarah took the lead and opened their trunk. By the dim light of a single lamp she found nightgowns, dressing gowns, and toothbrushes for herself and Poppy. She preferred digging through the trunk herself rather than risking having Poppy find what was hidden at the bottom—something she now realized was apparently worth killing for. Or was it? She had no idea whether or not the precious sword was the reason for all this. Trying not to think about it, she encouraged Poppy to get ready for bed while Sarah did the same. As soon as they were ready and dressed in prudishly modest nightgowns—for which Sarah was now grateful, given that she hadn't anticipated sleeping in the same room with Darius Noble—they climbed into bed and Sarah attempted to relax, as she knew Poppy was doing. Sarah was wearing her dressing gown as well, knowing she needed to unlock the door for Darius when he returned. But she told Poppy there was no need for both of them to wait for him. Poppy insisted that she couldn't possibly sleep, but her exhaustion was surely as deep as Sarah's, and within minutes Sarah could hear Poppy's breathing settle into an even rhythm that signaled she was sleeping.

With the lamp still emitting a subdued glow over the room, Sarah closed her eyes and held the bedcovers tightly in her fists, as if doing so might help keep her safe, or perhaps at least help her understand what it all meant. She felt responsible for Poppy, who would not have come on this absurd journey if not for her concern for Sarah's safety. And now it seemed they were all at risk. She opened her eyes when keeping them closed brought to mind far too vivid a memory of Evans's dead body pushing her to the ground, and how he'd fallen over her arm and shoulder and she hadn't been able to move. She'd given it very little thought at the time, but after she'd realized he was dead, the very idea made her shudder, and she wondered if she would ever be free of the memory and how it had affected her.

Sarah's mind became so caught up in what had happened and wondering what they might do now that she gasped when Darius knocked softly at the door, using the exact rhythm he'd told her he would use. She hurried to open the door for him and he slipped inside, whispering as he locked the door, "I parked the carriage some distance away and unharnessed the horses. I woke up the owner of a livery and paid him well to attend to the horses and also to lie should anyone ask if he's seen a man matching my description. I truly believe we're safe for now. There are too many inns and pubs in this town for anyone to search them all, and as I said, I know this innkeeper and I trust him."

"You've come here before?" Sarah asked him. "When you've been protecting someone?"

"I have," he said, "and I've not been found here yet. If I had, we would have gone elsewhere." He sighed and added, "I know how difficult this must be for you. After we've gotten some rest and had a good meal, we'll talk about what to do next."

"You have a plan?" she asked, certain he couldn't possibly solve this problem.

"I do," he said with confidence. "But don't worry about anything for now except getting some sleep. Without rest, your senses aren't as sharp as they should be, and you're more likely to get hurt. Since it's my job to keep you safe, *I* am going to get some sleep."

He'd removed his coat as he'd been talking and hung it over the back of a chair, but she was surprised to see him reach behind his back to pull a pistol out from beneath his waistcoat, which had obviously been tucked into the waistband of his breeches. Even though she'd said nothing, he responded to her silent surprise by saying, "Did you honestly think I *wouldn't* be carrying a gun?"

"No, I suppose not," she said as he set it down on the small bureau. "Actually, I'm glad to know you do."

He nodded, and Sarah went back to bed, discreetly removing her dressing gown before slipping between the covers. Her head had barely connected with the pillow before exhaustion lured her into a deep slumber.

# Chapter Five
## WORTH KILLING FOR

SARAH AWOKE TO THE SOUND of the door closing softly, followed by a combination of pleasant aromas. She squinted against bright sunlight, then had the horrible thought that perhaps someone other than Darius had come into the room. She sat bolt upright with a gasp, then took a deep breath when she saw Darius setting a large tray on the little table in the room, which had two chairs on either side of it.

"Did I scare you?" he asked, glancing in her direction with a little smile. "Sorry," he added and seemed to mean it. "I woke up starving, so I knew the two of you must be feeling the same. I'd prefer that neither you nor Poppy leave the room until we're actually ready to go—and that will be a while—so I got enough breakfast for all of us."

"It smells delicious," she said earnestly, suddenly so hungry she felt as if she couldn't get to that table fast enough. And she was actually glad to hear him say he didn't want her or Poppy to leave the room. She suspected that she'd quickly grow weary of being stuck within this small space, but for now it represented safety, and after what had happened last night, nothing felt more important than simply being safe.

"I'll let you and Poppy sit at the table," Darius said gallantly. "I can sit anywhere with a plate and be happy."

"I think Poppy is still very much asleep and I don't see any reason to wake her," Sarah said softly, then wondered how to ask what she needed to ask. She decided to simply choose not to be embarrassed over practical matters and said, "Would you mind very much giving me just a few minutes of privacy?"

He looked confused and she nodded toward the curtained area in the corner of the room. Even though it would prevent him from seeing anything untoward, she preferred to take care of her private business completely privately.

"Oh, of course," he said and headed toward the door. "I'll be in the hall. Just . . . open the door when it's safe for me to come back in."

"Thank you," she said and watched him leave the room, grateful he was so gracious—and perceptive.

Getting out of bed made Sarah realize the room was a bit chilly and she was glad for the fire burning in the grate, although she suspected it hadn't been burning long; therefore, it hadn't had a chance to really warm up the room. Once she had taken care of private matters, she found a pair of stockings in her trunk and put them on, then she put on her dressing gown, tied it around her waist, and opened the door into the hallway. She didn't want to take the time to get dressed while their breakfast was getting cold, and she knew she was more than adequately modest. She'd been dressed exactly this way many times when both she and Halford had spent time in her father's room during his illness.

"All set?" Darius asked, coming back into the room, where he closed the door and locked it.

"Yes, thank you," she said and sat down, surprised when he helped her with her chair. "Thank you," she said again, and he sat across from her. She quickly surmised that there was an enormous amount of food on the tray, but she felt so hungry she wasn't about to try and be ladylike and hold back for the sake of not appearing too gluttonous. She enjoyed every bite of the scones with butter and jam, boiled eggs, and fried pork; and the tea was both calming and delicious. She didn't even care that it wasn't her favorite flavor.

They both ate in silence, as if Darius was as hungry as she and they were enjoying their meal too much to want the distraction of conversation. When Sarah finally felt full and content—as long as she didn't allow herself to recall the horrible memories hovering close to the surface in her mind—she leaned both elbows on the table so she could cradle her third cup of warm tea in her hands and hold it close to her face, closing her eyes to inhale the comforting aroma and the caress of the steam on her skin. Even though her eyes were closed, she knew Darius was finished eating by the way he sighed contentedly and leaned back in his chair, scooting it a little farther from the table.

"Are you all right?" he asked, startling her slightly with the way his voice broke the silence.

Sarah didn't want to think about all the reasons she was *not* all right. But his inquiry was kind; his tone expressed genuine concern. She knew he deserved an honest answer, but at the same time she didn't want to talk about it. "I'm as all right as I can possibly be, I think," she stated truthfully. "We're safe for now . . . thanks to you. I don't want to think about anything except . . . the present."

"I understand," he said kindly. "I really do. There's no need to talk about it right now. I just want you to know that I do have a plan, and I have every reason to believe all will be well." Sarah opened her eyes and looked at him expectantly, wanting to hear about this plan of his, resisting the urge to express her most prominent thought, which was her desire to tell him that if his plan required leaving this room she was entirely against it. She knew such an idea was ludicrous, but she couldn't express the depth of her fear without thinking too hard about the reasons for it. And she just couldn't do that now; she just couldn't.

"We'll talk about it when Poppy can join the conversation," he said as if he'd read her mind. "That way I won't have to repeat everything twice."

Sarah only nodded, amazed that Poppy was still sleeping, and feeling envious. If Sarah were asleep, she wouldn't have her mind wandering continually toward thoughts that were just too awful to contemplate. Returning her attention to her tea, she barely glanced toward Darius as he stood up, but she gave him her full attention when he said, "I'm going out; there are some things I need to purchase and—"

"Do you need money?" she asked, surprised by how startled he looked in response to the question.

"No, Sarah," he said matter-of-factly, "Mr. Halford gave me more than enough to cover any expenses that might arise."

Sarah nodded again while she wondered where Halford would come up with that kind of money, but the answer was obvious. He had worked as an assistant to her father for many years—in matters both personal and professional. Of course he would have access to her father's money. *Her* money, she reminded herself; her father was dead. Murdered. Everything had fallen to her now, even the threat of death. It all seemed like a very bad dream.

"Lock the door after I leave," he said, putting the pistol back in its hiding place and tugging his waistcoat down over it, "and don't open it for anyone but me. While I was downstairs getting breakfast, I could see if anyone suspicious looking came up the stairs, but now I'll be leaving the inn. I'll be back before the two of you get hungry again. There's no reason to open the door unless it's me. Do you understand?"

He said it with such severity that Sarah realized she had sucked in her breath and was finding it difficult to let it out. She finally nodded in silence yet again and managed to start breathing again.

Darius nodded in return and left the room. Sarah rose to lock the door, since he'd told her he wasn't leaving until he heard evidence that she'd done so.

Sarah stared at the closed door and listened to the sound of Darius's footsteps as he left. She didn't want to admit she felt afraid in his absence. Not wanting to feel fear any more than she wanted to feel dependent upon this man she barely knew, Sarah forced her feelings inward and was glad to hear evidence that Poppy was coming awake. They said very little to each other while Poppy ate her breakfast and they both got dressed and helped attend to each other's hair so that they looked reasonably presentable. It seemed that neither of them actually wanted to speak aloud of Evans's death—and the horrible way it had occurred—and their exhausting and frightening journey to arrive where they were now, especially when neither of them actually knew *where* they were or what would happen next.

Darius returned not a moment too soon when Sarah felt as if the unusual silence between her and Poppy would drive them both mad. She unlocked the door following his distinctive knock, surprised to see him loaded down like a packhorse. He had two sets of large saddlebags slung over each shoulder, and his arms were full of a number of packages, which he seemed to barely be managing to hold onto. Sarah and Poppy each hurried to take a couple of packages before he heaved everything else onto the bed. Sarah closed the door and locked it before asking him in a quiet voice that didn't disguise her concern, "What on earth is all—"

"We can't travel by carriage any farther," Darius stated without apology, "therefore we will be riding the horses that were pulling the carriage, and we will be traveling through the woods, staying completely away from any roads. Hence," he motioned elaborately toward the items covering the top of the bed, "saddlebags and supplies." Before Sarah could form words to express any one of her many questions, he added, "I assume you ladies can ride."

"Sarah can, of course," Poppy said. "She is a proper lady in every respect and was therefore taught to ride in her youth. I, on the other hand, am a maid, and I have never ridden a horse."

"There's no need to worry," Darius said. "These animals are gentle and well-trained. You can follow me, and Sarah will follow you. The horse will follow my lead with very little need of any help from you. I'll show you what to do. It's easy; I promise."

Poppy sighed and Sarah recognized what she'd quickly come to learn about Darius Noble: he had a natural way of calming fears and concerns by saying exactly what needed to be said. A part of her almost didn't want to trust him, but she couldn't think of a single reason not to. And what choice did they have? There was evidence enough that Darius was determined to keep her and Poppy safe, and nothing else mattered right now.

Poppy appeared alarmed in spite of Darius's reassurance, but she nodded in agreement, as if she trusted him to know what was best, and that he would keep his promise to help her. Darius began opening the packages on the bed to reveal that they contained a generous supply of jerked meat and several fresh apples, which Sarah suspected would be crisp and delicious since this was the time of year when apples always tasted best. There were also some rounds of cheese and some bread. There were flasks, which Darius explained would be filled with water for each of them. Sarah silently appraised these things and wondered how long they would be traveling on horseback, and what exactly this portion of the journey would entail. But she refused to complain or even question Darius or his methods. She felt nothing but grateful to be in his care, and she knew without a word spoken between them that Poppy felt the same.

"Where exactly are we going?" Sarah asked him.

"To the home of some dear friends of mine," he reported with confidence. "That's all you need to know for now. We will be safe there for as long as we need to be."

Darius then pointed out the saddlebags—which were the largest Sarah had ever seen—and explained that they would need to pack all their belongings—along with the food and water—into the bags. They would be leaving the trunks behind. Since they had four horses, which had been pulling the carriage, one would carry their possessions and supplies. He also mentioned very casually that he had already sold the carriage for a fair price and it had been taken to the home of its new owner, some distance from the village where they now were. It was evident Darius had planned everything very carefully, which helped Sarah feel a little better, until a thought occurred to her and she gasped before she could think to hold it back.

"What?" Darius asked with a demanding voice that was not unkind. Both he and Poppy stared at her with a look that made it evident she could not avoid telling them the reason for her concern. She couldn't possibly go any farther on this journey without sharing the truth about what was in the bottom of the trunk. There could be no box containing and concealing the sword, given their change of plans. She knew she could trust Poppy, and she likely would have told her about the sword before now except that so much had been happening. She wondered for a long moment if she could trust Darius with something so valuable. In her mind she saw him running away with the priceless heirloom and abandoning her and Poppy. But she quickly realized she had no choice but to trust him; they were entirely dependent upon his care and protection. And instinctively she believed him to be a man of integrity.

Sarah sighed and forced the words out of her mouth. "There is something in the bottom of the trunk that can't possibly be put into a saddlebag, but it's highly valuable and we must take it with us."

"I see," Darius said, drawing out the words and turning his head slightly to look at her sideways, as if he were trying to discern whether he could trust *her*. When he said nothing more, and Poppy remained silently expectant, Sarah just opened the lid of the trunk, pushed aside the clothing covering the box and lifted it out, hearing Poppy let out a noise of surprise.

"Is *that* why you wanted to use the large trunk and have us share it?" she asked.

"Yes," Sarah said.

Darius's tone reeked of suspicion as he asked, "Does this have something to do with the danger you're in?"

"I have no idea," Sarah said, putting the box on the bed. "I didn't know it existed until after my father's death, and as far as I know, no one else is even aware of its existence. But I sincerely do not know for certain." She hurried to tell them about her final conversation with her father, and how in spite of most of it sounding like nonsense, she'd found the key, and then the hidden panel in the secret pantry where the box was hidden. She concluded by declaring that she knew her father had wanted this to be in her possession, and that she needed to protect it. When she had nothing more to say, Sarah reached inside her bodice where she'd carefully kept the paper on which she'd copied down the words she'd found regarding the sword. "I copied this out of a book of my family's history that I found in the library." She very briefly explained the story of William Charles Courtenay before she handed the paper to Darius who looked both alarmed and curious. As he unfolded the paper Sarah said, "Perhaps you should read it aloud for Poppy's benefit."

Darius cleared his throat quietly and began to read: "*This mighty sword has been blessed to hold great power to whomever shall possess it. To possess it is to possess great blessings upon the head of the possessor and all of the House of Courtenay, therefore if the rightful possessor of this great sword allows it to fall into the hands of evil, a great curse shall come down upon the House of Courtenay. So it has been blessed, recorded, and declared forevermore.*'"

"A sword?" Poppy said, incredulous. "You've been hiding and carrying around a sword?"

"May I see it?" Darius asked, still sounding suspicious. "I'm assuming it's very valuable—even for someone who doesn't believe in blessings and curses being attached to it."

Sarah swallowed hard but couldn't find any words. She reached beneath the neckline of her dress and drew out the long chain she always wore now. As she lifted out the key at the end of the chain, Darius asked in a slightly snide tone, "Is there anything else you're hiding in there I should know about?"

She absolutely knew he was not at all meaning the question to be improper or suggestive; he was completely focused on the paper in his hands and the key she had just revealed. Sarah didn't answer; she just lifted the narrow chain from around her neck and put the key into the lock on the box. As she opened it, Darius and Poppy moved closer, standing on either side of her. She lifted the lid, took a deep breath, and folded back the velvet fabric to reveal the sword, which actually sparkled as the angle of the sunlight through the windows reflected off of it. Poppy gasped yet again and took hold of Sarah's arm as if she feared toppling over. Darius muttered breathlessly, "Unbelievable!"

The three of them stood frozen, just staring at the exquisite piece, as if admiring the beauty of its craftsmanship made it difficult to speak. Poppy whispered, as if she feared the sword might overhear her, "Is that . . . an emerald? A real emerald?"

"According to what I read about the history of the sword," Sarah said, *not* whispering, "yes, it is."

"Remarkable!" Darius said in a tone combining awe and reverence. Without moving his gaze, he asked Sarah, "May I?"

"Of course," she said, knowing what he meant.

Darius reached his right hand toward the hilt, slowly and tentatively, almost as if he feared it might burn him if he touched it. She knew how he felt. He took hold of it firmly and lifted it up into plain view where all of them could see the fine details. "It can't possibly have been crafted as a weapon," Darius said, brandishing it carefully in a way that made it evident he knew exactly how to use a sword as a weapon.

"I'm not so sure," Sarah said. "I think the edges of the blade could slice a piece of paper."

Darius held it still and looked more closely at the blade. "I do believe you're right," he said and repeated, "Remarkable."

"Remarkable enough to kill for?" Poppy asked, her tone acrid.

"Someone else *must* know about this!" Darius said, looking at Sarah directly, as if to answer Poppy's question, that the sword *was* valuable enough to kill for—even without the belief of any attached curses or blessings.

"I have no idea," Sarah said, unable to keep from sounding astounded at the possibility of two men already having died for something that she would have gladly given away to have her father back. Darius carefully returned the sword to its resting place and turned more directly toward Sarah, silently asking for more information and focusing his full attention toward whatever she might tell him. "The history of the sword—including an accurate illustration of it—is in a book in the library. Any servant in the household could get into the library and read it there, or even remove a book without being noticed. Even though most of what my father said to me before he died didn't make sense, it was enough to guide me to the key and also the sword. But I don't know if that information is recorded somewhere that I don't know about."

"Perhaps not," Darius said. "If someone had known *where* to find it, then it wouldn't have been there for you to find."

"Fair point," Sarah said. "But I'm not convinced my father's death—or the danger I'm in—has anything to do with this."

"Your father's urgency in telling you about it makes me think there *is* a connection," Darius said with confidence. "Perhaps for some reason that day he figured out he was being poisoned and he wanted you to know about this before he died. Perhaps it was only meant to be passed on to an heir. Did he say anything to that effect?"

Sarah looked away, then closed her eyes, trying to remember. She'd tried and tried to recall exactly what her father had said and how he'd said it, but now remembering felt more important than ever. A memory of something he'd said came to her clearly, and she attributed Darius's specific question to helping spark the clarity. "He said . . . he couldn't go to the grave without me knowing about this, but his illness had never been severe enough to make anyone think he was anywhere near death. Therefore, I didn't take such a comment seriously. He was . . . agitated, and . . . said he was worried about me, and . . ." she gasped as it came back to her more clearly, "he said I needed to be careful, that he was concerned for my safety." She sat unsteadily on the edge of the bed, next to the box containing the sword. Looking up at Darius she asked, "Do you really think it's possible? That he figured it out? That he knew he was dying?"

"It's possible," was all he said, but his expression seemed to be saying that he *absolutely* believed it. Darius sighed and added, "Well, we can't possibly figure out the answers to these questions stuck here in this room, and given the situation it might be a good, long time before this mystery gets solved. The only thing that *really* matters is keeping you ladies safe, which is why we're leaving here tonight—past midnight when we won't be seen, especially with the direction we're going. The only problem is exactly how to take *this*," he motioned toward the sword, "traveling on horseback without making it too conspicuous on the chance that we encounter anyone."

"I should have told you about it sooner," Sarah said to him, her tone apologetic as she realized his burden of handling every detail of dealing with this precarious and complicated situation.

"It's not as if we had much opportunity to discuss such things," he said before he became quietly thoughtful. "But I have an idea. I need to go purchase a few more things, and then I think I can solve this problem."

"How?" Poppy asked.

"Let me see if it works before I make a fool of myself trying to explain," Darius said. "But before I leave, I think we all need some lunch." He headed toward the door, saying, "I'll get some food from the kitchen and be back soon."

Sarah nodded and locked the door after he left. Sarah and Poppy had very little to say to each other while they sorted through their things and began refolding clothing in a way that would make it fit into the saddle-bags. Sarah closed the box with the sword in it but left it on the bed, which made it impossible to ignore its existence and all the possible implications.

Darius returned with a lunch tray and set it on the table. He insisted that the ladies sit on the two chairs next to the table. He took his own plate to sit in an overstuffed chair where he held the plate with one of his large hands and used a fork with the other. The meal began in silence, but Sarah felt the urge to talk more about her swirling thoughts regarding the sword and all that it might mean. Now that her old friend and her new one knew about the sword, she felt relief at not having to hold all her thoughts inside and took advantage of the silence to say, "Forgive me, but . . . I can't stop thinking about the sword, and—"

"I can't stop thinking about it either," Poppy said.

"Nor can I," Darius admitted, and Sarah was glad to realize how comfortable they were all beginning to feel with each other—which was good considering how much time they were inevitably going to spend together; in fact, she had no idea how long they would be in Darius's care. She didn't want to think about that. One day at a time was all she could handle.

"So . . ." Sarah continued, "what if someone else *does* know about the sword? What if someone really is trying to obtain this treasure, and for some reason they believe I have it?"

"Or what if someone believes they have the right to it as long as you're no longer alive?" Poppy interjected.

"If anyone believes in curses," Darius said, as casually as if he were telling them lunch was delicious, "they wouldn't *want* possession of the thing. But if they *don't* believe in curses, you can't deny that—as you said, Sarah—a description of this great treasure is recorded in the family's history, and anyone—even any servant in the household—could have come across that information the same way you did. And perhaps oral traditions have been handed down about this great mysterious treasure that fueled an interest. It's possible."

"And maybe," Poppy said to Sarah in a voice that was both fearful and excited, "that same person knew about the conversation your father had with you the day he died; perhaps he was given a larger dose of poison after he'd said what he did in order to finish him off before he could say more."

"Poppy!" Sarah said in a tone that was more scolding than she'd intended. She softened her voice and added, "I just don't like to think of my father being . . . finished off."

"Sorry," Poppy said and clearly meant it. "But I also wonder if there was some reason he said what he said to you, *when* he said it. Had he been threatened? Or *had* he figured out in some way that he *was* being poisoned?"

"I also believe," Darius muttered, "that it could likely be more than one person." He pointed a finger at Sarah and smirked. "You could have a whole gang of servants in the household working together to try and find the treasure."

The thought made Sarah shudder. "But what point would there be to actually killing my father? Or me? Could they not just steal it and run off to a foreign land and change their names?"

"That would imply a family member," Darius said more seriously than he'd been thus far in the conversation. "Are you certain you don't have some distant cousin we're not aware of? Someone who could know the rumors of the treasure? Someone who wants all things Courtenay to himself?"

"It's not very likely, is it!" Sarah snapped at him, feeling too impatient to indulge in such far-fetched theories.

"Just a thought," he retorted, smirking again as if he enjoyed seeing her get so riled.

They finished their meal without any further speculations, and Darius took the tray with the dirty dishes down to the kitchen with him when he left to do his errands. As soon as he was gone, Sarah and Poppy resumed their organizing and folding in preparation for their journey. Silence settled over them again until it became so uncomfortable that Sarah said, "We usually can't stop chattering. This silence is . . . difficult."

"I feel the same," Poppy said with a sigh, "but I don't know what to say. It's all just so overwhelming."

Sarah drew in a deep breath of courage and said something that had been weighing heavily on her. "I feel bad, Poppy, that you've become caught up in all of this because of me. Whatever is going on has nothing to do with you, and I wonder if it would have been better if you'd not come or—"

"What?" Poppy retorted, sounding insulted. "My place is with you. This has nothing to do with my being employed as your companion. You are my best and truest friend. Do you think I would want you going through something like this *without* me?"

Sarah felt the sting of tears in her eyes and fought them back; she'd not cried since Evans had been killed, and she couldn't start now. The enormity of her fear and sorrow would surely require more than the release of a few little tears, and there wasn't time for any such grieving right now. She had to keep a level head and stay strong. Still, she was so deeply touched by Poppy's words that she couldn't keep the quiver out of her voice when she said, "I'm so glad because . . . I don't know how I would do this without you."

They embraced tightly, and Sarah sensed that Poppy was also trying very hard not to cry. Sarah was surprised when Poppy laughed instead as she eased back and took Sarah by the shoulders, saying in a voice that sounded more like herself, "Besides, do you think I would allow you to be traveling unchaperoned with that . . . *scoundrel.*" She laughed softly, which let Sarah know that Poppy didn't at all think Darius was a scoundrel, but she was certainly right about the need for a third person to be present in this situation, especially if they were to be sharing a room at an inn and traveling into the forest together.

"We couldn't have that," Sarah said, laughing herself, glad for the way doing so offered a tiny bit of relief to the torrent of emotion smoldering within her.

A moment later they heard footfalls in the hall and then Darius's distinctive knock at the door. Sarah opened it and he entered, this time carrying a stack of folded wool blankets with one wrapped package balanced on top of them.

"What are *those* for?" Sarah asked, feeling some alarm.

"Given the fact that we will be traveling through the woods to get to our destination, there will be no accommodations. We will be sleeping on the ground, I'm afraid."

Sarah and Poppy exchanged a somewhat fearful glance behind Darius's back while he set his load into a large chair. He turned to face both of them and added, "I know it's far from ideal. Thankfully it's autumn and not winter. Hopefully this sunny weather will hold for a few days and it won't be too cold."

"So, this is only for a few days?" Sarah asked, wishing she hadn't sounded so concerned.

"Yes, Sarah," he chuckled. "Only a few days." More soberly he added, "I assure you this is the best way for us to travel and remain safe. Unfortunately, that means sleeping on the ground, but we'll actually be traveling by night to reduce the possibility of being seen, and we will sleep during the day, which means it will be warmer."

"What a relief," Poppy said with such extreme sarcasm that Sarah couldn't hold back a giggle. She'd been feeling so thoroughly somber that the sound surprised even herself—but both Poppy and Darius stared at her with equal surprise.

"I believe the two of you are a wee bit silly," Darius said lightly.

"You can't even imagine how much," Poppy said with a lighter sarcasm.

"You're from Scotland," Darius said to her.

"You're just figuring that out now?" Poppy countered, pretending to sound offended.

"No," he drawled with a little laugh, "I'm just commenting on it now. I quite like the way you talk."

"As do I," Sarah said, giving her friend a warm smile. "I like everything about her."

"The feeling is mutual, dearie," Poppy said. "Now can we get on to what's important here?"

Sarah felt the urge to maintain the light mood, liking the way it soothed the strangeness and horror of all that had happened. Impulsively she said, "While you were gone, Poppy called you a scoundrel."

"Did she now?" Darius asked and let out a one-syllable laugh. "Well, maybe I am," he added and laughed more fully.

"Which is why," Sarah declared lightly, "*you* might be here to protect *us*, but Poppy and I will be on guard to protect each other from *you*." Sarah could hardly believe what she'd said until it was out of her mouth, which made her laugh even more.

"An excellent plan," Darius said, and they were all laughing, which Sarah felt certain was their way of letting go of all the stress they were feeling—and she far preferred laughter over tears.

Darius sobered his mood and looked directly at Sarah as he said, "I have an idea how to disguise the box containing the sword so that we can carry it with us and not have it look suspicious. May I have your permission to make some modifications to the box?"

Sarah actually had to think about it a long moment. She wondered how old the finely crafted box might be, and she briefly wondered if it would be some kind of affront to her ancestors to modify the box, but that thought was immediately replaced by the knowledge that keeping the sword safe was what was most important—next to keeping the three of them alive and safe.

"Of course," Sarah said. "Do whatever you need to do."

Darius nodded and set to work on the floor. The women watched in fascination as he carefully wrapped the sword in some thick, soft wool he'd purchased to keep it protected, then he used a hammer and nails to put some small pieces of wood in place over the top of it to create a false bottom, overlapping some of them in order to make them fit. Sarah wondered for a moment if the sound of his hammering would disturb other tenants at the inn; however, given that it was the middle of the afternoon, she doubted anyone would notice. Darius then took from the package he'd brought with him a variety of woodworking tools, which he placed carefully into the box, tacking nails only partially into the wood so they would help keep the tools in place. When he was finished, the interior of the box clearly looked as if it had been built to contain this set of tools, given how well he had fit them around each other. He then locked the box and handed Sarah the key before he took a length of heavy leather, about two inches wide, and nailed it to both ends of the box. Sarah wondered about the purpose of this, but she preferred to just wait and see instead of asking him questions when he was concentrating so hard on his project. Both Sarah and Poppy let out a little laugh when he lifted the strap over his head so that it rested diagonally across his chest, and the box of *tools* hung diagonally over his back.

"That's brilliant!" Poppy declared.

"Isn't it heavy?" Sarah asked, sincerely concerned about him carrying the box like that for however long they would be riding. The sword wasn't necessarily heavy, but the tools he'd put into the box surely were.

"A little," he said, "but I can manage, I assure you." He said it in a way that made Sarah wonder if he believed she'd been questioning his obvious masculine strength. She opted to not attempt any clarification and just echoed Poppy's declaration that it *was* indeed brilliant.

A short while later when all their things were mostly packed, and Darius had explained a few more details about their plans, he suggested they all try to get some rest, since they would be leaving after midnight and riding through the night. They all lay down where they had slept the previous night, but Sarah found it difficult to relax due to the storm of memories and fears she couldn't force away. She was surprised to come awake and realize that she *had* slept, and she could hear Poppy and Darius whispering while they were obviously eating supper and trying not to disturb her.

Sarah sat up in bed, and Darius said with a smile that caught her attention, "There she is!"

"You're eating without me?" Sarah asked in a tone that implied she was upset, but her light sarcasm belied that.

"I daresay you need every minute of sleep you can get," Darius said.

Sarah couldn't argue with that; she was dreading this exodus into the woods more than she dared admit. She ate until she was too full to eat anything else. She'd seen the food that Darius had packed into the saddlebags; and while none of it was at all detestable, she could foresee how quickly they would grow tired of eating the same thing for days. She wondered how long it would be until they had a real meal again.

The three of them finished packing, again weighed down by silence, as if they were all dreading this excursion. But Sarah completely trusted Darius's belief that this was the best way to remain safe. Given the fact that she couldn't go ten minutes without remembering every detail of the moment Evans had been shot, and her falling down beneath the weight of his dead body, she was willing to do practically *anything* to remain safe. So she kept her thoughts to herself, which meant she had nothing to say—and she suspected the others felt the same, or at least Poppy did; it was impossible to tell exactly what Darius Noble might be thinking. He was kind and compassionate and he seemed personally invested in the precariousness of the situation. But that didn't mean he was any more invested than he might be, regardless of whomever he might have been hired to protect. Sarah found the thought a little disappointing and she wondered why. She'd quickly grown dependent on Darius, heeding his every instruction, and trusting completely in his plan to keep her and Poppy safe. Was it her dependence on him that fueled her intrigue with him in a way she didn't understand? She often found herself watching him closely and darting her eyes quickly away if he looked at her, not wanting to be caught at it. But she was embarrassed to realize that Poppy had caught her. When Darius's back was turned, Poppy nudged her with an elbow and nodded toward Darius with an amused smirk.

"What?" Sarah mouthed silently.

"You *like* him!" Poppy mouthed silently in response.

Sarah shot her friend a glare of disgust and turned away, hoping to hide the possibility that her expression might betray how Poppy's comment had provoked a tingling in her limbs, a quickened heartbeat, and a fluttering in her stomach. *Don't be such a fool,* Sarah reprimanded herself silently. Darius Noble had been hired to protect her, and when this problem was solved, he would be on his way to save a different damsel in distress. She needed to focus on doing whatever it took to remain safe and indulging in a girlish attraction to a handsome and capable man was not conducive to that goal.

Forcing thoughts of Darius out of her mind—along with memories of Evans dying—Sarah made certain her things were all packed securely into saddlebags, then she sat and waited for the time when they would leave. When the others just sat too—locked in ridiculous silence—she was inexplicably relieved when Darius produced a deck of playing cards and set about teaching them an easy game that kept them distracted and offered an opportunity to laugh and tease just enough to keep Sarah's mind off of anything except this moment.

When it was finally time to go, Darius put the box of tools over his back and flung a set of saddlebags over each shoulder. The ladies each carried one set of saddle bags, and their trunks were left empty on the floor of the room. As Darius opened the door, Sarah noticed Evans's trunk containing the belongings he'd brought with him. She said to Darius, "What about—"

"It's taken care of," he interrupted, noticing where her attention was focused. "I've arranged for it to be sent back to Courtenay. I don't know whether there's anything meaningful in there, but his friends there will know what to do with his things."

Sarah just nodded, imagining Evans's body being returned to Courtenay as well, and the way everyone there would be horrified over his death. She forced the thought away, nodded at Darius and said, "You think of everything. Thank you."

Darius nodded in return and they left the room, walking very quietly to the stairs and down them. It felt strange to Sarah to be leaving this room where she had felt safe and secure. Just stepping out of it heightened the fear she'd been suppressing. At the bottom of the stairs they turned to go down a long hall toward the back of the inn, guided by a sconce on the wall, which emitted very little light. The inn was completely silent with the absence of any customers up and about at this time of night. But of course, Darius would have planned it this way.

Sarah and Poppy followed Darius out the back door of the inn where four horses were waiting—the same ones that had been pulling the carriage when they'd left Castle Courtenay. Sarah quickly noticed that three of them had saddles, and Darius would have had to acquire those as well. He really *did* think of everything. Standing next to where the horses were tethered was a man holding a lantern. Darius introduced him as the innkeeper and a trusted friend, but he didn't say the man's name.

"This is my sister," Darius said, motioning toward Sarah, and she tried to keep her surprise from showing.

"I can see that," the man said. "The same hair exactly."

"Yeah," Darius said casually while he put the saddlebags over the back of the fourth horse, which didn't have a saddle. "That's what our mother always said." He then motioned to Poppy. "And this is our cousin."

The man nodded toward Sarah and Poppy, and they simply nodded in return before Darius said, "I think we're ready to go." He held out a hand to help Poppy mount one of the horses while he kindly told her what to do and reminded her that the horse was well-trained and gentle. He put the reins into her hands and gave her some simple instructions but assured her the horse would just follow the horses in front of him and she would have to do very little. Poppy seemed to relax in the saddle, then Darius turned to help Sarah mount one of the other horses. As she put her gloved hand into his she could have sworn she felt literal heat emanating from his touch. Their eyes met for less than a second, but Sarah was once again overcome with all that tingling and fluttering.

Sarah settled herself quickly into the saddle and muttered a quiet "Thank you" to Darius as he put the reins into her hands. The innkeeper wished them a safe journey, and a minute later Sarah was following Poppy who was following the packhorse and Darius into the woods behind the inn. She was glad Darius knew where he was going, and all she and Poppy had to do was follow him, but she wished this part of their unsavory adventure was over. She was dreading this forthcoming journey with all her soul.

# Chapter Six
## SAFE HAVEN

SARAH HAD NO WAY OF tracking the hours, since there was no moon and she doubted she could have seen it moving across the sky anyway, given the thick trees through which they were traveling. Darius didn't seem to be following any actual trail, but he also seemed completely confident in where he was going. He'd been right about the horses following each other. Sarah could see that Poppy quickly relaxed as the horse she was riding remained dutifully behind Darius and the packhorse. Sarah's horse was equally dutiful, and she hardly had to do a thing to keep it in line behind the others.

Sarah began to feel cold, even through her cloak, and wished that one of the blankets secured to the pack horse was around her back and shoulders. When they stopped for a necessary break, she asked Darius if it would be too difficult to untie some blankets for them and he gladly did so. He also gave them each some cheese and jerked meat to eat as they rode, which was a little difficult to maneuver while holding a blanket around her with one hand, but Sarah managed. They continued to ride until the sun had been up for what Sarah guessed was a couple of hours, although she didn't trust her sense of time. They ate a haphazard breakfast from the food Darius had acquired before they prepared a place to sleep, deeply hidden in the trees with the horses tied nearby where they could graze. With a blanket beneath her and one under which she tried to get comfortable, Sarah felt certain she couldn't possibly sleep in such circumstances. She couldn't deny she'd lived a privileged—even spoiled—life. Still, few people had to actually sleep on the ground. But she was so thoroughly exhausted she fell asleep quickly and awoke to realize—even through the canopy of treetops—that the sun was moving toward the west horizon. Again, the three of them ate before Darius saddled the horses, and they began riding again as the air began to cool with the oncoming dusk.

They repeated the same routine for three more days. Or was it four? Sarah was astonished to realize she had honestly lost track. The bread became drier, the apples were gone, and the amount of meat and cheese was down to almost nothing. Late in the evening—what felt like a few hours after having started out—Sarah found it increasingly difficult to not complain or ask Darius how much longer this would go on. She had forced herself to remain silent, not wanting to come across as whiny or coddled.

When Sarah saw light shining dimly through distant windows, her relief was so great that she felt as if her body might melt right off the saddle. A minute later she heard Darius say, "We're nearly there. And they'll be as pleased that they've not yet gone to bed as we'll be pleased to have some real beds to sleep in."

"And if the house was dark?" Sarah asked him, mostly for the sake of conversation, which helped her avoid thinking about how sore, aching, and exhausted she was. And hungry, she had to acknowledge when her stomach rumbled loudly enough that she hoped the others hadn't heard it.

"We'll be there in minutes," he said instead of answering her question, which made her wonder if he *had* heard her stomach growling. She said nothing, not willing to be embarrassed over something she couldn't control. Darius added, "Even if it were the middle of the night, I would wake them; we have a standing agreement that I should never hesitate to do so. They would be unhappy with me if I did *not* allow them to help me—any time of the day or night."

"You've brought people here before, then," Sarah asked, "who needed protection?"

"I have," Darius said. "No one could find us here unless they already know where it is—and no one knows this location unless I trust them perfectly."

"But surely these people—your friends—are known to be here. They must go into town to purchase things and—"

"Of course," Darius said, "but no one ever questions that *I* am here, because I'm known in town as being a common visitor. And no one would *ever* know that I've brought company with me. It's out of the way enough that no one would notice there are extra people here, and the two of you will not go outside except at night when you can't be seen."

"We will really be safe here," Sarah stated more than asked.

"We will," he said, and Sarah turned her attention again to the lighted windows, surprised at how much closer they had become. She felt an almost giddy excitement for shelter, a good bed, and something to eat—anything besides jerked meat and dry bread.

Only a minute later, Darius dismounted his horse near the front of a house whose outline they could just barely make out. Sarah and Poppy followed his lead and dismounted. Sarah's every muscle complained over how long she'd either been in the saddle or sleeping on the ground. She heard a quiet moan from Poppy as she stretched her back and knew they were very much in the same condition. After the horses were tethered to a low fence not far from the house, Darius motioned for the women to follow him, saying, "I'll get our things after we get you inside where it's warm."

The women said nothing as Darius knocked at the door with the same unique rhythm he'd used at the inn where they'd stayed. The door flew open as quickly as if a harsh wind had forced its way into the house. A woman Sarah could barely see—since the light was behind her—stepped into the doorway and exclaimed, "Darius!" and flung her arms around him. He hugged her and lifted her feet briefly off the ground. "You've been staying away far too much," she added as he set her down.

"I couldn't agree more," he said with a little laugh. He then motioned toward Sarah and Poppy, who were standing in the shadows. "I've brought with me some lovely ladies who are in need of shelter for a while."

"And protection, I assume," the woman said as if she couldn't be more pleased by the situation.

"That too," Darius said and moved his hand to indicate that the women should come closer. "This is Sarah and Poppy," he stated. "Ladies, this is Daphne Nash. No one could possibly take better care of you than Daphne—and her husband David, who is . . ." He looked expectantly toward Daphne, silently expecting her to finish the sentence.

"He's already gone up to bed," Daphne reported. "He got up very early this morning to go into town for supplies. I was just about to go up myself, but I'm glad I was slow about it. Come in. Come in. I bet you're hungry and exhausted." She stepped back into the house and motioned elaborately with her arms. Sarah followed her in, with Poppy right behind her.

Darius said, "I'm going to take care of the horses," and Sarah heard him walking away before Daphne closed the door. Sarah took a quick glance around and her relief at being here deepened. Coziness and security seemed to emanate from every piece of comfortably inviting furniture and every item of tasteful and simple decor. They were standing in a small, square hall with polished wood floors, and a narrow staircase rose upward in front of them. To the right was a parlor with a huge couch and a few large chairs, all of them puffy and soft-looking, as if their only purpose was to provide comfort. A fire in the grate was burning down to coals, and a couple of lamps looked as if they had been waiting for Daphne to douse them for the night. To the left was a large dining table, built more for sturdiness and practicality than beauty—but it had a homey effect that was heightened as Sarah imagined the many chairs around the table filled with people enjoying each other's company.

Daphne motioned with her arm for Sarah and Poppy to follow her into the dining room, saying, "Sit yourselves down at the table. It'll only take me a few minutes to get you something half decent to eat. If you've been following Darius's usual plan, you're likely sick to death of jerked meat and dry bread."

Daphne laughed softly which made it easy for Sarah to say, "You know him well."

"That I do," Daphne said and laughed again as she went into a large kitchen that was in clear view from the dining table where she began bustling around to gather a variety of things, which she set on a large tray that had been left on a big work table. Sarah felt like she should offer to help but even her voice felt too exhausted to do so. As if Daphne understood without a word being spoken, she said, "You ladies sit tight; I can't imagine how sore and tired you must be. Tomorrow when the fire in the stove is hot, I'll fix you something more substantial, but this should help you feel better so you can get some decent sleep, and don't you worry about when you get up; sleep as long as you need."

"Thank you so much," Sarah said as Daphne set the tray on the table.

"Yes, thank you," Poppy added as they both eyed the slices of buttered bread, which were clearly fresh and soft. There were slices of what appeared to be cold lamb, and Sarah was already imagining it piled onto a slice of bread.

"Help yourself," Daphne said and poured out three glasses of milk, setting one in front of the chair where she clearly expected Darius to sit when he came in.

"Thank you," Sarah and Poppy both said together and began eating after Daphne had said grace over their simple meal, expressing gratitude that Darius and these dear women had arrived safely.

"This is delicious," Sarah said to Daphne who had sat down across the table from them.

"Yes, it is," Poppy added.

"I'm so glad," Daphne said, and Sarah finally took the time to assess this kind and generous woman. Daphne had dark-brown hair with some gray creeping back from her face. It was plaited on each side and then wound up and pinned at the back of her head. Her face showed her years in the way that her skin wrinkled from the corners of her eyes, across her brow, and into her cheeks when she smiled. If not for this facial evidence, she would appear much younger; she was slim and moved with easy agility and she had what seemed an innate energy. Even at this late hour, Daphne didn't seem at all too tired to do whatever her unexpected guests might need to be comfortable.

"So, you and your husband must know Darius very well," Sarah said.

"We do indeed," she said, her cheeks wrinkling more deeply as her smile widened. "He's a fine young man, and we respect the work he does; we want to do everything we can to help him, and given the way we're situated out here in the woods, it's the perfect place to stay hidden. You're welcome to stay here for as long as necessary. And you mustn't be afraid to speak up if you need something."

"You're so kind," Sarah said, and Poppy nodded in agreement, her mouth full.

Daphne's eyes narrowed slightly, and her brow wrinkled with concern. "We've been helping Darius long enough to recognize the signs."

"What signs?" Sarah asked and took another bite of the tender lamb slices she'd put on a slice of buttered bread.

"You're not only exhausted from the need to travel in a way that would keep you safe, but something dreadful happened to make such a journey necessary. I daresay you're both not only weary to the bone, but you're also in need of a good cry and some simple warmth and comfort." Sarah found it difficult *not* to cry right then and there as Daphne perfectly explained how she felt, and she knew Poppy would agree. She was glad when Daphne went on, which prevented her from having to speak. "I just want you to know that you're safe here, and after what you've been through—whatever it might be—you feel free to just stay in bed as much as you like until you catch up on the rest you need. There's no set schedule here you have to abide by; if you miss a meal, you can always just help yourself to whatever we have." She motioned nonchalantly toward the kitchen as if it represented a continual source of abundance that she was only too glad to share.

Sarah heard a door open in the distance—a different door than the one through which they'd entered—and Daphne said, "Oh, there he is. I'm certain that as soon as he takes your things upstairs, he'll be down to get something to eat." She laughed softly, and Sarah decided she loved Daphne's laugh; it had a soothing effect that made her feel as if everything *would* be all right. "It seems he always arrives hungry—not because he ran out of food, but because he got tired of eating the same thing for days."

"That sounds about right," Poppy said before she put the last bite of a slice of bread into her mouth. This made Daphne laugh again, which helped Sarah feel a little closer to truly being safe and daring to hope that this nightmare might eventually end, and she could once again live a normal life.

Sarah heard Darius going up the stairs after she caught a brief glimpse of him in the front hall with the box slung over his back—just as it had been every minute he'd been awake through their entire journey—and their saddlebags over his shoulders.

Daphne said, "We have a few guest rooms, along with some other odd places where people can sleep if necessary. I'm certain Darius will put your things in the two best rooms, which are right next to each other. As soon as you've had enough to eat, I'll take you up and make certain you have what you need."

"Thank you," Sarah said, feeling full but enjoying the glass of milk as if it were the nectar of life.

Sarah finished the last couple of bites of her food before she heard Darius come back down the stairs. He promptly sat down where Daphne had left a glass of milk and a plate of food, as if she knew exactly how he would want lamb stacked on his bread, and he knew exactly where he was expected to sit.

"Thank you," he said to Daphne and immediately added, "I put fresh water in their rooms already." Sarah assumed there was some kind of large container upstairs where fresh water was kept, since he hadn't been carrying water when he went up.

"Excellent," Daphne said. "Since I've kept the rooms cleaned and ready—just hoping you'd show up," she smiled and winked at Darius, "you should all be set to get some good sleep."

"I've been dreaming about just that for days," Darius admitted in a way that let Sarah know he'd apparently disliked their journey almost as much as she and Poppy—even though he'd frequently reminded them that at least it wasn't raining. Sarah was certainly grateful it hadn't rained, but she was even more grateful to be here now in Daphne's home, a woman with whom she already felt an affinity that was difficult to explain. Perhaps it was simply that Daphne was offering everything for which Sarah felt so desperate.

Whatever it might be, Sarah knew they would be staying here for some undetermined length of time, and she would surely have the opportunity to get to know Daphne much better. She was glad of that. If they were staying with someone cranky and difficult, the forthcoming stretch of her life could be miserable. But Sarah already felt safe and comfortable, and she could tell that Poppy felt the same.

"Although," Darius said, "I'll be keeping my things in the usual room, I'll be sleeping down here."

"Of course," Daphne said.

"Why?" Sarah asked, not knowing of any place to sleep down here on the ground floor except the sofa—which was surely too short for him—or the rug near the fireplace.

"So I'll be able to hear if anyone tries to get into the house," he said matter-of-factly and offered no further explanation before he asked Daphne, "You think David is already asleep?" He then took a man-sized bite and began to chew.

"Yes," Daphne said, and by her expression alone Sarah knew that Daphne felt love and admiration for her husband. "If he weren't, he would have heard the commotion and come down to see you, but he'll be up and around tomorrow after you've gotten some much-needed rest."

Daphne stood to begin cleaning up, since Sarah and Poppy had finished eating.

"May we help you?" Sarah asked.

"Certainly not!" Daphne said with kind firmness. "At least not tonight. Just give me a moment and I'll take the two of you upstairs."

After Daphne had gone into the kitchen carrying dirty dishes, Sarah said to Darius, "How long are we staying here?"

"I have no idea," he said between bites. "There are some things I have to try and figure out before I would consider it safe to move you." He took a long swallow of milk. "Is there a problem?"

"Not at all," Sarah said and gave him a tired smile. "I'm very glad to be here, actually."

"As am I," Poppy added with enthusiasm.

"Good," Darius said and smiled widely before he continued to eat.

Daphne led the way up the stairs and guided Sarah and Poppy to their rooms, which were side by side. Both had large beds covered with soft quilts, hand-stitched in beautiful patterns and colors of fabric. Both had a lamp left burning, fresh water, soap, and towels. Sarah knew which room was intended to be hers since the box containing the sword—and tools—was on the floor near the small bureau. Daphne pointed down the hall and told them which door belonged to the bedroom she shared with her husband, and she insisted they let her know if there was a problem or they needed anything—as if being awakened in the night with some petty request would be nothing but pleasant for her.

Once alone in the cozy and lovely guest room, Sarah couldn't get out of her dirty clothes fast enough. She'd been wearing them ever since the day they'd left the inn, and she tossed everything into a pile in the corner before she took advantage of the soap and water to get somewhat clean, thinking how nice a hot bath would feel. And she would be more than happy to prepare it herself; she simply had to ask Daphne where to find what she'd need, just as she intended to ask her where she would find what she needed to launder her dirty clothing. Sarah felt nothing but gratitude for Daphne—and her sleeping husband—for opening their home to Darius and his current subjects in need of protection. And she would not insult these people by being rude enough to expect that anyone would wait on her in any way. Growing up with Poppy at her side, the two of them had learned to blend their lives, and Sarah was grateful more than she ever had been for the way in which she'd often assisted Poppy with her work, which now made her feel capable of caring for herself, or at least she and Poppy could help each other—as they always had.

Digging clean underclothing and a nightgown out of the bottom of her saddlebag, Sarah relished the feel of the soft, clean fabric and crawled into the luxurious bed. As soon as she'd taken a few seconds to settle in comfortably, she found it strange to recall Daphne saying, *I daresay you're both not only weary to the bone, you're in need of a good cry and some simple warmth and comfort.* The words of this good woman echoed through Sarah's mind, as if to give her permission to actually let go of the tears she'd been fighting so hard to hold back for days. A little sob jumped out of her unexpectedly and she pressed the pillow over her mouth, not wanting Poppy or anyone else to hear her. Within a minute she was heaving with painful sobs, which she continued to muffle with the pillow. In spite of crying so hard, she didn't cry long before her surroundings of luxury and safety lured her to sleep.

* * * * *

Sarah came awake slowly, squinting against the light in the room, glad for the memory of Daphne telling her to sleep as long as she needed. Shifting and stretching, Sarah still felt sore from the challenging excursion through endless woods, but she did feel more rested than she had since she'd learned that her father had been murdered. Not willing to think about that—or anything related to it—Sarah was pleased to note that being in this house, with the warm welcome they'd already received, helped her feel better than she had hoped ever since Darius had announced they would be staying with friends of his. She didn't know what she'd been imagining, but it wasn't this.

Suddenly very hungry, Sarah got up and made her bed before she put on a simple dark-green skirt and a cream blouse with a high neck. The only problem was that she had trouble reaching the buttons down the back. Peeking into the hallway she saw that Poppy's bedroom door was still closed, and on the chance that she was still sleeping Sarah didn't want to bother her. She went back into her own room and closed the door quietly, not wanting to make any noise. With her hair pulled over the front of one shoulder, Sarah did the best she could with the help of the tiny mirror in the room to reach all the buttons and had to concede there were a couple that would have to remain undone. But her hair was long and full, so it would cover the buttons down her back, even tied back as it was with a black ribbon so she could work on laundry as soon as she got something to eat.

With her room straightened and the long, conspicuous box slid beneath her bed, Sarah went quietly down the stairs and found Daphne in the dining room, sitting at the table holding a dainty china cup that appeared a little out of place in this home that seemed to have been built and decorated for coziness and practicality. And yet, despite the practical, simple way Daphne was dressed, the cup looked very much at home in her hands.

Before Daphne became aware of her presence, Sarah quickly appraised the man sitting across the table from her, reading a newspaper. This had to be her husband, David. Sarah thought the married couple was very similar in the way that it was only the lines in their faces that gave away their age. David had broad shoulders and a firm build that was evident even with him sitting. His hair had gone completely gray—what very little there was of it. His head was bald on top, and the gray hair that went around his head was cut so short that it was barely visible. Still, this didn't detract from his overall youthful appearance. Sarah suspected they were near the age of her own parents—or how old they would be if they were alive—but they both had a more youthful air about them than her parents had ever had, even before their illnesses.

"Good morning," Sarah finally said before she chanced getting caught spying on them.

"Oh, there she is!" Daphne said as she set down her cup and stood, taking a few steps to embrace Sarah, who was taken off guard but couldn't deny the kindness and concern she felt from Daphne. "How did you sleep, little one?" Daphne asked even though they were almost exactly the same height. "You slept late; I hope that means you slept well."

"I did, thank you," Sarah said. "After sleeping on the ground during our journey, that bed was absolutely heavenly."

Daphne laughed softly. "Oh, I'm so glad!" She turned and motioned to her husband who had stood up when he became aware that Sarah had entered the room. "This is David, my husband."

"It's a grand pleasure to have you in our home," David said, stepping forward to cup one of Sarah's hands between both of his for a long moment. "I do hope you'll be comfortable and not too bored."

David spoke to her as if she were royalty or something akin to it. Sarah hurried to say, "You're both so very kind. I can assure you that we are very comfortable, and you mustn't make a fuss. We can certainly take care of our own needs, which will help keep us busy." Sarah looked around quickly and asked, "Have you seen Poppy yet?"

"Not yet," Daphne said. "She must still be sleeping."

"And Darius hasn't been awake long," David said with a chuckle. "That's how it usually is. I think he hardly sleeps a wink on the way here, and then he sleeps like the dead once he knows all is well. I believe he's getting cleaned up now."

Sarah considered the possibility that while she and Poppy had been sleeping in the woods, Darius might have slept much less than they had simply because he'd felt responsible for keeping them safe. She felt touched by yet more evidence that Darius was a good man. In fact, if he was on such good terms with people like David and Daphne, he surely had to be decent. She doubted they would tolerate any kind of a scoundrel or cad making himself so at home here the way he did.

"I've kept your breakfast warm in the oven," Daphne said, heading toward the kitchen, "although it's nearly lunchtime now."

"I'm so hungry I might be able to eat lunch in a few minutes," Sarah said, which made David laugh.

"May I help?" Sarah called toward the kitchen.

"Not today," Daphne called back.

"She might let you help . . . eventually," David said, motioning her toward a chair which he helped her with before he sat down again and poured her some tea into another of those dainty china cups, which matched the pot from which he was pouring. In more of a whisper he said, "She *loves* cooking for people; it makes her happy. Therefore, I recommend that except in rare cases we just let her do it."

"I'll keep that in mind," Sarah said, holding the hot tea close to her face, loving the feel of the steam. "But surely she'll let me do my own laundry . . . and prepare my own bath, and—"

"We'll work all of that out," David said reassuringly and with an expression that seemed to imply he knew exactly what she was thinking. He likely knew she was accustomed to having servants do a great deal for her, and with the kind of people who could afford the protection of someone like Darius Noble, they had likely had guests who expected to be waited on. She hoped that her willingness to help earn her keep would be conducive to also earning the respect of David and Daphne, because she liked them very much and having the respect of such people meant a great deal to her.

Before Daphne had returned from the kitchen, Poppy appeared in the doorway, looking refreshed and cleaner but still weary. Sarah wondered if the same weariness was evident in her own countenance. But she just smiled at her friend and asked how she'd slept. While Poppy was answering, Daphne came in from the kitchen, gave Poppy a jubilant greeting, and introduced David to her before she went back to the kitchen for more food. Sarah and Poppy enjoyed a hearty breakfast while Daphne sat with them, sipping her tea as if it were some kind of soothing concoction, and David continued to read the newspaper. They all shared some comfortable and easy conversation, although Sarah noticed they didn't ask any questions about where Sarah and Poppy came from, or their situation—except for commenting on Poppy's Scottish accent, which almost always happened when Poppy met someone new. David and Daphne offered little information about their own background. David explained that he now occupied much of his time with some woodworking in a section of their barn that had been transformed several years ago to accommodate his hobby. He was glad to be able to use that part of the barn and his tools more often now in this season of his life. It was evident that David had retired a few years earlier from a profession he had enjoyed and at which he had been very good in the nearest village. After breakfast, Sarah saw a clock and realized it was less than an hour until noon, when lunch would likely be served, and she was glad to recall hearing Daphne say last night that they were welcome to help themselves to anything to eat at any time, and they didn't have to abide by any set schedule. Sarah suspected that once they'd been here a day or two and had caught up on their rest, they would all be more likely to share meals. For today, she anticipated just finding herself a little snack should she require anything to hold her over until tea.

Before Sarah was finished eating, she said to Daphne, "After Poppy and I help you clean up in the kitchen, could you show us where we might do some laundry? I'm afraid we didn't bring an abundance of clothing and—"

"Yes, that would be very—" Poppy began but was interrupted.

"I will clean up the kitchen myself," Daphne insisted, almost indignantly, and David tipped down his paper to toss Sarah a discreet glance that seemed to say he'd told her to expect this. She just smiled back at him, glad that Daphne was looking elsewhere. "However," Daphne went on, "I'll be glad to show you where the laundry is done as soon as you're finished eating."

"Excellent," Sarah said and finished up at about the same time as Poppy. They both thanked Daphne profusely for the meal—and everything else— before Daphne led them through the kitchen, which was already very tidy, and through a door at the back.

They entered a room with a stove already burning and large pots of steaming water on top of it. Daphne motioned toward it and said, "We just light it every morning. Seems we always have something to launder, or someone needs a bath—which reminds me . . . I'm certain the two of you would love to bathe; I know I would after several days in the woods. There's a tub and extra towels in a large closet across the hall from your rooms. There's a barrel up there we try to keep filled with water, and there are buckets to get the water out of that, or to haul the water upstairs, but of course one of the men can do that for you if you just let them know when you want to—"

"Oh, we can do that," Poppy said at the same time Sarah said, "No need for that."

"Very well," Daphne said, "just don't be too proud to ask for help if you need it." The last seemed to imply that she'd already picked up on Sarah's determination to refuse to be treated any differently than anyone else in the house. Daphne added, "I'm certain the two of you are strong and capable and could take care of yourselves well enough, but men are just built with stronger arms, so we women need to make certain they're put to good use once in a while. Besides, they need *something* worthwhile to keep them busy." She smiled and turned to motion to the large tubs for washing and rinsing clothes, which could be tipped so that the dirty water would run down a cleverly made gutter that ran underneath the wall and outside. She pointed out large barrels of water and more buckets that could be used to transfer it to the wash tubs or the pots on the stove. She then drew their attention to a contraption that she said David had built for her years earlier, and something she was obviously very proud of. There was a clothesline at just the right height for an average-sized woman to reach, which was attached to some kind of pulley that moved the narrow rope when a lever was turned. Daphne opened a door to show them how simply turning the lever allowed her to send the clean clothes out into the sunshine to dry on a sunny day without her ever having to leave the house, but there was also enough clothesline inside on which to dry clothes on cold or wet days.

"Everything just smells so much nicer when it's dried out in the sun, doesn't it?" she said, pulling the door closed, which had two notches open at the top to accommodate the clothesline but not let in too much cold air from outside when it was shut tightly.

"Well, if that isn't the cleverest thing I've ever seen!" Poppy declared.

"I might have to agree," Daphne said, proud of her husband's ingenuity. "I think you ladies will find everything you need here. If there's *anything* else you need, I'm usually in the kitchen or relaxing in the parlor. If I leave the house, I'll leave a note on the table."

"Thank you," Sarah and Poppy said in almost perfect unison. Daphne smiled and left to go back into the kitchen. Poppy turned the lever back and forth a little as if she were simply fascinated by how it worked.

"Why don't we go get our dirty clothes and actually use it?" Sarah suggested.

"Excellent idea," Poppy said, and they did just that.

They went up to their rooms and returned quickly, each carrying an armload of dirty clothing. After they had filled the wash tubs with water— one soapy for washing and one clean for rinsing—Poppy recalled something she'd forgotten and went back to get it. A minute later Sarah heard the door from the kitchen come open and glanced up from her attention to the washboard to see Darius leaning a shoulder against the doorjamb.

"Good morning," he said. "Or rather, good afternoon."

She smiled at him but didn't say anything, taken off guard as she was by all the fluttering and tingling that had erupted within her at his appearance. She realized now that throughout most of their journey she'd been too tired and achy and focused on just getting through it that she'd stopped really paying attention to Darius, except for following his instructions. But now he was standing there, wearing clean clothes that reminded her of the day she'd met him. Everything looked somewhat worn and well used except for the fine waistcoat he wore, this one being a dark blue and cream brocade. His curly hair was damp, which made it look curlier and even blacker—if that was possible. Sarah wasn't certain she liked this attraction she'd come to feel for her protector. His place in her life was temporary, and she had absolutely no experience in dealing with men. She'd do well to keep her feelings to herself and just let them pass.

"Did you sleep well?" he asked as she switched her focus back to the lacy chemise she was washing.

"Very well," she said, "and you?"

"Far too well," he said with a chuckle.

"I'm certain you needed it," she said, but still avoided looking at him.

"I passed Poppy in the hall; she seems to be doing well. She told me you'd be here. I must say I'm impressed."

"With what?" she asked, not having any idea what he meant.

"A lady such as yourself doing your own laundry," he said.

"Under the circumstances," she said, "I would consider it rude to expect anyone else to do it for me."

"Hence," he added, and she could hear a smile in his voice, "I'm impressed."

"It's just a little laundry," Sarah said, putting the chemise into the rinse tub where she worked all the soap out before she wrung the water out of it with her hands and reached up to hang it on the clothesline, not caring that Darius Noble was watching her wash her underclothing.

Darius continued to stand there even though he said nothing more, so Sarah just kept at her task, trying to ignore him. She bent over to pick up a dirty blouse from the floor and tossed it into the tub where she pushed it up and down the washboard once it was sufficiently wet. She gasped when she realized Darius was standing right behind her, then she felt his fingers on her upper back and froze.

"Sorry if I startled you," he said just behind her ear, "but . . . you have a couple of buttons that are . . ." Sarah held her breath as she felt him fasten them, realizing her hair had fallen forward over her shoulder when she'd bent over. She knew he wouldn't have been able to see anything beneath them except her upper back, which she knew was always visible with ladies' evening gowns. It was more his closeness that unnerved her.

Sarah cleared her throat and silently commanded her quickened heartbeat to slow down as she said in an even voice, "Poppy was still asleep when I got dressed and I couldn't quite reach."

"All fixed," he said and moved away, glancing over his shoulder as he headed out the door. "Will I see you at tea?"

"Of course," she said, wondering why the question seemed so important to him. She refused to give the matter another thought, fearing she would start to imagine implications that didn't even exist.

Before teatime came, both Sarah and Poppy had washed and hung all their laundry, which was drying out in the sun. They'd cleaned up their mess in the laundry room, leaving it pristine before they'd hauled buckets of water upstairs—some of it cold to replace the water borrowed from the barrels there, and some heated on the laundry room stoves so their baths could be comfortably warm. They each took a turn at having a bath in the tub, which they slid across the hall into Poppy's room. They helped each other wash their hair and properly style it afterward. It took only a few minutes for Sarah to comb through Poppy's sleek blonde hair, and it took a good deal longer for Poppy to make Sarah's hair look remotely presentable. But oh, how wonderful it felt to be clean!

When they'd been getting out the tub, Poppy had noticed the room had a device built there similar to the one in the laundry room that was meant for dumping water, which would apparently run outside. With their baths completed they worked together to dump bucketfuls of water down David's clever contraption, then they cleaned the tub and decided that tomorrow they would launder the towels and wash the rags they'd used, leaving them for now in a discreet corner of Sarah's room.

At tea Sarah quickly noticed how comfortable Darius was in this parlor with David and Daphne. But then, Sarah felt surprisingly comfortable herself. Both she and Poppy were included in the casual conversation while they enjoyed some excellent biscuits and little sandwiches, and some of the best tea Sarah had ever tasted. It was different than either of the teas Sarah and Poppy had previously preferred, and they laughed over the realization that they both liked the same flavor, which had never happened before. Sarah was surprised to hear Halford's name come up in the conversation. She felt so completely separated from her home that it seemed odd to hear about the connection. She recalled now that Halford had said he'd hired Darius because of his connection to a man who had been a trusted friend for a very long time. Sarah listened with interest to how David and Mr. Halford had grown up in the same village, although no reference was made to exactly where that had been; she only knew it wasn't anywhere nearby—and she actually had no idea where they were. But it was as if Darius wanted it that way; as if *her* not knowing meant that whoever might be trying to kill her was less likely to know, although she couldn't see any logic in that. Still, it didn't matter to her where she was, as long as she was safe. And she was, which made it possible to relax and enjoy the conversation.

David and Halford had gone into the military together and their friendship had deepened as they had literally saved each other's lives on different occasions. Sarah wasn't clear on exactly how David and Daphne had come to know Darius, but she enjoyed hearing some of Darius's stories from the time he'd worked for the royal family—although it wasn't Darius who told them. David and Daphne seemed inclined to brag about him, which didn't necessarily seem to please him, but he took it all in with grace and humor, insisting they were exaggerating. And he didn't hesitate to say that he'd *hated* that job, in spite of all he'd learned that helped him do the work he did now—which he far preferred. Sarah found it ironic that his experiences with the royal family reminded her of her ancestor, William Charles Courtenay. The similarity almost made her believe that Darius had somehow been destined to be her protector, but she immediately squelched the thought and scolded herself for romanticizing the situation.

"Well, I for one am grateful for the job you have now," Poppy declared.

"As am I!" Sarah added.

She was surprised at how quickly Darius's mood darkened. "Yes, well . . . for all my supposed skill and experience, I didn't keep Evans alive, did I." His statement was filled with harsh self-recrimination.

David was quick to say, "No man is perfect, Darius, and you can't be everywhere at once, nor can you predict every possible situation. We've had this conversation far too many times."

"Yes," Darius said, "far too many." On his way out of the room he said, "Thank you for tea, Daphne. It was lovely as always."

After they heard the door at the back of the house close loudly and knew Darius had gone outside, Daphne said with compassion, "We must be patient with him. He's very good at what he does, but he always takes the losses very personally."

"And he has trouble understanding," David added, "that in such a profession, there will always be losses."

Daphne looked a little alarmed and hurried to add, "That's not to say that the two of you aren't safe here!"

"You're *perfectly* safe," David added. "Evans was killed in a place where Darius had very little control over the environment or the circumstances. Such is not the case here."

Sarah looked down at the cup and saucer in her hands, surprisingly comfortable as she admitted, "Evans was standing right next to me; knocked me down when he was shot. Whoever pulled the trigger was trying to kill *me*."

"Yes," Daphne said, her compassion deepening, "Darius told us. But you mustn't feel guilty for that any more than Darius should. There are evil people out there, little one. Their horrible actions do not make you or Darius or any other innocent victim responsible. Do you understand?"

"I'm trying to," Sarah said softly.

"As is Darius," David muttered gravely.

"Even though I wasn't being shot at," Poppy interjected, "I saw it happen, and . . . I can't get it out of my head." Her voice quivered slightly, and Sarah was surprised, given that Poppy hadn't said a word about the incident before now. But perhaps it was high time they talked about it, even if she never would have expected to be discussing it with these people they barely knew. But David and Daphne were remarkable people, and Sarah felt increasingly grateful for how thoroughly safe she felt with them here in their home; not only her own and Poppy's physical safety, but safe enough to talk about the horrible things that had happened preceding their arrival. They all talked a while longer, with their hosts expressing tender sympathy over her father's death and all that followed. Both Sarah and Poppy shed a few tears, but Sarah didn't feel at all embarrassed, and Poppy didn't appear to be embarrassed either. If they had to be kept in hiding, Sarah couldn't think of a situation any better than this. She truly felt safe.

# *Chapter Seven*
## HARVEST

IT TOOK ONLY A FEW days for Sarah and Poppy to feel completely comfortable in the home of their gracious hosts. Sarah felt grateful beyond words to be so at ease in this house and with these people—given the fact that she had no idea how many weeks—or perhaps months—they might be staying. Darius had told them more than once that he needed to be absolutely certain of their safety before he would take them back home—or to a different location. She didn't exactly understand how he might know that—short of the killer actually being discovered and incarcerated—but for now she preferred not to think about the details. She and Poppy had been opening up more with each other during their time alone and talking about the impact of all that had happened. While it felt good to be able to share her feelings—and tears—with Poppy, they both agreed that trying to speculate too much about the future right now would only make them feel restless and agitated. They'd both concluded that for now it was better to just focus on the present. When they'd somehow ended up in a conversation with Daphne on the topic, she suggested that it was important to take time to grieve over the losses in life, and perhaps it would be more healing for the two of them to have some distance from home—and from the situation. Sarah couldn't help but agree with her. In fact, it was becoming somewhat of a ritual for her to start crying each night when she was alone in her bed. But crying herself to sleep was already making her feel that at least she wasn't continually on the verge of bursting into tears, or worse, unable to feel anything at all.

Both Sarah and Poppy developed a daily routine, which included keeping their own rooms tidy, doing their own laundry, and assisting each other with buttons and hair. They also quickly discovered that while Daphne loved to cook—and she enjoyed sharing her creations with guests—she wasn't necessarily fond of washing dishes, and there was always something in the house that could use some cleaning, which kept them busy. Sarah loved being productive, which made it easier not to dwell on the reasons for this situation.

While the women found projects inside the house to occupy themselves, Sarah couldn't help noticing that Darius was keeping himself busy *outside*. According to Daphne he had already repaired a few things in the house and also in the barn, and he'd cleared away a great many weeds. She mentioned that David appreciated the help as much as he enjoyed the company.

A week after their arrival, the men were making some repairs to the roof in anticipation of winter, while the women were busy in the kitchen. Daphne was making what she called her *famous* pork and venison pie, and at Poppy's request she was teaching her and Sarah how to do it. Sarah was fascinated with the techniques that made a perfectly flaky, crisp crust, and tender meat inside that didn't leak its juiciness though the golden deliciousness encasing it. Since they were making pastry for the meat pie, they made extra for dessert, and Daphne mixed sliced apples with sugar and some spices to cook inside more of that perfectly flaky crust. While they were peeling and cutting apples—and listening to the pounding of hammers on the roof—Daphne told them the apples had come from one of the trees behind the house. Since Darius wouldn't let Sarah or Poppy outside during the day—just in case—neither of them had known there were apple trees.

"But now that you mention it," Sarah said, "we have been eating a lot of wonderful, crisp apples."

"All grown right here," Daphne said proudly. "The men have been picking a few bushels every day and putting them down in the cellar."

"I didn't realize that," Poppy said.

"Nor did I," Sarah added, thinking how she might enjoy picking apples out in the sunshine if she were not forbidden to leave the house, given the possibility that sometimes David and Daphne did receive visitors from the nearby village, and they couldn't risk anyone at all being able to report that a woman in danger—or her maid—had been spotted there.

"They'll keep fairly well until next spring," Daphne added, "but of course they taste best when they're fresh. I'm so glad you are here to enjoy them!" She said the last as if having Sarah and Poppy in her home was the best thing that had happened to her in years.

"I couldn't agree more," Poppy said with enthusiasm, and Sarah made a gentle noise of agreement

"It was excellent timing," Daphne added, "for Darius to show up right at harvest time. I don't mind helping pick the apples, but there are things I'd rather be doing, and Darius can pick more than both David and I put together. He's very good at it."

"So, he's been here at harvest time before?" Sarah asked.

"A number of times, yes," Daphne said. "He doesn't stay only when he needs to keep someone safe; sometimes he just needs to get away."

"Forgive me if this sounds nosy," Sarah began, "but—"

"Oh, you can ask me anything you like," Daphne said with a little laugh while they continued to slice the freshly peeled apples.

"Do you and David have children?"

"Yes," Daphne smiled, "three. We have a daughter who married a fine man and they have three children. Unfortunately, he works in the shop he inherited from his father—in Liverpool. They have a good life there, but we only get to see them once every year or two." She sighed. "And we have two sons; one lives in Portsmouth with a new wife. He works for the navy office there and quite enjoys it; that's where his wife's family lives, and it's good that she's close to her family since her health is somewhat fragile. But they're happy. I get regular letters from them."

"And the other son?" Poppy asked.

"He works abroad," Daphne said with a sudden cloudiness in her voice, which subtly implied that her relationship with this son might not be so favorable. "We don't receive letters from him, but I'm certain he's doing fine. He was always very independent. Even as a young child he made it clear he could do just about anything on his own." She sighed again. "Children are all different. You just never know where their personalities will take them. But David and I have been very blessed. Thankfully we enjoy each other's company." She laughed softly. "I know of many couples who reach our time of life when their children are gone, and they just make each other miserable. We're both *very* grateful that's not the case for us. We could spend every minute together and never get bored."

"That's lovely," Sarah said. "My parents were like that, which was wonderful of course, but I'm certain it made my mother's death much more difficult for my father."

"Oh, it would!" Daphne said compassionately. "If nothing else, little one, it's nice to think of your father and mother being reunited."

"Yes," Sarah said sadly and pushed back the threat of tears, putting them on hold until she was alone in her room tonight.

That evening they all savored the delicious results of the ladies' labor in the kitchen. Daphne gave Poppy and Sarah far more credit than they deserved, although both of them admitted how much they enjoyed the opportunity to learn from such a skilled cook.

"At least you're learning something," Darius said lightly. "I learned how to pick apples years ago, and now I can't get out of it."

"You know when harvest season is, boy," David said to him. "No one says you have to come here when the apples need picking."

"I can assure you my need for protection wasn't scheduled to coincide with the harvest," Sarah said, glad that her comment didn't dampen the jovial mood at the dinner table.

They all talked long after they'd finished eating, then Sarah and Poppy helped Daphne clear the table, but before they had carried all the dishes into the kitchen, David entered, rolling up his sleeves and announcing that it was his turn to wash the dishes. She looked past David to see Darius rolling up his sleeves as well. "And yes," David smirked playfully, "he's going to help me."

"Very well," Sarah said after Poppy had smiled and left the room. She might have been more inclined to argue if it had only been David, but the idea of Darius Noble washing dishes was simply too delightful. "I'll leave you men to it."

Sarah found Poppy in the parlor reading a novel she'd borrowed from Daphne, and Daphne was doing some mending. "I think I'll go for a little walk," she told them. "Even though it's dark, I'd like to get a look at these apple trees that produce such a wondrous harvest."

"Oh, they're beautiful even at night," Daphne said, smiling at her, and Sarah went upstairs to get her cloak.

Sarah stepped out the back door into the autumn air that had cooled significantly since the sun had gone down. She immediately craned her neck to look up and was instantly overcome by the beauty of the stars in the night sky. She'd become so weary of nothing but the sky for shelter during their days of travel that she hadn't once stepped outside since they'd arrived. And now the fresh air and the glory of a star-filled sky felt both soothing and replenishing. When her neck began to ache from staring upward for so long, Sarah turned her attention to the three enormous trees in front of her that had not been planted symmetrically. But the lack of balance in their position from each other somehow made them all the more beautiful. Sarah walked beneath each of the trees, caressing their trunks and reaching up to touch the leaves she could reach. She wished she could pick an apple—just one—if only to feel the sensation of having it pop off the branch into her hand. But she could see no low-hanging apples at all. She assumed the men were using a ladder to get the apples that were higher up in the huge trees, but she didn't see a ladder anywhere around. Perhaps it had been put away for the night.

Examining the trees more closely, Sarah noticed that one of them had branches perfectly placed for an easy climb. She didn't need to go up very far; she just wanted to pick an apple. Sarah took off her cloak and laid it on the ground; even though she felt a little chillier, she knew wearing a cloak to climb a tree wasn't a good idea. She found it remarkably easy to put a foot onto a low branch, then her other foot onto one a little higher up. After doing that a few more times, she looked around to find herself next to a large branch that stretched outward, and above it she could see the glimmer of a few shiny apples.

Sarah moved in a very unladylike manner out onto the branch using both her hands and feet until she eased herself into a fairly comfortable sitting position, with her legs hanging down. From there it was easy to reach up and take hold of an apple. She laughed as it plopped into her hand, making her feel rather victorious. She wanted to eat it then and there, but at the same time she wanted to wait and just savor the effort she'd put into finding the perfect piece of fruit. So she just sat there and held it, enjoying the night air and not feeling as cold as she might have expected. After some minutes passed, she realized she couldn't sit up here much longer; in truth it wasn't terribly comfortable. But as she looked back in the direction from which she'd come, getting down didn't look nearly as easy as getting up here. Thankfully it was dark, and she was alone, because she knew she couldn't do it without hitching up her skirt and petticoat around her waist. She decided she would have to go ahead and eat the apple where she sat if she wanted to truly enjoy it. She had no pockets, and if she threw it down it would get bruised.

Sarah was about to take a bite when she heard Darius say, "What on earth are you doing up there?"

His voice startled her, since she hadn't heard him approaching; she didn't know if he'd purposely tried to be quiet, or if she just hadn't been paying attention.

"I wanted to pick an apple," she declared as if it were a perfectly reasonable response.

"There's hundreds of them in the house," Darius said, sounding amused.

"I wanted to pick one myself," she said, trying to sound falsely haughty, but she laughed and lost all pretense.

Darius laughed too and said, "Did you accomplish your quest?"

"I did," she said and held it up to show him, even though she knew he likely couldn't see any details of what she had in her hand.

"And how exactly did you plan on getting down?" he asked.

Refusing to admit she'd been a little alarmed over that very question, she simply said, "In a way that no gentleman should observe. Therefore, I suggest you go back into the house while I do so."

"I see," he said and laughed again, leaning his hand against the trunk. "What are you doing out here, anyway?"

"Do you honestly think I would go to bed without making certain you're safe?" he asked. "When I was told you'd come outside, I came looking for you. And here you are—in the last place I would have expected to find you."

"Perhaps you don't know me as well as you think you do," she said, again trying to sound haughty but it faltered into a laugh.

"I'm certain that's true," he said, "but that works both ways."

"Oh, I'm certain you know a great deal more about me than I do about you," Sarah pointed out more seriously. "In truth, I know absolutely *nothing* about you."

"You know what you need to know," he said in a light tone, as if he were determined to keep this conversation friendly and not tread into things he didn't want to talk about. He was private about his personal life. She did know *that* about him.

"If you'd like, I'll catch you," he said, "and then you won't have to climb down."

"What?" she gasped, astonished at the very idea. "You want me to just *fall* out of this tree?"

"I do," he said. "It's easy. Trust me. I'll catch you. You're not that far up; you won't get hurt, I promise."

"But . . ." she said then immediately realized how silly she would sound to try and protest, so she changed her mind about what she wanted to say and added, "I don't want to hurt my apple. It's perfect, you know."

Darius laughed. "You hold on tightly to your apple, and I'll catch you."

"Are you *sure?*" she asked, surprised she was actually considering this.

"Of course I'm sure," he insisted. "Just . . . fall . . . and I won't let you get hurt. I promise." She hesitated but didn't speak and he added, "Trust me, Sarah. Your life is in my hands already, you know. I can catch you."

Sarah looked down to where he was standing with his strong arms outstretched. She was surprised at how quickly she was able to affirm that she *did* trust him, and she *did* know he was capable of making certain she didn't get hurt. She didn't blame him at all for what had happened to Evans, but she suspected he blamed himself. That last thought distracted her from the present situation until she brought herself back to the moment and wondered why it would occur to her now in *this* situation. She decided that perhaps Darius needed to know that she trusted him despite what had happened, and maybe allowing herself to fall into his arms was just the way to do so—however silly it might seem.

"Are you ready?" she asked.

"I'm ready," he declared.

"Are you certain?"

"I'm certain," he chuckled. "Are we going to be out here all night?"

"I'm coming," she announced, then she took a deep breath and slipped off the branch. For less than a second, she was falling, then she felt his strong arms beneath her, and the way his knees bent then straightened again as his body gracefully held her weight as if it were nothing.

"There!" he laughed triumphantly, and she expected him to set her on her feet, but he didn't. "How's your apple?"

Sarah glanced down to see it still firmly in her hand. "Fine," she said, surprised—but not unpleasantly so—by how close his face was to hers.

"And how are you?" he asked.

"I'm fine," she said, unable to keep from staring at him. Even in the darkness she could see his every feature. All the tingling and fluttering she'd been trying to avoid overcame her with such force that she was actually glad he'd not yet put her down, because she feared she might topple over from dizziness. "How are *you?*" she asked, hoping he didn't hear the quiver in her voice.

"Oh, I'm perfectly fine," he said and reluctantly guided her feet to the ground, letting go of her slowly. She teetered slightly—just as she'd feared she might—but he held to her arms and simply asked, "Are you certain you're all right?"

"Yes," she insisted, "just a little . . . unsteady."

"Well," he said, still holding onto her, "after such a tremendous fall, that's understandable."

His light sarcasm made her laugh softly, but as she looked up at his face, she wondered if he suspected the reason for her lack of balance. The last thing she wanted was for him to have the slightest suspicion that she'd developed some kind of school-girl infatuation over the man protecting her. But she would have never called herself a very good actress; her parents had always known when she'd been fibbing as a little girl, and she hadn't been very old when she'd determined that she should always be honest because she could never get away with lying. Looking into Darius's eyes now, she wondered if he could see the truth there, and if he did, she wondered if he might scoff at it, make fun of it, or simply disregard it.

Sarah kept telling herself to look away, but she just couldn't. It felt as if some invisible magnetic force kept her gaze locked with his. She was so preoccupied with trying to hide any evidence of the way she felt about him that it startled her to realize what she saw in *his* eyes. A barely audible gasp escaped her lips and it became even more difficult to try and look away.

"I've never met anyone like you," he said as if he were attempting to justify his reasons for staring at her. "A perfect lady, and yet so kind and respectful of others. Raised as an heiress and yet you clean and cook and do your own laundry. And you climb a tree just to pick an apple when you have no idea how you'll get down."

Sarah felt her breathing quicken as she took in what he was saying. Following his lead, she attempted to justify *her* reasons for staring at *him* by echoing his own words. "I've never met anyone like you, either," she said. "You're kinder and more respectful than any gentleman I've ever known— perhaps with the exception of my father. And you make me feel safe, even though . . ."

"Even though what?" he asked when she didn't finish.

"Even though I know practically nothing about you," she said, realizing she'd wanted to say this for several days. "You've asked me and Poppy a great many questions about ourselves, our lives, our preferences. You've told us a great deal about David and Daphne. But they tell us nothing about you, and you certainly offer no information about yourself. I have no idea if you even have a family, or where you come from, or—"

"With the work I do," he said, "I've always considered it prudent to be conservative about sharing my private life."

"Conservative would be an understatement," she said, marveling that they were still staring at each other, and he'd not let go of her upper arms. "Are we not friends? You said you'd never met anyone like me. If I'm different than your other . . . *clients*, could you not open up just a little bit about yourself?"

"Why?" he asked as if her answer would be deeply important.

Sarah had no trouble saying, "Because I'm interested; because I care. Your work must be very lonely. Do you not ever wish to just . . . share something of yourself with someone else?"

"I have friends," he said.

"And yet they share nothing about you, either," she said. "Is there something you're trying to hide?"

"No," he said quickly and sincerely. "I just . . ." His hesitation made it evident he had difficulty sharing whatever he was about to say. "I . . . don't want to get too attached . . . to anyone I'm hired to care for. It's always temporary."

Sarah wanted to tell him that his eyes were contradicting what he'd just said about not wanting to become attached. While she was waiting for him to offer some further explanation, she was completely taken off guard when he bent down and kissed her. She took in a sharp breath before she focused all her attention on enjoying the sensation of his lips pressed meekly against hers in a kiss that was lengthy but unassuming and tender. She'd never been kissed before, but her lips instinctively moved closer to his, as if by their own will they longed to be thoroughly engaged in this experience.

When their kiss ended, she heard him whisper her name in a dreamy voice while her eyes came slowly open, loving the view of his face so close and from this angle. She was enjoying the opportunity to take in every detail of his features when he stepped back and let go of her so suddenly that she almost lost her balance.

"I'm sorry," he said as if he'd just been caught in someone's home stealing their silver. "I'm so very sorry. I shouldn't have done that."

"Why not?" she asked, trying to figure out why she suddenly felt totally rejected. She couldn't keep from sounding a bit snide as she added, "Am I so repulsive, or—"

"It's not that, Sarah," he said, stepping backward. "It's nothing like that, I can assure you. It's just . . . I'm supposed to be keeping you safe; I was hired to protect you. This is just not . . . appropriate." He turned and walked away, saying over his shoulder, "Please go inside so I can lock the doors and make certain all is well."

"All is not well," Sarah said so quietly that only she could hear. She stood there for a minute or more trying to review what had just happened—and how it had affected her. She'd gone from curious to elated to devastated in a matter of a couple of minutes, which left her almost as disoriented and fraught as she'd been when she'd found out her father had been murdered.

Suddenly feeling cold when she hadn't noticed the temperature at all since Darius had found her in the tree, she headed toward the door of the house. She was almost there when she recalled her cloak on the ground near the tree and she turned back to get it.

"What are you doing?" Darius asked, and she realized he had circled around part of the yard and was standing in the shadows on the other side of the tree, waiting for her to go inside. She wondered why he sounded angry when *he* was the one who had kissed *her*.

"Getting my cloak," she said. "I left it on the ground."

She picked it up and said nothing more before she walked through the back door into the house, going straight up the stairs to her room. She didn't want to see anyone or talk to anyone. She just needed to be alone so she could try and accept that she had fallen in love with Darius Noble, but apparently as long as he was working to protect her, such feelings didn't matter. She was nothing short of amazed to realize he had similar feelings for her—or at least she assumed he did by the way he'd kissed her—but according to what he'd said, such feelings were nothing more than a dreadful inconvenience under the circumstances.

Sarah locked her bedroom door and tossed her cloak over a chair before she sat on it and sighed. She sighed again before tears came. She didn't know if she was still crying over the death of her father, the realization he'd been murdered, or the way Evans had been killed by a bullet intended for her. Or perhaps now she was crying for something else entirely. Or maybe all of it combined. She decided it didn't really matter *why* she was crying; she just kept doing so while she methodically got ready for bed, climbed beneath the bedcovers, and extinguished the lamp on her bedside table.

"Darius," she whispered into the darkness and cried some more until she once again cried herself to sleep.

\* \* \* \* \*

Sarah dreaded going down to breakfast the morning after her apple-picking adventure, but she finally worked up the nerve, only to arrive in the dining room and find that Darius had eaten early and was doing some work out in the barn.

"Or he might be using my woodworking tools," David said casually and sipped his coffee. "He does that occasionally to ease his boredom."

Sarah sat down next to Poppy, glad when the meal proceeded with casual conversation that had nothing to do with Darius. By the following morning at breakfast, Sarah was amazed at how skillfully he was managing to completely avoid her. She kept hearing one excuse after another from either David or Daphne, neither of whom seemed at all concerned or confused. Perhaps it was common for Darius Noble to have bouts of avoiding people and keeping to himself. Sarah wondered if the situation might have been better or worse if she'd had no idea regarding the reasons for his antisocial behavior. Knowing that it surely had something to do with their kiss beneath the apple tree and his immediate regret, she found it difficult not to think about him almost constantly—as if she hadn't had trouble with that *prior* to their strange little romantic encounter. Now that she knew she wasn't the only one feeling this way, Darius's absence left her confused and sometimes agitated.

Sarah worked slowly at washing the lunch dishes—another meal which had been eaten with Darius absent—wondering where he was and what he was doing. If she hadn't been strictly forbidden to leave the house in daylight, she would likely have wandered the yard and gone out to the barn to find him and confront him and get him to tell her the truth. As it was, Sarah was stuck in the house, too distracted by her thoughts to focus on reading or even sticking to a task for very long. She glanced at a little clock in the windowsill, alarmed by how long it was taking her to get the dishes done. She'd volunteered, since Poppy had confided that she was behind on her personal laundry, and Daphne had gone to check the supplies in the pantry and cellar to make a list of what was needed, since David was going into town to get some grain for the animals living in the barn. Sarah had been told there were chickens and cows, and of course horses. She knew well enough they would not be enjoying milk and eggs without the former, but she had yet to see them with her own eyes. And right now, she just wanted to go to the barn with the excuse of seeing the animals, hoping she might find Darius there. But he'd be furious with her if she left the house, and that would only make this situation worse.

"Darius went into town with David," Daphne said and startled Sarah.

"Is it safe for *him* to be seen in public?" she asked.

"Oh, he's known to show his face around here somewhat regularly," Daphne said. "I doubt anyone will think a thing of it. No one around here knows what he does for a living; they only know he's connected to us and visits often."

"I see," Sarah said and rinsed off a plate she'd just washed, wishing *she* could go into town. She didn't really mind being stuck here in this house; it was a pleasant home with good company. But she was finding it increasingly difficult to not see Darius while at the same time wondering *why* he had kissed her, *what* he was feeling, and *why* he'd become so upset about it.

"I thought you might like to know he couldn't possibly overhear us while we're talking," Daphne added.

"What?" Sarah asked, turning to see an intensity seeping into Daphne's expression.

"Never mind this," Daphne said and urged Sarah away from the dishes, handing her a towel on which to dry her hands. "We need to talk."

Sarah felt a little afraid as she followed Daphne into the parlor and they sat down to face each other.

"Darius told me what happened," Daphne said, and Sarah felt her face turn warm—which meant it was also turning bright pink.

"He did?" she asked, not knowing what else to say.

"I'm afraid there's very little Darius *doesn't* tell me," she said. "David knows too."

"Knows what exactly?" Sarah asked, wanting to clarify that they were talking about the same thing before she made a comment that embarrassed herself further.

"How he feels about you, little one," Daphne said as if she'd told Sarah something deeply tragic. "And what happened outside night before last."

"I see," Sarah said again and looked down at her hands as she folded them tightly in her lap. Without looking up she said, "And did he tell you I'm the reason he's not showing himself at mealtimes?"

"He *is* reluctant to see you," Daphne said in a way that made talking about sensitive matters seem so easy. "But it's likely not for the reasons you might think."

"How does he—or anyone else—know what I might think?" Sarah asked, looking again at Daphne.

"He doesn't; we don't," Daphne said, "although it's been evident since the day you arrived that you feel something for *him*." Sarah looked abruptly toward the window, hating the very idea of her feelings having been so obvious to those around her. "The thing is, little one," Daphne said, "he believes that if what he feels for you were not reciprocated, he would be able to dismiss all this more easily. He sincerely cares about you, but he doesn't want you to get hurt."

"What do you mean?" Sarah asked, noting that Daphne's wording seemed a little strange. Daphne hadn't said that Darius didn't want to hurt her; she said he didn't want Sarah to get hurt. Given that he was being paid to protect her, she couldn't help wondering if there was a connection. Or perhaps she was only imagining things. But since Daphne was making it so easy to be straightforward, Sarah waited expectantly for an answer to her question.

"He usually doesn't want people to know," Daphne went on, "but from what he said to me, I think he wants *you* to know; he just doesn't want to have to tell you himself. Still, you must know that this is very close to his heart; I'm trusting you—as he is—to respect the matter and keep it confidential."

"Of course," Sarah said, her heart quickening as she sensed from Daphne's tone and expression that she was about to hear something truly dreadful.

"To put it simply," Daphne began, "Darius has only loved one woman, and she was killed while he was responsible for her safety." Sarah gasped, and Daphne added, "I don't think he's ever forgiven himself, and I think he fears that if he indulges in his feelings for you, he will be distracted and put your life at risk, because that's what he believes happened before."

Sarah took all this in before she asked, "Why didn't he just tell me himself?"

"Darius is a gentle soul, little one," Daphne said. "For all that he is intelligent and perceptive and physically capable of just about anything, he's not unlike most men when it comes to sharing such difficulties. In truth, the two of you haven't known each other very long. He tells me he trusts you, but I'm certain that in spite of the years that have passed, he still finds it difficult to talk about."

"That's understandable," Sarah said, and couldn't think of anything else to say except, "What should I do?"

"Be patient," Daphne said with a kind smile. "I suspect you'll be here a long while yet, and the two of you will have more time to get to know each other better."

"Not if he won't be in the same room with me," Sarah said, a little miffed about that in spite of what she'd just learned.

Daphne laughed softly. "He'll come around. Just . . . be patient with him. I thought that if you knew the reasons why this is difficult for him, it might help you understand, because I can tell you've felt confused."

"That I have," Sarah admitted. She sighed and added, "I'm very sorry for his loss."

Daphne nodded and looked down, as if she couldn't think about it without becoming emotional herself. She looked back up and said, "It's impossible to know if anything might come of the way you and Darius feel about each other, little one, but I can assure you he will not allow himself to even consider any kind of relationship with you—beyond friends—until he is no longer responsible for your well-being." She stood up as if to indicate that was all she had to say.

Before Daphne could leave the room, Sarah said, "Thank you for telling me."

Daphne smiled and nodded and hurried away so quickly that Sarah wondered if she was actually on the verge of tears. It was readily evident that Daphne and David cared very much for Darius; she wondered if they had known this woman he'd loved who had been killed. Perhaps she had come here with him. The idea seemed likely.

Sarah sat there alone for several minutes reviewing everything Daphne had said. It was a little unnerving to think that David and Daphne knew everything about Darius's feelings—and what had happened under the apple tree. But her sorrow on Darius's behalf—combined with her concern for him—eased her temptation to feel embarrassed.

Needing a distraction, Sarah returned to the kitchen to finish washing the dishes, which meant she had to heat more water to get them properly clean since the water she'd been using had turned cold. By the time she was finished, Sarah knew she needed to talk to Poppy. It wasn't like her to keep secrets from her dearest friend. She completely trusted Poppy, and therefore concluded that she had avoided the subject mostly because she hadn't wanted to admit to her feelings for Darius when she barely understood them herself. But it wasn't fair for Poppy to be the only person in the house who didn't know what was going on.

Sarah found Poppy in her room, reading.

"May I talk to you?" Sarah asked, closing the door behind her.

"I wish you would," Poppy said, alluding to the likelihood that Poppy had been waiting for Sarah to confide in her.

"Forgive me," Sarah began, "for not being more straightforward with you. Everything has just been so . . . overwhelming . . . and confusing, and . . ."

"I know," Poppy said. "There's no need to apologize. I just want you to still be able to confide in me, and to know that I would never tell a soul anything you share with me."

"I know that," Sarah said and proceeded to tell her the whole story, beginning with her first inklings of attraction toward Darius up to the point of the conversation she'd just had with Daphne. Poppy was compassionate and kind as always, and she reassured Sarah that she wouldn't repeat a word of what Sarah had just shared.

Now that Sarah had no secrets from *anyone* in this house, she and Poppy were able to talk about other things. Sarah was glad to feel more relaxed with Poppy than she had since she'd found the sword and had started keeping secrets. In spite of this strange situation with Darius—and not having any idea how the situation might resolve itself—Sarah was relieved to feel like her friendship with Poppy was finally back to normal. Until now she hadn't realized how much tension there had been between them; it had been subtle and she'd chalked it up to her grieving and also her fear regarding all that was happening. But now she could see those things had been complicated by Sarah not opening up to Poppy the way she used to. Hopefully now everything would go back to normal—at least between her and Poppy.

# Chapter Eight
## THE COCOON OF WINTER

THE FOLLOWING DAY SARAH WAS pleased to realize she *did* feel more relaxed around Poppy since she'd shared all her secrets with her dearest friend. If she'd realized how much subtle tension her holding back had been causing them, she would have had that conversation a long time ago.

Breakfast with Poppy and David and Daphne was relaxed and enjoyable—in spite of the obvious absence of Darius. After supper was over and Sarah hadn't seen any hint of his existence all day, she asked Daphne while they were washing dishes, "How does he manage to eat his meals and avoid me? This is ridiculous."

"He manages to eat . . . barely," Daphne said. "But I agree with you; it's ridiculous. Personally, I believe he's lost perspective, probably thinking far too much about what happened years ago instead of focusing on the present. But I've said all I can say."

"Then I should talk to him," Sarah said and saw Poppy's eyes widen from where she was drying a pan that Daphne had just rinsed and handed to her.

"I wouldn't argue with that," Daphne said, and Poppy's expression filled with mock fear as she glanced toward Sarah, but Daphne didn't see her.

"Has he had supper yet?" Sarah asked.

"No," Daphne said, "it's in the oven keeping warm."

Sarah hurried to dry her hands, anxious to act on her instincts before she lost her nerve. "Is he in the barn? It's dark outside; I can go to the barn, can't I?"

"I don't see why not," Daphne said, seeming pleased. Sarah opened the oven to see a small frying pan there covered with a lid. "Careful, it's hot,"

Daphne said and handed her a small, clean towel with which Sarah carefully removed the pan from the oven, holding it in both hands while Daphne closed the oven. Daphne also hurried to lift the lid slightly and stick a fork into the pan, with the handle poking out slightly.

"Good luck," Poppy said as Sarah left the kitchen.

"And God bless!" Daphne called a little louder.

As Sarah went out the back door and headed down the well-worn path toward the barn, where the lights from its windows guided her in the right direction, she felt increasingly nervous and knew she could use all of the luck in the world right now—or more accurately, she needed divine intervention, which made Daphne's words especially significant.

Sarah pulled open the barn door while balancing the warm pan on her other hand. She tentatively stepped inside to see a single lantern burning nearby which illuminated a typical-looking barn—as far as she knew. The only other barn she'd ever seen inside was the one at Castle Courtenay where cows, chickens, and pigs were kept. At Courtenay, the horses were kept in the stables; here all the animals were in the same structure but separated into different pens and stalls.

Sarah quickly realized that the woodworking space she'd heard so much about was actually a large room built into the corner of the barn, with a door that stood between her and Darius. She could hear a scraping noise and knew Darius was in there, because David was in the parlor reading. She wondered if she should knock, but opted to just go in there and take him off guard just enough to get him to listen to her—even though she wasn't completely certain what she intended to say. But she silently uttered a quick prayer, took a deep breath, opened the door and stepped inside.

Darius looked up in surprise and for the first time since he'd kissed her, they were standing face-to-face. He set down the tool he was holding and brushed his hands together, creating a shower of sawdust that fell from them.

"Hello," she said. "I brought your supper. You need to eat."

"Thank you," he said as she set the pan—including the towel beneath it—onto the only empty space on the worktable where he'd clearly been very busy with a project. But Sarah was too preoccupied with *him* to be paying much attention to what he'd been doing.

As her nervousness set off the tingling and fluttering his presence often provoked, Sarah knew she just needed to say what she'd come to say and get it over with. This didn't have to be complicated; she just had to make a simple clarification.

"There's no reason for you to avoid me, Darius. I'm not going to read any implications into what happened between us, and I don't have any expectations. We barely know each other, so whether or not we have feelings for each other at this point is irrelevant as far as I see it. I know it's your job to protect me and you don't want anything to complicate the situation, so—"

"Daphne told you," he stated.

Sarah didn't have to ask what he meant; she knew exactly. "Yes, she told me. She thought I should understand the situation rather than continue to feel confused." Darius looked at the floor; she couldn't tell if he was attempting to hide some kind of frustration he felt toward Daphne for sharing the drama of his past, or if he might feel guilty for not having told her himself. She hoped it was the latter. But it really didn't matter. She just needed to hurry and finish saying what she'd come to say.

"Darius," she said, and he looked up again, "for now I think we should just forget about what happened; even if there's anything substantial behind what we feel, the timing is all wrong. Therefore, we just need time. Until this trouble in my life is resolved, nothing else matters. But you've told me I'm likely to be here for months, and I refuse to live here and have you avoid me like this. It's not necessary. Can't we just be friends? Like we were before?"

The silence following her question became strained until he sighed and said, "Yes, we can be friends. Forgive me; I've behaved very childishly."

Sarah hoped she wasn't treading too far into his personal life when she said, "I can understand why you would be upset, but what happened to her wasn't your fault."

"How can you possibly know that?" he asked with a forced calmness in his voice.

"Because I know Evans's death wasn't your fault, and if the bullet had hit me, that wouldn't have been your fault, either. I may know very little about you or your past, but I have enough common sense to know that you can't do the kind of work you do without accepting that you're human and there is much outside your control. If you blame yourself for everything that goes wrong when you're just trying to do the best you can, you're only going to end up making yourself miserable. At least that's my opinion; you don't have to agree." He said nothing; in fact, he looked a little shocked. Sarah ignored his expression, knowing she had no idea what he was thinking.

Satisfied with having voiced her thoughts, Sarah turned away from him, saying over her shoulder, "Enjoy your supper." Before she left the room, she added, "I'll see you at breakfast."

She closed the door behind her before he could respond, and she deeply hoped she *would* see him at breakfast and they could put to rest this ridiculous awkwardness. She couldn't deny how she felt about him, and she couldn't think about what Darius had said to her—or his kiss—without feeling a little giddy. But she also completely understood why the situation would create a great dilemma for Darius, and she had grown to respect him as much as she'd grown to love him. On both counts she knew she needed to step back and behave maturely enough to keep her feelings to herself until he was no longer her protector. By then, perhaps she would have come to realize that what she felt was nothing but a childish infatuation, or the result of her reliance on him to keep her safe. Or perhaps he would lose interest in her, and her feelings would be irrelevant. Either way, for now Sarah consciously shelved her growing affection for Darius Noble and committed herself to doing exactly what she had told him they both should do—and simply be friends.

\* \* \* \* \*

That night as Sarah was trying to go to sleep, her brief encounter with Darius kept running through her mind. Seeing him again had added a spark to the feelings she'd been trying to ignore. After much stewing, she finally concluded that her feelings simply were what they were. She wasn't *trying* to feel this way anymore than she had the power to make herself *not* feel this way. It was how she acted upon her feelings that mattered; her mother had taught her that. Sarah therefore decided that she needed to allow herself a little segment of time each day when she was alone to examine those feelings and acknowledge them, which was far more conducive to having a proper attitude about them than attempting to pretend they didn't exist. And the rest of the day she would behave appropriately and not give any indication to Darius or anyone else that she desperately wanted to be in the same room with him every waking minute, that she wanted to know everything about him—his hopes and dreams and fears. But she had to check herself continually to remember that they were—and for now could only be—friends.

Sarah finally slept, and the following morning when she went down to breakfast, she was pleased to see Darius already at the table, talking with David about something to do with the care of the animals. Poppy was also seated at the table and all three of them looked up simultaneously when she entered the room. "Good morning," they all said at the same time but in a garbled lack of unison.

"Good morning," she replied just before Daphne entered with a bowl of scrambled eggs, which she set on the table before she seated herself. Sarah sat down as well.

Only a few minutes into the meal Sarah began to experience relief as it bathed over her like a warm, summer rain. Darius was very much himself again—and his behavior felt genuine and not at all forced. Everything truly *did* feel as it had before he'd kissed her—even the way she was overcome with a keen awareness of him and the way he made her feel, which she was trying to suppress and keep hidden. And she wondered if it was the same for him. But they all talked casually and comfortably while they enjoyed Daphne's cooking.

David and Daphne talked about how all the apples had been picked and stored away, so the harvest was officially over, except for a couple of pumpkins and some winter squash that they would pick when the weather became colder. Daphne talked with anticipation about the recipes she looked forward to using with the vegetables they had recently harvested, and the few that were being left on the vine just a little longer. She also mentioned that she would be making apple tarts today, which provoked a pleased response from David and Darius. And she would be making applesauce tomorrow to go with a pork loin she would be cooking. This too was pleasing to David and Darius. They were clearly familiar with the positive results of Daphne's culinary skills; Sarah and Poppy just knew that anything Daphne made tasted good.

Near the end of the meal, Darius looked at Sarah across the table and said, "I keep forgetting to tell you that nothing has turned up in the investigation concerning your father's death. I know that's not good news, but I'm not surprised, to be truthful. I still believe the best course for you and Poppy is to remain here until more time passes. It's my experience that guilty people tend to relax more when months pass and they begin to believe they've gotten away with their crimes. I hope you're all right with that, with remaining here for now like we discussed."

"Yes," Sarah said. "We're very comfortable here." She glanced at Poppy who nodded in agreement. "As long as we're not wearing out our welcome, then—"

"Never!" David drawled with a laugh right before Daphne said, "The two of you are the most delightful guests we've ever had!"

Sarah smiled at her hosts, then looked again at Darius. "May I ask how you know this? How you're being kept informed?"

"Of course," he said. "I should have told you sooner; it just kept slipping my mind. Letters from Halford."

"But . . ." Sarah said and paused while she tried to articulate what felt like a flaw in this. "Couldn't someone see his letters? And where they're addressed? I don't trust *anyone* in that house anymore except for Halford, and my aunt of course."

"He writes his letters to David," Darius explained. "They've been friends all their lives, and Halford has been writing regularly to David for as long as he's lived and worked at Courtenay. No one could possibly see anything suspicious in his letters or find a connection to us being here. And even if someone *read* his letters—which they couldn't without unsealing them—they would not be able to discern the information he's giving us, because his messages to me are benignly mingled into the letter, based on a method he and I decided on before we left there."

"I see," Sarah said, glad to know that Darius was regularly hearing from Halford, even though she was indeed disappointed that the reason for her father's death was still a mystery. While she had the chance she asked, "And what happens if months pass and there still isn't any clue as to what happened? About who is behind this?"

"If nothing has changed by spring, we will change our tactics. But that's for me to handle, nothing for you to worry about."

"And is my aunt well? Has he said?"

"Yes," Darius told her with a tender smile, as if he appreciated and understood her love for her aunt. "She is well except for missing you."

"I miss her too," Sarah admitted, then confessed with a little laugh, "Well, she is the most eccentric woman I've ever known, and sometimes she can be overly dramatic, but I love her dearly."

"I know you do," Darius said. "When she and Halford met with me about seeing to your protection, she couldn't stop weeping over the fact that you would have to leave for so long."

Sarah smiled at him, then looked down, feeling suddenly sad. "Yes, well," she forced a chuckle, "Aunt Penelope weeps a great deal over every little thing. I'm certain she'll be fine."

"As will you," Darius said with a confidence that inspired her. He *was* himself again, and she was deeply glad for it! He looked at Poppy and added, "Both of you. I'll do everything in my power to keep you both safe."

Sarah noticed that he didn't promise to keep them safe; he promised to do everything in his power to do so. She appreciated hearing that his declaration was realistic and hoped that with time he would find peace over knowing he'd done everything in his power to keep Evans safe—and the woman he'd loved and lost.

"We know you will," Sarah said with confidence.

"Well, then," Daphne said cheerfully, "in the meantime we can get busy preparing for winter. I love winter, actually. I enjoy the coziness of being safe and snug here in our home when it's cold outside. And for some strange reason I love the look of the trees when they've lost their leaves, and I especially love it when it snows. Snow is so beautiful! I do hope we get some good snow this winter!"

"I hope so too," Darius said in a way that made Sarah suspect it wasn't for the same reasons, but he didn't elaborate before he stood up from the table and walked away, saying only, "I'll be in the barn if you need me."

Sarah watched him walk away, willing her stomach to stop fluttering. She turned her thoughts to gratitude over having things back to normal between them and knowing that her aunt and Halford were all right. She thought of what Daphne had said about her anticipation and enjoyment of winter and decided she could easily adopt Daphne's attitude. She felt safe and comfortable, and apart from missing her aunt, she felt no desire to return to Courtenay. It had become a frightening place, tainted with difficult memories. She far preferred to remain here in this safe haven where life was simple and good. With that thought most prominent in her mind, Sarah stood up and began to clear the table with Poppy assisting her. Daphne had become accustomed to their insistence on always doing so after meals and she remained seated, pouring herself another cup of tea. Sarah and Daphne exchanged a smile and Sarah realized she had also grown to love these kind people who had taken in both herself and Poppy. The thought of leaving here eventually felt even more difficult than leaving Castle Courtenay. But she didn't need to concern herself with that right now. She thought instead of apple tarts and good conversation and the warmth and comfort of this place she had come so quickly to call home.

\* \* \* \* \*

As autumn was swallowed up by a harsh winter storm that left a blanket of snow in its wake, Sarah settled more comfortably into her life in this safe haven, and she came to fully appreciate Daphne's theory on her love of winter with the way being snug and warm indoors created a feeling of contentment and coziness. Poppy had told Sarah more than once that she agreed completely, which wasn't a surprise since they were so much alike. But it was nice that the two of them were so compatible with Daphne, which made it easy to be comfortable in her home, and to share in the daily chores as well as learning from her in the kitchen as they worked together to prepare meals.

Darius was seeming more relaxed, which helped Sarah feel the same. Her affection for him only seemed to grow day by day, but she was finding it easier to enjoy being his friend and allowing time to pass while she refused to indulge in any expectations regarding the future. There were just too many complications to resolve.

Sarah loved looking out of any given window in the house and delighting in the way the snow made everything so lovely beneath its equalizing white blanket. Darius admitted that he too loved snow, not only because it was beautiful but because it made it easy to see any signs that unwelcome visitors might have been on the grounds.

"Do you think there *has* been someone?" Sarah asked in alarm.

"No," he said, remaining perfectly calm, "but it's just a fact that snow makes it easier to be certain. I'm not suggesting you're in any danger, Sarah. But snow once helped me greatly in keeping someone safe; that's what I'm saying."

"I see," Sarah said. "I never would have thought of such a thing."

"That's why *I* am protecting *you*," he said with a little laugh and they smiled at each other until the gaze they shared made it evident that neither of them had experienced any change in their feelings toward each other—except perhaps in their growing stronger. Sarah felt both alarmed and relieved. While she knew their feelings made the situation more complicated, she was glad to know that Darius shared her affection—even if nothing could be done about it. She prayed that one day—when her life was no longer in danger—the situation between them would be different.

As winter settled in more deeply, Daphne began talking about Christmas preparations, and David was equally enthusiastic over his anticipation of the holiday. Their discussion of plans merged into days spent decorating the house with garlands made from pine boughs the men had gathered in the woods, along with ribbons of red and gold that Daphne had collected over the years and kept carefully stored away between Christmases. Daphne engaged the help of Sarah and Poppy in making wreaths for the front door and the back, declaring that she considered them some form of bringing the Christmas spirit into the home each time one of the doors was opened while a wreath was hanging on it. They also made one to hang over the fireplace in the parlor. The house began to smell like Christmas with the bounty of pine distributed throughout, and Sarah relished both the aroma and the appearance. Even though Castle Courtenay had always been decorated beautifully for Christmas, its enormity had diluted the aroma of the decor so that she'd never noticed it the way she did now.

The effect was amplified when Daphne began one baking project after another that filled the house with a continual, invisible cloud of spices. She made gingerbread and mince pies in great quantity so that there was plenty for them to enjoy, and also enough for her and David to deliver to friends in the village as gifts of Christmas greeting. Daphne also made sweets by cooking sugar at a high temperature for what seemed a ridiculously long time, and then doing different things with it in order to create a variety of fanciful delights. Sarah and Poppy both loved helping Daphne in the kitchen each day as Christmas drew closer. Sarah was learning a great deal from Daphne, although she absolutely knew she would never be capable of developing Daphne's skills for making biscuits and cakes and candies turn out just right. Of course, Daphne had been practicing for years, but Sarah chose to just admire her skills and enjoy helping rather than really trying to learn. Poppy, on the other hand, seemed intent on paying close attention, wanting to learn how to follow Daphne's example and create delicious wonders for holidays in the future, making them a part of her own traditions. Sarah teased that she was delighted by Poppy's intentions, since they were determined to always be close no matter what course their lives took; therefore, Sarah felt confident she could always be able to enjoy Poppy's newfound hobby.

A few days before Christmas, the men brought a small pine tree into the parlor, which they all helped decorate using ribbons and candles and some charming mementos Daphne had collected over the years that made the tree not only lovely but sentimental. Sarah noticed after the tree was decorated that a few wrapped gifts were put beneath it, and a troubling thought occurred to her. She first discussed the matter with Poppy, then they went to find Daphne just before she was heading upstairs to go to bed.

Sarah spoke for both her and Poppy. "We would very much like to give Christmas gifts to you and—"

"There's no need for that, little ones," Daphne assured them with a smile.

"I'm absolutely certain it's not required," Sarah said, having expected this reaction. "But we *want* to; you've all be so kind to us, and . . . it's Christmas. But, as you know . . . we are in hiding and therefore can't go shopping, so . . ."

Daphne sighed and took in what Sarah was saying. "I understand," she said. "I'm certain we can help you."

They talked for a few more minutes about the best way to handle the situation, and the following day when Daphne and David went into town on a variety of errands, they went with money that Sarah and Poppy had given them, and some ideas for gifts they could purchase on their behalf. Since David and Daphne would be splitting up to do some of their shopping, they would be able to accomplish what Daphne had begun to call *the secret Christmas mission*. When they returned from town each of them separately gave Sarah and Poppy what they'd purchased, and the money that was left over. They each felt pleased and more comfortable now that they had gifts for each other as well as the people with whom they were sharing this home—people who had come to feel like family. The gifts were simple and practical, but it was the meaning behind the giving of gifts that mattered more to Sarah—and she knew Poppy felt the same way. They enjoyed wrapping the gifts in some lovely tissue paper Daphne kept with her Christmas decorations. Having handled it carefully, it had been reused many times, which gave it an even more delicate effect. The gifts were tied with used but well-preserved ribbon and placed beneath the tree, which made Sarah feel as if they were truly ready for Christmas, and she was surprised to realize she actually felt excited. She wondered how she might feel if she was back at Castle Courtenay trying to celebrate a holiday without her father, knowing that Penelope would likely cry over her brother's absence more than she would put any effort into attempting to enjoy Christmas traditions that meant a great deal to Sarah, most of which had been instilled in her by her mother. Sarah was a little taken aback to realize she didn't miss being at home. With her father gone, it just wasn't the same—and it never would be. She loved Penelope dearly, but her aunt loved to be alone and read most of the time, and she enjoyed socializing with ladies near her own age in the area. Despite the fact that Sarah and her aunt cared very much for each other, they had never really enriched each other's lives. Sarah hadn't thought about it that much until she had come to see how much Daphne and David—and even Darius—all shared a great deal of conversation over their meals, and as they worked together on projects of various kinds. They often played cards together, or they would talk about the books they were reading—something Penelope had never been interested in doing. Sarah sometimes looked around at the home she was living in, and the people here, and she wondered how she could ever go back to Castle Courtenay. She mentioned her feelings to Darius and he was clearly surprised, declaring that he'd expected her to be impatient about returning home, the way all his previous clients had been. Sarah was determined to just enjoy her present life and not think about what might happen next. For now, she was safe and happy and greatly anticipating Christmas Day with the exchanging of gifts and a wonderful Christmas dinner that Daphne was already preparing, unwilling to accept much help since she insisted this was something she considered a Christmas offering to those who sat around her table for the holiday, and she loved doing it herself.

The day before Christmas Eve was stormy, with more wind than snow, which just made it terribly cold outside. David and Darius remarked more than once how glad they were that they didn't need to go into town for anything at all until perhaps after the new year. With the exception of going out to the barn to care for the animals, the men remained inside, near the comfort of the fire in the parlor, which was where Sarah and Poppy had made themselves comfortable to read, since Daphne was insisting that no one was allowed in the kitchen. But they could hear her humming Christmas carols while she worked.

Sarah often broke away from the novel in her hands to just look out the windows at the snow. The wind was blowing it around so violently that it was impossible to see any distance from the window at all. But the house was safe and warm, and sitting here in the parlor near the fire with the aromas of Christmas filling the house, Sarah felt completely content. She thought it funny that she was generally more preoccupied with her feelings for Darius than she was about the danger in her life. Being so distanced from her old life, the events that had made it necessary for her to be in Darius's care felt surreal and impossible to comprehend.

That evening after supper, Sarah and Poppy helped Daphne clean a great many dishes—since she had been doing extra baking and cooking for the holiday. But the three of them sang Christmas carols while they worked together, sometimes laughing over how bad they sounded. But there were some familiar songs they did rather well at singing, and Sarah felt warmed by the sweet spirit of Christmas that encompassed her.

Sarah and Poppy went upstairs to bed, but the two of them ended up talking in Poppy's room for quite a while. As Sarah confessed with some apprehension that she wasn't missing Castle Courtenay or the people there at all, she was surprised that Poppy *wasn't* surprised. She had sensed the contentment Sarah had been feeling, and in fact admitted that she very much liked it here, even if they could never leave the house during daylight hours.

But in the deepest part of winter, neither of them would have gone out much anyway. It was as if being here in this house, while the storms of winter raged outside, they were in a safe cocoon where nothing could harm them, and all was well. And Sarah wanted to hold onto that feeling, here where it was so much easier to not think about the horrible things that had happened, and the threat against her own life.

Sarah hugged Poppy and said good night before she went to her own room to get ready for bed. She felt thirsty and noticed that the glass of water she kept on her bedside table was empty. Knowing the barrels of water left upstairs were for cleaning purposes and not considered safe for drinking, she took her glass down to the kitchen to fill it. As she neared the bottom of the stairs, she heard what sounded like a pan dropping in the kitchen, followed by Daphne saying with a laugh, "I'm getting clumsy in my old age."

"You're not old," Sarah heard Darius say as she stopped around the corner from the kitchen, realizing the sound of her approach had been lost in the sound of the pan dropping. It occurred to her that she didn't want to interrupt them if they'd been having a serious conversation, and she waited to make certain that wasn't the case.

Sarah was actually surprised to hear David say, "Now back to the point. You can't avoid this, Darius."

As Sarah realized they *were* having a serious conversation, she wanted to just creep back up the stairs but realized she couldn't do so without making noise; she knew for a fact that a couple of floorboards between where she stood and where the stairs began would creak when she stepped on them.

"And," Daphne added, "you can't expect your two closest friends to not come for Christmas dinner when they've been coming for so many years. Neither of them has any family to speak of; you know that. They *always* come for Christmas dinner."

"I know that," Darius said, sounding deeply concerned.

"But you can't have them here for dinner without telling them exactly what you do for a living," David said. "I'm not sure why you haven't been willing to tell them before now, anyway. We all know you can trust them with *anything*."

"I know that too," Darius said, "but . . ."

He didn't finish, and Daphne stated, "But since you lost Mary, you don't trust *anyone*."

"It's not about that," Darius said defensively.

"It *is* about that," David said. "Everything has been about that since her passing, and we all know it. I think—we both think—that sharing the truth with your friends would be a good step toward healing from all of that and moving on with your life. It's been years; it's high time."

"Well," Darius said with a sarcasm she'd never heard from him, "I'm glad to know the two of you have my life all figured out."

"You know it's not like that!" Daphne scolded.

More humbly Darius said, "Yes, I know. Forgive me."

More gently Daphne added, "We just want you to be happy, and sometimes circumstances force us to do things that we put off doing because it's difficult. So . . . it's Christmas. Sarah and Poppy are here, and your friends are coming to Christmas dinner. It won't take much explaining for you to simply tell them why these delightful young women are here, and I doubt they'll hardly think a thing of it. I think you've likely made it out to be much worse than it really is because you keep putting it off."

"That's highly possible," Darius said.

"And there's the other point," David interjected. "You can't have your friends here for dinner if you don't tell the girls the truth."

"I agree with him on this too," Daphne said firmly. "Sarah and Poppy are not like anyone else you've ever brought here. You trust them completely; we know you do. And we also know how you feel about Sarah. You can't deny that we all hope when this is all over that . . . well . . . you know."

Sarah's heart quickened at the mention of her name in such a context. But at the same moment she realized she had overheard far too much of a conversation that was clearly meant to be private. Knowing she couldn't go back to the stairs without being discovered, she steeled herself to just make her presence known.

As she took a deep breath and told herself to just walk into the kitchen right this second, David said, "You need to tell Sarah, Darius. It's only going to get more difficult if you—"

"Tell me what?" Sarah asked, walking into the kitchen. All three looked astonished; she just held up her glass and said, "I need some clean water."

"How long have you been standing there?" Darius snapped, as if—with his extremely perceptive mind—he'd realized he hadn't heard her approach.

"Probably too long," she admitted. "Since the pan dropped, which is why you didn't hear me. I didn't want to interrupt, and then I didn't know how to leave without making it worse. Forgive me."

"There's nothing to forgive," David said. "I think it's high time we're done with any secrets in this house."

"Because your friends are coming to Christmas dinner?" Sarah asked, looking at Darius, although she knew from what she'd heard that there was more to the situation than telling his friends that he had been hired to protect these women whom they would be meeting Christmas Day.

"His occupation is the secret he's been keeping from his friends," Daphne said as if telling Sarah was nothing. "It's the secret we've been keeping from you and Poppy that needs to come to an end."

Sarah hurried to say, looking at David and Daphne, "Darius was hired to protect me. He has the right to keep secrets; I'm not offended, or anything like unto it."

"That's very gracious of you," Daphne said with a wan smile toward her. "Nevertheless . . ."

David looked at Darius and said, "Do you want me to tell her or—"

"I think I'm man enough to handle it," Darius said, not sounding happy about this at all.

Sarah was surprised when Daphne took the glass from Sarah's hands and set it on the counter, as if what she was about to hear might shock her so badly she could very well drop the glass and break it.

"Get on with it, then," David said authoritatively when Darius didn't say anything else.

Darius sighed loudly and motioned with his arm toward David and Daphne. "Sarah," he said, "meet my parents."

"What?" Sarah said on the wave of a gasp. She looked at each of their faces, all looking expectantly at her, waiting for a reaction.

"Noble is my middle name," Darius added. "It's my mother's maiden name; I took it on as a surname to protect my family." He sighed again, even more loudly. "When I told my parents I had quit working for the royal family and I intended to make myself available to be hired to protect people in danger, they were eager to offer our home as a refuge if it was ever needed. It works perfectly since it's so secluded, and it's far enough away from town that few if any people ever come here to visit." He sighed once more. "I grew up in this house."

Sarah allowed herself a minute to take all of this in while the strangest sensation erupted inside of her and became so strong she couldn't hold it in. "It's incredible!" she laughed. She looked at all their faces again, laughing again as their astonishment over her reaction made the situation seem even funnier. "It makes perfect sense, doesn't it?" She laughed even harder.

"So, you find it amusing?" Darius asked, trying to sound offended, but she could see a sparkle of relief in his eyes.

"I find it absolutely . . . delightful," Sarah declared and laughed some more.

Now that the tension had been broken, they all laughed while both David and Daphne hugged her as if they were meeting her for the first time all over again. Sarah felt so deeply comfortable with the reality that these people were Darius's parents that she almost wondered if something deep inside her had suspected such a connection all along—even if it had never occurred to her conscious mind.

Sarah turned to face Darius and said, "A pleasure to meet you, Mr. Nash."

He gave her a smile that was only slightly sarcastic, but still his eyes sparkled. She wondered if he had feared she might be angry to learn he'd kept such a thing from her, and he was now deeply relieved.

"Well," he said, turning to his parents, "we can hope that my friends will respond half as well to realize I've been lying to them for years."

"They'll be fine," David insisted. "I wouldn't be surprised if they find the whole thing as humorous as Sarah finds it."

"We'll see," Darius said doubtfully and picked up the glass Sarah had brought with her, which he filled up from a large pitcher of water that always sat in a corner of the kitchen. He handed it back to her, which made her wonder if he wanted her to leave, or perhaps he was just letting her know there was nothing more to be said. "You'll tell Poppy?"

"Immediately," she said, even though she knew Poppy had probably gone to bed. "Thank you," she said, glancing at the glass, then she walked back toward the stairs, chuckling in a way that she felt sure would irritate Darius.

# Chapter Nine
## BETTER THAN HOME

SARAH SET THE GLASS OF water down in her room and hurried to Poppy's door where she knocked lightly before opening it without waiting for an answer; she was prepared to wake her if she had to. This was news that couldn't wait until morning. She found Poppy sitting up in bed reading, her expression one of surprise.

"What?" Poppy asked, setting the book aside as Sarah closed the door and sat down on the edge of Poppy's bed. "I assume there's a reason for that silly smile on your face."

"You are not going to believe what Darius just told me," she said. Sarah started at the beginning with all she'd overheard, leading up dramatically to the point where Darius had revealed the startling truth that David and Daphne were his parents. Poppy laughed so hard that she snorted, which made Sarah laugh too.

"It's unbelievable!" Poppy declared. "But at the same time, *not* so unbelievable."

"That's what I thought," Sarah said.

"All D names," Poppy said. "What did they tell us about their children when we first arrived?" She sniggered. "I wonder if the other two have D names, as well."

Sarah tried very hard to remember what Daphne had said about their children. A daughter married with three children in Liverpool. A son with a new wife in Portsmouth. And . . . ? A son who worked abroad? Sarah found it difficult to not start laughing again. Was that how they had chosen to define the situation, so they could tell the truth, if only barely? Now she clearly recalled Daphne saying, *We don't receive letters from him, but I'm certain he's doing fine. He was always very independent.* Of course they didn't receive letters from him; he was living under their roof when she'd said it.

Sarah caught Poppy up on everything she'd recalled, and they decided to do their best to discreetly ask about Darius's siblings—mutually agreeing that they likely had names starting with the letter D.

Having shared the news, they both went to bed, but it took Sarah a long time to quiet her mind and go to sleep. She felt a sweet anticipation of Christmas she hadn't felt since her mother's death, and she was delighted to realize that she was actually on very good terms with Darius's parents. And she loved them dearly!

The following day dawned with cloudy skies, but the snow and wind had stopped. It was a relatively normal day, except that Sarah observed Darius and his parents with new interest, simply because she now knew they *were* his parents. Given that Sarah and Poppy now knew the truth, he called them Mother and Father, except when he reverted to habit and called them by their given names; they didn't seem to notice or care either way. And Poppy was quite pleased with herself when they learned that Darius's siblings were named David Jr. and Delilah.

When the sun went down on Christmas Eve, Daphne declared their holiday had begun. With Sarah and Poppy's help, there was a pot of delicious-smelling stew simmering on the stove, and bread plaited in the shape of a wreath that was on the pan rising until it was time to go in the oven. Daphne was completely responsible for the beautiful artistry of the bread. Together they had also prepared Daphne's version of mincemeat, which didn't actually contain any meat in spite of its name; it was a mixture of raisins, chopped apples, and spices that had simmered and filled the house with an aroma that Sarah felt certain smelled the way Christmas was supposed to smell. She realized that having been raised in a social class where her meals had always been served far from the kitchens, she'd never had the pleasure of actually enjoying the sights and smells of their creation. The pot of mincemeat had been set aside, as well as a significant amount of pastry dough that Daphne had prepared. While the stew continued to simmer, and the bread was baking, each person gathered in the kitchen to make their individual mince pies by rolling out dough to spread in the bottom of small tins, and also over the top, once the mincemeat filled the tin. Daphne talked about how this had been a tradition since her childhood in the large family from which she'd come. After constructing the basic miniature pie, each person then used leftover dough to cut and form little decorations that would make every pie unique. Darius decorated the top of his pie with a hilarious rendition of a bird. David teased him terribly, but his pie was topped with some version of a Christmas tree that was so silly that Darius had plenty of reason to tease his father in return. Sarah just enjoyed seeing them interact this way, especially now knowing the true nature of their relationship.

Poppy made a lovely little arrangement of flowers on her pie, while Sarah did holly leaves and berries inspired by a photo she recalled in a children's Christmas storybook her mother had read to her when she'd been a child. Daphne's pie ended up with a mixture of flowers and birds—that actually looked like birds—and it was truly a work of art.

"It's plain to see who's been doing this since childhood," David said as everyone oohed and aahed over Daphne's pie.

"And who has been doing it for more than thirty years?" Daphne asked, nodding toward her husband's pie, which made them all laugh.

"And since childhood?" David said, turning his attention to Darius's pie.

"Who would dream this was the first time for you girls?" Daphne said to Sarah and Poppy.

Darius tried to say it was simply because they were women and had a more natural affinity for such things, until his mother lightly scolded him for saying that—with rare exception—men and women were capable of doing whatever they set their mind to. She reminded him that she was very good at swinging an ax to cut firewood when she needed to, and his father had certainly done his part to help care for their children when they'd been babies. She was competent at caring for the animals, and David knew his way around the kitchen.

"And don't forget," David said, "the baker in town—who is well known for creating baked goods that are lovely as well as delicious—is a man."

"Point taken," Darius said, raising his hands in surrender. "But I will not be setting my mind to become an expert at decorating pies."

"Fair enough," Daphne said and took the bread out of the oven before she slid in the mince pies to bake while they ate their stew.

During the meal David talked about how this stew recipe had been his grandmother's Christmas tradition. His father had learned a profession in his youth that had eventually made him very well off, but his father's parents had been very poor. Food had often been scarce, and having stew for Christmas—with chunks of meat and rich savory gravy—had actually been a luxury. Daphne and David had continued with the tradition of eating stew for Christmas Eve as a reminder of how blessed they were, and to keep perspective regarding people who were not so fortunate. Sarah felt moved almost to tears, especially when she considered how many baskets of treats, baked goods, and apples David and Daphne had distributed throughout the past week.

David went on to say that on the following day they would have a more traditional Christmas feast, but this meal was a different kind of tradition. Sarah was anticipating Christmas Day for a number of reasons, but she wondered if she could enjoy anything more than making mince pies and sharing stew and bread with this wonderful family. She tried not to even look at Darius, fearing he would see that her feelings for him had not diminished—or perhaps worse, she feared she might see evidence that his feelings for her were still the same. If anything, learning the true identity of David and Daphne—and realizing this was the home where Darius had grown up—had only made her feel more rapport with him.

Before they were finished eating, Daphne took a break to get the mince pies out of the oven. Sarah was amazed to realize that Daphne could tell more by the smell than the clock that they were sufficiently baked. Daphne left them to cool and returned to the dining table to finish her meal. Since they were all so full, they decided to wash the dishes and get the kitchen in order before enjoying their dessert. Given that it was a holiday, they all worked together in the kitchen to clean up, and Sarah enjoyed the bounteous teasing and laughter, garnished with the remarkable aroma of the cooling mince pies.

After enjoying their dessert, which had cooled to the perfect temperature to be eaten, they gathered in the parlor where Darius built up the fire and David lit the candles on the Christmas tree before he sat and opened the family Bible to read the story of the nativity. Sarah was so touched by the experience she felt near tears; never in all her life had Christmas been celebrated in such a way—not even when her mother had been alive. At Castle Courtenay the holiday decor had been lavish, and there was certainly a bounty of many good things to eat. There had always been a great many parties to attend, but Sarah had never truly enjoyed them; she'd never made friends among the young ladies her age in the community. Poppy had been her best friend and she always preferred spending time with her. As long as Sarah didn't think about the circumstances that had landed her and Poppy in this situation, she felt delightfully content, and knew if she were still at home—with her father's absence—she would have only been depressed, sharing trite gifts that had been put beneath a Christmas tree the servants had decorated. Right now, she loved discreetly stealing glances at Darius when he wasn't looking, and she loved exchanging smiles with Poppy and Daphne while David continued to read.

When they all went their separate ways to go to bed—the candles on the tree having been safely extinguished—Sarah didn't need any celebrations the following day to feel happy; she felt perfectly happy now. But given the fact that tomorrow *was* Christmas Day, and they *did* have special plans, she felt a childlike anticipation, which made it difficult for her to fall asleep.

The following morning Sarah felt giddy when she woke up to a clear blue sky and sounds coming from the kitchen downstairs. She hurried to get dressed, then she and Poppy helped with each other's hair, even though—as usual—there was very little that could be done with Sarah's hair that wouldn't take hours. Poppy efficiently pinned back enough hair from each side to keep it out of Sarah's face, and her thick, unruly black curls were left to hang around her shoulders and down her back, whereas Sarah could quickly and easily pin Poppy's blonde hair into a neat bun at the back of her head.

As soon as they were both ready for the celebrations of Christmas Day, they went downstairs together to find David and Daphne working together in the kitchen to make a finer-than-normal breakfast. They offered to help, but their hosts insisted they were enjoying themselves and that the girls— as they'd come to be called in this household—should just relax and get themselves a cup of tea from the pot that was sitting on the dining table beneath a tea cozy, hot and ready.

While Sarah was pouring tea into two cups for her and Poppy, David reported that Darius had gone out to take care of the animals and would be back in soon. While Sarah and Poppy enjoyed their tea in the parlor, sitting near the Christmas tree, they heard Darius come in the back door. A moment later he appeared with an armload of firewood, which he put down in its appointed spot near the fireplace. He stirred the fire with a poker and added some wood, at the same time smiling toward Sarah and Poppy and wishing them a merry Christmas. They returned the greeting, and Sarah felt certain his eyes lingered on her longer than necessary, and that his smile became more evident as she caught his gaze. She smiled back, and he looked away, but a quick glance toward Poppy made it clear that she had noticed. Sarah's stomach turned over and she could feel her heart beating in her throat. At such moments she couldn't help hoping that there might be some way for her and Darius to share a future. She allowed herself to indulge in such a possibility for a brief moment, feeling giddy and ecstatic over the very idea. Then she forced herself back to the moment—and the reality of all that stood in the way of such a possibility. Even when he was no longer responsible for keeping her safe, they led completely different lives. She would have to go back to Courtenay, and he would get hired to protect someone else. The idea of *anyone* else being here in this home, sharing life with this family she'd come to love, left her feeling almost sick. Therefore, she pushed that and every other difficult thought about the future quickly out of her mind. Today was Christmas, and nothing mattered except enjoying every moment of the day to its fullest.

After enjoying a lovely breakfast and working together to clean up the kitchen, they all gathered in the parlor and exchanged gifts. Sarah was touched by another family tradition, which was to tell the others something they were grateful for before opening a gift. She was quick to say how grateful she was to be here and for the great kindness the Nash family had offered to her and Poppy, but she was surprised to hear Daphne and David sincerely express their gratitude for having Sarah and Poppy in their home, and how they'd never had such delightful guests. Darius said how grateful he was that Sarah and Poppy were safe, and he also expressed sincere gratitude for his parents, their love and support, and the closeness he shared with them. The gifts they exchanged were simple and inexpensive, but all very much appreciated by the recipients, which made the giving all the sweeter.

After cleaning up the parlor—with the help of the girls—and carefully putting away the ribbons and tissue paper so they could be used again next year, Daphne got busy in the kitchen with the final preparations of Christmas dinner. She'd had a leg of lamb in the oven since before breakfast, which she declared would make it especially tender, and her special seasonings filled the house with the anticipation of enjoying her exceptional cooking. She reluctantly allowed the others to help her in the kitchen when she realized that without help, dinner would be served late, and she wanted to be done working in the kitchen before Darius's friends arrived. Together they peeled and cut potatoes that were cooked and mashed with milk and butter. Carrots and sweet potatoes were also prepared in a special way according to Daphne's instructions, and she heated up some applesauce she'd made earlier, adding more sugar and cinnamon.

After Daphne and David each told the girls a little bit about Darius's friends, they all sang some Christmas carols together while they worked. Even while Poppy and Sarah were laying the table with Daphne's finest dishes and some lovely candlesticks that were only brought out for special occasions, they continued to sing. Sarah couldn't help noticing that Darius had a fine, deep singing voice. And since he seemed to be growing more and more comfortable with Sarah and Poppy around, he was becoming less inhibited. Sarah just listened to the sound of his voice and restrained herself from looking directly at him, again forcing herself to think only of today.

Daphne was just finishing up the final details of dinner when David announced while looking out the window, "They're here, Darius."

Sarah glanced to where David was looking and saw two men riding horses out of the thick woods and toward the house. One was much shorter than the other, but they were all bundled up against the cold and she couldn't make out anything specific about these special friends Darius had known most of his life.

"They'll take their horses to the barn," Darius said, grabbing his coat. "I'll go talk to them." He said it with some trepidation and Sarah knew he was about to tell them the truth about the work he did, and apparently that meant admitting he'd not been truthful with them about many things for the past few years.

"I hope it goes well," David said with a sigh after Darius had left the house.

"I hope it goes quickly," Daphne said lightly, "or dinner will be cold."

Sarah ventured to admit to her true feelings over what was happening. "I feel like this is my fault. It's evident Darius doesn't want to tell them, and if we weren't here then—"

"Your being here is a blessing, little one," Daphne said with firm kindness. "We've been trying for a couple of years to get him to confide in his friends, and this has forced him to do what he should have done a long time ago. It's just happened that he's never had anyone here with him at Christmas time before."

"They're good men," David added. "There's no question about their being trustworthy; they'll keep his confidence. And Darius needs to learn to trust again—especially with the people who care about him."

Sarah said nothing more. She just exchanged a knowing look with Poppy, which let Sarah know her friend understood her own conflicted feelings— many of which she would never talk about with David and Daphne.

"Oh, look," David said, now monitoring a different window, "they're coming in."

"That didn't take long," Daphne said, surprised but pleased. "I hope that means it went well."

"They're men," Poppy said. "Did you expect them to analyze the situation over and over?" This comment made Daphne laugh, and David tossed her a comical glare before he shrugged as if to say he couldn't deny that men generally weren't inclined to discuss things the way women did. "I suspect he told them, and they asked a couple of questions before they all agreed they're hungry."

Daphne laughed again. "I daresay you're right, little one," she said, moving to her husband's side to look out the window. "They're talking and laughing," she observed.

"Nobody looks upset," Poppy noted.

"I daresay," David said, "this has all been much more difficult in Darius's head than actually facing up to the reality."

Sarah wished she could understand more fully why this situation—and trusting people—was so deeply difficult for Darius. She knew he'd lost the woman he loved, and he blamed himself, but she knew very little otherwise. She'd come to know his character and personality well while they'd lived under the same roof, but she knew practically nothing about his past and the things that haunted him.

Hearing the back door open startled Sarah back to the present with another silent reminder to simply enjoy the day and not concern herself with such things. She followed the example of the others and hurried to sit down in the parlor to look as if they'd been relaxing and talking rather than spying on Darius and his friends out the window. She could hear Darius talking and laughing, and the voices of two other men. She knew they were hanging their coats and hats near the door, then footsteps in the hall preceded their appearance in the parlor.

David and Daphne both stood up to greet Darius's friends with hugs and great enthusiasm at seeing them again after many months. Sarah was glad for the opportunity to get a better look at these men while their focus was on Darius's parents. One of the men was extremely short—probably a head shorter than Daphne—and one leg was shorter than the other. He wore a special shoe with a very high sole which helped even out the difference, but he still had entered the room with a strained gait. He'd clearly been born with this physical challenge, but his smile was bright, and his countenance radiated in a way that was enhanced by his yellow-blond hair and large blue eyes. His features were handsome, perhaps more so than the other man who was an inch or two taller than Darius, with brown hair that he kept brushing out of his eyes as if he was long overdue for a haircut. His nose was noticeably larger than most, and his chin noticeably smaller. But he too had a kind countenance, although he seemed to lack the confidence his friend exuded.

Once greetings were properly concluded with David and Daphne, the two men turned toward Sarah and Poppy who were standing side by side, some distance back, attempting not to be too intrusive.

"This is Sarah," Darius said, motioning toward her; she noted that he didn't use any surname, and she felt certain he didn't want his friends to know.

Sarah nodded and said, "Hello," with a genuine smile. She felt more than pleased to be meeting Darius's closest friends and hoped to be able to get to know them better.

"And this is Poppy," Darius added, and she too greeted the guests.

"Ladies," Darius continued, "these are my dearest friends." Motioning to the shorter man with the disabled leg he added, "This is Jimmy."

"A true pleasure to meet you," Jimmy said, his smile widening—if that were possible.

Sarah and Poppy both nodded toward him, returning his smile before Darius motioned to the other man and said, "This is Reggie."

"A pleasure," he said with a little smile and a slight nod; he was clearly quite shy—at least he was toward her and Poppy; he'd shown no sign of shyness in greeting David and Daphne, but then he'd known them since his childhood.

"Well, dinner is in the ovens keeping warm," Daphne declared, "but it won't last much longer without drying out. So take your seats and let's get on with this feast."

Sarah found it mildly amusing that in spite of Daphne's order for every-one to be seated, they instead followed her to the kitchen to help carry things to the table. When everything was laid out and they were ready to sit down, Darius helped Sarah with her chair in a very gentlemanly manner; they'd been eating here together for months, but this being a holiday apparently called for more formality. David assisted Daphne, and surprisingly the shy Reggie silently assisted Poppy with her chair. The men were all seated, and David initiated a special blessing on the food during which they all joined hands around the table. Meals in this house had always been preceded by a blessing, but never had they held hands, and Sarah assumed this was another holiday tradition.

Following David's lovely prayer, everyone at the table began dishing up food onto their plates from the serving dishes closest to them and then pass-ing them around the table until everyone had some of everything.

They had barely begun eating when Jimmy said, "I have an announce-ment to make."

"Oh, how exciting!" Daphne declared since Jimmy's tone made it clear his news was good.

"I'm getting married," he said. Following a long moment of stunned silence, laughter and congratulations exploded in the room. Jimmy went on to explain how the butcher's daughter—Laura—had caught his eye soon after she'd arrived with her father when he'd moved here and opened up his shop. The village had needed a butcher, since the only one they'd had was getting very old and his work was becoming less than ideal. This old and respected butcher had since closed up his shop and moved away to live with his married daughter. But the new butcher's daughter was a young woman Jimmy described as lovely and kind. They had begun sharing conversation every time he'd gone into the shop, which he'd enjoyed so much that he'd started making up excuses to go there even when he didn't need to. He'd finally invited her to go on a walk with him; walks had turned into sharing lunch with her and her father, who liked Jimmy very much—and the other way around. Jimmy proudly declared that Laura didn't care at all about what he called *his oddities*, that she loved him for who he was inside, and it made no difference to her that she was much taller than he was, and that she had to walk very slowly to accommodate him when they walked together. She had already begun helping out in the cobbler shop where he made his living, while still helping her father in the butcher shop. Their wedding was planned for late summer, and Jimmy expressed hope that Darius might be able to attend.

"I hope I can," Darius said sincerely. "I'm so very happy for you, my friend. You're a good man; you deserve a good life, and it looks like you're well on your way."

"I'd like to think so," Jimmy said. He then winked toward Sarah and Poppy who were sitting side by side across the table from the men. "So, you ladies had best not be flirting with me; I'm already taken."

Sarah laughed softly, and Poppy said, "I'm utterly disappointed, but I shall attempt to restrain myself." She turned to Sarah and added, "Funny how not one of the men I knew who worked in the household . . . back home . . ." Sarah knew she'd stopped herself from saying the name of their home, knowing that Darius still preferred to not give away any specific information about themselves. It wasn't that he didn't trust his friends; he had simply told Sarah and Poppy that sometimes when people know things, they let them slip without thinking about it, and he didn't want his friends to have the burden of needing to keep too many secrets on his behalf. Poppy cleared her throat as if to keep herself from saying anything she shouldn't and added, "None of those men were even half as polite as your friends, Darius."

Sarah noticed that Reggie smiled directly at Poppy, which caused Darius to share an astonished glance with his parents who were seated at opposite ends of the table, which required him to turn his head. He'd barely done so before Reggie said to Poppy, "You can flirt with *me*. I'm not taken."

Sarah saw the mouths of Darius and his parents fall open in a most unflattering way; their amazement couldn't be disguised. Sarah had barely met these men, but Reggie's shyness was as evident as Jimmy's confidence. What was it about Poppy that had so quickly emboldened him to push past his natural reticence and say such a thing? Poppy gracefully eased the tension by smiling at Reggie and saying, "I'm very glad to know that. I wouldn't want to be too presumptuous and embarrass myself."

"No need to worry about that," Reggie said with a sparkle in his eyes that implied he had developed some kind of crush on Poppy since he'd come through the door just a short while ago.

Poppy and Reggie exchanged another smile and they all continued to enjoy the amazing meal while Darius and his friends reminisced about humorous antics from their youth, with Daphne and David piping in about how some of those antics had gotten them into trouble. But they all laughed about such things now. Sarah observed these three men who had been friends since childhood and found the contrasts among them intriguing. Reggie was extremely shy, and while he certainly wasn't ugly by any means, no one would look at him and think he was handsome, although his eyes were kind and his smile lit up his face. Jimmy was—by appearances—dramatically different than most people. In fact, Sarah didn't even have to ask to be able to guess with confidence that there likely wasn't one other person in this village who had any significant physical defects. And yet Jimmy was confident and happy. And then there was Darius, who was without a doubt more handsome than any man had a right to be. His features were perfectly balanced, his build was strong and masculine, and his black curly hair was striking and—to Sarah—utterly irresistible. She felt curious about how these three men had become so close when they had been boys.

Poppy asked both Jimmy and Reggie some questions about themselves and they discovered that Jimmy's mother had died giving birth to him, and his father had been a heavy drinker who was embarrassed by his son's disabilities. He talked about how his father had called him a freak and had blamed him for his mother's death. Sarah winced at the very idea, but Jimmy talked about it matter-of-factly, making it clear he'd come to terms with it, and his confidence was based in knowing that the things his father had said weren't true. He told Sarah and Poppy how the cobbler and his wife had taken a special interest in Jimmy, and he'd spent a great deal of time in their home. Since his father was drunk much of the time, he'd hardly noticed. When his father died, the cobbler and his wife took him in, raised him with love and proper guidance, and trained him in the craft of this good man he called his *real* father. The cobbler and his wife had since passed away, but Jimmy loved the work he did in the shop he'd inherited, which he felt honored their legacy.

Reggie came from a large family; his parents having managed a dairy farm where everyone was expected to work as soon as they were old enough. He still worked on the family farm, providing milk, cheese, and butter to the community. He told of how clearly he remembered meeting Darius when he'd been helping *his* mother sell their dairy products in town, and Darius had been with his mother who was making purchases. The two boys had started playing in the middle of the street, getting very dirty, while their mothers were visiting. After that, their mothers arranged for them to play together at each other's homes, which worked out nicely since Daphne had become good friends with Reggie's mother during the process of getting their boys together to play. Reggie and Jimmy had already been friends prior to that time, since the cobbler's wife was in the habit of bringing Jimmy to play with Reggie and his siblings. The three of them had simply formed a bond that had never dissolved through the years. Reggie's parents had also passed on, and his siblings had all moved away to pursue occupations elsewhere; many of them were married with children. Reggie had been left to run the dairy, which he was obviously proud of doing.

They sat together at the table visiting long after they were all too full to eat anything more. At a break in the conversation they all pitched in to help clear the table and clean the dishes. Leftover food was put in covered dishes and set just outside the kitchen door in a wooden chest David had built for this purpose. It kept any animals from being able to get to the food, while the winter air kept it cold until it could be heated up and eaten later for supper and for days to come.

With the kitchen clean and in order, they all gathered in the parlor for what Sarah and Poppy now realized was a tradition of playing games. Sarah felt mildly nervous when they started playing charades. She'd seen it played at the parties she'd attended among the stuffy people of her social class, but she'd always insisted on just observing. Poppy, on the other hand, was eager to get involved, as if she enjoyed the possibility of making a fool of herself. Sarah agreed to play but only if she could go last, which gave her the opportunity to observe and learn. After everyone else had made complete fools of themselves, she didn't feel nearly as self-conscious. By the time she took her turn, it was evident they were playing this game more for the laughter it provoked than for any attempt to see who might win or lose. They all took two more turns at trying to get others to guess something by using wild gestures before they had all laughed themselves into exhaustion and melted into the sofa and chairs in the parlor to just visit. Daphne encouraged everyone to share their favorite Christmas traditions, or to talk about their best Christmas memories. This began a very tender and endearing conversation that Sarah took in with wonder. She'd never felt such warmth in her whole life, and she wondered how that was possible. Her parents had loved her very much; she'd never wanted for anything—or so she had believed.

That enveloping warmth continued as they played a game of cards, which again seemed more for the purpose of teasing each other and provoking laughter than any concern about who might win, although when Reggie came out the winner, he made a comical fuss about it, insisting with good humor that his friends should finally admit he was the smartest of the three. Poppy boldly encouraged Reggie's declarations in a way that pleasantly surprised Sarah. Observing her friend's interaction with Reggie—and the glances they were exchanging—she had to wonder if there really was some kind of attraction between them.

Hunger pressed them to warm up some leftover food for a light supper. Daphne cautioned them all not to get too full, because it was time to enjoy the traditional Christmas dessert of a pudding she'd put on the stove to steam while they were playing games. The pudding was as delicious as everything Daphne produced in her kitchen, but Sarah found it both comical and tender how Reggie and Jimmy exaggerated their compliments of how extraordinary it was, and how her Christmas pudding brought back the memories of all the Christmas dinners they'd shared.

When their guests were finally preparing to leave—which meant the conclusion of their official Christmas celebrations—Sarah was surprised to see some discreet whispering between Daphne and Jimmy only a moment before Daphne said, "Now, Reggie, I want you to come back and visit soon. Jimmy is very busy with his fiancée but I'm thinking you need to get out more, and we're all kind of stuck here and getting tired of each other's company. We'd just love to see you again soon."

Sarah couldn't help noticing how both Reggie and Poppy were extremely pleased but trying not to show it. She saw Darius bow his head as if that were the only way not to reveal how amused he was. Reggie eagerly agreed that he'd love to come back soon and spend more time with them, while Jimmy too seemed to be trying not to smile too broadly; he clearly saw the conspiracy of Daphne's intentions. Given the way he and Daphne had been whispering, he was likely in on the scheme, but Sarah wondered if anything romantic might truly evolve between Poppy and Reggie. The idea left her ill at ease, but she chose not to think about that right now.

When bedtime came, Sarah reluctantly told everyone good night and thanked them for a wonderful day. She was surprised when Darius hugged her, but then everyone else was hugging so it would have appeared odd if he *hadn't* hugged her. She desperately wanted to hold onto him much longer than the few seconds he had his arms around her, but she was keenly aware of the well-established boundary between them.

Once she was in bed, Sarah recounted every tender moment of the best Christmas of her life. She wanted to hold all her memories close and etch them clearly into her mind so that she would never forget them. She wondered if this would be the only Christmas she might ever spend with Darius and his parents, and the very idea pained her. She felt so perfectly at home here that she couldn't even imagine how deeply sad she would feel next Christmas when she was at Castle Courtenay with her sweet but overly dramatic aunt, sharing a very formal and dull holiday while she could only dream about the celebrations she'd enjoyed here in Darius's home. And what if something permanent emerged between Poppy and Reggie? The very idea of Sarah returning to Courtenay while Poppy remained here to marry and settle down made her tangibly ill. And yet she loved Poppy enough to want her to be happy. Reminding herself not to jump to conclusions over something that had practically no substance at this point, Sarah took her mind back to all the pleasantries of Christmas, which lulled her into a peaceful sleep.

## Chapter Ten
# THE UNEXPECTED VISITOR

As winter reached anxiously toward the growing warmth and color of spring, Sarah settled so comfortably into her new secluded life that she found it increasingly difficult to imagine life back at Castle Courtenay. A part of her never wanted to go back, especially when she considered facing all that had happened to her father. The box containing the sword was gathering dust underneath her bed, and she preferred to leave it there indefinitely.

Even with the passing of months, Sarah didn't feel any less comfortable and content living here with Darius and his parents. Being mostly shut indoors with other people of different personalities inevitably brought on challenges, but nothing that couldn't be resolved or avoided, and nothing that wasn't completely normal in the realms of human relationships. Sarah noticed how both Darius and his father would get mildly cranky if they didn't get out of the house every day for a significant amount of time. They both worked on projects out in the room in the corner of the barn, although Sarah began to realize that nothing significant ever came of the work they did out there; it was merely something with which to occupy their time, given that David was retired, and Darius's job right now was mostly just waiting. The men occasionally went into town together to get supplies, or sometimes they just rode away together on horseback. Either way, they always returned in better spirits, which meant the fresh air and the distance from the confinement of the house helped keep their moods in balance.

Sarah noticed similar tendencies among the women. Daphne never lost her temper or spoke unkindly to anyone, but there were times when everyone knew she was in a foul mood because one of her baking projects had gone awry—or sometimes for no apparent reason at all—and they all knew it was best to just keep their distance and ignore her subtly testy manner until it settled down, which would usually happen within an hour or two. But sometimes it took a day or more before she shed her silent irritability and became more like herself.

Sarah and Poppy had discussed their observations of the family with whom they were living, which led them to talking about their own need to sometimes just be left alone. They often took walks around the outside of the house at night to get fresh air and clear their heads, sometimes together and sometimes on their own. As much as Sarah and Poppy cared for each other and loved sharing most facets of their lives, they could still occasionally get on each other's nerves. But at least they were able to acknowledge such feelings when they surfaced, and respect each other's need for distance and solitude. And now that they'd lived in the Nash home for several months, they had both learned the idiosyncrasies of their temporary family members, and how to recognize bad moods and frustrations when they occurred. Still, even with their faults, Darius and his parents maintained their status of being good people, and Sarah felt nothing but gratitude to enjoy such safety and comfort. Sometimes she missed having someone else doing her laundry and making her bed, and there were some days when cleaning dishes was nothing but tedious. But such tasks were part of normal living, and even while she sometimes hated doing them, Sarah felt a growing empathy for the majority of people in the world who had to work every day of their lives. And overall, she found that given the choice, she much preferred doing some kind of work each day, rather than being waited on and cared for by others.

Reggie was coming to visit and have supper at least twice a week, and it hadn't taken long for everyone to realize that he was completely smitten with Poppy—and she with him. She'd talked with Sarah about her feelings, and the dilemma of what considering a future with Reggie would mean in regard to her friendship with Sarah, as well as her official position of working to help care for Sarah's needs. Sarah had assured Poppy more than once that she needed to follow her own heart and make her decisions based on what she knew to be right for herself, and not on anything to do with Sarah. "No matter what happens or where we end up," Sarah had told her, "we will always be the best of friends—even if that means regularly exchanging letters." Even as she said such things, her heart broke a little to think of living without Poppy; but she would not be so selfish as to deny Poppy her greatest possible happiness simply because she didn't want to be without her closest friend.

On an evening when the apple blossoms were in bloom, Sarah went outside after supper to enjoy their lovely fragrance as she wandered idly beneath the trees and reached up to touch the little white flowers. She marveled that so many months had passed, and even with her not being allowed outside in daylight, or ever being able to leave this place, she still didn't feel at all frustrated or unhappy with the situation. Looking back to when she'd been told she was being put into Darius's care and she and Poppy would have to leave Castle Courtenay, if she'd known then how long she would be gone, and that they would be so secluded, she would have boldly protested. But the kindness of Darius and his parents, and the level of comfort and safety she shared with them, had made all the difference. She felt deeply grateful and incredibly blessed. The present felt perfect and she didn't even want to think about the fact that it wasn't going to last. She knew David continued to receive letters from Halford, which were intertwined with carefully coded messages about the situation back at Castle Courtenay. Nothing at all had changed, and she wondered when it might be necessary to just accept that her father's killer would never be discovered, nor would the person who had killed Evans in his attempt to kill her. She couldn't hide forever, but she wondered if that meant she would live the rest of her life never feeling safe.

Sarah was startled by the sound of footsteps approaching and turned to see that it was Darius. Even in the darkness there was no mistaking his build or the way he moved.

"Sorry to bother you," he said, stopping an arm's length from her.

"You're not bothering me," she said, wondering if he was simply checking on her to make certain she was safe—as he had professed he was doing on numerous occasions when he'd found her out here in the evenings—or if he had some other motive.

"How are you?" he asked. "I'm amazed to see how well you've managed with being so confined here."

"I like it here," she said but didn't go into the reasons.

"Well, I can assure you that no other client I've brought here has been so gracious and easy to please—or care for."

"Well," she said, imitating his tone, "I can assure you that I've never encountered such kind and gracious people as your parents." She laughed softly and added, "You're not so difficult to be around, either."

"I'm glad to hear it," he said with a little chuckle.

"I daresay you must be growing tired of being stuck here with me and Poppy when nothing at all has changed."

"I could never grow tired of your company, Sarah," he said with a tenderness that made her heart quicken. "And Poppy is just . . . delightful, and easy to be around."

"Yes, she is," Sarah said, unable to keep from sounding sad.

"Is something wrong?" he asked.

Sarah wondered for only a moment if she should tell him the truth or just keep her feelings to herself. She sighed and said, "I'm very happy for Poppy . . . and Reggie. It's becoming more and more evident that marriage may be in their future."

"Yes, it seems that way," Darius said. "I've never seen Reggie so happy, and his shyness has practically disappeared since he's met her."

"Which makes me dread having to go back more than ever; I'll miss her so much. That's all."

"I can understand how difficult that must feel," he said. Following a stretch of taut silence, he added, "Is there anything I can do?"

"No, but thank you," Sarah said. "Well, when you're back at home you could check in on Poppy and make certain everything is going well."

"Of course," Darius said, but there was the slightest hint of disappointment in his voice, although she couldn't discern its source.

A moment later he added, "There's something I need to talk to you about."

"Has there been news from Halford?" she asked with more eagerness than she felt.

"Nothing new," he said, "but given how much time has passed, I believe we're not going to get any answers without changing the situation. Let me make it clear that I was hired to keep you safe and I take that very seriously. And in my opinion, you are not safe until we know who killed your father and why, and also who tried to kill you."

"You could be stuck with me for a very long time," Sarah said.

"I wouldn't consider that a problem," he replied with a tenderness that once again quickened the beating of her heart. "But let me discuss one thing at a time." She wondered if that meant he actually had something to say about his feelings for her, but she didn't dare hope. She didn't have time to wonder long before he continued. "I stick to the belief that guilty people become more relaxed when time has passed and it appears they have gotten away with their criminal acts. Now that we've allowed months to go by with everyone back at Courtenay having no idea where you are, I believe it's time to change the situation." He took a deep breath as if he might be nervous to proceed. "I would like to suggest that we go back. I will have my father write to Halford to arrange it. People there will likely know that I'm still there to protect you, but I will appear to be very bad at my job, which will make it appear easy to do whatever it is the guilty party is intent on doing."

"Kill me, you mean?" Sarah asked, her alarm clear in her tone.

"I won't let anyone hurt you," he insisted. "I know what to do, Sarah. I've already talked to Reggie about going with us. He'll be helping me, and so will Halford. But our tactics to keep you and Poppy safe will not be evident to those around us. You need to trust me, Sarah, when I tell you that it's time. If we don't go back . . . if we don't change the situation . . . we have no chance of finding out what really happened and why, and if we don't figure it out, you may never be safe—and I can't live with that."

Sarah thought about everything he'd said for a long moment before she said more gently, "I do trust you, Darius."

She heard him let out a long sigh of relief. "Good, I'm glad to hear it, because I have a confession to make."

"I'm listening," she said when he didn't go on.

He still hesitated at least a half a minute before he sighed loudly and finally said, "I've had a long time to think about some things you said to me . . . and things my parents have said to me—many times over. I think I'm finally coming to accept that it *wasn't* my fault Mary died, that I really did do everything I could have done, or at least all that I knew how to do. I believe now that the grief and shock of losing her distorted my perspective regarding the situation, and then I was just so . . . stubborn that I allowed myself to settle into those conclusions without really exploring the reality of the circumstances."

When he seemed unable to continue, Sarah said, "That sounds completely reasonable, and I wholeheartedly believe it's long overdue for you to forgive yourself and move on with your life."

"You've spent far too much time with my mother," he said with a little laugh. "You sound just like her."

"Or maybe I'm just more like her than most people might believe, given our different backgrounds."

"I think you might be right," he said, looking more directly at her than he had in months. In spite of the darkness and the overhanging branches that blocked the glow of a partial moon, she could feel the intensity of his gaze.

"That makes perfect sense," he said. "My mother is—in my opinion— the most amazing woman in the world. It stands to reason that I would fall in love with someone very much like her."

Sarah gasped softly and reassured herself that he really had said what he'd just said. She'd admitted to herself long ago that she'd fallen in love with him, even though a part of her had expected that with time her feelings would diminish. She'd known he was attracted to her, and she'd sensed that his feelings hadn't changed, but she was still surprised to hear him use the word *love* regarding those feelings.

"You don't have to say anything," he said when the silence grew awkward. "I know that last time we talked about our feelings for each other, I was insistent that I couldn't allow myself to feel any such thing for you because it would distract me from keeping you safe. But time has passed, and my perspective has changed regarding many things. Just having you around has made me look at life through a different lens, Sarah; by doing nothing at all, you have helped me heal from the losses in my life. I want to thank you for that."

"But I didn't do anything," she said. "You just told me that very thing."

"I want to thank you for being who you are, for awakening in me a feeling of hope and light in my life when I had doubted I would ever feel that way again." He took a deep breath and let it out slowly. "The point I'm trying to get to is . . . well, I've been wondering for a while now what to do . . . or say . . . given the way my perspective has changed . . . and my feelings have grown . . . but I didn't know what to say . . . or how to say it . . . and a couple of nights ago my father cornered me before I went to bed and he said something that made me realize what a fool I was being."

"Were you?" she squeaked. "Being a fool, I mean?"

"Absolutely!" he said and took a step closer, which required her to tip her head up slightly in order to keep looking at his face. "I've wasted all these months, convincing myself that remaining distant from you might keep you safer, when a part of me knew all along that I was simply afraid of confronting my true feelings, and I was using my distorted beliefs as an excuse to not become involved with you in any way."

Sarah could hardly breathe as his words became more and more unmistakable in their meaning. His silence implied that he expected her to say something. The only words that came to mind were, "So . . . what exactly did your father say to you?"

Darius was quick to answer. "He said that I was likely going to be a great deal more distracted by trying to avoid the truth about my feelings than I would be if I just admitted the truth to myself—and to you. He said that if I truly wanted and needed to be your protector, I needed to firmly face the truth. So, that's what I'm doing. All things considered, I'm hoping you might be willing for us to return to Castle Courtenay together—not just because you might need me to keep you safe—but because you've taken pity on me enough to agree to let me court you."

Sarah gasped again and tried to speak but couldn't. In spite of knowing him well enough to be absolutely certain he was telling the truth, and that she could trust him without any doubt, she still found herself asking, "You're not just suggesting this because it would give you a feasible excuse to stay at Courtenay, are you? Because if we need to put on a ruse for the sake of being able to find the killer, we can certainly—"

"I swear to you that this comes from my heart, Sarah. No ruse necessary. Unless of course you don't agree and would prefer to—"

"No," she said abruptly, not wanting him to change his mind—or worse to have him believe for even a moment that she didn't share his feelings. She smiled, even though she wasn't certain he could see her face well enough to tell. "It would be an honor to be courted by you, Mr. Nash."

"Really?" he asked as if he had entirely expected her to refuse him.

"Really," she said sincerely, and he laughed softly with an elated delight, to which she related completely.

"Then," he took another step toward her, and she tipped her head back a little farther to look up into his face, "might I suggest we start over where we left off . . . last autumn when you came out here to pick an apple?"

"I think that's an excellent idea," she said, hoping that meant he was going to kiss her, and she was not at all disappointed. Experiencing his kiss again after all these months made her realize she'd not exaggerated its magical effect on her. She took hold of his upper arms at the same moment he took hold of her shoulders, as if they both feared toppling over from the dizzying phenomenon of their kiss.

\* \* \* \* \*

Sarah awoke to see rain sliding down the window of her room, but she laughed softly with perfect contentment as she recalled her encounter with

Darius last night beneath the apple trees, and how everything had changed. They'd talked a long while after sharing that magical kiss, and he'd kissed her once more at the foot of the stairs before she'd come up to bed. Sarah knew there was potential danger for her back at Castle Courtenay, but the very idea felt so distant and even unimportant in contrast to knowing that Darius Noble Nash loved her. She didn't care where they ended up living, as long as they could be together. Nothing mattered more to her now than her longing for their courtship to end in marriage. Oh, how she prayed that would be possible! Darius was a good man, and she knew very well that he'd come from a good family; she loved his parents dearly.

Hearing sounds from the kitchen below, Sarah hurried to clean up and get dressed, pulling her hair back haphazardly into a ribbon—not wanting to wait for Poppy—and hurried down the stairs while consciously trying *not* to appear as if she were hurrying. She was so anxious to see Darius that her heart thudded against her ribs, but she wasn't at all prepared to find him standing at the foot of the stairs, leaning his shoulder against the wall until he saw her and stood up straight, smiling as if he might be even more glad to see her than she was to see him.

"Good morning," he said in a soft voice that implied he didn't want to be overheard. "I was hoping to see you for just a moment before breakfast."

"And here we are," she said as he took her hand before she stepped off the bottom stair and stood to face him.

With little warning he bent to kiss her, then he smiled and said, "Good morning, Sarah."

"Good morning, Darius," she said, and he kissed her again.

"I suppose we should show ourselves before anyone comes looking."

"I suppose we should," she said, feigning an exaggerated disappointment that made him laugh softly.

More seriously he said, "I think we need to tell them . . . now . . . at breakfast, unless there's a reason you want to wait."

Sarah thought of how she hadn't yet told Poppy, given that she hadn't seen her since Darius had opened his heart to her last night. But she knew Poppy would be so happy that she'd forgive Sarah for not sharing this wonderful news with her first.

Darius kept hold of Sarah's hand as they walked into the dining room, where Poppy was already sitting with a cup of tea. Sarah hadn't wanted to wake her, but now she knew that Poppy hadn't wanted to wake *her*—which was typical of their relationship. David was also sitting there perusing a newspaper, his hot cup of tea sitting on the table nearby. Sounds from the kitchen indicated that Daphne was working on breakfast.

Poppy looked up at Sarah and smiled a silent greeting before she said, "I've already offered to help her; you know how she is."

"Unless invited, we stay out of the kitchen," David said absently and turned a page of the paper.

Poppy then noticed that Darius and Sarah were holding hands, and she couldn't help but see the obvious happiness on both their faces. Poppy met Sarah's eyes, her countenance showing nothing but approval and excitement. Before they could say anything, Daphne came out of the kitchen holding a bowl of steaming scrambled eggs, and a plate of crisp sausages.

"We can eat now," she declared, setting the dishes on the table. Then she glanced quickly at Sarah and Darius standing there—instead of already being in their seats. Seeing their clasped hands, her eyes widened before she let out a delighted laugh.

"Does this mean what I think it means?" Daphne laughed again.

"What?" David said and turned abruptly to where Daphne and Poppy were staring. When he saw what had caught the attention of the women, his face broke into a grin.

"It means," Darius said, "that we are officially courting. I suppose time will reveal whether she can tolerate me for the rest of her life."

What followed was a flurry of laughter and hugs and expressions of how glad they all were, and how they all agreed it was about time. Darius heartily agreed, and they were all finally seated to share their breakfast. While they ate, Darius told the others about the need to return to Castle Courtenay in order to hopefully bring more information—or better yet the killer—into the open. Sarah knew he'd discussed this plan with his parents, but this was the first Poppy was hearing about it. She looked downhearted and Sarah reached for her hand across the table, giving it a squeeze.

"What is it, dearest?" Sarah asked her friend. When Poppy hesitated, Sarah reminded her, "You know you can say anything here. These people are more family to us than we've ever had."

"I can't deny that, dearie," Poppy said. "It's just that . . . when we left Courtenay, I desperately wanted all this to be over quickly, so we could go back, and life could return to normal. And now I dread going back; I don't want to leave here."

"I feel exactly the same way," Sarah said. "But Castle Courtenay is our home—at least for now—and if we don't go back, we'll never solve this problem. We can't live the rest of our lives in fear, and unfortunately you are too closely tied to me for you to avoid being caught up in this problem. I'm sorry about that."

"There's no need to apologize," Poppy said vehemently. "I'll just be glad when all of this is over and . . . we can make choices on how we live our lives based on something truly meaningful—instead of doing what's necessary to remain safe."

"Amen," Daphne said firmly.

Darius announced, "Reggie is going with us." Poppy's expression became much more pleased even before he added, "He's sharp and agile, and he served in the military for a few years, so he has more than enough training to help me keep the both of you safe. It only makes sense to bring him with us."

Poppy smiled at him, then blushed deeply, lowering her eyes in embarrassment, but laughing softly in a way that made it clear she knew that everyone was well aware of how much she'd grown to care for Reggie—and how he cared for her. And she couldn't help but be pleased to know that returning to Courtenay didn't mean leaving Reggie behind. The outcome of the romantic relationships that had evolved through their misadventures was yet to be seen, but Sarah knew she would always feel safer with Darius around; to her it seemed his love for her only gave him added incentive to protect her in every possible way. But until all this was solved, none of them could make life-altering decisions. They could only pray that it would be cleared up soon, so they could all move on with their lives safely.

They all sat at the table after they'd finished eating and talked about their plans to leave early the following morning, traveling on horseback the same way they'd arrived. Reggie would meet them at the edge of the village at dawn, and unlike last time, they would actually be traveling by daylight. And they were taking *two* packhorses, one of which would be carrying two small tents and some extra bedding, so they could sleep warmly and have protection against the possibility of rain. With the amount of time that had passed, Darius wasn't concerned about anyone paying any attention to their departure, although he said they would still mostly be traveling over meadows and moors and through wooded areas—instead of staying on or too close to the roads—just as an added precaution.

While they were clearing the table, Daphne started talking about the food she wanted to prepare for them to take along, which sounded much better—and had more variety—than what they'd been eating on their journey here. While Sarah and Poppy were helping Daphne in the kitchen, Sarah felt a sudden heartache at the thought of leaving this house—and especially being separated from David and Daphne. She forced back the threat of tears and reminded herself that this was only temporary. She would surely see them again—hopefully sooner rather than later.

A couple of hours later, Darius came to the kitchen to interrupt their baking projects to teasingly ask his mother's permission to take his sweetheart for a walk. Daphne pretended to be frustrated over losing one of her helpers, but both she and Poppy were smiling with obvious delight.

"But I'm not allowed out of the house in daylight," Sarah reminded him. It was a rule Darius hadn't let up on in spite of the months that had passed.

"Which is why," Darius said, "we're only walking to the parlor where we can hopefully have some privacy in order to talk."

"Oh, how exciting!" Sarah said with light sarcasm, and the other women chuckled.

Darius held out his arm with mock formality for Sarah to take it. She did so, and they walked through the dining room and across the hall to the parlor, where they sat close together on the sofa and he put his arm around her shoulders.

"Oh, this is nice," he said and pressed a kiss to the top of her head.

"Yes, it is," she agreed.

Darius began talking to her about how it might be to return to her home—both in regard to their blossoming relationship and the potential danger there that had brought him into her life to begin with. They were only a few minutes into the conversation when David entered the room and said, "Someone is approaching the house, and it's not Reggie. I wouldn't think it's a problem given that it's broad daylight, but—"

Darius stood abruptly and told Sarah to get Poppy and go upstairs until he let them know it was safe to come down. Sarah felt truly afraid as she followed Darius's orders. Did he really think that after all this time, someone approaching their home on horseback could be a potential danger?

"Sarah," he called to her when she was halfway up the stairs, Poppy ahead of her, "it's probably nothing, but it's better to be careful." Sarah nodded, grateful for his reassurance. She and Poppy went to Sarah's room and locked the door. But only a moment later Sarah *unlocked* it and crept silently into the hall.

"What are you doing?" Poppy whispered.

"I seriously doubt this has *anything* to do with us," Sarah replied in a voice barely audible. "I'm just . . . curious."

"You know what they say curiosity did to the cat, don't you?" Poppy whispered, following close behind her. They each sat down in the hall on either side of the opening that went down the stairs, leaning back against the wall where they couldn't be seen.

Sarah peeked around the corner to see that Darius was hovering near the bottom of the stairs, as if he would die before he'd let anyone dangerous get past him. She could hear the front door opening and was glad that David spoke loudly enough to be heard when he said, "What in heaven and earth are you doing here, my friend?"

"If you let me in, I'll explain," Sarah heard a man say in a voice that sounded incredibly familiar.

Sarah looked at Poppy and mouthed more than spoke, "Is that Halford?"

"The two of you can come down," Darius said with an ironic chuckle. "I know you're both right at the top of the stairs."

Sarah peeked around the corner to look at him. "You said to go upstairs; you didn't specify where exactly." She exchanged a smile with him and added, "Is this exceptional hearing you have a requirement of your occupation?"

"Probably not," he said as the women came down the stairs. "But it doesn't hurt any."

Darius guided Sarah and Poppy into the parlor in time to see Halford greeting Daphne with a hug before David invited him to sit down. He'd barely done so when he saw Darius there with Sarah and Poppy, and he stood back up out of respect for the ladies.

"Oh, my dear sweet girls!" he said and stepped toward them, giving them each a kiss on the cheek. "That castle is like a mausoleum without you."

They both told Halford how good it was to see him before they were all seated and David demanded an explanation as to his arrival. Considering all the uncertainty going on, and how very careful they had been about every little thing, Sarah could understand why David sounded mildly miffed.

"I would have written but my coming here was not planned . . . or rather not planned just yet. I was going to visit my cousin and his family, but I arrived to find the house closed up and a neighbor told me they'd gone on holiday. It was my plan to come here after leaving there and see how you're all doing, but I'd planned to be there long enough to write and warn you about my arrival. As it was, I knew that any letter I wrote would not get here before I did. It certainly was not my wish to alarm you."

"It's not a problem," Darius said. "We're glad to see you."

"Indeed we are," Daphne declared, and Sarah felt a little disoriented to see Halford—a man she had known her entire life—so obviously comfortable in this place and with these people whose existence she'd known nothing of not so many months ago. But all the pieces came together now in her mind as she recalled Halford telling her he'd hired Darius because he was known and trusted by a dear friend of his; he didn't bother mentioning that Darius was the son of said friend.

David took Halford upstairs to one of the remaining guest rooms while Darius went outside to take care of his horse, and Daphne set some food out on the dining table with the assumption that their unexpected visitor would be hungry. When Halford came back downstairs with David, he was glad for Daphne's offering—not because he was too terribly hungry, he admitted, but because he loved everything that came out of Daphne's kitchen. They all sat at the table with him and Daphne provided a hot pot of tea so they could hear Halford's update of everything going on back at Castle Courtenay, except that it ended up being a very short conversation since nothing had changed. "Life is every bit as boring there as it ever was," he said. "I miss your father terribly." He looked at Sarah. "He was not only my friend and good company, he gave my life purpose and fulfillment in being able to assist him. With him gone they try to find things to keep me busy, but I don't feel very useful. I confess that if it weren't for knowing you were coming back eventually, I likely would have left before now to seek employment elsewhere."

Sharing Halford's growing detachment to Courtenay, Sarah said, "You must do what you feel drawn to do. You were always very good to my father—and to me—but I don't want you fashioning your life around me."

"I suspected you might say that," Halford said with a familiar smile. "But I'm not certain what I'll do yet. We have many unanswered questions, and I don't know that I can move on until they're answered." He turned to Darius and asked, "Do you have any plans to help move this conundrum along?"

"We do," Darius said. "In fact, we're leaving tomorrow." He didn't offer any further explanation, and Sarah suspected it was for much the same reason he held back many details of the situation from Jimmy and Reggie; it wasn't that he didn't trust them, but rather that he didn't want them to carry the burden of information that could become a problem if they let it slip even in a situation that appeared benign.

Avoiding any more talk about the danger Sarah might be in and what Darius intended to do about it, he announced to Halford that he and

Sarah were courting. Halford was so pleased he could hardly stop laughing as he looked back and forth between the two of them.

"So," he finally asked, "will you settle down at Courtenay or stay here in the country?"

Sarah and Darius exchanged a glance that seemed to indicate they each hoped the other would answer the question. And Sarah realized in that moment she actually preferred the idea of living out her life here, of raising their children under the same roof as their grandparents, where they could play beneath the apple trees. She saw herself helping to care for David and Daphne as they got older and living close to Poppy who would be raising her own children with Reggie and helping him on the dairy farm. They would trade butter and cheese for apple tarts and be there for each other through life's ups and downs for the rest of their lives. She became so lost in her momentary fantasy that she was startled to hear Darius chuckle tensely and say, "I haven't even convinced her to marry me yet, Halford. We have plenty of time to make such decisions."

Sarah agreed with him, but she felt so completely detached to Castle Courtenay in that moment that she wondered why they were even going back. Of course, whoever believed she was a threat worth killing wouldn't know she'd had a change of heart. The issue of her safety had to be resolved, but she hoped it wouldn't take too long. She wanted to get on with her life, and already she was dreading the very idea of being away from this house—and David and Daphne—for even a day.

When Daphne returned to the kitchen to work on her baking projects, Sarah and Poppy went with her, having grown weary of the conversation when it had turned to horses and hunting. But Sarah enjoyed hearing the distant talk and laughter of these three men she loved and respected, all enjoying each other's company. She was glad to know that everything was all right back at Castle Courtenay, but that didn't make her want to return. It occurred to her that everything might *appear* to be all right, but in reality, it was *not*. Her father had been murdered, and someone had tried to kill her, at the cost of a man's life. The strange sword was still beneath her bed upstairs, its value in relation to the traditions of Courtenay still a mystery. Until those mysteries were solved, Sarah could not move forward with her life, and she believed Darius knew that, even if they had never voiced it.

Sarah enjoyed having Halford around throughout the remainder of the day, mostly because it was evident David and Darius were enjoying his company. Daphne also obviously liked him very much and had known him for many years—as long as she'd known David, apparently—but it was obvious the men enjoyed talking about things that held little interest for the women. With the exception of sharing meals and tea, the men and women seemed to naturally divide; throughout the bulk of the afternoon, the men were out in the barn—or more likely tinkering with the woodworking tools—probably just talking rather than being engaged in some kind of project, while the women continued to bake. Sarah always loved helping Daphne in the kitchen, and she was surprised to realize how much she'd learned in the months since she'd been here. Both Sarah and Poppy agreed they could likely now teach the cook at Castle Courtenay a few things that could improve the meals there. Daphne was delighted by such a possibility, but again Sarah felt nothing but dread about returning there. She thought that having Halford here might have made her homesick, but in truth it was having the opposite effect. She'd known him all her life, but it was her father he'd been close to. He cared for Sarah and respected her; he wanted her to be cared for and happy. But it was becoming increasingly evident that the bond that had ensured Sarah's relationship with Halford was her father, and now that he was gone, they had very little to say to each other. She hoped that he *would* find work elsewhere, mostly because she couldn't imagine him ever being happy at Courtenay with her father gone. She suspected that part of his reason for staying as long as he had was due to the same reason that Sarah's life was stuck in this strange kind of limbo where she couldn't feel safe and she couldn't move forward. Halford surely knew he was the only connection between her and what was going on at home—through his carefully worded letters back and forth with David. And until this mystery was solved, Halford likely felt as much in limbo as Sarah.

When Sarah and Poppy went upstairs to go to bed, the others were still visiting in the parlor, but by the time Sarah actually crawled into bed the sound of conversation that had been floating to her ears had ceased and the house was completely silent. She imagined Poppy and Halford comfortably settled in their guest rooms—much as she was—and David and Daphne going to bed in the room they'd shared for decades. And she thought of Darius sleeping down in the parlor—as he'd been doing ever since their arrival. She had many times expressed her concern for his comfort, but he'd assured her that with the blankets and pillows Daphne kept stored in a cupboard in the hall he was more than comfortable, and that he'd never be able to sleep upstairs when he believed doing so would compromise her safety. After all these months, Sarah truly doubted there was any threat of someone breaking into the house to try and harm her, but she smiled at the thought of Darius's convictions in keeping her safe, and how the current state of their relationship made her feel safer—and perhaps more content— than she'd ever felt in her life.

Sarah was startled out of sleep so abruptly that her heart threatened to pound right out of her chest. While she was attempting to orient herself to being awake—and the reason for it—she heard Darius whisper close to her face, making her gasp, "Someone is in the house. Listen to me carefully. Someone broke a window and climbed through it. I already woke Poppy. I want the two of you to stay together. Sit on the floor in the corner; try to stay out of sight and remain *absolutely* quiet. Do you understand?"

"Yes," she answered with a quivering whisper. She couldn't believe this was really happening. After all this time, she'd come to feel completely safe here. She'd *always* felt safe in this house. Did this really have something to do with her? And if so, *why now?*

Sarah followed Darius's instructions and quickly slipped out of bed, taking a blanket with her, and scurried to the corner of her room where she found Poppy already sitting crouched on the floor. They sat close together with the blanket over them, leaving only their faces exposed. Poppy said nothing, and Sarah thought it best they didn't so much as whisper, but the silence prodded all her worst fears to the surface, and again she wondered why now?

Halford! His appearance was the only thing that had changed; he was a tangible connection to Castle Courtenay. But they all trusted him completely. And he hadn't even been initially intending to visit them at this time; he was supposed to be at his cousin's home. It just didn't make sense!

# *Chapter Eleven*
## THE THIEF

Instead of trying to figure out the answers, Sarah forced herself to focus on remaining quiet—and hopefully safe. She then saw the shadow of Darius coming into the room and closing the door behind him. He pressed himself back against the wall next to the door so as to be behind it if it came open. Sarah could see that he was holding a pistol near his head and pointed upward, ready to aim it at their intruder if necessary.

Sarah couldn't resist whispering, "Are your parents—"

"Everyone is properly armed and prepared," he whispered back. "Now be still."

Sarah reached for Poppy's hand and they held so tightly to each other that Sarah knew Poppy's fingers had to hurt as badly as her own. After a silent minute that felt like an hour, Sarah heard the unmistakable sound of the stairs creaking beneath the weight of someone ascending. She'd become very accustomed to this sound during her months of living here. The silence was abruptly shattered by the sound of fists hitting flesh, groans, and something heavy hitting the floor; it sounded like a gun, Sarah thought, a rifle perhaps. Far worse was the indisputable sound of a person falling to the floor, and Sarah felt relatively certain it was David. She wanted to shout at Darius and insist that he make certain his father was all right, but she bit her tongue, reminding herself that Darius knew what he was doing, and she needed to trust him.

Sarah sucked in her breath sharply and heard Poppy do the same when the door came slowly open. She focused on keeping her breathing as steady and quiet as possible as the shadow of a large, burly man carrying a gun in one hand crept carefully around the room, clearly looking for something. His head turned in the direction of where Sarah and Poppy were sitting but he moved on. A moment later Sarah realized he'd gotten on his knees and was reaching beneath the bed and she knew—she *knew*—what he was looking for. And she'd been foolish enough to think that putting that box beneath the bed might keep it hidden. It was the most obvious place where something like that might be kept. She told herself that their safety was far more important than the contents of the box, but it still made her sick to think of someone taking it—especially when it seemed to be the reason lives had been lost, even if she didn't understand the connection.

Sarah could barely see shadows in the room, but she knew Darius had stepped out of the shadows toward this man, his pistol aimed toward the man's chest. "Put it back," Darius ordered in a voice so intimidating and harsh it made her shudder; she'd never heard him speak like that before, but then she'd never heard him confront an armed criminal. She wondered if this was actually the man who had killed her father—and Evans. In the darkness he didn't seem at all familiar, but he could have been hired by someone else, and she certainly couldn't claim to know every single person who worked at Courtenay well enough to recognize them like this in the dark. Her questions dissolved beneath a fear comparable only to the moment when Evans had been shot and killed and she'd been knocked to the ground in the process. Sarah hardly realized what was happening before the intruder abruptly swung the box toward Darius, knocking the gun out of his hand. She heard the pistol hit the floor and slide. Catching a subtle glimmer and movement on the floor she realized the pistol was within her view. She turned to see if Poppy had noticed it, but her eyes were squeezed tightly shut. Sarah felt panicked and terrified to realize Darius no longer had a weapon, and the man now struggling with him had a much larger build.

A shot rang out and Sarah involuntarily screamed before she even thought to hold it back, but as soon as she heard the sound come out of her mouth, she knew she'd given away her presence in the room.

"Ah, there's the little lady," the despicable voice of the intruder said, making it clear he was uninjured. She wondered if Darius was dead on the floor on the other side of the bed. The very idea made her so sick inside— and so angry—that she lunged for the pistol on the floor and jumped to her feet, aiming it toward the looming figure in the darkness.

Darius apparently saw her when she heard him mutter, "No!" There was a strain in that one word that let her know he'd been injured, and she had no idea how badly. With more strength in his voice he ordered, "Just let him take it. Don't risk your life for—"

"This just makes it easier t' do what I come t' do," the man declared maliciously, and Sarah saw him produce a second pistol after he'd reached inside his coat. She knew he was aiming it at her. She could feel her life being measured in seconds. She either had to pull the trigger or die. With a desperate prayer in her mind and her deepest instincts pounding in her chest, she recalled the training her father had given her with firearms and pulled the trigger in the same moment that Darius lunged at this man out of nowhere, like some kind of jungle cat with strength and agility she never would have imagined in a man—especially a wounded one. She heard the man yelp and wondered if her bullet had hit him. She felt horrified over the possibility that she might have hit Darius, given that she hadn't known he was going to launch himself in the very vicinity where she'd been aiming. Again she heard struggling and knew both men were still alive. She heard the sound of fists hitting flesh but couldn't see enough to have any idea what was actually happening. She then heard an especially hard blow before the intruder jumped to his feet, grabbed the box, and ran out of the room.

"Darius?" Sarah said, frantically feeling around on the floor to find him. "Darius? Are you all right?"

"I'm alive," he said in a strained voice. "You wounded him; I know you did. Shoulder or arm, I think. The important thing is that you're safe and—"

In a portion of a second Sarah was glad to know that Darius *was* alive, even if she didn't yet know what his injuries entailed, and she was certainly glad that *she* was alive. But she felt furious about the entire situation—and right now all of it was represented by this hired thug who had come into their home in the night, threatening their lives and their safety—and he'd stolen something he had no right to. Her fury drove her toward the door, saying over her shoulder, "Poppy, watch over Darius. I'll be right back."

She heard both Poppy and Darius protesting but she ignored them and hurried carefully down the hall. She found David on the floor at the top of the stairs and took a moment to lean over and touch his face, grateful to feel its warmth, and the way he responded to her touch.

"Are you all right?" she asked.

"A little beaten up," he said in a strained voice. "But I'll be fine."

Sarah noticed that the rifle he'd been holding was on the floor, and she knew she hadn't heard a shot fired before the intruder had entered her room; therefore, the gun was still loaded.

"I'll be right back," she declared and grabbed the rifle, hurrying down the stairs.

"Do you even know how to use that thing?" David called.

"My father taught me," she called back and rushed out the front door, which had been left open. Once outside, she could see the thief mounting a horse with the box slung over his back the same way Darius had carried it while they'd been traveling. She knew she had only one shot and she aimed carefully, but her target was riding away, and it was dark. She pulled the trigger and heard a distant clink, which let her know she'd probably hit the box, and the bullet had gone through the wood and made contact with its contents. She felt angry to think that the box he'd stolen had probably saved his life.

Sarah lost track of the minutes she stood in front of the house, holding the rifle at her side, looking into the distance, reviewing everything that had just happened. She had far more questions than answers—in fact many more questions than she'd had before. She wondered how Darius was—and the others. Was anyone else hurt? She knew she should hurry back inside and find out, but she felt frozen where she stood until she felt a gentle hand on her shoulder, which initially startled her.

"Little one," Daphne said, taking the rifle from her. "He's gone. Everything will be all right."

"Darius is hurt," Sarah reported. "And David."

"I know," she said. "And we need to attend to them. I need your help."

Upon hearing the word *help*, Sarah was set free from her dazed state and she rushed back into the house and up the stairs. A lamp was on the floor on the landing above her to illuminate the way. She arrived there to find David sitting on the floor, leaning back against the wall. Halford was kneeling next to him, assessing the damage. He had blood coming from his nose and the corner of his lips, but Halford quickly said, "I'll take care of him. Darius is . . ."

He didn't finish before Sarah ran back to her room, where a lamp was burning there also. She found Darius lying on the floor, with Poppy kneeling next to him. He too had blood on his face, but it was the blood oozing through the towel that Poppy had pressed tightly to his thigh that left her terrified.

"What happened exactly?" Sarah demanded, kneeling on the other side of Darius. She was grateful for the way Daphne knelt next to her and lifted the blood-soaked towel to examine the wound, because Sarah didn't know if she could bring herself to do it—and she knew nothing about how to deal with such things.

"When we were struggling . . ." Darius muttered, and she could tell he was in pain. She suspected that now that the intruder was gone, he had lost the unnatural energy to fight off the threat to their lives in spite of being injured. "His pistol went off . . ." Darius added, not lifting his head from the floor or opening his eyes. "Hit me in the leg."

"Then why did you think you could attack him all over again?" she demanded, sounding angry, which she knew was only a disguise for her fear. "I could have shot you!"

"I didn't know you had a gun," he said defensively, looking at her briefly. "I thought he was going to kill you."

"And I could have killed *you*!" she sobbed as the reality of all that had just happened began to settle in—and how much worse it could have been.

"But you didn't," he said, reaching for her hand as he closed his eyes again. "You hit him; I know you did."

"Fat lot of good that did!" Sarah protested, now concerned only about Darius as she turned to watch Daphne examining the wound. She tore away the fabric of his breeches that were soaked with blood and Sarah could see the hole where the bullet had entered, mostly because that's where the blood was gushing out. Daphne carefully lifted his leg to look underneath, which made Darius groan, but Daphne carefully laid it back down and declared with relief in her voice, "The bullet went straight through, so there's nothing to be removed—which is *very* good! And it's just in the muscle; nowhere near the bone."

"Praise heaven," Darius muttered.

Daphne added, "We just have to stop the bleeding, which means a great deal of pressure on the wounds."

Sarah was incredibly glad that Daphne knew what she was doing as she insisted that Darius roll onto his side so they would have access to both wounds—where the bullet had entered, and where it had exited. She insisted he stay right where he was on the floor until the bleeding had slowed down. She left to get more towels and returned to kneel again on the floor where she ordered Poppy to take a break since she'd already been pressing a towel over the wound for several minutes. Daphne handed Sarah a towel and told her to fold it until it was small and thick and then to press it over the wound with all her strength, while Daphne did the same from the other side. Darius groaned slightly when they began pressing hard, but Sarah could only think of how grateful she was to have him alive—and it seemed he would recover from this wound. She refused to think of any other possibility at this moment.

Sarah focused entirely on pressing with all her strength against the gaping bullet hole in Darius's leg, as if she could literally keep his life from draining out. She didn't realize she was crying until she felt the splash of wet tears on her cheeks.

"He's going to be all right," she heard Daphne whisper and looked up, more grateful for her reassurance than embarrassed over being caught crying.

"You're his mother," Sarah whispered back. "This can't be any more difficult for me than for you."

Daphne's eyes glistened with moisture in the shine of the single lantern nearby. "He'll be all right," she repeated with confidence, and Sarah wondered if she knew he would be, or if she was trying to be positive. Sarah looked down and saw so much blood on the rags pressed over both sides of the wound that she had to bite her tongue to keep from gasping.

"We need clean rags," Daphne said to Poppy who presented them immediately.

"Let me take a turn," Poppy said and nudged Daphne over, pressing a rag over the wound herself.

"The bleeding will slow down soon," Daphne insisted, wiping hair out of her face with a clean forearm, since her hands were covered with blood. But again, Sarah couldn't tell if she was speaking from some kind of experience, or simply trying to make herself believe it.

Darius said nothing; he didn't move or make a sound. Without relinquishing the pressure over the wound, she leaned over his face, almost afraid she might find him dead, but he turned his head slightly to look up at her, saying with a wan smile, "I'm going to be all right, Sarah. It hurts, but it's not going to kill me."

"And how can you possibly know that?" she countered, wishing her voice hadn't betrayed how strained she felt.

"Because he's been shot before," Daphne said, sounding angry. "Maybe it's about time you retire from this kind of work."

"Maybe I should," Darius said and closed his eyes again, as if he were trying to block out the pain. Daphne looked surprised and Sarah could well imagine they'd argued about this in the past, but he'd never before agreed with her.

Three bloody rags later, Sarah noticed that much less blood was soaking into it. Daphne noticed too and declared with glee, "It's slowing down. Now we have to bandage it up tightly and get him to his bed so we can elevate his leg."

Sarah and Poppy assisted according to Daphne's instructions to press clean folded rags over each side of the wound, which she bound to his leg very tightly with a long strip of cloth. "These will probably need to be changed frequently during the coming hours, but the important thing is that it's slowing down; the pressure is working."

Darius insisted he could get to his bed if the women would just help him get up on his good leg and offer him some support. They did so very carefully, but he immediately became dizzy, and it was evident his leg hurt more when he was standing upright.

"You're staying right here," Sarah said, guiding him toward her own bed with his arm draped over her shoulders, and with Poppy on his other side assisting in the same way. "It doesn't matter which room I sleep in."

Daphne pulled down the covers on the rumpled bed Sarah had barely slept in. They helped Darius sit down and then carefully guided his legs up onto the bed. Daphne situated the wounded thigh on a couple of extra pillows she'd grabbed while the girls were helping Darius to the bed. She spread a couple of towels over them to protect them from the bleeding before she gently situated Darius's wounded leg on the pillows and situated his ankle on a pillow placed over the footboard of the bed. Sarah noticed there was no need to remove his boots since he was barefoot, wearing breeches and a shirt that was untucked and wrinkled. She knew now that he'd always slept in his clothes while he'd been sleeping down in the parlor so that he could hear if someone entered the house in the night. After all these months it had actually happened. The reality of all that had just occurred still hadn't fully sunk into Sarah, but she shuddered involuntarily as she watched Daphne spread a blanket over Darius and ask him if he was comfortable.

"I'm fine, Mother," he said. "Thank you." He reached out a hand, but it was impossible to know if he was reaching toward Daphne or Sarah, since they were standing right next to each other. But they both held up their hands at the same time to indicate how much blood was on them, so neither of them took his hand.

"Ooh," Darius said with a smirk, "that's disgusting. You should wash up or—"

At that moment Halford guided David into the room. He appeared to be walking a bit gingerly, but he was on his feet.

"I'm fine," David said as Halford helped him into a comfortable chair. "A bit banged up, but nothing that won't heal."

"And what about you?" Halford asked, standing next to the bed and leaning over Darius. "Are you—"

They all gasped when Darius took hold of the collar of Halford's dressing gown so firmly and abruptly that Halford was caught off balance and barely managed to keep himself from toppling right on top of Darius. "Who did you tell?" Darius demanded, his nonchalant attitude about being wounded completely smothered by a sudden rage. "The timing *cannot* be a coincidence! You must have told *someone* you were coming here! Either that or you're part of this mess and—"

"How can you say such a thing?" Daphne said just as David demanded, "Darius! Calm down!"

Darius reluctantly let go of Halford's dressing gown while Sarah wondered how he could still be so strong after losing so much blood. But he still looked angry, and his gaze was fixed firmly on Halford as if he didn't trust him enough to even blink.

"Jonathan is one of my dearest friends," David said to Darius. Sarah took in the fact that this was Halford's given name. Not once in all the years she'd known him had she heard him called such, and even while he'd been here no one had used his name. Apparently, their conversations hadn't required it. Sarah overlooked this trivial revelation and listened expectantly to what would be said. "He would never do anything to bring us harm, Darius; you know that. And he cares for Sarah and Poppy almost as if they were his own."

"It's true, Darius," Halford said, looking intently at him. Sarah didn't possess Darius's intuitive skills, but she felt relatively certain that Halford wouldn't be looking Darius straight in the eye if he was in any way guilty. "I would never want to see any of you get hurt. I swear to you my coming here was impulsive when my cousin's family wasn't at home."

"But someone must have followed you," Darius said, only slightly less angry. "It seems that time passing has not diminished the culprit's vigilance as I'd hoped. Someone must have been watching you closely, knowing you're the one who hired me, and likely figuring out there was some connection between us. *Someone* followed you!" Darius practically shouted. "There's no other possibility of anyone finding this place. No one in the village knows Sarah and Poppy are here. It's a miracle they weren't hurt or killed, and clearly what just happened to me and my father could have been so much worse."

"Yes," Daphne said with the firmness of a mother, "it could have been *so* much worse, and the fact that it wasn't *is* a miracle. So let's be grateful for the miracles and get some rest." She turned to her husband and ordered, "You sit with him while I clean up, and then I'll take over while the rest of you get some sleep."

"I don't need someone to sit with me," Darius insisted.

"That bandaging has to be changed frequently," Daphne retorted. "You're not in charge anymore."

Darius let out a groan of frustration and Daphne left the room. Sarah followed her, longing to wash the sticky blood off her hands. And Poppy was right behind, likely wanting to do the same. Besides that, she had no desire to be in the same room with David, Halford, and Darius while there was so much tension in the air. Sarah didn't know what to think. She couldn't find a single reason not to believe Halford, or not to trust him. But she couldn't deny Darius's logic, although that didn't mean Halford intentionally did anything wrong. How could he have known someone might have been following him?

By the time Sarah got to the kitchen where Daphne was washing up, she had concluded that she was too tired and upset to think too hard about any of it right now. She wondered if they were safe, if more than one man had come, or if he would send others. But she didn't feel the strength to care about that right now either.

As soon as the three women were cleaned up, Sarah told Daphne she would get a couple of hours of sleep and then take a turn sitting with Darius. Daphne nodded her appreciation and said to both Sarah and Poppy, "You saw how I bandaged the wounds?" They both nodded. "Do you think you can do that again on your own, because it should be done every hour or so?"

"Yes," they both said at the same time and Daphne nodded again. "I'll gather up some supplies and leave them in the room with him. Come along, Sarah. I'll show you where you can sleep. Do you need anything from your room right now?"

"No, I'm fine," Sarah said and was led to Darius's bedroom once she'd hugged Poppy good night at the top of the stairs. After Daphne had left her there, Sarah knew if she'd ever opened the door to this room and looked around, she would have known Darius had grown up here. It clearly had evidence of a boy growing into a young man and into the Darius she knew now. She wanted to explore the room further, but exhaustion drew her to the bed, which had obviously been made up with clean sheets beneath the bedcovers a long time ago, and Darius hadn't slept in it since they'd returned. Sarah extinguished the lamp and snuggled down into the bed, trying to block out the sounds of gunfire, the blood, the fear, and grateful to drift into sleep quickly, knowing she'd agreed to watch over Darius in a couple of hours.

Sarah came awake so abruptly she thought someone might have nudged her. When she realized she was alone she took a deep breath, trying to escort herself more smoothly into wakefulness. She finally leaned up on one elbow to light the lantern on her bedside table, which allowed her to see the clock. It had been nearly *three* hours since she'd told Daphne she would take over watching out for Darius.

Sarah jumped out of bed, put on her dressing gown and hurried to freshen up before she went down the hall to find Daphne sitting in a chair she'd moved close to Darius's bedside, holding his hand even though he appeared to be asleep.

"Forgive me," Sarah whispered, sitting on a chair she moved noiselessly next to Daphne's. "I didn't intend to sleep so long. You should have wakened me."

"I've been fine," Daphne whispered. "If I'd needed you, I would have come to get you."

Sarah was glad to hear that and asked, "How is he?"

Daphne carefully eased the bedcovers off the wounded part of Darius's leg. Some blood was visible on the bandaging, but not nearly as much as Sarah might have expected.

"And how are you?" Sarah asked.

"Grateful," Daphne said with a quiver in her voice.

"As am I," Sarah said, and Daphne used her free hand to take hold of Sarah's, giving her fingers a squeeze. "If he'd been killed," Sarah continued to whisper, "not only would I have been heartbroken, I don't know if I could have ever forgiven myself."

"This is not your fault, little one," Daphne said. "I only hope the guilty party will be caught and punished."

"Amen to that," Sarah said, then both women gasped when Darius said, "I can hear you, you know."

"I thought you were asleep," Daphne said, slapping him lightly on the shoulder with a little laugh that swallowed up the tears Sarah knew had been threatening to overtake her.

Darius chuckled. "As if I could sleep with the way my leg hurts."

"I'd send for the doctor and have him give you something for that," Daphne said with some disdain, "but I know how you feel about bringing the doctor here for such things."

"You mean it's happened before . . . here?" Sarah asked.

"Yes," Darius said and opened his eyes to look at Sarah in the dim lamplight. "When Mary . . ."

He didn't finish, and she asked, "Mary died . . . here?"

"Yes, little one," Daphne told her, sounding as sad as if it had happened last week.

"Thankfully," Darius said in a more chipper tone, "my mother worked as a nurse when she was younger, and she's always been able to fix me up just fine."

"I wouldn't count on that being possible next time," Daphne said, sounding angry; Sarah understood completely. She still felt so terrified over the possibility of losing Darius, that she could comprehend—if only partially— why a mother would not want her son involved in such a dangerous business. Since Sarah and Darius were officially courting—and marriage had been mentioned more than once as the outcome they both hoped for—Sarah had been foolish enough to assume that Darius would stop working to protect people in danger. It wasn't as if they needed the money, but she honestly didn't know whether he was the kind of man who would be too proud to allow a wealthy wife to provide a living for him and their children.

Or perhaps he had some instinctive need to do dangerous work, and she would never be able to talk him out of it. Clearly, they had a great deal to discuss before they could ever consider marriage.

As if she hadn't expected a response from her son, Daphne stood up and said to Sarah, "Before I get some sleep, little one, I need you to help me with something. And just so you know, David and Jonathan are both downstairs, each with a couple of loaded guns to make certain no one else gets into the house. They'll take turns resting. We're as safe as we can possibly be."

Sarah just nodded and asked, "What do you need my help with?"

Daphne turned up the wick on the lamp so that the room was brighter before she got clean rags and bandages from the top of the bureau—and to Sarah's surprise—a bottle of whiskey. While she was wondering if she'd insist on Darius drinking some to ease the pain, she said to him, "This is the part you hate." Darius opened his eyes abruptly, saw the whiskey, and moaned. Daphne said, "You know it's necessary or—"

"Yes, I know," he growled. "Just . . . get it over with."

"What?" Sarah asked.

"The liquor helps prevent infection," Daphne stated. "And this is the strongest we have in the house." Sarah couldn't recall seeing anyone drinking liquor since she'd arrived, and she wondered if they kept it on hand more for medical reasons than for any other purpose.

Sarah did everything Daphne asked her to do as they removed the bloody rags and bandaging from the wound and placed a fresh folded towel beneath Darius's thigh. Daphne warned him and immediately poured liquor into the wound, which made Darius groan and squirm. Sarah hated to see him in so much pain and suppressed her temptation to believe this was her fault. Once he was able to breathe normally again, Daphne told Darius to turn carefully onto his chest as much as he could manage so she could access the back side of the wound. Sarah held a towel in place to catch the liquor as it overflowed, red in color as it mixed with blood. Darius responded again with sounds of acute pain, then gradually recovered while Daphne and Sarah hurried to place clean rags over the wounds and tightly bind them there with bandaging wrapped around his leg. They helped him get comfortable again with his leg propped up on pillows, and Daphne asked him if he needed anything.

"Nothing except Sarah," he said, reaching for her hand as she sat down in the chair Daphne had been occupying. "Although, after seeing me in this condition, I don't know if you still want me around."

Before Daphne left the room, she said to Darius, "Before I get some rest, I'm riding out to meet Reggie and let him know of the change in plans. Yes, I'm taking a gun with me, and yes, your father will make certain I get back safely."

Darius nodded as if he wanted to protest but knew there was no other choice. Reggie would be expecting to meet them for the intended trek back to Courtenay, and they couldn't leave him waiting.

Daphne slipped out of the room after squeezing Sarah's shoulder and saying, "I'll let you know when I'm back, and after that you know where I'll be sleeping if you need anything."

"Yes, thank you," Sarah said, then turned to Darius and responded to his earlier comment, "More than ever! So much so that I confess I'm in agreement with your mother." She took a deep breath and just said it—now while her emotion was high as a result of what had happened earlier. "I don't want you in danger, Darius. I want to grow old with you."

"Then maybe it's time I retire," he said; only then did she recall that the subject of his doing so had come up once before, and he had implied he might agree. Perhaps this wouldn't be a problem after all. "It's going to take a while for me to be well enough off to safely guard someone else; by then I could be getting pretty old." He smiled and squeezed her hand. "I love you, Sarah."

"I know," she said, and he chuckled. "I love you too, Darius," she added, and his expression became immediately sober.

"I *didn't* know," he said.

"You didn't?" she asked, greatly surprised. "I should have thought it was obvious."

"Perhaps," he said. "But you've never said as much."

"Well, I should have," Sarah said and stood up long enough to push Darius's black curls back off his brow to kiss him there. She looked into his eyes, so grateful to know he'd be all right, and impulsively kissed his lips, noting no sign of pain or weakness in his kiss. She smiled again and sat back down, saying, "You should try and get some rest."

"I suppose I should," Darius said. "You won't leave?"

"If I do, I won't be far away," she said and kissed his hand. "If I'm not here it will be your mother or Poppy and they can come find me. Now rest."

"As you wish, m'lady," he said and closed his eyes.

Sarah watched him as his breathing gradually became more even and she knew he'd fallen asleep; perhaps his exhaustion had overcome the pain. Only then did she allow silent tears to slide down her cheeks, overcome by the vivid image of how much Darius had been bleeding, and the shocking reality that he'd been shot—and if the gun had been aimed just a little differently, he could have died. She knew her own life had been in danger as well, and she could only be grateful that they were both alive and together; she didn't want to think of trying to create a life without him, any more than she wanted to think of *him* trying to create a life without *her*. Both options broke her heart. They needed to be together, which meant they needed to remain safe until they could discover the culprit behind all of this and make certain the danger was over. But she wondered if that would ever be possible.

Sarah didn't leave Darius's side while he slipped in and out of sleep, clearly in pain. Daphne returned safely from getting a message to Reggie and then she was off to get some sleep. Sarah's continual need to review all that had happened during the night was mingled with her deepening love for Darius and wondering what the future might hold for them. She felt shocked each time she recalled those brief minutes in which Darius had been shot by the intruder, and how Sarah could have accidently shot Darius again—given that she hadn't known he was going to lunge at the intruder while he had a gun pointed at Sarah. She felt shocked all over again each time she realized that the box containing the precious Courtenay sword was gone. She wondered if she would ever see it again and realized she didn't care. The people she loved were worth far more to her than any monetary treasure could ever be. If all this danger had been related to the knowledge or possession of the sword, then she was glad to be rid of it, and she hoped that meant the danger was over. She would have gladly been eager to give the sword away if it could give her the freedom to live her life in peace. In that respect, the only thing that really bothered her was that someone needed to be held accountable for the deaths of her father and Evans. She hated the idea that the killer—or killers—might never be discovered. But she would rely on Darius's advice regarding that, and until he healed, they wouldn't be going anywhere or doing anything.

Poppy came in to sit with Darius so that Sarah could get some rest. Before Sarah left, the two of them worked together to change the bandaging and decided they'd done a fairly good job, considering that Daphne wasn't there to help them. Darius facetiously said he was proud of them, as if he weren't in any pain at all. They were all glad to see that there was very little blood since the last time the bandages had been changed. With this evidence of improvement, Sarah kissed Darius and left him in Poppy's care, glad for the opportunity to get some rest; she felt exhausted to her very core.

Sarah woke from a deep sleep and turned over to look at the clock. Her stomach growled with hunger the moment she saw that it was nearly time for lunch. She hurried to get cleaned up and dressed, hearing sounds from the kitchen downstairs, but she went straight to Darius's room to check on him. David was sitting in the chair next to the bed, bending over and talking quietly with Darius who looked pale in the daylight; and he had some bruising on his face as a result of last night's escapades. David's face too showed signs of the fighting that had taken place in the house, but as he shifted slightly in his chair, she knew he was hurting in other places besides his face.

Sarah waited only a second before she made her presence known by saying, "Good morning. I'm glad to see you're both still alive."

"Very much so," Darius declared, smiling to see her.

"Me more than him," David said somberly. "I'm grateful it wasn't worse."

"As we all are," Sarah said, scooting a chair next to his and squeezing his hand.

"Tell her what Halford told you," Darius said to his father, and Sarah recognized by the crease in his brow that he wasn't pleased with whatever David needed to say.

David turned gingerly to face Sarah. "Jonathan told me this morning that he'd lain awake for hours trying to think of anything he might have unwittingly said or done that could have brought this on. He's certain that he was always extremely careful about his correspondence with me, and no one could have connected him to us except for the fact that he'd been the one to hire Darius. Everyone in the house knew he was going to visit his cousin's family, but only one person had known he was also intending to visit old friends—and this person also knew these friends had a connection to the man who had been hired to protect you."

"Who?" Sarah demanded, waiting to hear a name she might not even recognize—a stable hand or a houseboy perhaps.

Sarah's chest tightened painfully when David said, "Mr. Curtis, the solicitor."

"What?" Sarah blurted and immediately uttered a firm disclaimer. "I trust him every bit as much as I trust Halford. He's worked with my father for as long as I can remember. He was a part of this plan from the beginning. Why *wouldn't* Halford mention it to him?"

"That's pretty much what *he* said," Darius interjected. "Curtis was involved with the plan to keep you safe; it was perfectly natural for Halford to mention that he was going to see how you were doing before he returned home."

"Someone else in the household must have overheard them . . . or someone knew more than we believed before we even set out." Sarah just couldn't stand for Curtis to be implicated in any of this, any more than she could tolerate the thought of Halford somehow being involved. "He just wouldn't do anything to hurt me or Poppy; he wouldn't!"

"Well, that's almost exactly what Poppy said," David told her. "Jonathan and I went outside early this morning, as soon as there was enough daylight to detect any clues. It's evident from the prints in the dirt that there was only one horse, and one man; so that's reassuring, I suppose."

"Except that someone who wants to hurt me now knows where I am and could come back," Sarah said, "or tell someone else. Or maybe now that this person has what I've been hiding, they'll be satisfied enough to leave us alone."

"I don't think we can count on that," Darius said with a scowl. Then it occurred to Sarah that David and Daphne likely hadn't known anything about what she'd been hiding, but Darius was quick to say, "I told my parents about that—not until this morning, but I *did* tell them."

They all sat in silence for a long minute, Darius's scowl becoming contagious. David finally stood with great care and said, "I think lunch is on." He paused and looked directly at Sarah. "Daphne won't tolerate having Darius left alone until that wound has completely sealed up and stopped bleeding. I'll leave you in his care if you think you can handle him." He said the last with a wink.

"Oh, I think I can handle him," Sarah said, smiling at David and then at Darius.

"Good," he said, moving toward the door. "I'll send someone up with lunch for both of you. If I bring it myself, you might not get it until next month."

Sarah and Darius both chuckled and she turned to look at him as soon as his father had left the room. "Are you in much pain?" she asked.

"Not as bad as it has been," he said, "but I can't deny that it hurts. I just keep reminding myself that the pain means I'm alive." He took her hand as she moved over to the chair where David had been sitting. "For the first time in years, Sarah, I have something truly wonderful to live for, and I don't want to miss out on one minute of the possibility of sharing a future with you."

"I don't want to miss it either," she said and kissed him. She then pressed her forehead to his, surprised by a surge of tears. "I couldn't bear to lose you, Darius," she said, not even trying to disguise the fact that she was crying.

# *Chapter Twelve*
## RETURN TO COURTENAY

THEIR TENDER MOMENT WAS INTERRUPTED by the sound of someone coming up the stairs. Sarah hurriedly regained her composure and took the tray from Daphne as she entered the room.

"Thank you," Sarah said. "I'll make sure he eats well."

"I hope so," Daphne said. "His appetite at breakfast was nothing impressive."

Sarah set the tray down on the bureau and Daphne left the room. With her back turned to Darius, Sarah uncovered one of the two plates to find a beef sandwich and some carrots from the cellar that had been sliced and steamed to freshen them up. She set the plate on Darius's chest, saying, "I assume your hands work and you can eat without assistance."

"I *can*," he said with mock defensiveness. "However, you'll need to prop me up a little more."

Sarah saw what he meant and moved the plate to the bedside table so that she could help put more pillows behind his back, making it possible for him to sit more upright. She then gave him back his plate and set two glasses of milk on the bedside table before she got her own plate and sat back down.

"I slept through breakfast," she said. "I'm starving."

While she was chewing a bite far too large for a lady, Darius asked, "And how are *you*? I know you weren't physically wounded last night, but I know it must have been terrifying, and—"

"I'm all right," she interrupted, "but only if I don't think about it too hard. This brings up so many uncertainties; not that there weren't uncertainties before, but . . . now it's closer to home, I suppose."

"Does that mean you consider this place home?" he asked with a facetiousness she knew was intended to imply that he believed her to be far too attached to Castle Courtenay to ever feel truly at home anywhere else.

Sarah dearly loved taking him by surprise when she said, "I've never felt more at home than I have here."

"Surely you're not serious!" he said, holding his sandwich halfway between the plate and his mouth.

"I'm *quite* serious," she said. "The longer I'm away, the less I want to go back. The only thing I miss at all is my aunt."

"Perhaps she could come here and live with us after we're married," Darius said lightly as if he didn't at all believe such a thing was possible. He took a bite, but while he was chewing, he realized Sarah still wasn't showing any sign of humor in her expression. He finished chewing and swallowed before he said, "You're an heiress, Sarah. You can't just . . . give up a place like Courtenay."

Sarah didn't comment. She just looked down at the plate on her lap, wondering if he was right. "Perhaps I can't," she said. "I respect the fact that everything I inherited from my father comes with great responsibility, and I need to honor what he left me. It's just that . . . I know everything is being managed very well in my absence—at least according to Halford. Apart from my aunt, I doubt anyone notices I'm gone. I was always close to Poppy—and my parents—but beyond Poppy and Halford, there was no one on the staff who ever showed much warmth toward me. Whereas . . . here . . . in your home, it's been . . ." She felt mildly choked up but swallowed carefully and added, "An entirely different experience."

"Sarah," he took her hand while they momentarily ignored their lunch, "you can't make such far-reaching decisions when you're in the midst of these extreme circumstances."

"I know; I really do. And I won't. I'm just . . . telling you how I feel."

"And I'm grateful for that," he said. "I want you to always be honest with me."

"And you with me," she insisted.

"I just want you to be happy," he added. "I would do almost anything short of criminal behavior to make you happy."

Sarah laughed softly. "I don't believe any kind of criminal behavior would be required."

"Let's hope not," he said lightly, but his eyes belied the seriousness of his words. "After what happened last night, I'm not so sure. But . . . that's not the point I'm trying to make." He leaned on one elbow so he could move a little closer to her. "I will go wherever you want to go, live wherever you want to live."

Sarah's heart quickened a little and she hesitated to speak her next thought, except they had just committed to being honest with each other, and she didn't want to wonder about the motivation behind his words. "That sounded a lot more serious than simply courting, Mr. Nash."

"You can't tell me you don't know I want to marry you," he said, taking her breath away. A part of her *did* know, but he'd never voiced it so directly. "And may I say that after losing Mary the way I did, I never thought I could feel this way again; I never believed I could have the strength . . . the ability . . . to fully commit my life to another woman. But I mean it from the very depth of my soul, Sarah. I don't believe I could ever be happy without you, and I also mean it when I say that I only want you to be happy. And if living at Courtenay makes you happy, then that's where we'll live. If you want to live here, so be it. My parents would be more than thrilled. And if you want to go elsewhere and start a new life completely, we'll do that. As long as we're together, I don't care."

"You really *do* mean it," she said after examining the intensity in his eyes.

"I really do."

Sarah took that in for more than a minute, still ignoring her lunch. There was too much fluttering going on in her stomach to even think about eating. She said aloud something she had thought many times. "I've come to know you well enough to be certain your interest in me has nothing to do with the fact that I *am* an heiress; and even if I *never* go back, I've still inherited a great deal of wealth."

"Sarah," he drew her name out on the wave of a long sigh. "I *don't* care about the money. I can work to provide for us if it came to that, even though I don't think keeping this job any longer is an option. Even assuming that my leg completely heals eventually, I don't want to put my life in danger any longer; I don't want you or my parents to be in danger; what happened last night certainly cemented that. I feel terrible to think my work has put my loved ones in harm's way, but if I hadn't been doing this job, I never would have met you. Still, I'm capable of working if I had to."

"But you wouldn't have to," she said. "Whether I go back to Courtenay or not, I have more than enough money for us to live on for the rest of our lives and still leave a fine inheritance for our children—unless you're one of those men who's too proud to be provided for by his wife's inheritance."

"I am neither that proud nor that foolish, Sarah. Money is just money. When people love each other, it doesn't matter where the money comes from. Look at my parents, for example."

"What *about* your parents?" she asked, having no idea what he meant.

He leaned a little closer and lowered his voice to a whisper, as if he were about to tell her a great secret, never to be repeated, but he smiled slightly as he said, "They both came from very wealthy families." Sarah gasped softly but let him continue. "My father was the third son of a baronet. He didn't inherit the title or the estate, but he inherited a great deal of money, which he used to create a simple life, the kind of life he'd always wanted to live. My mother also came from a wealthy family and inherited a very large dowry. Neither of them ever had to work, but my father *did* work because it was fulfilling for him; they could have afforded to hire servants, but they never did." He lowered his voice a little further, as if the secret was becoming deeper. "And just so you know, I don't *need* your money, Miss Heiress of Courtenay. I've never worked because I needed the money. Between my parents' fortunes, my siblings and I have each received a fine inheritance."

Sarah couldn't utter a sound while she took all of this in. From what Daphne had told her, Darius's sister was married to a man who worked in a shop in Liverpool, and his brother worked for the navy office in Portsmouth. As if Darius knew exactly what she was thinking, he said, "We were taught the value of work, Sarah, and that real happiness is found by keeping busy and serving the community—no matter how much money we might have."

"I see," Sarah said, looking at Darius as if she were meeting him all over again—at the same time rethinking all she knew of his parents in light of this new information. Her respect and admiration for these good people deepened. Wanting to ease the tension, she asked with mock severity, "Then aren't you worried about me marrying you for your money?"

Darius laughed and leaned toward her to kiss her. She met him halfway since he could only lean so far without disrupting his lunch or moving the wounded leg. With their noses nearly touching he said, "I'm only worried that you won't marry me at all."

"Are you asking?" She kept her gaze locked with his, wanting him to see the seriousness in her eyes. She absolutely knew they needed to be together for the rest of their lives, and she saw no reason to prolong the suspense. She also saw no point in their *courting* when they could be getting on with their lives. For all that there were mysteries to be solved regarding her situation, her relationship with Darius had nothing to do with any of that. She wondered if she should say so but felt certain he already knew.

"This is not at all how I imagined proposing to you, Sarah. You deserve far better than—"

"Only one thing matters to me, Darius. We are completely in agreement about what we want, so—"

"Will you marry me?"

"Yes," she said with a little laugh as delight erupted out of her. Darius laughed too as they kissed again.

"Well, I'm glad we've cleared that up," Sarah said and relaxed back into her chair, taking another bite of her sandwich. She chewed and swallowed and took in Darius's expression—a combination of amused and confused—as he settled back against the stack of pillows behind him. "Now we can start planning our future instead of wondering whether or not we'll be together." She smiled at him. "Now that I know we've both chosen to share our lives, I think it's easier to believe that everything will work out. And wherever we choose to live, it will be a choice we make together, and we will find a way to get past all this . . . *drama* . . . and get on with our lives."

"I couldn't have said it better myself," he muttered and returned her smile before he continued eating his own lunch.

\* \* \* \* \*

Throughout the afternoon, they watched over Darius in shifts while he managed to sleep better than he had during the night. Daphne declared that the wound was already looking much better, and the bleeding had completely stopped. Darius didn't experience nearly as much pain when she used the liquor again to clean it, and they felt confident he just needed to stay down until the wound was more stable—as Daphne had put it—and then he could work on getting his strength back after all the blood he'd lost.

David and Halford worked together to cover the broken window with wood, which had been measured and cut to fit perfectly where the glass had been. The two of them also hung string across every window on the ground floor, attaching bells or even kitchen utensils that would clank together and make noise if they were disturbed. David admitted this was a method Darius had used in the past to warn off intruders, and with Darius down in bed, both David and Halford admitted they were not as sharp or as quick as Darius had been, and they needed this extra measure of warning. The two men would be sleeping in the parlor for the time being, while the women and Darius slept upstairs, and each night before retiring they would place a small, tight rope across the opening at the bottom of the stairs, which would cause an intruder to trip if he attempted going up the stairs, giving everyone advance warning. They kept loaded guns in every room, and they all agreed to be united in their efforts to protect themselves, but not to indulge in fear. Daphne insisted that she refused to have her home filled with fear and anxiety, and that surely God would help protect them. This request had been a part of every prayer said over every meal since Sarah and Poppy had come here, and Daphne felt confident that their protection thus far had been an answer to those prayers, and that Divine protection would continue to serve them well. They would trust in God, do their best, and expect to remain safe. Sarah sincerely appreciated Daphne's attitude, because she preferred to enjoy the fact that she and Darius were engaged to be married. She felt a little giddy every time she thought about it, and she didn't want fear of the future, or the trauma of difficult memories, to mar her joy in any way.

That evening they all had supper around Darius's bed so they could eat together. They moved extra chairs into the room, and they all managed to hold their plates and eat with very little trouble. With everyone gathered all at once for the first time since their home and safety had been intruded upon, Darius took the opportunity to announce that he and Sarah would be getting married. They didn't know exactly when yet or what their plans would be after that, but he declared with a beaming smile that he was simply grateful to have Sarah in his life and to know that they would always be together—whatever path their lives followed. Everyone was more than thrilled, and Sarah noticed David beaming as much as his son and Daphne actually dabbing at tears while she laughed with perfect happiness. Was it possible that David and Daphne had wanted this to happen as much as she had? She knew they had grown to care for her—as she had for them—but it warmed her heart to know this marriage was something they wanted very much.

After supper Sarah and Poppy went to the kitchen to help Daphne clean the dishes and put everything in order, while David and Halford remained with Darius to help him get cleaned up and ready for bed, with the hope that he would sleep better tonight. The moment the women had entered the kitchen and set down the dishes they'd carried from Darius's room, Daphne turned and hugged Sarah tightly. Sarah returned the hug with equal vigor, noting over Daphne's shoulder that Poppy had a smile that consumed her entire face.

"Oh, little one!" Daphne said, pulling back to take hold of Sarah's shoulders. "I can't tell you how I've hoped and prayed this would happen. You have healed his heart more than you could ever know, and I'm so grateful that I never have to let you go. Now you will always be my daughter." She turned and reached out a hand toward Poppy, who took it, "And you will always be as good as my daughter because I know the two of you will always remain friends."

"Of course we will," Poppy said, and the three women shared a hug and a burst of laughter before they settled down to do the necessary chores. Sarah felt deeply content, except when she thought of returning to the place where her father had been murdered, and where a murderer was likely lurking secretly. But she didn't have to worry about that for now. Until Darius was healed enough to travel, they wouldn't be going anywhere—for which she was deeply grateful. In spite of the recent intrusion, she still felt safer here than she believed she could feel anywhere else.

Over the next couple of days, everyone took shifts sitting with Darius at Daphne's insistence—even though Darius insisted he was fine. But his mother didn't want him left alone until he was capable of doing more for himself without compromising the wound, which so far was looking very good. There were personal things Darius needed help with that required the assistance of Halford or his father, but they managed to work those things around the times when the women took shifts sitting with him. Sarah enjoyed her time with Darius when no one else was around. She always tried to insist that he sleep—especially when her shift was in the night—but he insisted that he just wanted to talk to her, and she couldn't deny that she was glad for it. Given his brush with death and their recent engagement, conversation between them took on a new depth as they talked more about their lives, their fears, their hopes. And Sarah loved him more every hour she spent with him.

Four days after the terrifying incident that had landed Darius in bed, Jimmy and Reggie came to visit him. Reggie had known about the situation since Daphne had let him know their plan had changed due to what had happened, and she'd asked that he quietly let Jimmy know without telling anyone else. Reggie would have been due for a visit soon anyway, since he never went very long without coming to see Poppy. Darius was pleased to see his friends when Sarah escorted them up the stairs, and they were thrilled with the announcement that Darius and Sarah were officially engaged. She went back downstairs to give the three friends some time together. While everyone else relaxed in the parlor, doing needlework or reading, they kept smiling at each other when bursts of male laughter floated down from the room where Darius was recovering.

Again, they all ate supper in Darius's room, squeezing in two more chairs, which made their gathering very cozy. But there was always more laughter with Jimmy and Reggie around, and they all had a delightful time. The moment they were finished eating, Poppy and Reggie volunteered to carry used dishes down to the kitchen, and it was evident they wanted some time alone. Everyone else remained surrounding Darius's bed talking about trivial things until Jimmy said with a seriousness that hadn't been present in the conversation thus far, "Darius, when you go back, I want to go with you. I know that Reggie is going with you, and I know his going isn't just about being with Poppy. We all know you have to go back there when the time is right, and it could be dangerous. I know I have limitations, my friend, but you know I'm good with a gun, and I can help keep you safe." He paused and nothing but silence replied before he went on. "You're not going to be your best self, Darius, and I want to help keep you safe." He looked around the room and nodded toward the door, as if to indicate Poppy and Reggie, who were not in the room. "All of you."

"And what about Laura?" Darius asked. "I don't think she'd like having you put yourself in harm's way when—"

"We all have someone we love, someone who loves us. I haven't told her anything about the situation, because I wouldn't do so without asking your permission, but I absolutely know she would want me to do this. She knows what a dear friend you are." He put his hands firmly on his thighs. "I'm going with you. That's all there is to it."

"Well, all right," Darius said lightly. "Who am I to argue with that?" More seriously he added, "Thank you, my friend. And yes, you should tell Laura. If you trust her not to repeat the details, then I trust her."

Jimmy nodded, and more silence fell until Sarah said, "And when do we get to meet Laura?"

"I haven't brought her here because I didn't think any of you would want her to know about your secret guests." He winked at Sarah.

"Well, it's likely time she knew the truth," Daphne said, "especially if you're going back to Courtenay with the others. Besides, the two of you will be married soon, which makes her family."

"Then I will bring her with me next time I come," Jimmy said, seeming pleased with the prospect.

"We will look forward to that," Darius declared, and the others agreed.

Later that evening after their guests had left and Sarah had helped Daphne clean up the kitchen, she sat beside Darius's bed, holding his hand. After what Jimmy had said earlier, she knew they were likely thinking the same thing—and it needed to be voiced between them—but she didn't want to say it, and she suspected he didn't either. Fearing they wouldn't be able to say a word about anything else until the matter was clarified, she cleared her throat and just spoke her thoughts. "I don't want to go back, Darius, but I know I have to—*we* have to. Perhaps my reluctance to go back to the place my father was murdered will be lessened when I actually return. Maybe I've made it far worse in my mind than it will be in reality. I do miss my aunt, and I know our likelihood of discovering the truth of what happened and why is more probable if we go back; either way we just have to go back. Whether I feel the need to stay there remains to be seen, I suppose."

"You're right," he said, squeezing her hand, "about everything. And whether or not you feel the need to stay is entirely up to you. I will stay with you wherever you decide to live." He sighed. "But yes, we need to go back. As soon as I heal enough to be able to travel, I think we just need to get it over with."

"I worry about how the results of your getting shot will hinder your ability to do what you're so good at."

"No need to worry about that," he said with a smile. "I may be your fiancé now, but I'm still officially your protector as well. And it's just as Jimmy said: I know I have my limitations, but you know I'm good with a gun." He smiled and added, "We'll be fine."

Sarah nodded and felt relieved to realize she believed him. She needed to follow his example of courage in going back and facing this situation head-on. She would never be able to truly get on with her life until she knew the truth, and she prayed that their return would help bring the truth to the surface.

\* \* \* \* \*

While spring eased gracefully into the warmth of summer, Darius regained his strength and his ability to walk. At first, doing so caused him a great deal of pain, but he worked on it slowly until he had only a slight limp, and the wound was healing up nicely.

Halford returned to Castle Courtenay with strict instructions from Darius on how to behave, and what he needed to pretend not to know. The household felt different with him gone, and Sarah hoped he would remain safe, and that whoever might have knowledge of his connection to Darius would not put him in any danger.

Laura proved to be a delightful addition to their household. She was very pretty and clearly very much in love with Jimmy. And once she knew the truth about the reasons Sarah and Poppy were living with the Nash family, Jimmy began visiting more frequently and bringing her along.

During one of their visits, while Reggie was there too, Reggie announced that he and Poppy were getting married. Everyone was thrilled, and they all laughed over the irony that these three men who had been friends since childhood were now all engaged to be married at the same time. They all promised to set their dates so that they could attend each other's weddings. In spite of Sarah being perfectly happy on Poppy's behalf, she felt a little pang over the realization that Poppy would definitely be living permanently in the nearby village once she and Reggie were married. Sarah didn't know how she could manage at Courtenay without her dear friend, but she talked it through with Darius and they both agreed she couldn't yet decide on whether she should remain there until they had more information. In spite of all that compelled Sarah to want to live out her life here in Darius's family home, she knew she had a responsibility to the estate she had inherited from her father. It had been easy to avoid thinking about that with all that had been happening, and how it had necessitated her being *away* from her ancestral home and the legacy it represented. But as the time drew closer for them to return, she found her sense of duty and obligation haunting her.

When Darius announced one morning at breakfast that he was feeling an urgency to return to Courtenay and assess the problem from the other end—as he put it—they decided to leave in two days. Sarah trusted Darius's instincts, and if he said he felt an urgency, she was more than willing to follow his lead. That evening Jimmy and Reggie came for supper and they discussed details of their journey, as well as what they planned to do once they arrived. They would be renting a carriage from a man in the village who owned the local livery, and who also sometimes offered people passage to the nearest locations where other travel arrangements could be made. The horses that had come from Courtenay, pulling the carriage Evans had been driving, were living happily in the barn behind the house. Sarah knew they'd been well cared for and regularly exercised and given fresh air. And now those horses would be taking them back to where they'd left so many months ago that Sarah had lost track.

Reggie and Jimmy would be driving the carriage and caring for the horses, under the guise of being servants of Darius's family as Darius returned to Castle Courtenay with his fiancée and her maid. They would all appear to be completely relaxed in regard to the previous danger, behaving as if they no longer considered it to be relevant. But in reality, they would all be extremely alert and watchful, and Darius had taught Sarah and Poppy some simple methods of putting things into place in their rooms to make certain no one could enter during the night to cause them harm. They were also committed to making certain they only ate food that had come directly from the same pots and serving dishes from which the staff was eating. Considering the fact that an official inquest had declared Oswald's death the result of poisoning, it wouldn't be strange to insist that these precautions be taken—for the safety of everyone in the house.

When the time finally came to leave, Sarah had a terrible time saying goodbye to Daphne and David, and she barely managed to keep from sobbing like a little girl as they embraced and whispered promises of seeing each other soon. But Sarah didn't know exactly how long it would be, or what their future might entail.

Once in the carriage with Darius and Poppy, Sarah couldn't hold back her tears, but Darius put his arm around her, guided her head to his shoulder, and encouraged her to cry if she needed to. Sarah felt a little better to look across the carriage and see that Poppy was dabbing at her eyes with her handkerchief. They had both become extremely attached to David and Daphne and the sweet feeling in their home. At least they were both traveling with the men they'd grown to love, but Sarah felt envious of Poppy given the fact that when she was married to Reggie she would inevitably return here and live in the village nearby where she could visit David and Daphne frequently.

Sarah was grateful to know that whatever her final decision might be, Darius would always be with her, would always stand by her side. But she didn't want to live a great distance from his parents who had come to feel like her own mother and father. She was sincerely torn between what she considered an important obligation to the legacy she'd inherited from her father, and the simple life she had grown to prefer. She had discussed her confusion with Darius to the point that the conversation had become wearying—always coming to the same conclusions. She couldn't make a fair decision until they returned to Courtenay and would hopefully be able to solve the mystery of her father's death—and Evans's. She still thought of him often and the price he'd paid to save her life, even if he'd done so without knowing it.

"Everything will be all right," Darius whispered and kissed the top of her head. "And I promise you that with time you will absolutely know which direction you should take with your life."

Sarah looked up at him. "How did you know I was thinking about that?"

"You're *always* thinking about that," he said with a little smile, and Sarah noticed that Poppy was smiling as well.

While Sarah was trying to think of a way to defend her obsession with the conundrum before her, Darius added, "Don't worry, my love. No matter what happens . . . no matter what you decide . . . I will always be with you."

"You've probably told me that a hundred times," Sarah said, settling her head more comfortably against his shoulder. "But I'm grateful for the reminder."

Darius kissed her head again and Sarah closed her eyes, determined to let go of her obsessive concern over a decision she couldn't possibly make at this time, and instead focus more on the present. When the time was right to face this choice, she would know; until then, all her fretting and stewing was completely pointless. She concentrated on the motion of the carriage and the miles it was putting behind them as they traveled toward Castle Courtenay. She wondered how far away they actually were, and what direction they were traveling. She honestly had no idea where they'd traveled—or how far—after Evans had been killed. As long as Darius knew where they were, she knew everything would be all right. He'd had that effect on her right from the start. She recalled how easy it had been to trust him and put her life in his hands, even when he'd been a stranger to her. And now she'd come to trust him with her heart, her future, her happiness. In the deepest parts of her soul, she absolutely knew she was safe with him in every respect. With that thought she fell asleep, realizing as she drifted off that she hadn't been sleeping well due to her dread of going back, but now that they were on their way, she felt more relaxed.

Sarah woke up when the carriage stopped for the horses to be fed and watered—and as Reggie joked when he opened the carriage door for them, the people needed to be fed and watered as well. Sarah and Poppy were glad for a chance to freshen up at the pub, and with several men in the place who appeared rather rough, they were both glad to not be alone. Just being together helped them feel safer. When they returned to the dining room of the pub, they found the men sitting at a table and joined them. They'd already ordered a meal, which was served a few minutes later. Sarah didn't realize how hungry she was until she tasted the stew, which was very good—although not nearly as good as what Daphne could produce. Her hunger made her realize they'd been on the road far longer than she'd realized. She was tempted to ask Darius exactly where they were and how many miles they had yet to go, but she decided she didn't really want to know.

After setting out again they traveled for hours before stopping at an inn where horses and people alike would be spending the night after having a good meal. Darius reminded Sarah and Poppy of all the necessary precautions before he left them in the room they were sharing, and they locked the door. As soon as it was locked, they also tacked a piece of string across the doorway with a bell tied in the middle. They'd come equipped with a number of such contraptions, which Darius had provided. No one would be able to enter the room uninvited without alerting them. Sarah couldn't deny that knowing such precautions were in place made it easier to relax and get some much-needed sleep—once she'd forced herself to stop obsessing over how it might be to return home.

They repeated their travel routine the following day, and once again they stayed at an inn that provided every necessary service for travelers. The next morning while they were all sharing breakfast in the dining room, Darius told the women they would be arriving at Castle Courtenay later that day. They would be stopping for lunch on the way, but they would likely arrive at Courtenay before tea was served, according to his rough estimates. The very idea created a fluttering inside Sarah. She couldn't discern if it was some form of excitement over returning home and seeing her aunt—and to simply be where she'd spent her entire life—or whether it was more from an indefinable fear. She couldn't be sure; perhaps it was both.

On the final stretch of the journey, Sarah found herself holding constantly to Darius's hand, sometimes squeezing his fingers so tightly that he would tease her about it and she would force herself to relax until she would get lost in thought over what to expect, and then she would inevitably squeeze his hand too hard all over again.

"It's going to be all right," Darius reminded her more than once. She could only nod at him and force a smile as so many memories and fears tumbled around and around in her mind.

"It's very beautiful," Darius said after many minutes of silence, which drew Sarah's attention to the fact that Castle Courtenay—with its surrounding grounds—had come into view out the carriage window.

Sarah took a deep breath, feeling strangely soothed just to see her home. "It *is* beautiful!" she said, a little breathless. But her fondness for this place came with the same horrifying reality that had been with her when she'd left here so many months ago. Her father had been murdered! At least one person here was not only completely lacking in integrity, they were capable of murder. She could only pray—as she had been all along—that the culprit could be found, the mystery solved, and life could go back to normal; she couldn't imagine ever being able to feel at peace until she discovered the truth. She didn't want to spend the rest of her life looking over her shoulder, wondering if the person guilty of killing her father might still want to do away with her as well for reasons she didn't understand.

Within a minute of the carriage stopping in front of the main door, three servants—an under butler and two maids—came flurrying out of the house with excitement over Sarah's unexpected return. Sarah knew them by name and greeted them warmly, but in the back of her head was a constant question regarding whether she could trust them; she had no idea who in this household might have contributed to her father's death— and the threat against her own life. But Sarah was proud of herself for the way she behaved as if she were nothing but delighted to be home. She quickly informed the servants that Darius was now her fiancé, over which they expressed sincere happiness on her behalf and offered appropriate congratulations. Sarah then asked for a room to be prepared for Darius, and for accommodations to be made for the men who had come with them. While Jimmy and Reggie were unloading the luggage from the top of the carriage, the servants scurried away to take care of everything and to inform the rest of the household that Sarah had returned. Once again Sarah was amazed at how agile Jimmy was at doing this job, considering his limitations. To watch him climb up and down from the box seat and help move luggage, one might not even notice his disability.

Darius helped his friends carry the luggage into the front hall where Sarah was glad servants would take it all upstairs, given that Darius still had a limp from his bullet wound, and she didn't want him exerting too much physical energy just yet. After Jimmy and Reggie left to take the carriage to where it would be kept, and to care for the horses, the door was closed, and Sarah stood with Poppy and Darius in the familiar hall of her home.

"This feels very strange," Poppy said quietly.

"Yes, it does," Sarah agreed.

"And yet you have come home," Darius said, "Lady of Courtenay."

Sarah turned more toward him, startled to hear herself referred to that way. He was smiling with a hint of mischief in his eyes, but something inside her felt deeply uncomfortable with such a title—or perhaps it was the attached responsibility. Or maybe it was the fact that inheriting Courtenay had also put her life in danger. Whatever the reason, she chose to ignore Darius's comment and was glad to see Mrs. Weatherford, the housekeeper, coming up the hall to greet them. She seemed nothing but pleased to have Sarah and Poppy back, and she congratulated Sarah and Darius on their betrothal.

"It didn't take long for the news to spread," Poppy commented.

"Not in a house like this," Mrs. Weatherford said with a sincerely happy grin. She then told them that fresh water was on its way up to their rooms, so they could freshen up, and then tea would be served in the parlor that was known to be Sarah's favorite. Mrs. Weatherford offered to personally escort Darius to the guest room he would be using; since she mentioned that it had a perfect view of the gardens, Sarah knew exactly which room she meant, and she would know where to find him.

"Thank you," Sarah said; both Darius and Poppy echoed her words and Mrs. Weatherford seemed pleased with their kindness. Sarah instinctively knew that the servants they'd encountered thus far had been far too genuinely pleased to see her to be hiding any guilt.

Sarah took only a few steps toward the stairs before she heard a familiar voice call her name, and she turned to see her aunt rushing from the direction of the library, wearing an elaborate dress made out of bright blue satin that rustled as she practically ran. "Is it true?" Penelope asked, already crying. "Is it really true? Are you really here?" By the time she'd finished expressing her disbelief she was standing directly in front of Sarah, smiling brilliantly through the tears running over her cheeks. "Oh, my dear sweet girl!" Penelope uttered, taking Sarah's face in her hands for a moment before she threw her arms around Sarah and they embraced tightly. "I've missed you so very much!"

"I've missed you too," Sarah told her aunt, eagerly accepting her embrace and returning it fully. She truly had missed her aunt—in spite of her eccentricities, and her tendency to be overly emotional. "It's so good to see you!" Sarah said, pulling back to look at her.

"And you!" Penelope said, then turned to look at Poppy. "And it's good to see you, my dear."

"It's good to be back," Poppy replied, but Sarah could tell she was being gracious and was probably lying. Poppy had found a new life elsewhere with Reggie and couldn't wait to return, and Sarah knew it.

Penelope then settled her eyes on Darius with an appraising smile as she wiped her face dry with the handkerchief she pulled out of the cuff of her sleeve. "And what's this I hear? The two of you are betrothed?"

"It's true," Darius said to Penelope. "She's taken pity on me and agreed to make me happy for the rest of my life."

"Well, I think it's just wonderful!" Penelope declared, putting both hands to the sides of her face as if that might help contain her glee. "Why don't you all go and freshen up and I'll see you at tea and we can catch up. I can't wait to hear what you've been doing all this time."

Penelope embraced Sarah again before she turned and went back the way she'd come. They all started up the stairs while Sarah tried to orient herself to actually being here. She was overcome with a strange dichotomy of knowing she should feel completely at home here—and she could only hope that she would feel that way again—while at the same time feeling that home felt far away with David and Daphne. She wondered what they were doing right now. She imagined David working on some project out in his wood-working room in the corner of the barn, while Daphne was busy with her own projects in the kitchen, humming as she worked. And she imagined they both were likely adjusting to the house being quieter and less crowded.

Sarah forced her thoughts to the present, trying not to feel or appear afraid even though she knew their greatest purpose for being here was to try and uncover the truth. And she was very likely in danger.

# Chapter Thirteen
## ONE PIECE OF INFORMATION

POPPY DECLINED COMING DOWN TO the parlor for tea. Even though she was technically a servant, and in any other household she would never be included in such a situation, she had long ago become more a part of the family. Penelope and Sarah's father had grown accustomed to Poppy being around for practically everything, but today Poppy was going to have tea with the servants—since that's where she would find Reggie and Jimmy, and she wanted to be with her fiancé. She had her own announcement to make, and Sarah felt the division between them growing wider as the paths of their futures were falling into place. Well, at least *Poppy's* future was clear. Sarah knew she and Darius would always be together, but the details of her life remained vague and uncertain.

Sharing tea with Darius and her aunt was mildly awkward at first when she still felt so disoriented. But Darius quickly eased the tension by speaking comfortably with Penelope and telling her a version of their mis-adventures that deviated only slightly from the truth. Penelope had been involved with hiring Darius to protect Sarah, and therefore knew they had been hiding somewhere all this time. She was interested in hearing the details and was amused that the friends they had been staying with turned out to be Darius's parents.

Penelope became overwhelmed by one of her tearful outbursts as she spoke of the household receiving the news that Evans had been killed, and how she had not only been saddened and horrified by his death but had become even more concerned for Sarah's safety. But Halford had assured her that he was in communication with people who knew of the whereabouts of Sarah and Poppy and their protector and that all was well. She spoke tearfully of the funeral service and burial of the man who'd given his life for

Sarah. He'd had no family, but he'd had many dear friends here at Courtenay and in the nearby village, and the service had been well attended.

Sarah found it difficult to eat any of the delicious little sandwiches and cakes that had been served with tea while Penelope talked about Evans's death until she realized that eating gave her a good reason not to speak. Since she had no idea what to say, she preferred keeping her mouth full. She marveled at how well Darius had learned to read her thoughts and feelings when he filled in the silence by telling Penelope how upset Sarah had been over Evans's death, and how losing him had made the danger readily evident. Penelope dabbed at new tears to hear this, and to hear how difficult the situation had been on them—both emotionally and physically, since Darius had told her about their trek on horseback through the woods and having to sleep on the ground. But Sarah noticed that he hadn't mentioned anything about the armed intruder who had shot him in the leg and stolen the sword. He had told Sarah earlier to follow his lead on how much information they shared with others, and she was more than glad to do so. Her own mind felt heavy and disoriented; she was only too happy to know that Darius would effectively handle the situation in the best possible way.

Over the next few days, Sarah was amazed—although she realized she shouldn't have been—at how easily Darius seemed to feel completely at home at Castle Courtenay. He was kind and respectful to the servants, and quickly acquainted himself with most of them by wandering around and chatting with people while they were doing their work, and he usually pitched in to help. Sarah often accompanied him, mostly because she just wanted to be with him, and partly because she felt safer in his presence. At first, she was convinced that his efforts in talking with each and every person who lived and worked here was for the sake of solving their ongoing problem—and she knew that was part of it—but she quickly began to see his genuine interest in others.

In honoring her position as the heir of Courtenay, Sarah met with those who were employed to oversee the household and the estate to be assured of the condition and circumstances of all that had taken place in her absence. Darius joined her for those meetings, but he didn't utter a word, as if he were letting her know by his silence that he had complete confidence in her being able to handle her responsibilities without any assistance from him. Sarah was grateful for the times she had lingered in her father's study when he'd been having such meetings, which gave her some idea now of what she should expect of those who were in her employment and earning a generous wage to see that everything was cared for according to the expectations of the late Oswald Courtenay—and which she insisted must remain the standard of care for the estate and the people living there.

Sarah was glad to have those meetings over with, and to be comfortably reassured that everything was in order. Her father had done well in choosing the people he hired, and she felt confident they were still doing their jobs according to her father's wishes because they had respected him a great deal.

When they were finished with the final appointment, Sarah turned to Darius and said, "You see? They didn't need me at all. Everything here runs perfectly without my presence."

"Perhaps," he said, "but that doesn't necessarily mean you shouldn't be here. Things are always subject to change, and someone has to be certain that those changes don't allow anything important to become overlooked."

"Are you saying I *should* stay?"

"You know how I feel about that; the decision has to be yours."

"Do *you* want to live your life here?"

"I would manage," he said with a smile. "It's a beautiful place to raise a family."

"No more beautiful than your parents' home; it's a different kind of beauty."

"That's true, with different benefits on either hand."

"I miss your parents, Darius."

"I miss them too," he admitted.

"I think our children should have their grandparents in their lives every day, not just for an occasional visit."

"Perhaps we could convince them to come and live here," he said and smiled more broadly as he waved his arm to indicate the enormity of the home in which they were sitting. "There's plenty of space."

"Yes," she laughed softly, "we're not short of space, but . . . I can't imagine them wanting to give up the life they live; it's practically idyllic."

"I think we should let them decide. I believe that being a part of our lives—and our children's lives—might hold more sway than you think. My siblings don't share the closeness with them that I do. It's not that anything is wrong; they're just not as compatible. My parents could never be happy uprooting their lives to go and live with either of them. But we've always been close, and I know they love you dearly; I believe they'd do just about anything to be a part of our lives."

"Really?" Sarah asked, hope mingling with her surprise. She took a deep breath and let it out slowly. Perhaps that was the answer; she was torn over the fact that staying at Courtenay would separate them from Darius's parents, but perhaps this could solve that problem. Still, there was a more pressing issue standing in the way, and despite her dwindling hope that it would ever be solved, she couldn't shake the instinct that it *had* to be made right before she could peacefully move forward with her life.

On the third day of sharing meals with Darius and her aunt, Sarah realized that he and Penelope were getting along so well that it had become almost entertaining. Penelope loved hearing the stories of what she called his adventures, and he could easily make her laugh—which was refreshing in contrast to her general tendency to cry over every little thing. Sarah could see clear evidence that Darius had meant it when he'd said that he would stay with her wherever she chose to live. Darius was obviously adaptable, and she believed he could be happy here if she was, but she could only be happy here if she felt completely safe, and that would never happen until the mystery was solved and the person—or people—responsible for all of this death and danger were brought to justice.

Poppy understandably wanted to be with Reggie as much as possible, and she had continued taking her meals with the staff so that she could eat with Reggie and Jimmy, who were always on subtle but high alert regarding anything that might be construed as dangerous or suspicious. The only time Sarah and Poppy were seeing each other was first thing in the morning and before bed to help each other with hair and buttons, when they could catch up on each other's activities. Sarah missed being with Poppy the way she'd been accustomed for many years, but they had both tearfully discussed the possibility that perhaps this was helping them prepare to live different lives, far away from each other. Sarah knew—as Poppy did—that life was always subject to change and such separations were to be expected, especially when it came to getting married and settling down to start their own families. Still, it was difficult.

Each evening after supper Sarah enjoyed walking hand-in-hand with Darius through the magnificent gardens of Castle Courtenay. He often commented on how beautiful it was, and she began to think more and more that he could be content remaining here after their marriage.

During their walks he told her that he still had no clue who might have any culpability. He hadn't encountered one person who came across as guilty. There were a few stable hands who were somewhat standoffish, and Sarah knew who they were, but as Darius pointed out, that didn't make them guilty of any crimes, and without proof they had nothing to go on.

This felt deeply discouraging to Sarah, but she knew that Mr. Curtis, the solicitor, was coming to meet with them the following morning. He'd been away on behalf of a client, but word had been left with his wife that Sarah was back and wished to see him, and they'd received a message earlier that day, which let them know that Mr. Curtis would be arriving at ten the following morning. Darius held out great hope that the solicitor would be able to give them some kind of information that would be helpful, but Sarah knew that Darius also felt some anger toward Mr. Curtis. Ever since Halford had told him that Curtis was the only person he'd told where he was going prior to the horrible incident that had occurred at Darius's home, Darius had harbored some ill will and suspicion toward Mr. Curtis. Sarah couldn't imagine Mr. Curtis possibly intending her—or her father—any harm, although she was beginning to wonder if she had any substantive idea of whether he was truly trustworthy. She had lived under the same roof with Halford, and he'd been as close to her father as she had been to Poppy. She'd known Mr. Curtis for years—as had her father—but only through occasional visits. Her father had trusted him, but her father had been murdered. While Darius was anticipating their meeting with Mr. Curtis, hoping they might get some answers, Sarah was dreading it and could only say that she would be glad to have it over and done with. Even if he was guilty, he wasn't going to admit it. She knew Darius was perceptive, but that didn't mean at least one person in this household—or the solicitor—might not be very good actors.

The entire situation weighed very heavily on Sarah as she went to bed that night. Of course, it had been weighing on her ever since her father's death had been declared a murder, but she had been safely hidden away for a long time; she'd had a comfortable distance from this place. And now she was feeling a definite desperation to find out what had happened and why, but a part of her was beginning to believe that would never happen, that the killer would go free, and she would never feel completely safe for as long as she lived.

At breakfast Darius said nothing about the meeting with Mr. Curtis and she wondered if there was a reason he didn't want Penelope to know. Sarah had grown accustomed to doing as he'd asked and following his lead regarding what was said or not said to anyone in the house, but sometimes his precautions seemed extreme. Darius had assured her more than once that he knew Penelope was prone to worry and anxiety, and he didn't want to tell her anything that might cause her alarm or agitate her, when that knowledge wouldn't do her any good.

After the meal, Penelope left to attend a ladies' luncheon with some friends at one of their homes. It was a weekly occurrence that rotated among the ladies who participated. Given the fact that Darius hadn't told her about Mr. Curtis's visit—just as he hadn't told her about many other things—she thought it was best that Penelope wasn't in the house. If Darius ended up getting angry with Mr. Curtis as she feared he might, she didn't want Penelope getting in the middle of any kind of argument. Sarah had reminded Darius to stay calm, and he assured her he would, but no one spent more time with him than she did, and no one had heard him talk about this more than she had. She knew that for all his efforts to remain positive and protective, he had some very difficult feelings about the intrusion that had taken place at his parents' home. The wound in his leg had surely contributed to him naturally being upset over the danger that had found its way into their safe haven.

Sarah and Darius waited in the study that had been the room where Oswald Courtenay had managed all the business of the estate. They had been in this room together a number of times the last few days as Sarah had met with those running the household and the estate, but the very thought of meeting with Mr. Curtis under the present circumstances was making her stomach smolder.

"Shouldn't Halford be here by now?" Sarah asked, squeezing Darius's hand too tightly—something she'd developed a habit of doing whenever she felt anxious. He often teased her about it by pretending that it hurt far more than she knew it did. His hands were large and strong, and she could always feel his strength coming through his grasp—just as she did now, sitting next to him on a small sofa near the window.

"He's coming," Darius said, not at all concerned. He lifted Sarah's hand to his lips and kissed it, which reminded her to relax her grip.

She looked at him and asked, "Do you really think Mr. Curtis will know something that could help?"

"I don't know, but I hope so."

"And you'll stay calm?" Sarah asked.

"Sarah, my darling," he said, looking into her eyes, "I know you're well aware of how difficult my feelings have been over what happened, and how desperately I want answers—as much as you do—but have you ever known me to lose my temper?"

Sarah thought about it. She recalled how angry he'd been with Halford when he'd questioned him about who might have followed him when he'd visited; but for all that he'd been upset and very firm in his questions, she could never say that he'd lost control of his temper. "No," she finally said.

"Then why do you think I would do that today? I'm well aware that getting angry with someone is much less likely to create a situation conducive to solving any problems."

Sarah thought about his question a long moment and was surprised with how quickly she knew the answer. "My father had a temper; he was a good man, but he shouted at me a number of times over things that were fairly insignificant. And I saw him get angry with other people. I suppose something in me just assumed that any man would do the same." She kissed *his* hand. "But I was wrong. And you're absolutely right. I should know you better than that."

He smiled and kissed her lips. "So . . . just trust me; let me handle the situation in the way I believe is most likely to get the information we need— if he has any information to offer; he might not. But rest assured that even if I *appear* to have a temper, I am completely in control of my emotions and my actions."

Sarah thought about that. "So . . . you're going to *pretend* to be upset with the hope of . . . what? Scaring the truth out of him?"

"Maybe," Darius said. "We'll see how it goes. I'm just going to follow my instincts."

Sarah sighed and looked away, her thoughts spinning. "I pray this works. I don't think I can keep living like this . . . not knowing . . . wondering if we're safe, and—"

"We've both been praying very hard, Sarah," Darius reminded her. "Now we just need to do the very best we can and see what happens. We need to recognize there are many things we have no control over, and for all that we hope for a good outcome, we have to let go of our expectations, because if it doesn't turn out the way we hope, we could go crazy."

Sarah looked into Darius's eyes, taking in his humble but confident countenance—and his obvious love for her. She touched his face and asked, "Where did you learn to be so wise?"

He chuckled and said, "If I *am* wise, the answer to that question is obvious. You *have* met my parents, have you not?" She laughed softly. "I have lived a blessed life, Sarah, if only to have been raised by such extraordinary people."

"And I am blessed to have been taken into such a wonderful family," she said.

Darius kissed her, but he pulled away quickly when the door opened and Halford entered, looking as nervous as Sarah felt. However, she didn't feel as nervous as she had prior to hearing the things Darius had just said. She only prayed that their appointment with Curtis would be fruitful.

Halford took a seat in one of the comfortable chairs facing the sofa, which left his back toward the door. He offered no greeting but simply said, "I hope he's not late. I want to get this over with."

"As we all do," Darius said. "Please try to relax and remember what we talked about."

"What did you talk about?" Sarah asked, realizing she hadn't been present during any such conversation.

Darius looked at her and said, "We have no reason to believe Curtis is actually guilty of doing anything wrong, but I've met him, and I know the type of man he is. If he *has* done anything wrong, I'll be able to tell. There's the possibility that even if he *did* have a part in this, he might have been threatened or coerced. We are going to give him the benefit of the doubt and assume he's innocent until there's evidence to the contrary."

"Well, thank you for telling me that," Sarah said with sarcasm. "I would have liked to know your thinking before now."

"Sorry," he said and clearly meant it. "I'm adjusting to having a woman in my life."

"I forgive you," Sarah said with a mock snideness that made Halford chuckle, but at least it eased the tension a bit. "Is there anything else about the situation you'd like to fill me in on before Mr. Curtis arrives?"

Darius thought about it. "Just that . . . often people don't think they know anything helpful, but if you ask the right questions and get them to really concentrate, they often recall things that might seem insignificant but are actually very helpful. I'm hoping Curtis knows more than he thinks he does—whether or not he's guilty."

"Curtis is a good man but easily intimidated, I think," Halford said. "He respected your father and cared for him, but he was also intimidated by him. I hope he hasn't been intimidated by someone with evil motives, and I also hope that Darius can use his intimidation tactics to get some answers. He's the only one who knew where I was going, but I still don't believe he could be guilty of doing anything to hurt you or your father deliberately." He let out a weighted sigh. "I suppose we shall see." He glanced at the clock. "He's late."

"He'll be here soon," Darius said. "He's a punctual man, correct?"

"Yes," Halford said.

"And yet one can't always predict the time it takes to ride a horse a certain distance. He'll be here."

Silence settled over the room until they heard a distant knocking at the front door, which actually startled Sarah, and made Darius chuckle. Halford just looked more nervous. Darius ordered him to relax, which only resulted in Halford appearing even more nervous.

A maid opened the door of the study and guided Mr. Curtis into the room before she left and closed the door behind her. They all rose to greet him, and he entered the room with nothing but confidence and pleasure in seeing them. He first greeted Sarah by kissing her hand, saying sincerely, "Oh, my dear! It is so grand to see you alive and well! You've been sorely missed."

"It's very good to see you," Sarah said with an easy smile; she hoped her own instincts were accurate as she sensed no guilt in him whatsoever. He was a superior solicitor, but she couldn't imagine him being sharp enough to have acting skills excellent enough to look her in the eye and appear so genuinely pleased over her being alive and well.

"Hello, Mr. Noble," Curtis said, shaking Darius's hand, and Sarah was startled to recall that he was known by a surname that wasn't accurate—even though she'd heard him called such a few times since their arrival here. "I can't thank you enough for keeping this sweet young lady safe all this time."

"It's been my pleasure," Darius said.

Curtis then turned to Halford and shook his hand as well. "And it's good to see you, my friend. I trust you are doing well."

"Well enough," Halford said. "We need to talk."

Mr. Curtis's brow creased as he glanced quickly at each of them and picked up on the serious tone in the room. "Well, I assumed as much since you asked me to come. So, let's talk. I admit I'm anxious to hear how things have gone in your absence, and I'm hoping you have figured out something to help us find out who's behind all this madness."

They were all seated, Mr. Curtis taking the other comfortable chair that faced the sofa. They were all able to see each other's faces as the difficult conversation commenced. Halford had agreed to share with Mr. Curtis what had happened at the home where Darius had been hiding Sarah and Poppy. Curtis appeared to be genuinely astonished and horrified, and he even asked, "How on earth could someone have found you?"

"That's what we're wondering," Darius said, sounding angry.

"The thing is," Halford went on, "it happened the day after I'd arrived there, and . . ." he hesitated, his nervousness increasing, which put Mr. Curtis visibly on edge, "you are the only person I talked to about my plans, and . . ."

Mr. Curtis gasped as the implication sank in. "You can't possibly think . . ." He looked directly at Sarah, his eyes filled with sadness and astonishment. "Oh, my dear . . . I would never do anything to hurt you—or your father." He looked at Halford, then at Darius. "Are you saying what I think you're saying? That you think I could have something to do with this?"

"We don't know what to think," Darius growled with a low rumble. "We have very little to go on, and at this point we all feel hesitant to believe anything or to trust anyone. It's a miracle the damages weren't worse. Sarah *could* have been killed that night—as could anyone else who was in the house."

"And you were shot?" Curtis asked with horror, since Halford had mentioned that.

"Yes," Darius said, still with that rumble in his voice. "And I was very lucky. If I'd been killed or permanently maimed, I certainly wouldn't have been able to keep Sarah and Poppy safe, now would I?"

"I'm so grateful it wasn't worse!" Curtis said emphatically. "And I can promise you I had *nothing* to do with this! Nothing!"

"All right," Darius said more calmly, leaning his forearms on his thighs in order to look more intently at Mr. Curtis. "Then talk to us; help us figure out what happened and why."

"Perhaps someone overheard us." Halford suggested the only possible answer they'd come up with thus far.

"No!" Curtis insisted. "That's not possible. I remember very well where we were when you told me. It was in *this* room, with the door and windows closed, and we were speaking softly. We were *not* overheard."

"Then how?" Sarah asked. "What other possibility is there that someone would have known to follow Halford? Could it be as simple as someone knowing Halford had hired the man who was protecting me, and if Halford left here, he should be followed? It's possible but it doesn't seem very likely, does it?"

"No, it doesn't," Mr. Curtis said, his voice almost frantic as he was obviously thinking very hard. Sarah felt convinced of his innocence even before he looked up at her with the sparkle of moisture in his eyes. "Oh, my dear! If I have inadvertently done something to bring harm to you in any way, I don't know if I can ever forgive myself."

"If you didn't intentionally do or say anything," Sarah said, "then there's nothing to forgive."

Curtis gave her a wan smile, but his distress clearly consumed him even before Darius asked, "Is there *anything* you remember that could help us figure this out? Anything? Often, we observe or hear things that may seem completely benign or insignificant, but it can help put pieces together. Please think, Mr. Curtis. Is there anything? Just . . . relax and think through any interactions you've had where this situation was being discussed, and tell us if you recall anything . . . unusual, even if it didn't seem to be at the time."

They all remained completely quiet while minutes ticked away on the clock and Mr. Curtis kept his eyes closed as if he were mentally reviewing a great deal of information. He shifted in his seat a few times and sighed loudly every minute or so. His eyes finally came open and glanced over each person in the room, but they settled on Sarah before he said, "There is only one thing I can think of, but . . . I'm sure it's nothing. I wish I could be more helpful."

"Just tell us what it is," Darius said, "and let me decide if it's helpful."

"Well," Curtis drawled, still directing his attention to Sarah, "the only person I spoke to about this was in the room when we all met together before you left here with Mr. Noble. Your aunt was concerned about your safety, and I know Mr. Halford kept her updated on the letters he was receiving by way of a mutual friend that let him know you were all right. But I can't exactly recall where we were when I mentioned to her about Halford's intention to check on you while he was away. We *could* have been overheard; I'm not certain." He blew out a long breath of frustration. "I wish I could be more helpful; I truly do."

"Yes, I know," Sarah said kindly.

Mr. Curtis asked if he should speak with the police again and get them involved with this investigation—given that more crimes had been committed. Darius insisted that he didn't want the police involved; he believed they would only complicate the situation and wouldn't likely be able to figure out anything they didn't already know. He confided in Mr. Curtis that his intention was to continue to give the impression throughout the household that they had given up on trying to find the culprit, and his presence here was simply due to his being Sarah's fiancé.

"You're engaged?" Curtis asked, and Sarah realized that fact hadn't come up in the conversation. Before either of them could answer, he added, "Is that just . . . a ruse to explain your presence here, or—"

"No, it's real," Darius said, taking hold of Sarah's hand for the first time since Mr. Curtis had arrived. His relaxed tone let Sarah know that Darius believed the solicitor was telling the truth. He had to be at least as discouraged as she was over the lack of information Curtis had offered, but he sounded nothing but delighted as he said, "As difficult as all of this has been, I've been blessed to have found the love of my life."

"As have I," Sarah said, smiling at Darius.

"Oh, that's wonderful news!" Mr. Curtis said. "And you'll stay here, of course?"

Sarah felt comfortable admitting, "I'm not certain yet, to be truthful. I'm still trying to decide what's best."

They talked with Mr. Curtis about the positive and negative aspects of the options of where and how Sarah and Darius might go forward with their lives. The solicitor offered some professional information that Sarah found helpful regarding her responsibilities, and also her rights as an heiress.

When Mr. Curtis was leaving, Darius thanked him for his time and the information he'd offered. Sarah was a little surprised, since she couldn't recall him saying anything helpful at all. But the moment Mr. Curtis had left the house and Halford had gone upstairs, Darius said quietly to her, "We need to speak with your aunt, right away."

"Why?" Sarah asked. "You can't possibly think that—"

"One piece of information leads to another, Sarah," he said with such intensity that she felt truly afraid for the first time since they'd arrived. While she was trying to convince herself that her fears were exaggerated, Darius added even more quietly, "And we need to increase our vigilance regarding your safety."

"Why?" she asked again in a squeaky whisper.

"Because I sincerely believe you are in far more danger here than I had anticipated." Sarah didn't speak as Darius looked in both directions down the hallway as if he expected a villain to jump out and kill them both at any moment. He looked directly at her and added, "Except when you are in your room with the usual precautions in place, I am not leaving you alone. And yes, that means you cannot leave your room until I come there in the morning to escort you to breakfast, and I will escort you back to your room before bed."

Sarah felt too stunned to speak. He'd picked up on something Mr. Curtis had said, and she had no idea what it was. And she didn't know how to ask, or even if she wanted to know. She trusted Darius implicitly; she had right from the start. She wasn't going to start questioning his motives now. Or his instincts. But she dreaded speaking with Penelope even more than she had dreaded Mr. Curtis's visit. It would surely be nothing but a great deal of crying on her aunt's part, which would get them nowhere. More and more she believed they were simply never going to find out who was responsible for her father's death, and that of Evans. Perhaps she just needed to resign herself to that fact, learn how to remain alert enough to be safe, and get on with her life.

# *Chapter Fourteen*
## THE CULPRIT

Sarah and Darius shared lunch together, talking only about speculations of sharing their life together, and nothing about their forthcoming visit with Penelope—or the reasons for it. Sarah didn't want to question Darius's thinking or his methods, but she honestly couldn't think of a single reason to believe Penelope could help them at all. And Sarah was undoubtedly unnerved by Darius having told her that she was in a great deal more danger than he'd suspected. She wanted to ask what he meant exactly, but he was steering away from talking about it and she didn't press too hard, not *really* wanting to know. She tried to think back to their visit with Mr. Curtis, and yet for all her efforts she couldn't recall anything the solicitor had said to put Darius on a keener alert for her safety.

After lunch they went for a walk in the gardens where they mostly talked about his parents, speculating over what they might be doing now, which made Sarah miss them terribly. But it didn't necessarily diminish her growing belief that she needed to remain here at Castle Courtenay and honor her father's legacy.

When they estimated it was nearing time for Penelope to return from her ladies' luncheon, Darius took Sarah to the study to wait, and he instructed a maid to immediately tell Sarah's aunt upon her return that they wished to speak with her. Sarah was prepared to settle in and wait, fearing her nerves would only grow minute by minute. However, they'd only been in the study a short time when Sarah just happened to be looking out the window as Penelope's carriage came to a halt in front of the house. The driver jumped down from the box seat to open the carriage door, and Sarah's heart began to pound painfully in her chest.

"Darius!" she whispered frantically, as if she feared being overheard even though no one else was in the room. "Come here, quickly!" Everything in her mind flipped over with a terrible fear that Darius had indeed figured something out she never could have guessed. He rushed to her side at the window where she was peeking discreetly between the sheer curtains. "Look at the driver, Darius. He's built like . . . and moves like . . . the man who . . ."

"Shot me," Darius finished with certainty. "He's one of those stand-offish stable hands, isn't he?" His statement was laced with anger. "I don't know why I didn't recognize it before. You're right, Sarah. It was dark but there's no doubt it's the same man."

"What do we do now?" she asked, suddenly breathless.

"I'm thinking," he said as they watched Penelope step out of the carriage with the assistance of the culprit. She wore a ridiculously lavish purple dress, with fabric so bright it was almost blinding. And she was apparently oblivious to the true nature of her driver. Was Penelope also in danger? Sarah felt so angry in that moment that she wanted to personally claw at this man's face with her fingernails—as if she were capable of doing such a thing to a man who was so bulky and strong.

While Darius was still thinking, he headed toward the door and Sarah followed. He flung it open to see Penelope about to come into the room.

"Oh, my!" she said with a startled laugh. "I was told you wanted to speak with me."

"We do," Darius said with a smile that Sarah recognized as phony, but she doubted Penelope knew him well enough to notice the difference. "If you could just . . . wait for a few minutes . . . I've just remembered something I forgot to tell one of the stable hands. I won't be long."

"And . . . I'm going with him," Sarah said to her aunt, which made Darius glare at her discreetly. "But we'll be back straightaway. Just relax. You must be fatigued after your outing."

"Indeed," Penelope said, not seeming at all concerned about their unusual behavior.

Sarah closed the door to the study as they left, and she had to almost run to keep up with Darius's determined stride—which he managed surprisingly well even with the remaining limp from his wound. "Where are you going?" she asked in a low voice, not wanting them to be overheard.

Also speaking quietly, Darius said, "I would prefer to go alone."

"And I would prefer to know what's going on," she insisted.

"I just need to speak with . . . our *friend*." That last word came out of his mouth with acrid sarcasm.

Sarah was trying too hard to keep up with him to make any further comment until they entered the carriage house where the villainous fiend was unharnessing the horses. For this reason, Sarah could understand why Darius had wanted to hurry. Of course, he would be here for only a few minutes after he'd left Penelope at the front door. And he was here alone.

"What?" the culprit growled after a cursory glance at them. Sarah believed his name was Rick, even though she'd had so little interaction with him.

"I just have a couple of questions for you," Darius said, moving close enough to Rick that he took a step back, apparently not liking the intensity radiating from Darius.

"I don't know nothin' that concerns ye," Rick insisted, and Sarah felt chilled as she clearly recognized his voice; he was indeed the man who had invaded the Nash home and threatened their lives.

"I'm not so sure," Darius said, meeting him eye to eye; they were similar in height, but Rick was burlier, and Sarah felt nervous as she hung back to observe from a distance. She thought of what they'd believed this man was responsible for, and she feared he could seriously hurt Darius—and her. If only there had been time to summon Reggie and Jimmy. She questioned her own wisdom in coming here with Darius, but on the other hand she didn't believe Rick would hurt Darius in broad daylight when she was standing there as a witness, not so far from the door, knowing she could easily outrun him the short distance from here to the house. Darius took a step closer to Rick, who leaned his upper body back but didn't move his feet. "I would like to know exactly why you followed Mr. Halford to discover our whereabouts—where you tried to kill us."

"I don't know what ye're talkin' about," Rick said perhaps a little too quickly but with obvious guilt in his eyes; he was not a good actor by any means. Sarah couldn't believe it. Only minutes ago, she had noticed the possibility that this could be the culprit, and as soon as she heard his voice, she knew he was the one. But she still had trouble believing it was true in spite of recognizing him so clearly; and how would they ever prove it?

"Don't you?" Darius asked and abruptly reached out to grab Rick's upper arms, squeezing hard.

"What do ye think ye're doin'?" Rick demanded angrily, shrugging him off. But Darius immediately grabbed Rick's shoulders with renewed pressure and the man squealed with pain. Sarah gasped. Darius was brilliant! He knew how much the wound in his leg still pained him if it was bumped or overused. Their assailant had been shot that same night.

Without any warning, Darius ripped Rick's shirt to reveal a wound in his shoulder that wasn't healing nearly as well as the one in Darius's leg. Rick's astonishment was swallowed by fear as Darius took him hard by the shoulders again and hissed, "Who sent you? Tell me now!" Darius reached one hand back beneath his waistcoat and pulled out the pistol he always carried, immediately pressing the barrel to Rick's chest.

The man lost all pretense of being fearless. He looked down at the pistol and back at Darius's face. "She's not as sweet as everybody seems t' think, ye know."

"Who?" Darius asked with a low growl, and Sarah gasped again before putting her hand over her mouth, feeling suddenly sick as impossible pieces started coming together in her mind only a moment before Rick nodded toward her.

"The old hag," he said, glancing at Sarah. "Yer precious aunt. She'd kill ye before she'd let anyone but me see her real self."

"And why you?" Darius demanded, not seeming as surprised as Sarah felt. Had he figured it out already? Is that what he'd learned from something Curtis had said? Is that why he'd wanted to speak to Penelope as soon as she returned?

"I'll do just about anything fer a price," Rick said with an evil smirk, and Darius struck him hard with his fist. It took Rick off guard enough that he actually fell to the ground.

Sarah rushed outside, realizing the smoldering in her stomach had gotten dramatically worse. She ran around the corner of the carriage house to a cluster of bushes where she threw up, unable to believe that her beloved and trusted aunt could actually be behind such evil. Could it be true? Obviously, Sarah believed it *could*, or she wouldn't be throwing up.

Only a moment after she'd finally been able to calm her ongoing heaving, she heard Darius call her name and turned to see him holding to Rick's arm with one hand and pointing the gun at him with the other. Rick's hands had been tied behind his back.

"Are you all right?" Darius asked her.

Sarah shook her head, unable to lie and not wanting to speak. He looked concerned but obviously couldn't do anything to help her right now. She followed as he forced Rick into the door of the house that was nearest the kitchens. Since it was a common gathering place for the servants, it wasn't a surprise to see a maid appear in the hall. She stepped back and gasped as she saw what had to be shocking.

"Have someone send for the police," Darius said to her. "And tell them to hurry. When that's done, find Mr. Halford and tell him to go to the study immediately."

The maid agreed and rushed away. Neither Darius nor Rick said a word as the latter was forced through long hallways of the house to the study where Penelope was waiting. Sarah followed a few paces behind, concentrating very hard on subduing the urge to throw up again as she considered the possibility that Penelope—dear sweet Penelope—might have actually murdered her own brother, and then had sent someone to kill Sarah, killing Evans in the process. It just couldn't be possible! Could it? She still couldn't even fathom such a thing, and yet she'd heard what Rick had said, and she'd already judged that he was a very bad actor. What reason would he have to lie? He'd already been found guilty; he would surely be eager to share the blame.

As they approached the study, Sarah's heart began to pound with dread, which at least distracted her from her nausea. She saw Darius motion with his head for her to go ahead of them and open the door, which she did even while she fought to subdue her shock and horror and appear calm as she entered the room to see Penelope look up from where she was sitting comfortably, reading a book.

"Hello, my dear. I hope everything's all right. You've certainly piqued my curiosity about whatever it is that—"

"No," Sarah said, "everything is *not* all right."

Penelope looked completely ignorant of what could possibly be the problem until Darius guided Rick into the room, the gun still pointed at him. Sarah watched her aunt closely, desperate for any evidence that she was innocent in all of this. But her aunt's normally sweet and loving demeanor vanished and was replaced so quickly by something sinister and evil that Sarah couldn't even recognize her. She'd known this woman her entire life; she was family—Sarah's *only* family! Sarah just couldn't believe it. She wanted to throw up again, but instead she just shouted, "How could you? You *killed* him! You killed my father . . . your own brother!"

Hurling accusations at her aunt, Sarah wished she would hear some kind of denial, some kind of feasible explanation of why such a gross misunderstanding might have occurred. But Penelope didn't even *try* to pretend she was innocent; it was almost as if the real her was so deeply exhausted from pretending that she had no power to hold it back.

"He *deserved* it!" the stranger she'd known as her aunt hissed back at Sarah. "The way everyone loved and admired him *disgusted* me!" Penelope's eyes took on a dazed and bizarre quality that Sarah could only perceive as revealing something in her that might accurately be described as insane. "Ever since we were children, he always behaved as if he had the right to inherit *everything*, and—"

"He *did*!" Sarah countered.

"Of course you'd believe that, you little brat!" the older woman snarled, and Sarah wanted to cry like a baby but was in far too much shock. She felt Darius's hand on her arm, offering silent reassurance even while he kept a gun pointed at Penelope's lapdog. She wondered how many years this vile form of servitude had been taking place, with Rick doing her bidding, no matter how evil.

"I'm older than he was," she continued to rant. "What kind of rotten world determined that a man can inherit all the property and the money? We know we can have a woman as queen, but we can't have a woman inheriting an estate. No!" she bellowed. "Except in *your* case!" Sarcasm dripped from her lips in her reference to Sarah. "No! You had the luck of being born *without* a brother. And even in my brother's absence does everything come to me—his sister? No!" Each time she said the word *no* her voice became huskier and louder. It was as if realizing she'd been caught had released some kind of monster inside her, and now that it had been let loose there was no holding it back. "No!" she shouted yet again. "It all went to *you*! You who have no idea what the legacy of Courtenay even means." She paused and let out a sound that was part hysterical laughter and part unquenchable anger. "Where's the sword?" she demanded, stepping closer to Sarah, which made Darius take a step closer to Sarah, who could well imagine how fast he could turn the gun toward Penelope if he had to.

Sarah exchanged a quick glance with Darius and could read in his eyes that he knew something she didn't know, but he needed her to appear ignorant—which wouldn't be difficult since she knew absolutely nothing. As far as she knew, Rick had stolen it the night he'd shot Darius. Sarah turned back to Penelope and said, "What are you talking about?"

"Don't pretend with me you little *wench*!" Penelope stepped forward with amazing speed and slapped Sarah hard.

Darius pointed the gun at her and forced her to step back while Sarah held a hand over her stinging face; the pain was so bad she almost felt dizzy. If she'd had any doubt regarding her aunt's insanity, it had completely vanished with the physical evidence of her cruelty.

"Say what you need to say, old woman," Darius growled at her. "But keep your distance and keep your hands to yourself."

Penelope glared at him but seemed willing to obey his orders, and he took a step back, turning the gun again toward Rick. A quick glance at the man sitting with his hands tied behind him showed that he actually seemed pleased with Penelope's behavior; perhaps he'd grown tired of doing her bidding and knowing he'd been found out made him only too happy to make certain Penelope paid for her own crimes. Now that Sarah was seeing this side of her aunt, she could well imagine her to be manipulative and threatening. She couldn't believe this was the same woman! What had all the crying and supposed sensitivity been over the years? An act? Or was she somehow mentally predisposed to behave as two completely different personalities? Or maybe she was simply so skilled at manipulating even those closest to her, that perhaps they just couldn't see it.

"You know the sword I'm talking about," Penelope said to Sarah as if she were a naughty child. "I know he told you how to find it before he died, because I overheard that conversation."

"He was barely coherent," Sarah said. "Most of it was nonsense."

"Not nearly as much nonsense as you might have thought," Penelope shot back.

"He knew he was dying!" Sarah retorted with renewed horror. "Because *you* were poisoning him!"

"He was such a gullible fool." Penelope laughed maniacally. "And you're so much like him." Then she reverted to horrible harshness. "So, where is it? I know you had it! But *this* fool . . ." she motioned toward Rick, "came back with nothing but a box of tools; a box with a bullet hole in it. Too bad you didn't have better aim," Penelope said to Darius. "You could have killed him, and I wouldn't have had to deal with the buffoon any longer." She glared at Rick. "For all his willingness and skills, he obviously can't keep a secret."

"Oh, I didn't shoot him," Darius said and tipped his head toward Sarah. "She did."

Rick let out a dismayed grunt, as if having been shot at by a woman were somehow demeaning. Penelope looked surprised, but maybe just a tiny bit afraid as she realized Sarah might not be exactly the kind of woman she'd believed her to be. Well, the feeling on that was certainly mutual!

"Where's the sword!" Penelope shouted at Sarah. "I know you have it! And I know that whoever possesses it is the rightful heir of Courtenay— laws or no laws!"

"If you believe such a thing, you have an entirely distorted perception of reality," Sarah said, which was truer than she could imagine. "It's just a sword."

"It's worth a *fortune!*" Penelope snarled. "And it belongs to *me*! I am the only one who should possess it! Possessing it is the only way to be free of the curse of the Family Courtenay! And I am the rightful heir!"

"I am absolutely certain that no such curse exists," Darius said, surprisingly calm. "You've simply chosen to see certain events as a curse because that's how you *wanted* to see them. If anything, your distorted beliefs about trying to possess the sword and believing *that* would make you the rightful heir have done nothing but curse your own life. Either way, I don't think inheriting the estate would do you much good now. You've just confessed to murder—and to hiring someone else to commit murder on your behalf."

Penelope looked horrified, but at that very second Mr. Halford opened the door, and with Reggie and Jimmy in tow, entered the room. "Forgive us for being so slow to come. We were—" He took in the man sitting in the chair with his hands tied, and the visage of Penelope that was nothing like what he'd ever seen before. "What on earth is going on?" he asked, sounding alarmed.

"That's a long story," Darius said, "but . . ."

Taking advantage of the distraction and the open door, Penelope dashed out of the room with the agility and speed of someone much younger. Darius said to Halford and his friends, "Follow her. Don't let her out of your sight. If she goes to her rooms don't let her out. The police should be on their way."

Halford looked confused and horrified at the implications, but he nodded and did as Darius had asked. With Penelope gone, Sarah collapsed into a chair, so undone she could hardly breathe. She tried to recall all her reasons for loving and trusting her aunt, but there were too many to count. She considered how involved Penelope had been in supposedly keeping Sarah safe after her father's death. How disappointed she must have been when Darius had hidden Sarah away so cleverly that she couldn't be found! And how frustrating it must have been that Halford's communication with his friends had been so apparently benign and without clues as to Sarah's whereabouts. Her aunt had actually wanted her dead and had gone to great lengths to make it happen. And she was responsible for Evans's death! It was too horrifying to comprehend.

Darius sat down close beside her and put his arm around her, keeping the gun pointed at Rick while he whispered, "It's horrible, I know. But it's going to be all right . . . with time; I promise."

Sarah nodded absently, still attempting to take all of this in. They sat in silence while Sarah was mostly oblivious to Rick looking bored and very unhappy over his inevitable fate. She was barely aware of Darius's soothing presence. For all the negative emotions that felt stuck behind a wall of shock, she felt a deepening relief to realize that it was over. They'd solved the mystery; they'd found the culprits. She could finally feel safe again; she only had to get used to the idea that her beloved aunt was a killer—and likely insane.

A maid came through the open doorway to report that Mr. Halford had sent her to tell them that Penelope had indeed locked herself in her rooms. He and one of the under butlers were guarding the doors so she couldn't leave, and one of the stable hands had returned from town to report that the police were on their way and it wouldn't be long before they would be here.

The maid left, and not many minutes later, police officers arrived. Sarah felt as if she were hearing everything from a distance as Darius explained the situation and Rick said nothing at all. The police were very familiar with the unsolved case of Oswald Courtenay's murder; they would simply need to interview the culprits themselves and go through another inquest before their guilt was decided by a judge. But they took Darius's word—and Sarah's—as enough evidence to justify arresting both Rick and her aunt. Sarah had managed to tell the police everything she had heard Rick and her aunt confess, even though her own voice had sounded as far away as everyone else in the room who was speaking.

Only a minute or so after two police officers had taken Rick away, another came running down the stairs. Sarah could hear him speaking to his fellow officers in frantic tones but couldn't understand what he was saying. Darius motioned for Sarah to remain seated—for which she was grateful— and he went out into the hall to find out what was happening. He came back a few minutes later, looking more somber than she'd ever seen him.

"What?" Sarah demanded, wanting only to crawl into her bed and be completely alone and cry for hours.

"Penelope's dead," he reported, and she sucked in her breath. "Apparently she hadn't discarded the leftover poison she used to kill your father. There was an empty vial in her hand."

Sarah put a hand over her mouth as her tears finally exploded. She felt utterly horrified but at the same time somehow relieved—and she felt guilty for feeling relieved. But as much as she despised everything her aunt had done, the thought of her going to prison, and what the inevitable judgment would be for murder, she truly felt relieved that Penelope would never have to face any of that. And clearly Penelope had had the same idea.

Darius sat again beside Sarah and held her while she cried and cried until she finally found the presence of mind to say, "Will you help me to my room? I . . . I need . . . to . . ."

"I understand," he said. "Of course. It's over now, my darling."

"Yes," Sarah said and came unsteadily to her feet, grateful to have Darius there to lean on, "it's finally over."

\* \* \* \* \*

During the days leading up to Penelope's funeral, Sarah didn't leave her room and she was rarely able to get out of bed. It took every ounce of strength she could muster to attempt coming to terms with the realization that this woman she had loved and trusted her entire life had always carried a secret side to herself—a side that was evil and purely selfish, full of distorted ideas and beliefs, and willing to stop at nothing to get what she wanted—although Sarah still had trouble understanding exactly why that might be. Penelope had always lived comfortably here at Courtenay; she'd been treated with respect and she'd had money enough to buy anything she wanted, do what she wanted, travel wherever she might want to go. What exactly was it that had made her feel so cheated, so deeply angry, so malevolent toward her own brother and niece—enough to kill? But given the fact that Sarah was Penelope's only living relative, she had to accept that her questions would go unanswered. There was no one left to talk to who might have any insight into her aunt's inexplicable behavior.

Poppy and Darius spent a great deal of time with Sarah in her rooms—given the fact that she didn't want to go out, mostly because she didn't have the motivation to get cleaned up or put on more than a dressing gown over her nightgown. And worst of all, she couldn't stop crying. She felt more like Aunt Penelope than she ever had: crying uncontrollably and unable to keep it from happening. But she wondered how genuine this side of her aunt might have been all these years. Had her tears been a part of masking her true identity? Had they been the means of manipulation and disguise? Or had she truly been a woman with two distinct facets to her personality?

After days of crying, thinking, pondering, and talking everything through with Poppy and Darius over and over, Sarah finally concluded that she could never understand her aunt's challenges, or her motivations, because Sarah couldn't think the same way as her aunt no matter how hard she might try. It just wasn't within her capacity or her character. And she came to recognize that her grief over losing her aunt was more about what she'd discovered about her rather than her death; her death was horrible, surely, but Sarah couldn't deny feeling some relief in not having to face any of the further consequences of Penelope's actions. Sarah was gradually able to expel her need to grieve and turn her thoughts to gratitude. She could now move forward with her life and not have to fear for her safety. It was a miracle that they'd discovered the truth, all things considered—and she gave Darius full credit for being so sharp and perceptive. Darius, however, was quick to point out that it was Sarah who had recognized the guilty stable hand, which led to the unraveling of the whole ugly story.

The morning of Penelope's funeral—which would be a simple, private service—Sarah bathed and had Poppy help wash her hair and style it as much as it was possible. She put on the black dress she'd worn to her father's funeral and felt ready to face this day and get it over with, if only so she could put all of this behind her—officially, once and for all. Penelope was gone, and Rick was in the custody of the police. His crimes would be dealt with according to the law. She'd given her official statements, and it no longer had anything to do with her.

Standing at Penelope's graveside with Darius on one side of her and Poppy on the other, Sarah listened absently to the vicar treading carefully with his words as he attempted to speak respectfully of the dead while avoiding anything that might sound hypocritical in regard to what he now knew about Penelope's evil deeds. A thought occurred to Sarah that had completely left her mind since their horrible encounter with Penelope prior to her death; she'd been so caught up in her confusion and grief that she hadn't given it another thought.

"Darius," she whispered discreetly, leaning toward him without drawing attention from anyone else standing solemnly around the grave, "where is the sword? Was it not in the box that was stolen?" She thought of how she'd shoved the box under her bed when they'd arrived at their safe haven, and she'd left it there to gather dust. She'd stopped wearing the key around her neck and had left it in a drawer, beneath other things. But obviously the sword had *not* been in the box, and Darius was the only one who would have taken any thought or effort to remove it.

She looked up into his eyes, silently repeating her question. Darius smirked very subtly and winked. "What sword?"

Sarah couldn't bring herself to speak about it any further right now. Clearly, he'd taken it out of the box and had hidden it elsewhere. That was all she needed to know. Given Penelope's distorted desires to have that sword—and what she'd believed it represented—Sarah wasn't certain she ever wanted to see it again.

After the service was over, while Darius was talking with Reggie and Jimmy—since his friends had come to the funeral to offer their support; and of course, Poppy was never far from Reggie—Sarah took advantage of the opportunity to speak privately for a few minutes with Mr. Curtis. She just had a couple of questions for him regarding the estate she'd inherited, and she was pleasantly surprised with how well he knew the answers without having to do some investigating and get back to her.

That evening after supper, Sarah slipped away to the drawing room and looked out the window over the gardens below, taking in the beautiful view from this particular room which had been carefully planned. She pondered her memories of having grown up here at Castle Courtenay, and she thought of her parents and missed them more than she had in a long time. She wondered how they would feel about all that had happened, and her ability to make the best decision in moving forward with her life.

"Are you all right?" Darius asked, startling her; she hadn't heard him enter the room.

"Just . . . thinking," she said, turning back to the view.

Darius stood beside her and asked, "May I guess that your thoughts might include whatever it was you discussed with Mr. Curtis earlier?" She looked up at him in surprise and he smiled. "From your expression during that conversation, it was obviously very important, but you haven't said anything, so I'm assuming it has to do with the reasons you're particularly . . . lost in thought this evening."

Sarah drew back her shoulders and took a deep breath. She'd told Mr. Curtis what she wanted him to do on her behalf, but once she said it to Darius, it would truly be real. "As it turns out," she said, "there are many wealthy Americans who are interested in purchasing English estates—for the sake of prestige or something." She heard him take a sharp breath and took that to mean he hadn't expected the direction this conversation was taking. Still looking at the gardens, glowing in the setting sun, she went on. "As I see it, the Courtenay family line is gone. When I marry you, I will take on your name, and I will feel only joy over that. It's nothing to me any more except a house that's too big and too ornate. I don't want to live in a place where my father was murdered, and where my aunt took her own life. It would always haunt me." She sighed. "Mr. Curtis told me that it's possible—and commonly done—to make certain the buyer will keep all the household staff intact—as well as the tenant farmers—so that everyone maintains their employment and their homes. I can sign some papers and walk away from the responsibility completely." She finally looked up at Darius, her voice breaking with emotion as she added, "And I'm surprised at how comfortable that decision feels; I know it's right. I feel completely at peace, and I'm hoping we can leave tomorrow. I miss your parents. I miss the house that felt more like home to me than this place ever did. I miss the apple trees and the woods and the barn. I miss helping your mother in the kitchen, and—"

"I miss all those things too," Darius said with a loving smile. "If you want to leave tomorrow, then we will."

Sarah saw the contentment in his expression and asked, "Did you know I would make this decision?"

"I had no idea what you would choose in the end."

"Did you *hope* I would make this decision?"

"I meant it when I said I want to spend my life with you, and it doesn't matter where. Although, I will not deny that I too miss my parents. I think we could have been happy here, and I think I would have found a way to manipulate my parents into coming to live with us. But . . . this feels good to me too, Sarah—especially after all that we now know."

Sarah smiled at him as her peace expanded. "I love you, Darius Nash."

"And I am so glad of that," he said with a little laugh before he kissed her.

# *Epilogue*

SARAH'S HEALING FROM ALL THAT had happened increased exponentially from just being back under the same roof with Daphne and David—and having Poppy there as well. They settled quickly and easily back into the life they'd become familiar with, and Castle Courtenay felt a lifetime away—which was exactly how Sarah wanted it to feel.

The day after they returned home, Darius asked Sarah to come upstairs with him, and he showed her how he had wrapped the sword in fabric and tied it to the bedsprings underneath his bed—after discreetly searching for the key among Sarah's belongings. He explained that since this was the room they would share following their marriage, the sword that represented her legacy would always be nearby, and one day they would hand it down to their eldest child.

"You don't need a castle or an estate to carry on a great legacy," he told her. "I believe your aunt was misguided and likely not entirely sane, and we can't judge her for that. But your parents were good people, Sarah. And you are the rightful heir of Courtenay; this sword belongs to you. The people who purchased the estate have nothing to do with that."

Sarah deeply appreciated his insight, which helped her feel even more at peace. She was also grateful for his insight in removing the sword from the box and hiding it. Sarah didn't care about its monetary value, but the fact that it had been passed down through her family for many generations— and she was the last of her bloodline—meant a great deal to her. For her, the beautiful heart-shaped emerald embedded in the sword was tenderly symbolic.

Along with having the sword in her possession, Sarah had brought with her the books from the library that contained her family's history. She had left practically everything else with the house except her personal belongings. But this was *her* history, and no one else's—and it was also something she wanted to be able to pass down to her children.

* * * * *

Sarah and Darius were married in the autumn, soon after the apples had all been harvested and the leaves on the apple trees had been transformed into brilliant colors. Jimmy and Laura had been married a couple of months earlier, and Poppy and Reggie's wedding date was set for a couple of weeks afterward. As close as they had all been and were all quickly becoming friends, stepping into this new season of life together felt wholly appropriate, and Sarah knew in her heart that she never could have felt so perfectly surrounded by love if she'd remained at Courtenay. This was truly her home now, and it always would be.

A year after Sarah and Darius were married, David and Daphne invited their friends over to celebrate the conclusion of the harvest. After sharing an amazing meal and working together to clean it up, they all sat on blankets and pillows spread out beneath the apple trees, enjoying what would likely be one of the last truly pleasant days of autumn. Sarah and Poppy had expanded their close friendship to include Laura—Jimmy's wife—which made any time the three couples got together enjoyable, and Darius's parents had taken them all in with great love. The three women were all in different stages of pregnancy and loved speculating over the unknown factors of when exactly each of the babies would be born, and the gender of each one—and the known factor that the three children would grow up to be friends because they would so often be spending time together throughout the coming years.

Sarah leaned back on a pile of pillows Darius had situated perfectly behind her, knowing she was frequently prone to backaches as the baby inside her grew larger. She closed her eyes and inhaled the now-familiar aroma of autumn in the air in this place that was now home for her. She doubted she could ever feel more content than she did in that moment. Then Darius sat beside her and kissed her, while at the same time putting a hand over her rounded belly, silently expressing love for their unborn child. She looked into his eyes and smiled before he kissed her again and she had to admit she might have been wrong. She was very likely to grow more and more content with every passing year.

# About the Author

ANITA STANSFIELD HAS MORE THAN fifty published books and is the recipient of many awards, including two Lifetime Achievement Awards. Her books go far beyond being enjoyable, memorable stories. Anita resonates particularly well with a broad range of devoted readers because of her sensitive and insightful examination of contemporary issues that are faced by many of those readers, even when her venue is a historical romance. Readers come away from her compelling stories equipped with new ideas about how to enrich their own lives, regardless of their circumstances.

Anita was born and raised in Provo, Utah. She is the mother of five and has a growing number of grandchildren. She also writes for the general trade market under the name Elizabeth D. Michaels.

For more information and a complete list of her publications, go to anitastansfield.blogspot.com or anitastansfield.com, where you can sign up to receive email updates. You can also follow her on Facebook and Twitter.